Praise for *The Châtelet Apprentice*

'Reading this book is akin to time travel: it is an exhilarating portrait of the hubbub and sexual licence of Paris during an eighteenth-century carnival. . . The period detail is marvellously evocative, Le Floch is brave and engaging, and even though the story takes place almost 250 years ago, it is curiously reassuring that in many ways, Paris, and human nature, have not changed at all.' *Economist*

'Parot succeeds brilliantly in his reconstruction of pre-revolutionary Paris, in splendid period detail' *Times*

'A solid and detailed evocation of pre-revolutionary France – the poverty and squalor, side by side with the wealth and splendour, are brought lovingly to life. And the plot has all the twists, turns and surprises the genre demands.' *Independent on Sunday*

'A terrific debut. . . Working without modern investigative techniques in a police force reliant on torture, Le Floch confronts the ethical dilemmas of the period in a novel that brilliantly evokes the casual brutality of life in eighteenth-century France.' *Sunday Times*

Jean-François Parot

Jean-François Parot is a diplomat and historian. *The Châtelet Apprentice* is his first novel, and the first in a series of Nicolas Le Floch mysteries which have been published to much acclaim in French.

Michael Glencross

Michael Glencross lives and works in France as a translator. His most recent translations into English include *The Dream* by Emile Zola and *Around the World in Eighty Days* by Jules Verne.

THE
CHÂTELET
APPRENTICE

JEAN-FRANÇOIS PAROT

Translated from the French by Michael Glencross

For Madeleine and Edouard

This work is published with support from the French Ministry
of Culture / Centre national du Livre

A Gallic Book

First published in France as *L'énigme des Blancs-Manteaux* by Éditions Jean-Claude
Lattès

Copyright © Éditions Jean-Claude Lattès 2000
English translation copyright © Gallic Books 2007

First published in Great Britain in 2007 by
Gallic Books, 134 Lots Road, London SW10 0RJ

This edition published in Great Britain 2008 by Gallic Books

A CIP record for this book is available from the British Library

ISBN 978-1-906040-06-2

Typeset in Fournier by SX Composing DTP, Rayleigh, Essex

Printed in the UK by CPI Bookmarque, Croydon, CR0 4TD

2 4 6 8 10 9 7 5 3

CONTENTS

NICOLAS LE FLOCH'S
PARIS

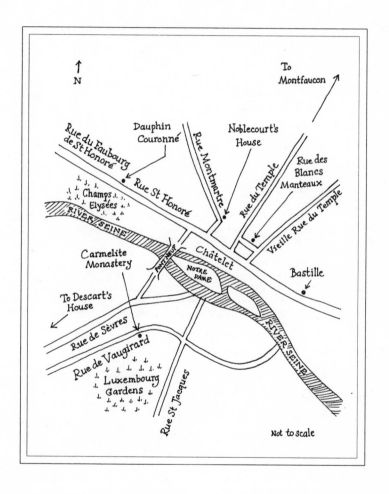

DRAMATIS PERSONAE

NICOLAS LE FLOCH : an investigator appointed by the Lieutenant General of Police in Paris

CANON FRANÇOIS LE FLOCH : Nicolas Le Floch's guardian

JOSÉPHINE PELVEN (known as FINE) : Canon Le Floch's housekeeper

MARQUIS LOUIS DE RANREUIL : Nicolas Le Floch's godfather

ISABELLE DE RANREUIL : the marquis's daughter

MONSIEUR DE SARTINE : Lieutenant General of Police in Paris

MONSIEUR DE LA BORDE : First Groom of the King's Bedchamber

GUILLAUME LARDIN : a police commissioner

PIERRE BOURDEAU : a police inspector

LOUISE LARDIN : Commissioner Lardin's second wife

MARIE LARDIN : Commissioner Lardin's daughter by his first marriage

CATHERINE GAUSS : a former canteen-keeper, the Lardins' cook

HENRI DESCART : a doctor of medicine

GUILLAUME SEMACGUS : a navy surgeon

SAINT-LOUIS : a former black slave, Semacgus's servant

AWA : Saint-Louis's companion and Semacgus's cook

PIERRE PIGNEAU : a seminarist

AIMÉ DE NOBLECOURT : a former procurator

PÈRE GRÉGOIRE : the apothecary of the monastery of the Discalced Carmelites

LA PAULET : a brothel-keeper

LA SATIN : a prostitute

BRICART : a former soldier

RAPACE : a former butcher

OLD ÉMILIE : a former prostitute, a soup seller

MASTER VACHON : a tailor

COMMISSIONER CAMUSOT : the head of the Gaming Division

MAUVAL : Commissioner Camusot's henchman

OLD MARIE : an usher at the Châtelet

TIREPOT : a police informer

CHARLES HENRI SANSON : the hangman

RABOUINE : a police spy

PROLOGUE

Prudens futuri temporis exitum
Caliginosa nocte premit Deus...
'Knowing the future,
God conceals the outcome in darkest night . . .'
HORACE

On the night of Friday 2 February 1761, a horse-drawn vehicle was laboriously making its way along the highway that leads from La Courtille to La Villette. The day had been gloomy, and at nightfall, sullen skies had unleashed a fierce storm. If anyone had been keeping a watch on this road they would have noticed the cart pulled by a scrawny horse. On the seat, two men stared into the darkness, the black flaps of their capes partly visible in the gleam of a shabby lantern. The horse kept slipping on the wet ground and stopping every twenty or so yards. Two barrels thudded against each other, jolted about by the ruts in the road.

The last houses in the *faubourgs* disappeared, and with them the few remaining lights. The rain ceased and the moon could be glimpsed between two clouds, casting a bluish light over a countryside enveloped in a shapeless, drifting mist. Hillsides covered with brambles now rose up on either side of the track. For some time the horse had been tossing its head and tugging nervously at the reins. A persistent smell hung in the cold night air, its lingering sweetness soon giving way to an appalling stench. The two shadowy figures had pulled their cloaks down over their faces. The horse stopped, let out a strangled whinnying and flared its nostrils, seeking to identify the foul smell. Even when lashed with a whip, it refused to get going again.

'I think this nag is giving up on us!' exclaimed Rapace, one of the men. 'I'm sure it can smell meat. Get down, Bricart, take it by the bit and get us out of here!'

'I saw the same thing at Bassignano in 1745 when I was serving in the Dauphin's Regiment with old Chevert. The beasts pulling the cannons refused to go past the corpses. It was September, it was hot and the flies . . .'

'Stop, I know all about your military campaigns. Grab the beast by the neck and hurry up. It just won't move!' shouted Rapace, hitting it twice on its skinny rump.

Bricart grumbled and jumped down from the cart. When he reached the ground, he sank into the mud and had to use both hands to pull out the wooden stump fitted to his right leg. He went up to the crazed animal, which made one last attempt to signal its refusal. Bricart seized the bit but the desperate beast jerked its head away, striking him on the shoulder. He fell flat on the ground, uttering a stream of obscenities.

'It won't budge. We're going to have to unload here. We can't be far.'

'I can't help you in this mud; this damned leg is useless.'

'I'll get the barrels down and we'll roll them towards the pits,' said Rapace. 'It should only take two goes. Hold the horse; I'm going to look around.'

'Don't leave me,' whined Bricart. 'I don't like it here. Is this really where they used to hang people?'

He rubbed his bad leg.

'So much for the brave old soldier! You can talk when we've finished. We'll go to Marthe's tavern. I'll treat you to a drink, and a trollop, too, if you feel like it. They stopped hanging people here before your grandfather's time. Now there's only dead cattle from the city and beyond. It's the knacker's yard – it used to be at Javel but now it's here at Montfaucon. Can't you smell the stench? In the summer, when there's a storm brewing, you even get a whiff of it in Paris, all the way to the Tuileries!'

'You're right, it stinks and I can feel presences,' murmured Bricart.

'Oh, shut up. Your presences are nothing more than rats, crows and mongrels: horribly fat ones, all fighting over the carcasses. Even the scum off the streets come here to scrape around for something to eat. Just thinking about it makes my mouth feel dry. Where did you hide the flagon? Ah, here it is!'

Rapace took a few swigs before handing it to Bricart, who emptied it greedily. They could hear high-pitched squeals.

'Listen: rats! But enough talk, take the lantern and stay with me, to give me some light. I've got the axe and the whip: you never know who we may come across, not to mention the smashing-up we've to do . . .'

The two men moved cautiously towards some buildings which they could now make out in the beam of the lamp.

'As sure as my name is Rapace, here's the knacker's yard and the tallow vats. The lime pits are further on. Walls of rotting flesh, piles and piles of it, believe me.'

Nearby, crouched behind a carcass, a shadowy figure had stopped what it was doing, alarmed by the whinnying of the horse, the swearing and the light of the lantern. The figure trembled, thinking at first that it was the men of the watch. By order of the King and the Lieutenant General of Police they were patrolling more and more, in order to drive away the poor starving wretches who fought with carrion eaters for left-overs from the feast.

This huddled ghost was merely an old woman in rags. She had known better times and, in her prime, had even attended Regency dinners. Then her youth faded and the beautiful Émilie had stooped to the most abject form of prostitution, along the *quais* and at the toll-gates, but even that had not lasted.

Now, diseased and disfigured, she survived by selling a foul soup from a portable stewing pot. This concoction, which was largely made out of scraps stolen from Montfaucon, risked poisoning her customers and infecting the city and its *faubourgs*.

She saw the two men unload the barrels and roll them along before emptying their contents onto the ground. Her heart was pounding so hard that she could not hear what was being said and dared not grasp what they were doing. Instead, old Émilie strained her eyes to make out the two dark shapes – red, she thought – now lying close to the building containing the tallow vats. Unfortunately the light from the lantern was dim and renewed gusts of wind made its flame flicker.

What she saw she did not understand and could not bring herself to imagine, paralysed as she was by a fear beyond words. And yet the old woman was gripped by a curiosity which made the horrible scene even more incomprehensible to her.

One of the two men was laying out on the ground what looked like items of clothing. With a tinder-box he struck a light that flared up briefly. Then a sharp crackling sound could be heard. The old woman huddled closer to the rotting flesh, no longer even aware of its acrid emanations. She was fighting for breath, oppressed by an unknown terror. Her blood froze, and all that she saw as she lost consciousness and slid to the ground was a light that was growing bigger.

Where the gallows once stood all was silence again. The cart moved off into the distance, and with it the muffled echo of conversation. Darkness closed in and the wind blew like a gale. What had been left behind on the ground gradually began to come to life: it seemed to be writhing and devouring itself from within. Faint squeals could be heard and a frantic scuffling began. Even before dawn, the huge crows were awake and coming closer, soon followed by a pack of dogs . . .

I

THE TWO JOURNEYS

'Paris is full of adventurers and bachelors
who spend their lives rushing from house to house and men,
like species, seem to multiply by circulating.'

J.-J. ROUSSEAU

Sunday 21 January 1761

The barge glided along the grey river. Patches of fog rose up from the water, swathing the banks and refusing to yield to the pale light of day. The anchor, weighed one hour before dawn as the regulation required, had had to be dropped again because the darkness was still impenetrable. Already Orléans was receding into the distance and the currents of the River Loire in spate carried the heavy craft swiftly along. Despite the gusts of wind that swept across the deck, a cloying smell of fish and salt filled the air. It was transporting a large cargo of salted cod, as well as some casks of Ancenis wine.

Two silhouettes stood out at the prow of the boat. The first belonged to a member of the crew, his features tense with concentration, peering at the murky surface of the water. In his left hand he held a horn similar to those used by postilions: in the event of danger he would sound the alarm to the skipper, who was holding the tiller at the stern.

The other was that of a young man, booted and dressed in

6

black, with a tricorn in his hand. Despite his youth there was something both military and ecclesiastical about him. With his head held high, his dark hair swept back and his intense stillness, he looked impatient and noble, like the figurehead of the boat. His expressionless gaze was fixed upon the left bank, staring at the bulk of Notre-Dame de Cléry, the grey prow of which parted the white clouds along the shore and seemed to want to join with the Loire.

This young man, whose resolute attitude would have impressed anyone other than the bargee, was called Nicolas Le Floch.

Nicolas was rapt in contemplation. A little more than a year earlier, he had followed the same route in the opposite direction towards Paris. How quickly everything had happened! Now, on his way back to Brittany, he recalled the events of the past two days. He had taken the fast mail-coach to Orléans, where he planned to board the barge. As far as the Loire, the journey had been marked by none of those colourful incidents that normally relieve the boredom of travel. His travelling companions, a priest and two elderly couples, had watched him all the time in silence. Nicolas, accustomed to the open air, suffered from the confined space and the mixture of smells inside the carriage. Five disapproving looks soon put an end to his attempt to open a window. The priest had even made the sign of the cross, presumably on the assumption that this desire for freedom was the work of the devil. The young man had taken the hint and settled back into his corner. Gradually lulled by the monotony of the journey he had drifted off into a daydream. Now the same reverie came over him on the barge and, once again, he saw and heard nothing more.

Everything really had happened too quickly. After receiving a solid classical education from the Jesuits in Vannes, he had been working as a notary's clerk in Rennes when suddenly he had been summoned back to Guérande by his guardian, Canon Le Floch. Without further explanation he had been fitted out, given a pair of boots and a few *louis d'or*, as well as plenty of advice and blessings. He had taken leave of his godfather, the Marquis de Ranreuil, who had given him a letter of recommendation for Monsieur de Sartine, one of his friends, who was a magistrate in Paris. The marquis had seemed to Nicolas both moved and embarrassed and the young man had not been able to say goodbye to his godfather's daughter, Isabelle, his childhood friend, who had just left for Nantes to stay with her aunt, Madame de Guénouel.

With a heavy heart he had left the old walled town behind him, his sense of abandonment and separation intensified by his guardian's visible emotion and the heartrending cries of Fine, the canon's housekeeper. He had felt lost during the long journey over land and water that was taking him to his new destiny.

As Paris had drawn near he had become aware of his surroundings again. He could still remember how scared he had felt when he first reached the capital. Until then, Paris had been little more than a dot on the map of France hanging on the schoolroom wall in Vannes. Astounded by the noise and bustle of the *faubourgs*, he had felt bewildered and vaguely uneasy before this enormous plain covered by countless windmills. The movement of their sails had reminded him of a group of gesticulating giants straight out of that novel by Cervantes which he had read several times. He had been struck by the crowds in rags that constantly came and went through the toll-gates.

Even today he could remember when he'd first entered the great city: its narrow streets and enormously tall houses, its dirty, muddy thoroughfares and multitudes of riders and carriages, the shouts and those unspeakable smells . . .

On arrival he had wandered around lost for hours, often ending up in gardens at the bottom of dead-ends or finding himself back at the river. Eventually a pleasant young man with eyes of differing colours had taken him to the church of Saint-Sulpice and then to Rue de Vaugirard and the monastery of the Discalced Carmelites. There he was given an effusive welcome by a portly monk, Père Grégoire, a friend of his guardian, who was in charge of the dispensary. It was late and he was given a bed in the garret straight away.

Taking comfort from this welcome, he had sunk into a dreamless sleep. It was only in the morning that he discovered his guide had relieved him of his silver watch, a gift from his godfather. He resolved to be more wary of strangers. Fortunately the purse containing his modest savings was still safe inside a secret pocket that Fine had sewn into his bag the day before he left Guérande.

Nicolas found the regular pattern of life in the monastery reassuring. He took his meals with the community, in the great refectory. He had begun to venture out into the city equipped with a rudimentary street map on which he marked in pencil his tentative explorations so as to be sure of finding his way back. There were many aspects of life in the capital which he disliked, but its charm was beginning to work on him. He found the constant bustle of the streets both appealing and disconcerting;

on several occasions he had almost been run over by carriages. He was always surprised by how fast they went and how they suddenly appeared from nowhere. He quickly learnt not to daydream, and to protect himself against other dangers: stinking muck that splashed his clothes, water from the gutters that poured down on passers-by, and streets transformed into raging torrents by a few drops of rain. He jumped, dodged and leapt aside, like a Parisian born and bred, in the midst of all the filth and a thousand other hazards. After each outing he had to brush his clothes and wash his stockings: he only had two pairs and was saving the other for his meeting with Monsieur de Sartine.

On that front there was no progress. On several occasions he had gone to the address written on the Marquis de Ranreuil's letter. He had greased the palm of a suspicious doorkeeper only to be ushered off the premises by an equally disdainful footman. The weeks went by slowly. Seeing how unhappy he was and wanting to give him something to do, Père Grégoire suggested that the young man work alongside him. Since 1611 the monastery of the Discalced Carmelites had been producing a medicinal brew sold throughout the kingdom, made from a recipe that the monks kept a closely guarded secret. Nicolas's task was to crush the herbs. He learnt to recognise balm, angelica, cress, coriander, cloves and cinnamon, and discovered strange and exotic fruits. The long days spent using the mortar and pestle and breathing the fumes of the stills befuddled him so much that his mentor noticed and asked what was on his mind. Père Grégoire immediately promised that he would inquire about Monsieur de Sartine. He obtained a letter of introduction from the prior that would smooth Nicolas's path. Monsieur de Sartine had just been appointed Lieutenant General of Police, replacing Monsieur Bertin. Père Grégoire accompanied this good news with a stream of comments so detailed that it was obvious the information had only recently been acquired.

'Nicolas, my son, here you are about to encounter a man who might influence the course of your life, providing you know how to please him. The Lieutenant General of Police is the absolute head of the service to which His Majesty has appointed the task of maintaining law and order, not only in the streets but also in the daily lives of all his subjects. As criminal lieutenant of the Châtelet prison, Monsieur de Sartine already had considerable power. Just think what he will be able to do from now on. Rumour has it that he will not refrain from making arbitrary decisions . . . And to think that he's only just turned thirty!'

Père Grégoire lowered his naturally loud voice somewhat and made sure that no indiscreet ear could catch what he was saying.

'The abbot told me in confidence that the King has given Monsieur de Sartine authority, in the last resort and when the situation is critical, to decide matters alone, outside the court and with the utmost secrecy. But you know nothing of this, Nicolas,' he said, putting a finger to his lips. 'Remember that this great office was created by our present King's grandfather – God be with that great Bourbon. The people still remember his predecessor Monsieur d'Argenson, who they called "the creature from hell" because of his twisted face and body.'

He suddenly threw a pitcher of water over a brazier, which sizzled, giving off acrid smoke.

'But enough of all this. I'm talking too much. Take this letter. Tomorrow morning go down Rue de Seine and follow the river as far as Pont-Neuf. You know Île de la Cité, so you can't go wrong. Cross the bridge there and follow the Quai de la Mégisserie on the right-hand side. It will take you to the Châtelet.'

Nicolas got little sleep that night. His head was buzzing with Père Grégoire's words and he was only too aware of his own insignificance. How could he, alone in Paris, cut off from those he loved and twice orphaned, have the audacity to face such a powerful man who had direct access to the King and who, Nicolas sensed, would have a decisive effect on his future?

He tried unsuccessfully to banish the restless images haunting him and sought to conjure up a more soothing picture to calm his mind. Isabelle's delicate features appeared before him, causing him further uncertainty. Why, when she knew that he would be gone from Guérande for some time, had his godfather's daughter left without saying goodbye?

He saw again in his mind's eye the dyke amid the marshes where they had sworn their eternal love. How could he have believed her and been foolish enough even to dream that a child found in a cemetery might so much as look upon the daughter of the noble and powerful Marquis de Ranreuil? And yet his godfather had always been so kind to him . . . This bittersweet thought finally carried him off to sleep at about five in the morning.

It was Père Grégoire who woke him one hour later. He washed and dressed, carefully combed his hair and, with the monk urging him on, stepped out into the cold of the street.

This time he did not lose his way, despite the dark. In front of Palais Mazarin, buildings were gradually emerging from the gloom as day was breaking. The banks of the river, like muddy beaches, were already a hive of activity. Here and there groups of people huddled around fires. The first cries of the Paris day were ringing out everywhere, signs that the city was rousing itself from slumber.

Suddenly a young drinks seller bumped into him. After almost dropping his tray of Bavarian tea the boy went off, swearing under his breath. Nicolas had tasted this drink, made fashionable some time ago by the Palatine princess, the Regent's mother. It was, as Père Grégoire had explained to him, a hot beverage, sweetened with syrup of maidenhair.

By the time he reached Pont-Neuf, it was already thick with people. He admired the statue of Henry IV and the pump of La Samaritaine. The workshops along the Quai de la Mégisserie were beginning to open, the tanners settling down to their day's work now that the sun had risen. He walked along this foul-smelling bank with a handkerchief held to his nose.

The mighty prison of the Châtelet rose up before him, dour and gloomy. He had never set eyes on it but guessed what it was. Uncertain how to proceed, he entered an archway dimly lit by oil lanterns. A man wearing a long dark gown passed him, and Nicolas called out:

'Monsieur, I would like your help. I'm looking for the offices of the Lieutenant General of Police.'

The man looked him up and down and, after an apparently thorough examination, answered him with a self-important air:

'The Lieutenant General of Police is holding a private audience. Normally he sends someone to represent him, but Monsieur de Sartine is taking up office today and is presiding in person. Presumably you know that his department is to be found in Rue Neuve-Saint-Augustin, near Place Vendôme, but he still has an office in the Châtelet. Go and see his staff on the first floor. There's an usher at the door, you cannot mistake it. Do you have the necessary introduction?'

Wisely, Nicolas was careful not to reply. He took his leave politely and went off towards the staircase. At the end of the gallery, beyond a glass-panelled door, he found himself in an immense room with bare walls. A man was seated at a deal desk and looked as if he were nibbling his hands. As he approached, Nicolas realised that in fact it was one of those hard, dry biscuits that sailors ate.

'Good day to you, Monsieur. I would like to know whether Monsieur de Sartine will receive me.'

'The audacity! Monsieur de Sartine does not receive visitors.'

'I must insist.' (Nicolas sensed that everything depended on his insistence and he attempted to make his voice sound more assertive.) 'I have, Monsieur, an audience this morning.'

With instinctive quick-wittedness Nicolas waved before the usher the great missive bearing the armorial seal of the Marquis de Ranreuil. If he had presented the little note from the prior, he would doubtless have been shown the door immediately. This bold stroke shut the man up and, muttering something under his breath, he respectfully took possession of the letter and showed him a seat.

'As you wish, but you'll have to wait.'

The usher lit his pipe and then withdrew into a silence that Nicolas would dearly have liked to break in order to allay his anxiety. He was reduced to contemplating the wall. Towards eleven o'clock, the room filled with people. A small man entered, to the accompaniment of polite whisperings. He was dressed in magistrate's robes with a leather portfolio under his arm, and he disappeared through a door that had been left ajar, allowing a glimpse of a brightly lit drawing room. A few moments later the usher rapped on the door and he, too, disappeared. When he came back, he beckoned Nicolas to go in.

The magistrate's gown lay on the floor and the Lieutenant General of Police, dressed in a black coat, stood in front of a desk made of rare wood with gleaming bronze ornaments. He was reading the Marquis de Ranreuil's letter with intense concentration. The office was an ill-proportioned room, the bareness of the stone and the tiled floor contrasting with the luxury of the furniture and the rugs. The light from several candelabra added to the weak rays of the winter sun and to the red glow from the Gothic fireplace, illuminating Monsieur de Sartine's pale face. He looked older than he was. His most striking feature was his high, bare forehead. His already greying natural hair was carefully combed and powdered. A pointed nose sharpened the features of a face lit from within by two steel-grey eyes that sparkled with irony. Though short of stature, his erect bearing emphasised his slenderness without detracting from his air of authority and dignity. Nicolas felt the beginnings of panic, but he remembered what he had been taught at school and controlled his trembling hands. Sartine was now fanning himself with the letter, examining his visitor inquisitively. The minutes seemed unending.

'What is your name?' he asked suddenly.

'Nicolas Le Floch, at your service, Monsieur.'

'At my service, at my service . . . That remains to be seen.

Your godfather gives a very favourable account of you. You can ride, you are a skilled swordsman, you have a basic knowledge of the law . . . These are considerable attainments for a notary's clerk.'

Hands on hips, he slowly began to walk around Nicolas, who blushed at this inspection and its accompanying snorts and chuckles of laughter.

'Yes, yes, indeed, upon my word, it may well be true . . .' continued the Lieutenant General.

Sartine examined the letter thoughtfully, then went up to the fireplace and threw it in. It flared up with a yellow flame.

'May we depend on you, Monsieur? No, don't reply. You don't know what this will mean for you. I have plans for you and Ranreuil is handing you to me. Do you understand? No, you understand nothing, nothing at all.'

He went behind his desk and sat down, pinched his nose, then examined Nicolas once more, who was sweltering as he stood with his back to the roaring fire.

'Monsieur, you are very young and I am taking a considerable risk by speaking to you as openly as I do. The King's police needs honest people and I myself need faithful servants who will blindly obey me. Do you follow me?'

Nicolas was careful not to agree.

'Ah! I see you are quick to understand.'

Sartine went towards the casement window and seemed fascinated by what he saw.

'So much cleaning-up to do . . .' he mumbled. 'With meagre means at our disposal. No more, no less. Don't you agree?'

Nicolas had turned to face the Lieutenant General.

'You will need to improve your knowledge of the law,

Monsieur. You will devote some hours each day to this, as a form of diversion. You will have to work hard, indeed you will.'

He hurried across to his desk and grabbed a sheet of paper. He motioned to Nicolas to sit down in the great red damask armchair.

'Write. I want to see whether you have a good hand.'

Nicolas, frightened out of his wits, concentrated as best he could. Sartine thought for a few moments, removed a small gold snuff-box from his coat pocket and took out a pinch of snuff which he delicately placed on the back of his hand. He sniffed first with one nostril and then the other, closed his eyes in contentment and sneezed loudly, sending black particles flying all around him and onto Nicolas, who withstood the storm. The Lieutenant gasped with pleasure as he blew his nose.

'Come, write: "Monsieur, I think it appropriate for the King's service and my own that as from today you should take as your personal secretary Nicolas Le Floch, to be paid from my account. I should be obliged if you would provide him with board and lodging and submit a detailed account of his work to me." Take down the address: "To M. Lardin, Commissioner of Police at the Châtelet, at his residence, Rue des Blancs-Manteaux."'

Then, swiftly taking hold of the letter, he held it up to his face and examined it.

'So, a somewhat bastard hand, yes, somewhat bastard,' he declared, laughing. 'But it will do for a beginner. It has flourish, it has movement.'

He returned to the armchair that Nicolas had vacated, signed the missive, sanded it, folded it, lit a piece of wax from embers left in a brass pot, rubbed it over the paper and impressed his seal on it, all in the twinkling of an eye.

'Monsieur, the functions I wish you to perform with Commissioner Lardin require integrity. Do you know what integrity is?'

For once Nicolas dived straight in.

'It is, Monsieur, scrupulously fulfilling the duties of an honest man and . . .'

'So he can speak! Good. He still sounds rather schoolboyish but he's not wrong. You will need to be discreet and cautious, be able to learn things and to forget things, and be capable of drawing secrets out of people. You will need to learn to write reports about the cases assigned to you, and in an elegant style. You will have to pick up on what you're told and guess what you're not told and, finally, to follow up the slightest lead you may have.'

He emphasised his words by raising his forefinger.

'That is not all: you must also be a fair and faithful witness to all you see, without weakening its significance or altering it one jot. Bear in mind, Monsieur, that on your exactness will depend the life and honour of men who, even if they may be the lowest of the low, must be treated according to the rules. You really are very young. I wonder . . . But then again so was your godfather when at your age he crossed the lines under enemy fire at the siege of Philipsbourg. He was with Marshal Berwick, who lost his life in the action. And I myself . . .'

He seemed deep in thought and, for the first time, Nicolas saw a flicker of compassion light up his face.

'You will need to be vigilant, swift, active, incorruptible. Yes, above all incorruptible.' (Here he hit the precious marquetry of the desk with the palm of his hand). 'Go, Monsieur,' concluded Sartine, rising to his feet, 'from now on you are in the King's service. Ensure we are always satisfied with you.'

Nicolas bowed and took the letter that was held out to him. He was near the door when the mocking little voice stopped him with a laugh:

'Really, Monsieur, you are admirably dressed for someone from Lower Brittany but you're in Paris now. Go to Vachon, my tailor in Rue Vieille-du-Temple. Get him to make you some coats, undergarments and accessories.'

'I do not . . .'

'On my account, Monsieur, on my account. Let it not be said that I left the godson of my friend Ranreuil in rags. A handsome godson, to tell the truth. Be off with you and always be at the ready.'

Nicolas was relieved when he reached the river again. He took in a deep breath of the cold air. He felt he had survived this first ordeal, even if some of what Sartine had said was bound to worry him a little. He rushed back to the monastery of the Discalced Carmelites, where the good monk was waiting for him whilst furiously pounding some innocent plants.

Grégoire had to temper Nicolas's enthusiasm and managed to dissuade him from going off to Commissioner Lardin's residence that very evening. Although the watchmen did their rounds the streets were dangerous; he was afraid that Nicolas might lose his way and attract trouble, especially in the dark.

He tried to dampen the young man's eagerness by asking for

a blow-by-blow account of his audience with the Lieutenant General of Police. He made Nicolas go over the smallest detail and drew out the proceedings by adding his own comments and asking more questions. He constantly alighted on points requiring further explanation.

Inwardly, and despite his original foreboding, Père Grégoire marvelled at how Monsieur de Sartine had so quickly been able to turn this unknown provincial boy, still overawed by the great city, into an instrument of his police force. He rightly assumed that beneath this near miracle, performed with such speed, there lurked a mystery whose complexities he did not understand. He therefore looked on Nicolas with amazement, as if he were a creature of his own making who was now suddenly beyond his control. It made him feel sad, but not bitter, and he punctuated his remarks with 'God have mercy' and 'This is beyond me', repeated *ad infinitum*.

By now it was time for supper, so the pair of them hurried off to the refectory. Then Nicolas prepared himself for a night's sleep that proved no more refreshing than the previous one. He had to try to restrain his imagination. It was often feverish and unbridled and played unfortunate tricks on him, either by making the future look bleak or, on the contrary, by putting out of his mind what should have been a reason for caution or concern. He resolved once more to improve himself and, for reassurance, told himself that he knew how to benefit from experience. However, his familiar anxiety soon returned with the thought that the following day he would be starting a new life that he had to avoid conjuring up in his imagination. On several occasions this idea gripped him just as he was dozing off, and it was very late by the time he finally fell into a deep sleep.

*

In the morning, after he had listened to Père Grégoire's final words of advice, Nicolas said goodbye and they promised to see each other again. The monk had indeed grown fond of the young man and would have been happy to continue to instruct him in the science of medicinal herbs. As the weeks had gone by his pupil's considerable qualities of observation and reflection had not escaped his notice. He made him write two letters, one to his guardian and the other to the marquis, and promised to have them sent. Nicolas did not dare add a message for Isabelle, vowing that he would make good use of his new-found freedom to do so a little later.

Almost as soon as Nicolas had stepped out of the doors of the monastery, Père Grégoire went to the altar of the Blessed Virgin and began to pray for him.

Nicolas took the same route as he had the day before, but this time there was a spring in his step. As he passed the Châtelet, he went over his interview with Monsieur de Sartine, a conversation in which he had hardly said a word. So, he was about to enter 'the King's service' . . . Until then, he had not understood the full significance of these words. On reflection they had no meaning for him.

His schoolmasters and the marquis had mentioned the King, but all that seemed to belong to another world. He had seen engravings and a head on coins and he had mumbled his way through the unending list of sovereigns, which had meant no more to him than the succession of kings and prophets in the Old

Testament. In the collegiate church of Guérande he had sung the *Salve fac regum* on 25 August, Saint Louis's day. His intellect made no connection between the King, a figure in stained glass, the symbol of faith and fidelity, and the man of flesh and blood who ruled the State.

This thought occupied him until he reached Rue de Gesvres. There, aware once more of his surroundings, he was astonished to discover a street that crossed the Seine. When he came out on Quai Pelletier, he realised that it was a bridge lined with houses on either side. A young Savoyard chimney sweep waiting for custom, with a marmot on his shoulders, told him it was Pont-Marie. Looking back at this marvel several times, he reached Place de Grève. He recognised it from a print he had once seen, bought from a street hawker, which showed the torture and execution of Cartouche the highwayman before a large gathering of people in November 1721. As a child, he had daydreamed in front of it and imagined being part of the scene, lost in the crowd and caught up in endless adventures. With a shock he realised that his dream had become a reality: he was walking the stage where famous criminal executions had taken place.

Leaving the grain-port behind him to his right, he entered the heart of old Paris through the Saint-Jean arch at the Hôtel de Ville. When giving him directions, Père Grégoire had particularly warned him about this spot: 'It's a grim and dangerous place,' he said, clasping his hands, 'with everyone from Rue Saint-Antoine and the *faubourg* passing through.' The archway was the favourite haunt of thieves and fake beggars who lay in wait for passers-by under its solitary vault. He entered it cautiously, but only came across a water carrier and some day labourers going towards Place de Grève to find work.

He reached the market of Saint-Jean via Rue de la Tissanderie and Place Baudoyer. It was, so his mentor had told him, the largest in Paris after Les Halles; he would recognise it by the fountain in its centre, near the guardhouse, and by the many people who came to collect water from the Seine.

Accustomed to the good-natured orderliness of provincial markets, here Nicolas had to force his way through total chaos. All the goods were piled higgledy-piggledy on the ground, except for the meat, which was on special slabs. In the warm autumn air the smells were strong, foul even, around the fish stalls. He found it hard to believe that there could be markets bigger or busier than this one. The space for the stallholders was very cramped and it was almost impossible to move around, but this did not prevent horse-drawn vehicles from driving through, threatening to crush anything in their path. People were haggling and arguing and from the accents and the clothes he realised that many peasants from the nearby countryside came here to sell their produce.

Carried first one way then the other by the crowd, Nicolas went around the market three or four times before finding Rue Sainte-Croix-de-la-Bretonnerie. This street led him without mishap to Rue des Blancs-Manteaux where, between Rue du Puits and Rue du Singe, he found Commissioner Lardin's residence.

He hesitated and gazed at the three-storey house, bordered on either side by gardens protected by high walls. He raised the knocker, which produced a dull echo inside as it struck the door. The door half opened to reveal the face of a woman wearing a white mob cap, a face so wide and chubby that it seemed to be the continuation of a huge body, the top half of which was squeezed into a red jacket. This was framed by two arms, similarly proportioned to the rest, which dripped with washing suds.

'What do you want?' asked the woman, with a strange accent that Nicolas had never heard before.

'I've come to deliver a letter from Monsieur de Sartine to Commissioner Lardin,' said Nicolas, who immediately bit his lip, realising he had played his trump card rather too soon.

'Give me.'

'I must give it in person.'

'No one at home. Wait.'

She slammed the door shut. All that remained for Nicolas was to show the patience that, as his own experience had confirmed, was the main virtue needed in Paris. Without daring to move away from the house he walked up and down, examining the surroundings. On the opposite side of the road, where there was an occasional passer-by, he glimpsed buildings, a monastery or a church, hidden amidst tall, bare trees.

He sat down on the front steps of the house, tired out by his morning's expedition. His arm was numb from carrying his bag and he was hungry, since all he had eaten that morning in the refectory of the Carmelites was some bread dipped in soup. A nearby bell was chiming three o'clock when a sturdily built man, wearing a grey wig and leaning on a cane very like a cudgel, curtly asked him to make way. Guessing who this was, Nicolas stepped aside, bowed and began to speak:

'I beg your pardon, Monsieur, but I'm waiting for Commissioner Lardin.'

Two blue eyes stared at him intently.

'You're waiting for Commissioner Lardin? Well, I've been waiting for a certain Nicolas Le Floch since yesterday. Would you know him by any chance?'

'That's me, Monsieur. As you can see . . .'

'No explanations . . .'

'But . . .' stammered Nicolas, holding out Sartine's letter.

'I know better than you do what orders the Lieutenant General of Police gave you. I have no use for this letter. You may keep it as a souvenir. It will tell me nothing I don't already know and merely confirms that you did not comply with the instructions given.'

Lardin knocked and the woman reappeared in the doorway.

'Monsieur, I did not want . . .'

'I know, Catherine.'

He motioned impatiently, as much to interrupt his servant as to invite Nicolas inside. He took off his coat to reveal a sleeveless, thick-leather doublet and, removing his wig, uncovered a closely shaven head. They entered a library, and Nicolas was stunned by its beauty and tranquillity: the dying embers in the carved marble fireplace, a black and gold desk, the *bergères* upholstered in Utrecht velvet, the light-coloured panelling on the walls, the framed prints and the richly bound books lining the shelves all helped to create an atmosphere that someone more worldly than Nicolas would have described as voluptuous. He vaguely sensed that these refined surroundings were somewhat at odds with the boorish appearance of his host. The main drawing room at Château de Ranreuil, though still half medieval, had been until then his only point of reference in such matters.

Lardin remained standing.

'Monsieur, this is a very odd way to begin a career in which exact-ness is of the essence. Monsieur de Sartine entrusts you to my charge and I don't know to what I owe this honour.'

With a wry smile Lardin made his finger joints crack.

'But I obey and you must do the same,' he continued. 'Catherine will take you to the third floor. I can only offer you a meagre attic room. You will take your meals with the servants or out of the house, as you wish. Each morning you will appear before me at seven o'clock. You must, I am told, learn the law. For that you will go for two hours each day to Monsieur de Noblecourt, a former magistrate, who will assess your abilities. I expect you to be perfectly assiduous and unfailingly obedient. Tonight, to celebrate your arrival, we shall dine together as a family. You may go.'

Nicolas bowed and left. He followed Catherine, who settled him into a small attic room. To reach it he had to cross a cluttered loft. He was pleasantly surprised by the size of the room and by the presence of a window which overlooked the garden. It was sparsely furnished with a small bed, a table, a chair and a chest of drawers cum washstand with its basin and ewer and a mirror above it. The wooden floor was covered with a threadbare rug. He put his few possessions away in the drawers, removed his shoes and went to sleep.

When he woke it was already dark. After quickly washing his face and combing his hair, he went downstairs. The door to the library where he had been received by Lardin was now shut, but those to other rooms along the corridor were still open. This enabled him to cautiously satisfy his curiosity. First he saw a drawing room decorated in pastel colours, compared to which the library suddenly seemed positively austere. In another room a table had been laid for three. At the end of the corridor another door led to what had to be the kitchen, judging by the smells coming from it. He went closer. The heat in the room was intense and Catherine kept having to wipe her brow with a cloth. When Nicolas entered she was opening oysters and, to the surprise of the young Breton who was used to swallowing them live, she was removing the contents of the shells and placing them on an earthenware plate.

'May I ask what you are preparing, Madame?'

She turned around in surprise.

'Don't call me Madame. Call me Catherine.'

'Very well,' he said, 'and my name's Nicolas.'

She looked at him, her unprepossessing face lighting up and becoming more attractive. She showed him two capons she had boned.

'I'm making capon and oyster soup.'

As a child Nicolas had enjoyed watching Fine prepare delicacies, the canon's one weakness. Gradually he had even learnt how to make certain Breton specialities, such as *far*, *kuign aman* or lobster in cider. Nor was his godfather, the marquis, averse to turning his hand to this noble activity which, to the canon's great disgust, he described as one of the seven 'lively' sins.

'Cooked oysters!' exclaimed Nicolas. 'Where I come from we eat them raw.'

'What! Living creatures?'

'And how exactly do you make this soup?'

Going on his experience with Fine, whom he had needed to spy on for a long time in order to discover her recipes, Nicolas was expecting to be thrown out of the kitchen.

'You so good that I tell you. I take two nice capons and bone them. I stuff one with flesh of other and add bacon, egg yolks, salt, pepper, nutmeg, *bouquet garni* and spices. I tie it all with string and poach in stock gently. Then I roll my oysters in flour and I fry them in butter with mushrooms. I cut up the capon and lay out the oysters, pour on the stock and serve with a trickle of lemon and some spring onion, piping hot.'

Nicolas could not contain his enthusiasm and it showed; listening to Catherine had made his mouth water and he felt even hungrier. So it was that he won over Catherine Gauss, a native of Colmar, a former canteen-keeper at the battle of Fontenoy, the widow of a French guard and now cook to Commissioner Lardin. The formidable servant had adopted Nicolas for good. Now he had one ally in the household and he felt reassured by his ability to charm.

Nicolas was left with confused memories of the dinner. The splendour of the table with its crystal, silverware and sparkling damask tablecloth gave him a feeling of well-being. The warmth of the room with its gilded grey panelling and the shadows cast by the gleam of the candles created a cocoon-like atmosphere. This, added to his already weak state, made Nicolas feel languid, and the first glass of wine went straight to his head. The commissioner was not present; only his wife and daughter kept Nicolas company. They seemed of about the same age and he soon gathered that Louise Lardin was not Marie's mother but her stepmother, and that there was little love lost between the two women. Whereas Louise seemed anxious to come across as assertive and rather flirtatious, Marie remained reserved, observing her guest out of the corner of her eye. One was tall and blonde, the other slight and dark-haired.

Nicolas was surprised by the delicacy of the dishes served. The capon and oyster soup was followed by marbled eggs, partridge hash, blancmange and jam fritters. Nicolas, who was well versed on the subject, identified the wine as a Loire vintage, probably a Bourgueil, because of its blackcurrant colour.

Madame Lardin questioned him discreetly about his past. He had the feeling that she particularly wanted to clarify the origin and nature of his relations with Monsieur de Sartine. Had the commissioner given his wife the task of getting Nicolas to talk? She filled his glass so generously that the idea did cross his mind but he thought no more of it. He spoke a great deal about his native Brittany, giving them a thousand and one details that made them smile. Did they take him for an object of curiosity, some exotic foreigner?

It was only later, after he had got back to his garret, that he began to have his doubts: he wondered whether he had been too talkative. In fact he was so unclear as to why Monsieur de Sartine should have taken an interest in him that he easily convinced himself that he could not have let slip anything compromising. Madame Lardin must have been disappointed. He recollected also the irritable expression on Catherine's face when she served or listened to Louise Lardin, who was herself very distant towards the servant. The cook muttered under her breath, looking furious. When, on the other hand, she served Marie, the expression on her face mellowed almost to the point of adoration. It was with these observations that the young man ended his first day in Rue des Blancs-Manteaux.

This was the start of a new life for Nicolas, one arranged around a regular sequence of tasks. Rising early, he had a good wash in a garden lean-to which Catherine agreed to let him use.

He had extended his modest wardrobe of clothes at Vachon's, where the mere mention of Monsieur de Sartine's name had opened all doors as well as the credit book, and the tailor even went slightly beyond the original order, much to Nicolas's embarrassment. From now on, when he looked in a mirror, he saw the reflection of a dashing young man soberly but elegantly dressed and the lingering looks Marie gave him were confirmation of his changed appearance.

At seven o'clock he appeared before Commissioner Lardin, who informed him of his timetable. His lessons with the magistrate Monsieur de Noblecourt, a small kindly old man, and a keen chess player and flautist, were enjoyable moments of relaxation. Thanks to his teacher's knowledgeable advice he became a keen concert-goer.

Nicolas continued to explore Paris and the *faubourgs*. Never, not even in Guérande, had he walked so much.

On Sundays, he went to concerts of sacred music that were given then in the great hall of the Louvre. One day he found himself sitting next to a young seminarist. Pierre Pigneau, a native of Origny in the diocese of Laon, longed to join the Society of Foreign Missionaries. He explained to an admiring Nicolas his vow to dispel the darkness of idolatry with the light of the Gospels. He wished to join the mission in Cochin China, which for the past few years had been subject to terrible persecution. The young man, a tall, ruddy-faced lad with a sharp sense of humour, agreed with Nicolas about the poor performance of an *Exaudi Deus* given by the celebrated Madame Philidor. So indignant were they at the audience's applause that they got up together and left. Nicolas accompanied his new-found friend to the Seminary of the Thirty-Three. After arranging to meet up again the following week, they went their separate ways

The two young men soon took to ending their outings at Stohrer's, pastry-cook to the King. His shop in Rue Montorgueil had been a fashionable meeting place ever since its owner had supplied the court with cakes of his own creation that were especially to the liking of the Queen, Marie Leszczyńska. Nicolas greatly enjoyed the young priest's company.

In the beginning, Lardin, whose duties were not confined to a particular district, instructed him to accompany him on his assignments. Nicolas experienced the early morning routine of sealing up property, confiscating goods, making reports or merely settling the disputes between neighbours that were so common in *faubourg* tenements where the poorest people crowded together. He made the acquaintance of inspectors, men of the watch, guards on the ramparts, gaolers and even executioners. He had to steel himself for the horrendous spectacles of the torture chamber and the great morgue. Nothing was kept from him and he soon learnt that in order to function properly the police had to rely on a host of informers, spies and prostitutes, a twilight world that enabled the Lieutenant General of Police to know more about the secrets of the capital than anyone else in France. Nicolas also realised that, through his control of the postal service and all private correspondence, Monsieur de Sartine had at his disposal a precious network for penetrating people's innermost thoughts. As a result, he himself was suitably cautious and remained guarded in the letters he regularly sent to Brittany.

Nicolas's relations with the commissioner had barely changed, either for better or for worse. Lardin's cold, authoritarian manner was met by the young man's silent obedience. For lengthy periods, the policeman seemed to forget all about him. Monsieur de Sartine, on the other hand, did not hesitate to remind Nicolas of his existence. From time to time a little Savoyard chimney sweep would bring him a laconic note summoning him to the Châtelet or to Rue Neuve-Saint-Augustin. These encounters were brief affairs. The Lieutenant General would question Nicolas, who noticed that certain questions revolved oddly around Lardin. Sartine made him describe in minute detail the commissioner's house and the family's habits, even going so far as to ask about what they ate. Nicolas was sometimes a little embarrassed at being interrogated in this way and puzzled as to the meaning of it.

The Lieutenant General of Police ordered him to attend criminal hearings and to give him a written summary of the sessions. One day, he instructed him to report back on the arrest of a man who had circulated letters of exchange with disputed signatures. Nicolas saw the officers of the watch grab an individual in the middle of the street. He had bright eyes and a striking face, and he spoke French with a strong Italian accent. The man called out to him:

'Monsieur, you look like an honest person, look how they treat a citizen of Venice. They are seizing the noble Casanova. Bear witness to the injustice being done. It's a crime against someone who lives and writes as a philosopher.'

Nicolas followed him as far as For-l'Evêque prison. When he gave Sartine his report the Lieutenant General began to swear under his breath and exclaimed:

'He'll be free by tomorrow: Monsieur de Choiseul protects this scoundrel. He's an agreeable fellow, for all that.'

The apprentice policeman drew various conclusions from this episode.

On another occasion he had to offer to purchase some jewellery from a dealer in clocks and watches. The man was awaiting delivery of a large number of precious items before reselling them but he was also expected to go bankrupt. Nicolas was to pass himself off as an envoy of Monsieur Dudoit, a police commissioner from the district of Sainte-Marguerite, whom Monsieur de Sartine suspected of being in league with the dealer. The Paris Chief of Police kept his staff closely in check, wishing to avoid a repeat of the popular unrest of 1750, when there had been protests against the dishonesty of some commissioners. Even the world of gambling was no longer a mystery to Nicolas and he was soon able to distinguish between its recruiters, procurers, keepers, touts and lottery receivers, and the whole world of betting and card sharps.

Everything in Paris, in the world of crime, revolved around gaming, prostitution and theft, and these three worlds were interconnected in countless ways.

*

In fifteen months Nicolas learnt his trade. He knew the price of silence and of secrecy. He had matured and was now better able to control his feelings by restraining his imagination, which was still too wild for his liking. He was no longer the adolescent whom Père Grégoire had welcomed on his arrival in Paris. It was a different Nicolas who received a letter from Guérande informing him of the desperate state of health of his guardian. The sombre and stern silhouette standing at the prow of the barge, facing the raging Loire, on this cold January morning in 1761 was already that of a man.

II

GUÉRANDE

Passion da Vener
Maro dar Zadorn
Interramant d'ar Zul
Dar baradoʒ hec'h ei ʒur.
Dying on Friday
Dead on Saturday
Buried on Sunday
Going to paradise certainly.
Saying from Lower Brittany

Wednesday 24 January 1761

The Loire was kind as far as Angers. Rain which sometimes turned to snow had fallen incessantly and during the overnight stay in Tours the river level had continued to rise. Sometimes, through a break in the fog, a ghost town emerged, grey and lifeless. The banks slipped by unseen. On reaching Angers the barge was caught up in an eddying current. It struck the pier of a bridge, spun around several times and then, out of control and breaking up, it ran aground on a sand bank. The passengers and crew were able to reach the riverbank in a punt.

After reviving himself with some mulled wine at an inn for boatmen, Nicolas made enquiries about possible ways of getting to Nantes. He had been on the barge for several days. Would he reach Guérande in time to see his guardian again? He anxiously assessed the further delays that threatened to build up. The river was becoming less and less navigable and no boat would risk going downstream for the time being. The road seemed no better for the carriages and he gave up the idea of waiting for the next mail-coach.

Confident in his riding ability, Nicolas decided to get hold of a horse and to continue his journey at full gallop. He now had money saved up from the wages paid him by Lardin. He was about forty leagues away from his destination and planned to take the most direct route from Angers to Guérande. Nicolas felt capable of facing up to highwaymen. At this time of year he also had to reckon with the packs of ravenous wolves that roamed around in search of prey and would not hesitate to attack him. But nothing could shake his determination to get there as soon as possible. So he chose a horse, which cost him a king's ransom – the postmaster was reluctant to risk his precious animals in such weather – and he spurred it on as soon as he was beyond the city walls.

That same evening he slept in Ancenis and the following day headed off into the countryside. He reached the abbey of Saint-Gildas-des-Marais without mishap and was greeted with curiosity by the monks, who were delighted by this unexpected diversion. Near the monastic buildings, some wolves were tearing at pieces of dead flesh; they took no notice of him.

By daybreak he had reached the forest of La Bretesche. This was where his godfather, a friend of the Boisgelin family, used to hunt wild boar every autumn. Only the base of the castle towers could be glimpsed in the distance. He was entering a landscape familiar to him.

During the night the wind had turned into a gale, as often happens in these parts. His horse was struggling. The storm raged so loudly that it almost deafened Nicolas. The sodden track, which bordered a peat bog, was strewn with broken branches. The clouds were so low in the sky that the tips of the tall pine trees seemed to be ripping through them.

Sometimes the fury of the elements would suddenly abate. All was still, and in the restored silence the piercing cry of huge seabirds that had been driven inland could be heard as they hovered over the countryside.

But the storm soon resumed. The ground was covered with scudding shreds of white foam which stopped and then moved on. Some became caught in thickets or in the hollows of tree stumps, like sea snow. Others slid along the still-frozen surface of the marshes. A few leagues away the waves deposited white mounds flecked with yellow onto the beach which the storm tore and broke up, thinning out the remains which it carried inland. Nicolas could taste the salty trace of the ocean on his lips.

The old medieval town appeared through a clump of trees. It stood amidst the marshes like an island cut off from the black and white patchwork of land that surrounded it. Nicolas urged his horse on and galloped up to the walls that ringed the town.

He entered Guérande through the gateway of Sainte-Anne. The town seemed to have been deserted by its inhabitants, and the sound of his horse's hooves echoing off the ancient stones reverberated through the streets.

In the old market square he stopped in front of a granite house, tied his mount to a ring on the wall and with trembling legs stepped inside. He bumped into Fine, who, on hearing a noise, had hurried to the door to greet him.

'Oh, it's you, Monsieur Nicolas! Thank God!'

She embraced him tearfully. Beneath her white coiffe, the wrinkled old face of the woman he had cuddled up to for comfort as a child became tense, her cheekbones purplish.

'What a terrible misfortune, Jesus, Mary and Joseph! Our good master fell ill at Mass, on Christmas night. Two days later he caught a cold when he went to relight the Holy Lamp. Since then, everything has got worse, and now there's the gout as well. The doctor says it's started to affect his insides. There's no hope. His mind's gone. He was given the last rites yesterday.'

Nicolas's gaze fell on the chest upon which his guardian's cloak, hat and cane lay. The sight of these familiar objects brought a lump to his throat.

'Fine, let's go to him,' he said, in a voice choking with emotion.

Small and slight, Fine put her arm around the tall horseman's waist as they went upstairs. The canon's bedroom was in semi-darkness, lit only by flames from the fireplace. He lay motionless, his breathing irregular and rasping, with both hands clutching the top of the sheet. Nicolas fell on his knees and whispered:

'Father, I am here. Can you hear me? I am here.'

He had always addressed his guardian in this way. In truth it really was his father who lay dying there, the person who had taken him in, who had looked after him devotedly and always shown him great affection, whatever the circumstances.

In his despair Nicolas became aware of the love he had always felt for the canon, a love that he had never spoken of because he had taken it so much for granted. Never again would he have the chance to express it. He heard again the canon's voice say to him gently – and, he now realised, with such tenderness – 'My dear ward.'

Nicolas took the old man's hand and kissed it. They remained like this for a long while.

Four o'clock was striking when the canon opened his eyes. A tear formed in the corner of one eye and rolled down his hollow cheek. His lips quivered, he attempted to speak, gave a long sigh and then died. Nicolas's hand, guided by Fine's, closed his eyes. His face was serene.

The faithful housekeeper took things in hand with a sort of stubborn determination. As was the custom in her native Cornouaille, the area from which the canon also came, she made the sign of the cross above the dead man's head, then flung the window wide open to help the soul escape from the body. Then she lit a candle at the head of the bed and sent the maid off to inform the chapter and the banner-bearer's wife, who was well versed in these ceremonies. When she arrived, the church bell was tolling the death knell. The two women laid out the body, placed one palm against the other and tied the hands together with a rosary. They put a chair at the foot of the bed and placed on it a bowl of holy water and a sprig of laurel.

To Nicolas the hours that followed seemed interminable. Chilled to the bone, he had no awareness of what was going on around him. He had to respond to the greetings of all those who came to pay their last respects at the deathbed. Priests and nuns took it in turn to recite the litany for the dead. As was the custom, Fine served cider and pancakes to the visitors, many of whom remained in the large room, talking quietly.

Monsieur de Ranreuil was among the first to arrive, without Isabelle. Her absence had further stirred Nicolas's emotions on seeing his godfather again. Beneath his cavalier tone, the marquis had difficulty in disguising his sorrow at the loss of an old friend and, with it, thirty years of companionship. In the throng he scarcely had time to tell Nicolas that Monsieur de Sartine had written to say that he was pleased with him. It was agreed that the young man would go to Ranreuil after the funeral, which was to take place on Sunday.

As the hours slipped slowly by, Nicolas watched the changes to the face of the dead man. The waxen complexion of the early hours had gradually turned copper-coloured, then black, and the shrunken flesh had now hardened into the outlines of a death mask. His feelings of tenderness were disappearing before this decomposing object that could no longer be his guardian. He had to collect himself in order to put aside this impression, but it came back to him several times before the body was placed in its coffin on Saturday morning.

On Sunday the weather was fine and cold. In the afternoon the coffin was borne on a stretcher to the nearby collegiate church. In vain Nicolas looked for Isabelle in the crowd gathered there.

He followed the hymns and prayers without thinking, withdrawing into himself. He examined the stained-glass window above the high altar which portrayed the miracles performed by Saint Aubin, the patron saint of this holy place. The great Gothic arch of predominantly blue glass and stone gradually lost its radiance as the winter shadows lengthened. The sun had disappeared. In the morning it had revealed itself in the glow of sunrise; it had shone in splendour in the glory of midday and now it was declining.

Every man, thought Nicolas, has to go through the cycle of life like this. His gaze fell once more on the coffin draped in a black cloth decorated with silver flames that shimmered in the dim flicker of the candles around the catafalque. He felt overcome once more with sorrow and loneliness.

The church was by now smothered in darkness. Inside, as happens in winter, the granite was weeping. The smoke from the incense and the candles mingled with the moisture oozing from the dark walls. The *Dies Irae* rang out like a final cry of despair. Shortly, pending a permanent burial place, the sad remains would be set down in the crypt near the twin recumbent figures of Tristan de Carné and his wife.

Nicolas reflected that it was precisely here that he had been abandoned; almost twenty-two years previously Canon Le Floch had found him and taken him in. The idea that his guardian was returning to the earth at this very spot was in some mysterious way a consolation.

Monday was bleak and Nicolas felt the after-effects of the journey and his grief. He could not decide whether to visit the marquis who, after the service, had repeated his desire to see him.

Fine, oblivious to her own suffering, tried her best to take his mind off things. Yet despite all her efforts to cook him his favourite childhood dishes he would not touch them, making do with a piece of bread. He spent part of the day wandering through the marshes, staring at the sea-line merging into the pale horizon. He was overcome with a desire to go away and forget. He even went as far as the village of Batz, climbing up to the top of the church spire, as he always used to with Isabelle. He felt better up there, cut off from the world, looking out over the marshes and the ocean far below.

When he came home, soaked through, he found Master Guiart, the notary, waiting for him with his back to the fire. He asked Nicolas and Fine to listen to the reading of a very short will, the main provisions of which lay in the final section: 'I die without wealth, having always given to the poor the surplus that God was willing to grant me. The house I dwell in belongs to the chapter. I pray that providence sees to the needs of my ward. To him shall be given my gold repeater watch, to replace the one stolen from him recently in Paris. As to my possessions proper – clothes, furniture, silverware, paintings and books, he will understand that they be sold to procure an annuity at the rate of one in twenty for Mademoiselle Joséphine Pelven, my housekeeper, who for more than thirty years has devoted herself to my service.'

Fine was crying and Nicolas attempted to console her. The notary reminded them that the young man had to pay the servant's wages, and the doctor's and apothecary's fees, as well as for the hangings, chairs and candles for the funeral. Nicolas's savings were fast diminishing.

After the notary had left he felt like a stranger in his own house and could not bear to see Fine sitting there, grief-stricken. They stayed talking for a long time. She would return to where she came from, as she still had a sister in a village near Quimper, but she was worried above all about what would become of the person she had brought up. One by one the ties linking Nicolas to Guérande were snapping and he was drifting like a boat that had broken its moorings, carried away by swirling currents.

On Tuesday Nicolas at last made up his mind to respond to his godfather's invitation. He wanted to get away from the house on the old market square; Master Guiart had begun the inventory and valuation appraisement of the deceased's possessions, and Fine was finishing her packing.

He rode slowly and pensively, keeping his horse at walking pace. The weather was fine again but a hoar frost covered the moorland with white latticework. The ice in the ruts crackled beneath the horse's hooves.

As he neared Herbignac he remembered the traditional games of *soule*. This violent and rustic sport, which was as old as the hills, required physical strength, courage, a good pair of lungs and unfailing resilience as kicks and blows rained down on the players. Nicolas's body still bore the marks. An injury to his right eyebrow had left a scar that was still visible and his left leg, broken when he was kicked with a clog, still caused him pain when the weather turned wet.

Nevertheless he felt a certain elation at the memory of these frenzied runs in which the *soulet*, a pig's bladder stuffed with sawdust and rags, had to be carried to the goal. The difficulty was that the playing area had no limits and the person carrying the *soulet* could be pursued anywhere, even into ponds and streams, and there were many of those in this part of the countryside. Also, punching, butting and hitting the players with a stick was allowed and even encouraged. At the end of every match the exhausted and bloodied combatants came together for some friendly feasting after a trip to a washtub had removed the caking of clay or mud which covered them. Sometimes the chase even continued as far as the banks of the River Vilaine.

While these thoughts were going through his mind, the young man had neared his destination. As he watched the great oaks around the lake and the tops of the castle towers gradually rise up above the moorland, he strengthened his resolve to clear up the mystery of Isabelle's disappearance.

There had been no news or sign of her since he had left for Paris. At no point had she appeared, not even when Nicolas was in mourning. Perhaps she had forgotten about him, but more cruel than this was his present uncertainty. Although he dreaded the suffering of a definitive separation, he could no longer imagine a future in which his love might still be reciprocated. He was nothing, and his experience in Paris had taught him that birth and wealth always prevailed. His meagre talents counted for little.

The ancient stronghold, set amidst water and trees, was now within hailing distance. Nicolas crossed the first wooden bridge that led him up to the barbican, protected by two towers. He left his horse in the stables, then advanced onto a stone promontory as far as the drawbridge. Compared with the enormous bulk of the building, the entry gate was rather narrow – a reminder of the precautions taken in former times to prevent a rider entering on horseback. The central courtyard, massive and cobbled, lent an air of distinction to the main body of the building flanked by two gigantic towers which occupied its far end.

The chapel bell struck midday. Nicolas, who knew his way around the castle well, pushed open the heavy door of the great hall. A young fair-haired girl, simply clad in a green dress with a lace collar, sat near the fireplace working. At the sound of Nicolas entering she looked up from her sewing.

'You frightened me, Father,' she exclaimed without turning round. 'Was the hunting successful?'

Receiving no reply she became worried, turning to stare into the shadows.

'Who are you? Who allowed you to enter?'

Nicolas pushed the door shut and removed his hat. She let out a faint cry and restrained herself from rushing into his arms.

'I see, Isabelle, that now I truly am a stranger at Ranreuil.'

'Can it be you, Monsieur? How dare you come here after all that you have done?'

Nicolas looked bemused.

'What have I done, except trust you, Isabelle? Fifteen months ago I had to obey your father and my guardian, and leave without saying goodbye to you. You were, it seems, in Nantes, staying with your aunt. That's what I was told. I left and during all these months that I've been alone in Paris, not a word, not a single reply to my letters.'

'Monsieur, I am the one with grounds for complaint.'

Nicolas's anger grew in the face of such an unfair remark.

'I thought you had given me your word. I was very foolish to believe someone so unfaithful, someone . . .'

He stopped, out of breath. Isabelle looked at him, petrified. Her sea-blue eyes were brimming with tears, whether of anger or of shame he did not know.

'Monsieur, you seem very skilled in reversing roles.'

'Your irony hurts me, but you are the unfaithful one. You are the one who made me leave.'

'Unfaithful? In what way? These words are beyond me. Unfaithful . . .'

Nicolas began to pace around the room, then suddenly stopped in front of a portrait of a Ranreuil who stared sternly at him from his oval frame.

'They're all the same, century after century . . .' he muttered under his breath.

'What are you talking about, and what has it to do with us? Do you think he's going to come down from his frame and reply to your soliloquising?'

Isabelle suddenly seemed to him frivolous and detached.

'Unfaithful, yes, you. Unfaithful,' Nicolas repeated sombrely, drawing closer to her.

He stood over her, furious, reddening, with fists clenched. She was frightened and burst out sobbing. Once again he saw the little girl whose childhood sorrows he used to console and his anger subsided.

'Isabelle, what is happening to us?' he asked, taking her by the hand.

The young woman huddled against him. He kissed her.

'Nicolas,' she stammered, 'I love you. But my father told me you were going to Paris to be married. I didn't want to see you again. I made it known that I was in Nantes, at my aunt's. I couldn't believe that you had broken our oath. I felt lost.'

'How could you have believed such a thing?'

The suffering that had tormented him for so many months suddenly vanished in a burst of happiness. Tenderly he held Isabelle to him. They did not hear the door open.

'That will do. You forget yourself, Nicolas . . .' said a voice behind him.

It was the Marquis de Ranreuil, hunting whip in hand.

For an instant the three figures seemed rooted to the spot like statues. Had time stopped? Was this eternity? Then, everything restarted. Nicolas was to retain a terrible memory of this scene, one that would haunt him at night from then on. He let go of Isabelle and slowly turned to face his godfather.

The two men were the same height and their anger made them even more painfully alike. The marquis was the first to speak.

'Nicolas, I want you to leave Isabelle alone.'

'Monsieur, I love her,' replied the young man in a low tone.

He drew closer to her. She looked at each of them in turn.

'Father, you misled me!' she exclaimed. 'Nicolas loves me and I love him.'

'Isabelle, that is enough. Leave us. I must speak with this young man.'

Isabelle put her hand on Nicolas's arm and squeezed it. At this heartfelt gesture, he turned pale and faltered. She rushed out, gathering up her flowing dress.

Ranreuil, who had regained his customary calm, said in a low voice:

'Nicolas, please understand that all this pains me greatly.'

'Monsieur, I understand nothing.'

'I no longer wish you to see Isabelle. Do you understand?'

'I understand, Monsieur, that I am nothing but a foundling, taken in by a good man and that I must disappear.'

He sighed.

'But know, Monsieur, that I would have laid down my life for you.'

He bowed and was preparing to leave when the marquis stopped him, grasping him by the shoulders.

'My godson, you cannot understand. Trust me, one day you will. I cannot explain anything to you now.'

Ranreuil suddenly seemed old and tired. Nicolas freed himself and left.

At four o'clock the young man galloped away from Guérande with no hope of ever returning. All he was leaving there was a coffin still awaiting burial and an old woman crying in a grief-stricken house. He was also leaving behind his childhood and his illusions. He would never think back on this senseless journey home.

Like a sleepwalker, he passed through forests and rivers, towns and villages, stopping only to change horses. However, sheer exhaustion forced him to take the fast mail-coach to Chartres.

It was the very day on which old Émilie had spied two suspicious-looking individuals in Montfaucon.

III

DISAPPEARANCES

Y quieren que adivine
Y que no vea . . .
And they want him to guess
Without being able to see . . .
FRANCISCO DE QUEVEDO Y VILLEGAS

Sunday 4 February 1761

Entering Paris brought Nicolas back to earth with a jolt. He emerged from a long period of torpor.

Darkness had fallen long before the mail-coach reached the central post office in Place du Chevalier-au-Guet. His carriage had been delayed because of the waterlogged and sometimes flooded state of the roads. The Paris he was returning to was one he had never seen before. Despite the weather and the lateness of the hour, a wave of madness was engulfing the whole city. He was straight away surrounded, jostled, overwhelmed and taunted by groups of yelling revellers. Laughing beneath their masks, they cavorted around and got up to all sorts of mischief.

A procession in cassocks, surplices and square caps mimicked the funeral rites of a straw dummy. A wretch dressed as a priest and wearing a stole imitated the celebrant. All around them were prostitutes pretending to be pregnant nuns, weeping and wailing. The whole cortege advanced by torchlight, blessing the spectators with a pig's trotter dipped in dirty water. Everyone seemed caught up in the frenzy and the women were by far the most daring.

A masked prostitute threw herself on Nicolas, kissed him and whispered in his ear 'you look as grim as death' as she handed him a grinning skeleton's mask. He quickly freed himself from her embrace and went off under a hail of abuse.

Carnival had begun. From now until Ash Wednesday, the nights would be given over to riotous youths mingling with the rabble.

Shortly before Christmas Monsieur de Sartine had brought together all the commissioners of the districts, and Nicolas, although in the background, had been present at this council of war. After his bitter experience of the scandalous excesses that had marked the carnival of 1760, the first after his appointment, the Lieutenant General had no wish to see a repetition of events that had worried even the King. Fines and arrests were no longer adequate. Everything had to be anticipated and brought under control; every cog in the police machine had to function with absolute efficiency.

Now that he was confronted with the realities of the night, Nicolas understood Monsieur de Sartine's words better. All along his route bawdiness was the order of the day. He soon regretted not following the prostitute's advice by putting on a mask. Had he worn the same garb as the revellers, he would have passed unnoticed; he would not have had to brush with rampaging gangs who broke windows, extinguished lanterns and performed all sorts of dangerous pranks.

These are real saturnalia, thought Nicolas, noting how everything had been turned upside down. Prostitution, which was normally confined to a few specially designated areas, showed its various faces with total impunity. Night became day with its rowdiness, singing, masks, music, intrigues and enticements.

The Saint-Avoye district, which included Rue des Blancs-Manteaux, seemed calmer. Nicolas was amazed to see the Lardins' residence extensively lit up as the commissioner and his wife rarely had guests, and never in the evening. The door was not locked so he did not need to use his key. He heard a loud conversation echoing from the library. The door was open, and he went in. Madame Lardin had her back to him. She was standing up and talking angrily to a short, burly man in a cloak. Nicolas recognised him as Monsieur Bourdeau, one of the inspectors at the Châtelet.

'Don't worry! Look here, Monsieur, the fact is I haven't seen my husband since Friday morning. He hasn't been home since . . . We were supposed to be having supper with my cousin, Dr Descart, in Vaugirard. It may well be that his duties have detained him overnight: I have the misfortune to be married to a man who never tells me what he does with his time. But three days and now almost three nights without news, I just can't understand it . . .'

She sat down and dabbed her eyes with a handkerchief.

'Something has happened to him. I know it has, I can sense it. What should I do, Monsieur? I'm desperate.'

'Madame – I think I can tell you that Monsieur Lardin was assigned to uncover a clandestine gambling den. It's a very delicate case. But here's Monsieur Le Floch. He'll be able to help me tomorrow if by any chance your husband does not reappear, though I am sure that he will.'

Louise Lardin looked round, stood up and clasped her hands, dropping her handkerchief as she did so. Nicolas picked it up.

'Oh! Nicolas, there you are. I'm so pleased to see you. I'm so alone and at my wits' end. My husband has disappeared and . . . You will help me, Nicolas, won't you?'

'Madame, I'm happy to do so. But I share Monsieur Bourdeau's opinion: the commissioner has doubtless been held up by this case, which I know something about myself – it does indeed involve some delicate matters. Rest yourself, Madame. It is late.'

'Thank you, Nicolas. How is your guardian?'

'He's dead, Madame. I thank you for your concern.'

With a sorrowful expression she held out her hand to him. He bowed. Louise Lardin left the room, without so much as a glance at the inspector.

'You know how to calm down the ladies, Nicolas,' he commented. 'My compliments. I'm very sorry to hear about your guardian . . .'

'Thank you. What's your feeling? The commissioner is a creature of habit. He occasionally spends the night away from home but he always tells his wife in advance.'

'Of habit . . . and of secrets. But the main thing for this evening was to allay his wife's fears. You managed that better than I did.'

Bourdeau studied Nicolas and smiled, his eyes sparkling with a kindly irony. In whom had Nicolas noticed the same expression? Perhaps in Sartine, who often looked at him in the same way. He blushed without picking up on Bourdeau's words.

The two men conversed a few moments more and agreed to decide their next move at dawn. Bourdeau took his leave. Nicolas was on his way up to his attic when Catherine, who had been listening to everything in the shadows, suddenly emerged. Her broad, snub-nosed face seemed pallid in the light of the candle.

'Poor Nicolas. I pity you. How terribly sad. You are alone now. All goes badly, you know, here also. Very badly, very badly.'

'What do you mean?'

'Nothing. I know what I know. I am not deaf.'

'If you know something you must tell me. Don't you trust me any more? You want to add to my suffering. You're heartless.'

Nicolas immediately regretted his lack of sincerity towards the cook, whom he loved dearly.

'Me, heartless? Nicolas cannot say that.'

'Well then, Catherine, speak up. Remember that I haven't slept for several days.'

'Not slept? But, my little one, you must. Here, there has been a big argument between Monsieur and Madame last Thursday about Monsieur Descart, Madame's cousin. Monsieur accused her of flirting with him.'

'With that sanctimonious bigot?'

'Exactly.'

Nicolas was pensive as he went back to his bedroom. As he unpacked his bag, he thought about what Catherine had said. Of course he knew Dr Descart, Louise Lardin's cousin. He was a tall, lanky individual, who always reminded Nicolas of the wading birds in the marshes around Guérande. He did not like his receding profile, accentuated by the lack of a chin and a bony, hooked nose. He felt uncomfortable in his presence; with his preaching voice, his obsession with obscure quotations from the scriptures and his knowing nods, the man irritated Nicolas. How could the beautiful Madame Lardin allow herself to be taken in by someone like Descart? He was suddenly annoyed with himself for not being more concerned about Lardin's fate and, with that, he fell asleep.

Monday 5 February 1761

It was early morning when he left the sleepy household. Only a glum and silent Catherine was up, relighting her kitchen stove. Evidently the commissioner had not returned. Nicolas made his way to the Châtelet via streets littered with rubbish from the night's celebrations, like a receding tide. He even saw a clown in a soiled costume snoring amidst the filth in a carriage entrance. As soon as he arrived he set about writing two notes, one to Père Grégoire and the other to his friend Pigneau, to inform them of the canon's death and of his own return. While he was taking the notes to the post office, the usual little Savoyard chimney sweep appeared with a message from Monsieur de Sartine, asking Nicolas to drop everything and come over to Rue Neuve-Saint-Augustin.

When he entered the Lieutenant General's office Nicolas witnessed a strange spectacle. Sitting in his armchair, the most serious-minded man in France seemed deep in meditation, his brow furrowed. He kept crossing and uncrossing his legs, and tossing his head to the great despair of a hairdresser's assistant who was attempting to arrange his hair into neat curls. Two manservants were opening oblong boxes and carefully removing different styles of wigs that they placed, one after the other, on a dummy clad in a scarlet dressing gown. All Paris knew that Monsieur de Sartine had a strange hobby: he was a passionate wig collector. Such an innocent quirk could be tolerated in a man who had no other known weakness. But on this particular morning he did not seem satisfied by the display and was muttering menacingly.

Having protected Sartine's face with a screen the assistant hairdresser applied large quantities of powder to his head, and Nicolas could not help smiling at the sight of his chief surrounded by a whitish cloud.

'Monsieur, I am very pleased to see you,' said Sartine. 'Not before time. How is the marquis?'

As usual Nicolas was careful not to reply. But for once, Sartine repeated his question.

'How is he?'

He gazed intently at Nicolas. The young man wondered if Sartine, who was always well informed, did not already know all that had happened in Guérande. He decided to remain vague.

'Well, Monsieur.'

'Leave us,' said Sartine, dismissing the servants attending him with a wave of the hand.

He leaned against his desk, a position he often adopted, and, most unusually, invited Nicolas to be seated.

'Monsieur,' he began, 'I have been observing you for the past fifteen months and I have every reason to be satisfied with you. Do not get carried away, you know very little. But you are discreet, thoughtful and precise, which is essential in our profession. I shall come straight to the point. Lardin has disappeared. I do not know the exact circumstances and I have some grounds for concern. As you know, I exercised my discretion in assigning him to some special cases, and he was to report back only to me. Upon your life, Monsieur, do not breathe a word of what I am telling you in confidence. Lardin enjoys great freedom in all this. Too much freedom, perhaps. However, you are too observant not to have noticed that I do sometimes question his fidelity, do I not?'

Nicolas nodded cautiously.

'He is working on two cases,' continued Sartine, 'one of which is particularly delicate because it involves the reputation of my men. Berryer, my predecessor, dealt me this card, so to speak, when he left the position. I could have done without it. I must tell you, Monsieur, that Commissioner Camusot, the head of my Gaming Division and an essential cog in the police machine, has for years been suspected of protecting back-street gambling. Does he profit from it? Everyone knows that the dividing line between the necessary use of informers and unacceptable practices is a very fine one. Camusot has a henchman, a certain Mauval. He is a dangerous individual. Be wary of him. He acts as an intermediary to rig the card games with his agents. Then the police raids and arrests follow. And you know that, according to the regulations, the money confiscated . . .'

He gave Nicolas a questioning nod.

'A portion of the sums confiscated goes to the police officers,' said Nicolas.

'There speaks a true pupil of Monsieur de Noblecourt! My

compliments. Lardin was also working on another case, which I cannot tell you about. All you need to know and remember is that it is, in a way, beyond us. You do not appear particularly surprised by what I've said. Why must I speak to you like this?'

He opened his snuffbox, then snapped it shut, without taking a pinch.

'The truth is,' he went on, 'I have no choice in the matter, and I have to confess that in this instance I am forced to try a new tack. I have here a special commission for you that will give you full powers of investigation and the ability to call on the assistance of the authorities. I will inform the criminal lieutenant and the lieutenant of the watch. As for the district police commissioners, you already know them all. Respect the conventions, however: be firm with them, but do not get into open conflict. Don't forget that you are representing me. Solve this mystery for me, for a mystery it seems to be. Set to work immediately. Begin with the night reports, which are often very revealing. You will have to learn how to compare them and piece things together, even if they at first seem unconnected.'

He handed Nicolas an already signed document.

'This, Monsieur, is an open sesame that will unlock all doors, including those of the gaols. Do not misuse it. Do you have any requests?'

Nicolas addressed the Lieutenant General calmly:

'Monsieur, I have two things to ask . . .'

'Two? You are suddenly very bold!'

'First, I would like to have the services of Inspector Bourdeau to assist me in my task . . .'

'You're rapidly getting a taste for authority. But I approve your choice. It is essential to be able to judge men and their characters, and I approve of Bourdeau. What else?'

'I have discovered, Monsieur, that information does not come free . . .'

'You're quite right and I should have thought of that first.'

Sartine went towards the corner of the room and opened the door of a strong-box. He took from it a roll of twenty *louis d'or* and handed it to Nicolas.

'You will provide me with a full and faithful report of everything you undertake and you will keep an account of this money. If you run short, ask for more. Off you go. There's no time to lose. Do whatever it takes to find Lardin for me.'

Monsieur de Sartine certainly knew how to surprise Nicolas. He was so excited as he left the study that, had it not been for the roll of gold coins weighing down his coat pocket, he would have pinched himself to check if this were not all a dream. But his pleasure at having been singled out and given an important assignment soon gave way to a nagging anxiety. Would he prove equal to the task? He already had an inkling of the obstacles that would inevitably accumulate along the way. His age, his inexperience and the intrigues that such a signal favour could not fail to provoke would further complicate his task. And yet he felt ready to face this new challenge. He compared it to the challenges taken on by the knights of chivalry whose adventures filled the volumes in the library of the Château de Ranreuil.

This thought reminded him of Guérande; he still felt sorrow when he thought about his guardian, the marquis and Isabelle . . .

He read the terms of the warrant Sartine had handed him:

We hereby instruct that the bearer of the present order,
Monsieur Nicolas Le Floch, is, for the good of the State,
charged with a special mission and shall represent us in all
that he does and judges necessary to command in the
execution of the instructions that we have given him. We
instruct also all the representatives of the police and of the
watch of the provostship and viscountship of Paris to afford
him aid and succour in all circumstances, in which duty we
are confident that you will not fail.

Nicolas swelled with pride as he read this, and he felt invested
with a new authority. He suddenly realised what 'the King's
service' meant and how grand it was.

Convinced of being but a humble instrument in a task whose
ramifications were beyond him, he went to the office in the
police headquarters where the reports of the commissioners and
the rounds of the watch were kept. He would see Bourdeau later
and wanted to set about his investigation without delay, as
Sartine had ordered.

Nicolas was well known to the clerks and was therefore
greeted without any awkward questioning. He was given the
latest night reports and immersed himself in repetitive accounts
of the minor incidents that marked the days and nights of the
capital in this turbulent period of Carnival. Nothing caught his
attention. He was much more interested in pouring over copies
of the registers of the Basse-Geôle,[1] which listed the macabre
remains washed up by the Seine. A net laid out downstream of
Paris caught floating bodies that drifted in the waters of the

river. Yet here, too, the dull repetitiveness of the accounts provided him with no clue.

A male corpse, of one said to be called Pacaud, choked by the waters.

A male corpse of about twenty-five years, without wound or bruise, but presenting signs of choking by the waters.

A male corpse of about forty years, without wound or bruise, but from the signs we have seen consider that the aforesaid individual died of a seizure.

The headless body of a child, which we consider to have served for anatomical demonstrations and to have remained underwater for some considerable time.

Nicolas pushed away the register and realised the magnitude of the task he had been set. His doubts returned. Was it possible that Monsieur de Sartine had been making a fool of him? Perhaps he did not want Lardin to be found. Entrusting such an investigation to a beginner was perhaps a way of hushing it up. He set aside these unpleasant thoughts and decided to go to the Châtelet in order to visit the Basse-Geôle and to consult with Inspector Bourdeau.

The inspector's enquiries had been just as fruitless as his own. Nicolas did not know how to tell the inspector about Monsieur de Sartine's commission. He found it simpler to hand him the Lieutenant General of Police's orders, without saying a word. When he had read them Bourdeau looked up and, examining the young man with a kindly smile, said simply:

'This really is news. I always knew you'd go far, and fast. I'm happy for you, Monsieur.'

There was respect in his voice and Nicolas shook his hand, touched by these words.

'However,' continued Bourdeau, 'your problems are far from over. You must not underestimate how difficult it will be. But you have full authority and, if I can help, you know you can count on me.'

'On that very point, Monsieur de Sartine has allowed me to take an assistant. To tell the truth, I've asked for someone to help me. I've put forward a name. Yours, in fact. But I'm very young and inexperienced and I would quite understand if you said no.'

Bourdeau was pink with embarrassment.

'Don't worry. Here we are operating outside the rules. I've been observing you since you joined us and age has nothing to do with it . . . I'm flattered that you thought of me and I would like to work under you.'

They remained silent for a moment and then it was Bourdeau who continued:

'This is all very well but time is short. I've already spoken to Commissioner Camusot. He hasn't seen Lardin for three weeks. Did the Lieutenant General tell you?'

Nicolas reflected that Monsieur de Sartine was deluding himself about the secrecy of the enquiries and did not reply to the inspector's question.

'I should like to visit the morgue. Not that I've found anything in the reports, but no stone must be left unturned.'

Bourdeau held out his open snuffbox to Nicolas, who for once helped himself liberally. This little ceremony was a well-established routine in the Châtelet before facing the stench of the Basse-Geôle. Nicolas was well acquainted with this sinister place; he had been there with Lardin. It was a loathsome cellar, a vile hole, lit only by a half-window. A metal grating and a ramp separated the decomposing bodies from those members of the public allowed in to view them. To prevent the bodies from decaying too quickly, salt was thrown at regular intervals onto those that were most decomposed. It was here that the bodies washed up by the Seine or found on the public highway were identified – or cast back into anonymity.

Visiting time had not yet begun but a man was already there in the dank corner of the vault. He was carefully studying the sorry remains laid out on the flagstones and amongst them Nicolas was surprised to recognise those described in the reports. But there was a great difference between the coldness of the records and the sordid reality. He had not paid any attention to the silent, shadowy figure and it was Bourdeau who pointed out the unusual presence with a nudge and a wink. Nicolas went up to the stranger.

'Monsieur, may we know what you are doing here and who allowed you in?'

The man turned round. With his forehead against the grating, lost in contemplation, he had not heard them approaching. Nicolas jumped with surprise.

'Why, it's Dr Semacgus!'

'Yes, Nicolas, it is indeed me.'

'This is Inspector Bourdeau.'

'Monsieur . . . But you yourself, Nicolas, what ill wind brings you to this place? Still learning your trade?'

'Why yes, and what about you?'

'Do you know Saint-Louis, my servant? He hasn't been seen since Friday and I'm very worried.'

'Since Friday . . . Doctor, this place does not seem to me to lend itself to conversation. Shall we go back to the offices?'

They found themselves in the antechamber of the room where Nicolas had waited for his first interview with Sartine. Now the usher greeted him politely. Nicolas fondly remembered himself as a timid boy from Brittany, and then became annoyed with himself for being wistful about the past. His early life was over and done with; he had to devote himself entirely to his current assignment. They went towards a shabby-looking office used by the duty policemen. Nicolas requested that Semacgus wait a few moments and went in alone with Bourdeau.

'What a strange coincidence,' he said. 'You don't know the doctor and so you won't be as surprised as I am at the occurrence of two such similar events.'

He remained thoughtful for a moment, then went on:

'Guillaume Semacgus is a navy surgeon trained at the school in Brest. He spent a long time at sea on the King's ships, then sailed with the Compagnie des Indes. He stayed for several years in our trading post in Africa, at Saint-Louis in Senegal. He's a scholar and an eccentric, a well-known anatomist. He's also a friend of Lardin's. I've never understood why. It was at Lardin's house that I met him . . .'

An idea crossed his mind but he preferred to keep it to himself.

'He's served by two black slaves whom he treats very well. Saint-Louis acts as his coachman and Awa, his wife, as his cook. He lives alone in Vaugirard.'

Another idea occurred to him, which he likewise set aside.

'Let's go and take a formal statement from him.'

Nicolas opened the door and invited Semacgus to enter. In

broad daylight the man appeared well built, of a type that would not go unnoticed. He was much taller than Nicolas, who was himself of more than average height. He wore a dark coat of military cut with brass buttons, a brilliant white cravat and soft leather boots, and was leaning on a cane with an exotically sculpted silver pommel. His dark-eyed face was large and florid, and he radiated a calm authority. He sat down at a small table on which Bourdeau spread out his papers, having sharpened his quill. Nicolas remained standing behind the doctor.

'Dr Semacgus, you will be so kind as to give us your statement . . .'

'Nicolas, don't take this badly, but where does this self-assured tone come from and by what right . . . ?'

It was Inspector Bourdeau who replied:

'Monsieur Le Floch has been delegated special powers by Monsieur de Sartine.'

'Very well, but you will understand my surprise.'

Nicolas did not react to this.

'Doctor, what do you have to say?'

'As you wish . . . On Friday evening I was invited by a friend to a midnight meal. It's Carnival after all. I was taken to Rue du Faubourg-Saint-Honoré by Saint-Louis, my servant, who occasionally drives the small cabriolet I own. At three in the morning I could find neither my coachman nor my carriage.'

The quill scratched the paper.

'For the last three days I have been going around the hospitals and, as a last resort, I came to the Basse-Geôle, in case . . .'

'You came outside the opening hours,' commented Nicolas.

Semacgus managed not to show his annoyance.

'As you well know, I pursue the study of anatomy and Lardin has given me a note allowing me to enter at any time to examine the bodies laid out in the morgue.'

Nicolas suddenly remembered that this was true.

'Could you tell me the name of this friend who invited you on Friday evening?' he asked.

'Commissioner Lardin.'

Bourdeau was about to say something but a stern look from Nicolas stopped him.

'Where exactly was this party?'

The doctor smiled wryly and shrugged his shoulders.

'In a disreputable place well known to the police. At La Paulet's, the Dauphin Couronné in Rue du Faubourg-Saint-Honoré. You can eat on the ground floor, play *faro*[2] in the cellar and on the upper floors enjoy the girls. A real Carnival paradise.'

'Are you a regular customer?'

'And what if I were? But no, that isn't the case. I was invited by Lardin, which came as rather a surprise. I did remember that he was keen on this sort of entertainment, but he had never invited me to take part before.'

'Did you find it enjoyable?'

'You're very young, Nicolas. The food was choice and the girls were pretty. When the occasion presents itself I don't deprive myself of such pleasures.'

'At what time did you arrive?'

'Eleven o'clock'

'And you left when?'

'At three o'clock, as I already told you.'

'Did Lardin leave with you?'

'He'd made himself scarce long before. And with good reason, after all that commotion.'

'What commotion?'

'Well,' smiled the doctor, 'we were masked . . . Lardin had had a lot to drink, wine and champagne. A little before midnight, a man entered the room. He bumped into Lardin, or the other way round. Lardin tore the man's mask off. I was surprised to recognise Descart. As you may be aware, he's my neighbour in Vaugirard. I got to know him at Lardin's; Madame Lardin is his cousin. It's thanks to him that I found a house on my return from Africa. Descart at La Paulet's! This was the world gone mad. They came to blows immediately. Lardin was beside himself, frothing at the mouth. He accused Descart of wanting to take his wife. Descart retreated and Lardin left shortly afterwards.'

'Alone?'

'Yes. As for me, I went upstairs, with a girl. But does all this really have anything to do with the disappearance of Saint-Louis?'

'And the name of this girl?'

'La Satin.'

'Did Descart recognise you?'

'No, it was not yet midnight and so I still had my mask on.'

'Was he recognised?'

'I don't think so. He put his mask back on immediately.'

Nicolas felt slightly embarrassed to be giving such a grilling to a man he had always liked, a natural reaction given the kindness Semacgus had always shown towards him.

'I must inform you of another disappearance,' he said.

'Commissioner Lardin has not been seen since Friday evening. You are apparently the last person to have seen him.'

Semacgus's reply was simple and surprising.

'It was bound to happen.'

Bourdeau's quill started to scratch away again even harder.

'What do you mean?'

'That Lardin, despising the whole human race as he did, was bound to attract trouble.'

'He's your friend . . .'

'Friendship does not preclude clear-headedness.'

'May I point out that you're talking about him as if he is dead . . .'

Semacgus gave Nicolas a pitying look.

'I can see that the job is growing on you, police officer. Your apprenticeship is apparently over.'

'You haven't answered me.'

'It's only an intuition. My concern is much more for my servant, who you seem to be forgetting about entirely.'

'Saint-Louis is a slave. It's in their nature to run away.'

The brown eyes looked at Nicolas sadly.

'Those are rather conventional ideas for a young person and they don't suit you, Nicolas. Besides, Saint-Louis is free; I freed him. He has no reason to run away. Especially as his wife, Awa, is still at home.'

'Give an exact description to Monsieur Bourdeau. We will look for him.'

'I hope he'll be found. I'm very fond of him.'

'One more question. Did Lardin have that ever-present cudgel of his on Friday evening?'

'I don't think so,' replied the doctor.

He looked at Nicolas again, this time with a flicker of amused curiosity.

'That will be all, Doctor,' said the young man. 'See Bourdeau about Saint-Louis.'

When Semacgus had withdrawn, the two policemen remained deep in thought for a long time. Bourdeau drummed the desk with his fingertips.

'For a first interrogation, no one could have done better,' he said at last.

Nicolas did not respond to this comment which nevertheless pleased him.

'I'm going back to Rue Neuve-Saint-Augustin,' he said. 'Monsieur de Sartine must be told about all this immediately.'

Bourdeau shook his head.

'Not so fast, young man. It's time to eat instead. In fact it's well past lunchtime. Besides, the Lieutenant General is not available in the afternoons. Lunch is on me. I know a little hostelry that serves decent wine.'

After walking along Rue de la Grande Boucherie, which backed onto the Châtelet, they entered a small street, Rue du Pied-de-Bœuf. Nicolas had by now become used to the way of life and even the smells of this district. The butchers slaughtered cattle in their shops and blood ran down the middle of the streets, where it congealed at the feet of the passers-by. But this was nothing compared with the odours from the melting-houses for animal tallow. Bourdeau negotiated his way between ruts and puddles, oblivious to the stench. Nicolas, who had just returned from Brittany and could still feel the ocean's breath on his skin, put his handkerchief to his face, much to his companion's amusement.

The inn was welcoming. Its customers were shop boys and notaries' clerks. The innkeeper was from the same village as Bourdeau, near Chinon, and his wine came from there too. They sat down to a fricassée of chicken, bread, goat's cheese and a jug of wine. Despite the unappealing nature of the walk, Nicolas did credit to the *ambigu*[3] and tucked in heartily. The conversation was taken up with planning their campaign: informing Monsieur de Sartine; carrying out enquiries in Vaugirard and Rue du Faubourg-Saint-Honoré; questioning Descart and La Paulet, and continuing to go through the police reports.

It was almost five o'clock when they went their separate ways. Nicolas discovered that Sartine was not at his home; he was at Versailles, summoned by the King. He thought for a moment of going to visit Père Grégoire, but the Carmelite monastery was a long way off and it was getting dark, so he sensibly decided to return to Rue des Blancs-Manteaux.

Things had definitely been going on in the house during his absence. No sooner had he got inside than again he heard two people talking, this time in Madame Lardin's drawing room.

'He knew everything, Louise,' said a man's voice.

'I know, he made a terrible scene. But for heaven's sake, Henri, explain why you were in that place at all.'

'It was a trap. I can't tell you anything . . . Did you hear a noise?'

They stopped talking. A hand had been pressed against Nicolas's mouth, another pushed him into the darkness and dragged him into the pantry. He could see nothing and heard only heavy breathing. He was released. He felt someone's breath and smelled a fragrance that seemed familiar to him, then the footsteps receded and he found himself alone in the dark, watchful and motionless. A little later, the front door closed and he heard Louise Lardin returning to her rooms on the first floor. He waited a few moments more, then went up to his garret.

IV

DISCOVERIES

'The more light we have,
the less clearly we are able to see.'
THE PRINCE DE LIGNE

Tuesday 6 February 1761

As soon as he awoke Nicolas tried to remember down to the very last detail the scene that he had witnessed on his return to Rue des Blancs-Manteaux. The fleeting fragrance he had smelled could only have belonged to Marie Lardin. If Catherine the cook had grabbed him like that he would instantly have recognised her from the mixture of odours that always clung to her clothes. But why should Marie have dragged him away like this? She doubtless wanted to protect him, but from whom? He had identified the voices of Descart and Madame Lardin, and the meaning of their words was by now quite clear to him. But more than one conclusion could be drawn from them. Descart had a special relationship with Louise Lardin. He had recounted the Dauphin Couronné incident and she had been outraged by his presence at that establishment. But why had he spoken of a 'trap'? Was it a way of exonerating himself for having been there?

For Nicolas, this brief exchange took on a special significance in the light of the attack that was only intended to protect him. The fact that someone – Marie Lardin – had considered he was in danger simply for having overheard the conversation gave a disturbing dimension to all this. From now on his best option would be to play the innocent and disguise his curiosity from everyone in the house. They would all realise soon enough – if they had not done so already – that he had been appointed by Sartine to investigate the commissioner's disappearance.

While he was thinking, Nicolas caught himself humming an aria from Rameau's *Dardanus*. This had not happened to him since he'd left Guérande. Life was, it seemed, returning to normal. He was impatient to start his day's work. He had joined the police without deliberately choosing it as a career. A stranger to Paris, he had been taken in hand by Sartine and one thing had led to another. What was happening now, with its twists and turns, surprises, discoveries and sometimes pitfalls, filled him with a new energy, even if some questions remained unanswered and he still felt doubtful when he was in the thick of it. Semacgus's interrogation left him with a confused feeling of bitterness. He wondered whether he should remain at the Lardins' house when all the indications were that one day he would be obliged to question them, too.

As he finished his quick wash in ice-cold water, he was suddenly struck by the silence in the house. Admittedly it was a quiet neighbourhood but it suddenly seemed to be muffled, as if under a blanket. A glance outside gave him the explanation: day was breaking and the dawn cast a yellowish light over a garden covered in snow.

The canon's watch struck half past seven. When Nicolas went downstairs Catherine was not there, but she had left a pot of soup on the stove which he knew was for him. Freshly baked bread awaited him on the table. Every Tuesday the cook left the house early with two enormous wicker baskets to go to the Saint-Jean market. She walked as fast as her enormous bulk allowed to take advantage of the early hour. With a little luck she might find fish so fresh it was still alive; the barges transporting it from the Lower Seine were equipped with salt-water tanks for the pick of the catch.

He was about to go out when he heard Louise Lardin calling him. She was sitting at the desk in the library, writing in semi-darkness. Only a candlestick, its candle almost spent, lit up her tired and haggard face.

'Good morning, Nicolas. I came down very early. I couldn't sleep. Guillaume has still not returned. I didn't hear you come in yesterday evening. What time was it?'

The concern was new and the question direct.

'Well after eight o'clock,' said Nicolas, lying.

She gave him a quizzical look and he noticed for the first time that her usual smile was missing. How hard her tight-lipped face could appear, with her hair undone and no make-up.

'Where can he be?' she asked. 'Did you see Bourdeau yesterday? No one tells me anything.'

'The search is continuing, Madame. You may be sure of that.'

'Nicolas, you must tell me everything.'

She had got up and was now smiling. Forgetting how scantily dressed she was, she resumed her normal seductive pose. She reminded him of the enchantress Circe and his mind began to wander. He imagined himself suddenly transformed into a woodpecker like King Picus, or a swine like Ulysses' companions. He did not think Catherine's soup would protect him from Louise's evil spells. He was unable to keep a straight face at these mythological musings, which reminded him a little of his school days.

'So you find this amusing, do you?' asked Louise Lardin.

Nicolas pulled himself together.

'No, Madame, not at all. Excuse me but I must leave.'

'Go, Monsieur, go. No one is stopping you. Perhaps you will bring back good news. But, the more I look at you, the more convinced I am that I can expect nothing from you.'

He was on his way out when she called him back and held out her hand.

'Excuse me, Nicolas. I didn't mean that. I'm anxious and worried. You are my friend, are you not?'

'I am your servant, Madame.'

He hurriedly took leave of this woman whose obvious duplicity intrigued him. He could not identify exactly what kinds of feelings she aroused in him.

The snow had stopped falling, there was a sharp chill, but the day promised to be fine. At police headquarters Nicolas met Monsieur de Sartine on the staircase. The Lieutenant General was impatient and in a hurry and Nicolas was forced to give him an account of the initial results of his investigations right there on the steps. If he had been expecting some flattering approbation he was soon disappointed and had to make do with a vague grunt.

Nicolas did, however, venture to request permission to borrow a mount from the official stables as he wanted to make his way to Vaugirard to question Dr Descart. The answer, delivered in the haughtiest of tones by a furious Sartine, was that having been given a commission, a move that was perhaps already proving ill-advised, Nicolas should simply make good use of it, without worrying people with trivial details. He could take one, a score or fourscore horses, donkeys or mules, as long as it was in the King's service.

Mortified by this reply, Nicolas went off to meet Bourdeau. He recounted this altercation, but regretted doing so immediately, as if he had let slip a personal weakness. The inspector listened with amusement and attempted to convince him of the insignificance of the incident, which had damaged nothing more than his self-esteem. Nicolas blushed and readily agreed.

Bourdeau pointed out that Monsieur de Sartine had dozens of cases on his hands and that Lardin's disappearance was probably not the most important of them. He also had to answer to the Comte de Saint Florentin, a minister of the King's household, whose responsibilities included Paris, and above him the chief ministers, who all wanted a say and, lastly, the King himself to whom he had direct access and from whom he received his orders. Could there possibly be a more delicate post, with more constant worries? This was ample justification for his occasional changes of mood and for an immoderate love of . . . wigs. What were they, in comparison, other than mere cogs in the immense police machine? Nicolas should learn his lesson and get on with the job.

Still smarting, the young man took the hint and changed the

subject, thanking heaven for having granted him a companion who knew how to tell him the truth. After giving Bourdeau the task of reading the latest reports he went to the stables to choose a horse – there were no mules or donkeys to be seen – and set off for Vaugirard.

Nicolas crossed the Seine via Pont-Royal and arrived at the Esplanade des Invalides. There he stopped, awestruck by the splendour of the scene. The sun cast slanting shafts of light through dark clouds. With the help of the wind, an invisible ballet master directed constantly shifting and alternating plays of darkness and light that swept across this immense panorama. The curtain of shadow pierced by flashes of light gave way at each moment to its opposite: the brightness then flickered, swallowed up by a dark fiery glow.

In the middle of all this, majestically towering over the scene, the dome of the church of Saint-Louis seemed to swivel on its stone axis as it reflected the flitting shadows. The radiance of the dome was further highlighted by the horizontal line of the rooftops, their wet slates gleaming where the snow had already slid down. White heaps piled up around the attic rooms and the chimney pots, and came crashing down in blocks, topping the building with powdery whirls. Nicolas, an unrepentant dreamer before ocean skies, marvelled at the multifarious range of greys, blacks, whites, golds and deep blues. So much beauty stunned him and his heart was racing with joy. He found himself in love with a Paris that allowed him such feelings, and he understood for the first time the deep meaning of the sentence from the scriptures: 'And there was light.'

The wind that slapped his face brought him out of his dream and back to the nagging fear of confronting Descart. He spurred his horse on and felt giddy from the icy air. Holding his hat, lest it blow away, he sat straight in the saddle and raised his head high. His hair billowed freely, like the brown mane of his mount, and from a distance this moving mass of muscle, cloth and leather must have looked like a ghostly centaur. The repeated thud of hooves on the snow produced a dull swishing sound, their irregular beat only adding to the strangeness of the misty apparition crossing the esplanade. Beyond the Vaugirard toll-gate, dreary-looking hills stretched out from the city walls to the heights of Meudon. The windmills, like towers of ice, kept guard; from their frost-encrusted sails hung delicate lances of crystal. All was bright, silky and brittle. The giddiness of the ride and the sun's reflection in the snow again numbed Nicolas's senses, as he passed like a dark streak through a colourless world.

In the midst of a petrified army of vines there appeared snow-covered hovels and bourgeois dwellings. He had the feeling of being worlds away from the capital. At 'La Croix Nivert', a crossroads forced him to try to find his bearings. He had come to see the doctor once before, to give him a letter from Lardin. Descart had not even invited him inside or deigned to speak to him.

Nicolas eventually located the residence. It was a large building surrounded by high walls, the tops of which were crowned with fragments of glass set into the mortar. A dog began to howl and the horse shied so much that a less experienced rider than Nicolas would have been thrown from his saddle straight away. He calmed the angry beast by stroking its neck and whispering words of comfort.

Jumping to the ground, Nicolas hesitated a moment, and then pulled a handle that rang a bell in the distance. The dog began to howl again. Nobody came. Nicolas then noticed that the gate was ajar, and he went through the garden along a path with box trees on either side. The shutters were closed, but the door opened with one turn of the handle.

He was surprised to find himself on a sort of inner terrace. This turned out to be the upper part of a stone staircase which led down to an enormous room via two semi-circular flights of steps. He was struck by the strange odour of something musty, like damp felt, cold incense and extinguished candle, added to which was an all-pervasive sweet, metallic and acid stench that Nicolas was unable to identify.

The young man contemplated the scene below him, of a tiled room with windows at either end concealed by heavy curtains and a fireplace opposite the staircase. The high ceiling consisted of exposed beams blackened by smoke. Wooden shelves covered almost all the walls. Above the fireplace a large crucifix offered the harrowing vision of a Christ made of ivory, his arms stretched upwards. It caught Nicolas's attention: his guardian, the canon, would have required, if not a certificate of confession, at least a true and complete profession of faith from any parishioner owning one like this.[1] In a corner of the room, Descart, a blood-spattered apron covering his coat, was finishing the process of bleeding an elderly woman whose right arm, held in position by bandages and splints, appeared to be broken. The contents of a metal bowl in which a crimson pool shimmered darkly revealed that several basins of blood had already been drawn. The ashen-faced patient was leaning back in an armchair in a faint as Descart dabbed her temples with smelling salts. Nicolas cleared his throat and coughed. The doctor turned round.

'Can't you see that I'm operating?' he said angrily. 'Get out.'

The woman was coming round and she began to groan feebly, taking up all the doctor's attention.

'Monsieur,' said Nicolas, 'when you have finished what you are doing, I should like to speak with you. To question you in fact.'

Once again he was annoyed with himself for having been unable to find the right word in the first place, like a horse shying at an obstacle.

'To question me?' exclaimed the doctor. 'To question me! A flunkey to question me! I demand you leave.'

Nicolas, white-faced, rushed down the staircase and stood firmly in front of Descart, who stepped back a pace, his face twitching.

'Monsieur,' said Nicolas, 'I would ask you not to insult me. You may come to rue it in several ways. I shall not leave and you will hear me out.'

The woman, still dazed, looked at each man in turn.

'I shall unleash my dog and then you will leave, I guarantee it,' growled Descart.

He lifted his patient to her feet, supporting her on her good arm, and led her towards the door.

'Madame, go home. You need complete rest and a strict diet. I shall see you again tomorrow. Further bleedings will be necessary. Everything depends on the reaction between opposites. Go.'

No one had heard a man enter noiselessly who, for some moments, had been looking down at the scene in the semi-darkness.

'At this rate, honourable colleague, you'll soon have no patients left alive.'

Nicolas immediately recognised Semacgus's voice.

'All we need now is for the devil himself to put in an appearance,' exclaimed Descart, pushing the woman out of the room.

Semacgus went down the stairs and greeted Nicolas with a wink. He walked up to Descart.

'Dear colleague, I wish to have a word with you.'

'You, as well! But to say "colleague" is going too far. You put on your airs and graces, Monsieur Journeyman Surgeon.[2] One day I shall succeed in having you banned. A man who rejects bleedings, who lets nature follow its course and who treats people without having the qualifications.'

'Leave my qualifications out of this – they are just as good as yours. As to bleedings, in this enlightened century you are a throwback to the past.'

'Throwback to the past! He's insulting Hippocrates and Galen. "The teaching of the wise man is a source of life."'

Semacgus took hold of a chair and sat down. Nicolas sensed that in doing so he was seeking to contain the violence of his temperament. This position, he had observed, was a protection against excessive behaviour; anger comes upon one less quickly when seated than when standing.

'Your own teaching is a cause of death. When on earth will you understand that bleeding, though useful in cases of plethora, is harmful in many others? How can you treat this poor woman's fracture by weakening her? More than this, you starve her whereas you should be prescribing her good food and burgundy. That would help to cure her.'

'He blasphemes against the Scriptures,' yelped Descart. ' "The wicked is snared by the transgression of his lips." If your trivial reflections were to be examined seriously, you would know, as Batalli[3] teaches, that "blood in the human body is like water in a good spring: the more you draw, the more there is." The less blood, the more blood. Everything is expelled and dissolved; the fevers, the humours, the bile, the acrimonies and the viscosity. The more one bleeds, the better one is, you poor ignoramus.'

Traces of foam began to appear at the corners of his thin lips. He had instinctively taken hold of his lancet and was tracing scrolls on the shiny, bloodstained surface of the pan.

'Let's stop there, Monsieur. This is a very bad example. Poor Patin[4] demanded to be bled seven times and died. As far as authors go, I prefer to follow our friend Sénac, the King's doctor, whom you presumably know. When the intention is to divert blood from the head it is in fact diverted from the heel. You are neither learned nor polite nor honest, and I'm of a mind to ask you very directly . . .'

Nicolas decided to interrupt this argument which was beyond him, although he dimly understood that Semacgus's arguments bore the hallmark of common sense. This response was probably unfair because his judgement was clouded by his personal preference. But he was also embarrassed to see Semacgus fall for this game, reacting to Descart's provocations and becoming involved in this ridiculous quarrel.

'Gentlemen, that will do,' he interjected. 'You will debate this matter another time. Monsieur Descart, I am here on behalf of Monsieur de Sartine, the Lieutenant General of Police, from whom I have full powers to investigate Commissioner Guillaume Lardin's disappearance. We know that you were among the last people to have seen him.'

Descart took a few steps and poked the fire, which crackled and flared back to life.

'Anything can happen in this sinful world,' he sighed. 'This young fellow . . .'

'I await your answer, Monsieur.'

'I did indeed dine at the Lardins', ten days ago.'

Semacgus made a movement but Nicolas held him back, putting a hand on his arm. He could sense the anger building up inside him.

'And you haven't seen him since?'

'You have my answer. "You are my witnesses, oracle of God."'

'Have you met with Lardin since?'

'Certainly not. What is the reason for this inquisition?'

Semacgus could not stop himself speaking out, but his question was not the one that Nicolas feared.

'Descart, what have you done with Saint-Louis?'

'Nothing at all. Your negro is of no interest to me. He sullies the Lord's earth.'

'I've been told . . .' Nicolas intervened.

He was again surprised by Descart's reply.

'That I shot at him, on St John's Day. The devil was stealing cherries from my garden. He got no more than he deserved – a dose of grapeshot.'

'A dose that took me more than two hours to remove,' said Semacgus angrily. 'My servant did not steal from you, he was going past your house. Now he has disappeared. What have you done with him?'

Nicolas was interested to note the turn in the confrontation. Hitting two flints together produces a spark. Let's leave them to it, he thought to himself, and the truth might emerge.

'Explain then to this young man what you do with the slave's woman!' sneered Descart. ' "Their faces are darker than soot." Everybody knows what filthy business you get up to with her. The jealous beast threatened you and you killed him. That's all there is to it.'

Semacgus stood up. Nicolas squeezed his arm hard; he sat down again.

'It would seem that insolence and devoutness go hand in hand, Monsieur Ten Commandments. You may rest assured that I will not give you a moment's peace until I find my servant, who incidentally is not a slave but a human being like me, like Monsieur Le Floch, and perhaps even like you, Monsieur Bleeder.'

Descart was still obsessively gripping the lancet. The three men remained silent until Nicolas, in an icy voice and with an authority that took them by surprise, brought the curtain down on the scene.

'Dr Descart, I have listened to you. Rest assured that your statements will be checked and that you will be summoned to appear before a magistrate who will question you not only about Commissioner Lardin's disappearance, but also about that of Saint-Louis. Monsieur, I must bid you goodbye.'

As he quickly led Semacgus away, he heard Descart proffer a final biblical quotation:

' "I was a reproach among all mine enemies, but especially among my neighbours, and a fear to mine acquaintances." '

The cold air did them good. Semacgus's naturally florid face was by now bright red and a purplish vein was throbbing hard at his temple.

'Nicolas, I did not kill Saint-Louis. You believe me, don't you?'

'I do believe you. But I would also like to believe you about Lardin. You understand that you are among the suspects.'

'Now you, too, are talking as if Lardin is dead.'

'I didn't mean to.'

'But why did you stop me talking to him about the evening at La Paulet's?'

'You said it yourself: there's nothing to indicate that anyone recognised him. It would be your word against his. I await further evidence from witnesses to corroborate your statement. But why does he hate you so much, apart from your disagreements about medicine?'

'Don't underestimate them, Nicolas. They play a part in the long-standing rivalry between doctors and surgeons. I treat some of the poor; he believes that I am trespassing on his territory and losing him custom.'

'But you used to be friends, didn't you?'

'Acquaintances, at best. Because of Lardin.'

'Answer me this, was there anything between Louise Lardin and yourself?'

Semacgus gazed up at the brilliant blue sky. He blinked, looked at Nicolas's tense face and, laying his hand on the young man's shoulder, began to speak in a hushed voice.

'Nicolas, you are very young, let me say it again. To tell the truth, I fear that Louise Lardin is a dangerous woman, of whom you, too, should beware.'

'Is that an answer?'

'The answer is that I yielded to her once.'

'Did Lardin know?'

'I don't know, but Descart caught us.'

'A long time ago?'

'About a year.'

'Why doesn't Descart talk about it?'

'Because he himself is in the same position. Were he to accuse me, this accusation could be turned against him.'

'Who knows about this business with Descart?'

'Ask Catherine, she knows everything. And if Catherine knows, Marie will find out very quickly; she hides nothing from her.'

Nicolas held out his hand to Semacgus with a beaming smile.

'We're still friends, aren't we?'

'Of course, Nicolas. No one wants your investigation to succeed more than I do and for God's sake don't forget poor Saint-Louis.'

Nicolas returned to Rue Neuve-Saint-Augustin, sobered by what he had just learnt but cheered to be friends once more with Semacgus. He was pleased to think that Monsieur de Sartine would be deprived of certain information and that he would only give him a report when he had matters of more substance to submit to him. He still harboured some resentment towards him from their last meeting.

Bourdeau was waiting for him, looking busy and enigmatic. A report from the men of the watch had intrigued him. A certain Émilie, a soup seller, had been arrested on Saturday 3 February at about six o'clock in the morning by the toll-gate guards on their night rounds. When she was questioned at the police station of Le Temple, the details she had given were so extraordinary that they were taken to be fictitious and had been noted down only as a formality. The old woman had been released. Bourdeau had carried out his own investigation. She was known to the police for petty offences and as a former woman of easy virtue, who as she got older had descended into debauchery, then poverty. Bourdeau had jumped into a carriage, found old Émilie and had just questioned her at the Châtelet, where she was being held. He handed his report to Nicolas.

Tuesday 6 February 1761

Before us, Pierre Bourdeau, Inspector of Police at the Châtelet appeared one Jeanne Huppin, otherwise known as 'old Émilie', soup seller and garment mender, dwelling in lodgings in Rue du Faubourg-du-Temple, near La Courtille.

On being questioned she said in these very words 'Alas, my God, to think I am come to this. My sins are the cause of it all.'

Asked as to whether she did go to the place known as 'La Villette', at the knacker's yard in Montfaucon on the night of Friday 2 February, there to purloin the rotten meat found upon her, the which being illegal and contrary to regulations.

Replied that in truth she had gone to Montfaucon, there to seek sustenance.

Questioned as to whether this meat was intended for her purveyal of soup.

Replied that she had intended to use it for herself and that need and poverty had brought her to this pass.

Said that she would reveal matters providing she be promised it be taken into account, not for the excusing of her conduct but for acting as the good Christian that she was and for the cleansing of her conscience of a dread secret.

Said that being occupied in cutting with a great trencher a morsel of dead beast, she had heard a horse neighing and two men approaching. That she concealed herself from fright and fear of being surprised by what she took for a night round of the watch that surveys sometimes this place. Saw the aforesaid men empty by lantern light two casks of a matter that seemed to her bloody, all the which accompanied by garments. Added that she had heard a crack and seen something burn.

Questioned as to whether she could tell that which had burnt.

Replied that she was too afraid and that fright had taken away her senses. The cold having revived her, she had fled without seeking to examine anything whatsoever for fear of attracting towards her a pack of stray dogs that had gathered. She was crossing through the toll-gate of the city when the guards stopped and questioned her.

Bourdeau suggested going to Montfaucon straight away, in order to see what the situation was. Old Émilie needed to go with them to verify at the scene the accuracy and consistency of what she had said. If her claims were true, this would at least prove that a bloody incident had taken place during the night that Lardin had disappeared. Nicolas objected that at night there were plenty of sinister goings-on in the capital, and that there was nothing to suggest a link between this case and their investigation. However, he agreed to accompany Bourdeau.

Though generous by nature Nicolas was nonetheless thrifty with the funds entrusted to him, and he was reluctant to make a dent in Monsieur de Sartine's finances by hiring a cab. Old Émilie was removed from her cell at the Châtelet but was not told the purpose of the journey. Nicolas was hoping that the agony of her uncertainty would make the destitute creature panic, and so undermine her defences. She was now sitting next to Bourdeau. Nicolas, seated opposite her, could observe this former woman of pleasure at his leisure. He had never seen a sorrier sight than this pathetic relic of past glories. The old woman was wearing a jumble of rags, one on top of the other. Did the poor creature fear being robbed or was she seeking to protect herself from the cold? This heap of torn and filthy clothes looked as if it were parcelled up in a sort of greatcoat made of some unknown material that might have been felt if the passage of time had not transformed it into a sort of fluffy blanket. The garment revealed in parts the splendid remnants of rich fabrics, bits of yellowed lace, of paste and embroidery in silver and gold thread. A whole past life was summed up in the layers covering this human wreck. Out of a shapeless bonnet tied with a ribbon peered a face at once narrow and bloated, in which two care-worn, mouse-grey eyes darted to and fro, unnaturally highlighted by a bluish black that reminded Nicolas of the moustaches he pencilled in with charcoal when he was a child. Her twisted mouth was half-open and revealed a few stumps of teeth and the tip of a tongue that was still surprisingly pink.

After a while, the solemn way in which Nicolas was staring at her began to intrigue old Émilie. Out of habit she eyed him in a way that made him blush down to the roots of his hair. He was horrified at what her expression might mean. She immediately realised that she was on the wrong track, and resumed her slumped position. Then she rummaged around in a sort of green satin handbag, which had known better days, and spread out on her lap her remaining treasures: a hunk of black bread, a broken black onyx fan, a few sols, a small horn knife, a brass rouge box and a shard of mirror. She dipped a dirty finger into the rouge and, looking at herself in the triangular mirror, began to make up her cheeks. Gradually she rediscovered the customary and touching gestures of the woman she had once been. She blinked, moved her head back to take better stock of the result of her efforts, pursed her lips, smiled and tried to smooth her wrinkled brow. Instead of the beggar-woman opposite him, Nicolas thought he could see the silhouette of a charming, joyful young girl, who forty years earlier had enjoyed the company of the Regent every evening. Nicolas looked away, moved by this spectacle.

Soon they were outside the city walls and old Émilie, who had for some time been observing the landscape through the carriage window, recognised the direction they had taken. Pitiful to behold in her anguish, she looked at each of them in turn. Nicolas immediately regretted not having drawn the leather curtains and swore that in future he would pay more attention to this type of detail. Thus he was creating his own method of investigation, as circumstances dictated; the unwritten rules of his profession were impressing themselves upon him day by day. He progressed in his understanding of criminal matters by bringing to them his sensitivity, his skills of observation, the wealth of his imagination and his instinctive responses, which were vindicated after the event. He was his own master, in charge of blaming or praising himself. Above all he had learnt that a flexible approach, based on experience, was the only way to get closer to the truth.

The carriage stopped and Bourdeau got out to speak to some labourers who had approached them, intrigued by their arrival. On a nearby hill a lone horseman watched them from near a great oak tree, whose branches were heavy with a multitude of crows. Nicolas noted the fact without dwelling on it and helped the old woman down. Her hand was clammy and feverish; she could hardly stand and seemed terror-stricken.

'My God, I can't . . .'

'Come, be brave, Madame. We are with you. You have nothing to fear. Show us the place where you hid.'

'I recognise nothing with all this snow, good Monsieur.'

The sky was clear but the cold here was keener than in Paris. The snow crackled underfoot. They edged their way forward and eventually came upon some shapeless heaps, from which emerged hooves covered in frost. Bourdeau questioned one of the knackers.

'How long have these carcasses been here?'

'Four days, at least. With Carnival we haven't worked Saturday or Sunday. In any case the frost has set in in the meantime. Now we'll have to wait for the thaw to be able to handle the dead meat.'

Old Émilie held out her hand and pointed to one of the piles. Bourdeau swept away the snow covering it and revealed the body of a horse. One of its thighs had been cut into.

'Is it that one? Incidentally, what did you do with your trencher?'

'I can't remember.'

Bourdeau continued to work away, kneeling on the ground. A glint of blue flashed in the snow. He lifted up a butcher's cleaver.

'Would that be your implement by any chance?'

She grabbed it and held it tight against her as if it were something precious.

'Yes, yes, that's my knife sure enough.'

Bourdeau had to wrest it from her.

'I can't return it to you quite yet.'

Nicolas intervened.

'Don't fret. You'll get it back. Just tell me where you were watching from.'

This calm voice reassured her. Automatically, she bent to the ground and huddled up to the carcass, peering towards the corner of a brick building situated a few yards away.

'It's over there,' Nicolas said in a hushed voice, helping her to her feet and dusting the snow off her. 'Don't be afraid. The inspector and I will go on our own. Stay here and wait for us.'

They soon came upon several heaps covered with snow. Nicolas stopped, thought for a moment and then asked Bourdeau to go and find an implement to clear away the snow. It was quite obvious that these were not animal carcasses. While he was waiting he poked around in one of the piles. His fingers touched something hard, broken into several pieces, like the teeth of a giant rake. He forced himself to grip it with both hands and pulled hard. A heavy object came away from the frozen ground, and to his horror he saw rising up before him a lump of flesh that he immediately recognised as the remains of a human thorax. By the time Bourdeau returned with a broom, Nicolas, pale as a ghost, was vigorously rubbing his hands with snow.

A glance was enough for the inspector to grasp what the young man was feeling. Without exchanging a word they carefully cleared the ground all around, revealing a quantity of human remains mixed in with straw, and bones that were almost totally bare except for a few frozen and blackened scraps of clothing.

They placed the remains alongside each other and little by little reconstructed what had been a body. The state of the skeleton with its coating of snow showed well enough how savagely the scavenging rats and beasts of prey had attacked it. One didn't have to be a great anatomist to notice that many bones were missing, but the head was there, its jaw fractured. Near the spot where Nicolas had made his first discovery they found some clothes, a leather doublet and a blackish, torn shirt which appeared to be blood-soaked.

Their last find confirmed Nicolas's fears. Lardin's cudgel was revealed, with its strange sculpted designs on the silver pommel and the snake-like creature curled around the stick. The inspector nodded; he, too, had understood. Other clues followed: a pair of grey calamanco breeches, some stockings, sticky with a black substance, and two shoes whose buckles had disappeared. Nicolas decided to add these items to everything else they had found, and to examine them in more detail later. He gave Bourdeau the task of finding something suitable in which they could carry away their macabre harvest. The inspector soon came back with an old wicker trunk bought from a knacker who had kept his apron and tools in it. They quickly filled it up, carefully wrapping the bones in the clothes.

Meanwhile Nicolas seemed to be searching for something else and was ferreting around, crouching, with his nose to the ground. Suddenly he asked Bourdeau to give him a piece of paper and he began to trace some small craters that pockmarked the ground. They had left their impression in the clayey soil before it had been covered up by snow and hardened by frost. Nicolas made no particular comment. He did not wish to pass on the fruits of his reflections, even to Bourdeau. It was not that Nicolas mistrusted him but he was quite happy to lend a certain air of mystery to a turn of events that put the inspector at a disadvantage. He did not enjoy having to be so cautious but he felt it advisable so long as he himself was unclear about things and had not found a satisfactory explanation for some of his own observations.

He responded to his companion's quizzical expression with a toss of the head and a sceptical look. They carried the trunk away. They had forgotten about old Émilie who was watching them with a dazed expression and recoiled as they walked by. Nicolas grabbed her by the arm as they went past and took her back to the carriage. She was crying quietly and her tears made her make-up run, disfiguring her face so much that Nicolas took out his handkerchief and with infinite gentleness wiped away the black and red streaks that were streaming down her cheeks.

The return journey was gloomy. Nicolas remained silent, deep in thought. Night was falling by the time they went through the toll-gate. Nicolas suddenly ordered the coachman to drive into an adjacent street and to extinguish the lantern. As he jumped down he had just enough time to glimpse a horseman galloping along the main street; it was the same man who had been watching them in the knacker's yard.

At the Châtelet Nicolas had the trunk containing the presumed remains of the Commissioner put away for safe keeping in the Basse-Geôle. He also decided to keep old Émilie in his care so that he could question her again and he paid for her to be put in a cell with special privileges, and served a hot meal. He then withdrew to the duty room to write up a brief report for Monsieur de Sartine recounting his visit to Descart and the journey to Montfaucon, but omitting the conversation with Semacgus. His conclusion, subject to further checks that he planned to carry out, stated that the remains discovered could well be those of Guillaume Lardin.

V

THANATOS

'But here for our victim is the unaccompanied song
that fills mortals with dread.'

AESCHYLUS

NICOLAS had returned quite late to Rue des Blancs-Manteaux. The house was silent and he hoped Catherine had left him some food keeping warm in a dish on the stove, as she usually did. Sure enough he found that the table had been laid for him with bread and a bottle of cider. He noticed a stew containing a strange vegetable – a root vegetable that Catherine had first come across when working in the field kitchens in Italy and Germany, and now grew in a corner of the garden at the back of the house. These stewed 'potatoes'[1] filled the kitchen with their aroma. He sat down to eat, poured himself a drink and filled his plate. It made his mouth water to see the vegetables in their glossy sauce with a sprinkling of parsley and chives.

Catherine had given him the recipe for this succulent dish. You had to choose good-sized potatoes, then proceed extremely slowly, giving the various ingredients time to combine together and not getting impatient, which was essential if it were to be a success. First she carefully peeled her large potatoes, preferring to round them off. Then she diced some bacon and cooked the pieces gradually before removing them from the dish after they had given out all their fat but, most important, had not yet changed colour. Then, she specified, the potatoes had to be put into the boiling fat and left to slowly turn golden brown, together with some unpeeled cloves of garlic and a handful of thyme and bay. This way the vegetables would be covered with a crispy coating. As they continued to cook they would soften right through. Then and only then should you sprinkle a whole tablespoonful of flour over them, stir the dish vigorously and a few minutes later pour half a bottle of burgundy over it. After adding salt and pepper you leave the dish to simmer slowly for a good half-hour. The sauce thickens and becomes soft and smooth, like satin, giving a light and moist coating to the potatoes that stay golden and tender beneath the sweet-smelling crust. The secret of successful cooking, said Catherine, was to love doing it.

Nicolas's plate was not level and he noticed that it was resting on a piece of paper on which he recognised the cook's poor and almost childish handwriting. The message was brief: 'The slut insulted me this evening, tomorrow I will tell the whole story.' He finished his meal hurriedly. It was out of the question for him to go and find Catherine right then in order to question her; she rented a furnished room in a house a few doors away. He felt a twinge of remorse at the fact that, although he had lived at the Lardins' for more than a year, he had never been inquisitive enough to find out exactly where his friend lived. As he climbed the stairs Marie suddenly appeared on the landing and dragged him up a few more steps. She huddled up to him, so close that he could smell her fragrance. Her cheek brushed against his and he noticed that she was crying.

'Nicolas,' murmured the young woman, 'I just don't know what to do. This woman disgusts me. Catherine said horrible things to her that I didn't understand. They hit each other. She threw Catherine out. Catherine was a second mother to me. And what about my father? Where is he? Do you have any news?'

She clung to his coat. He was stroking her hair to calm her down when a noise made them start. She tore herself away from him, pushed him further up the stairs and pressed herself against the wall. A shadowy figure carrying a light walked to and fro on the landing, then all was normal again.

'Goodnight, Nicolas,' she whispered.

She rushed off to her room, light as a bird, and Nicolas returned to his garret, vowing that he would have a long talk with her. Normally when his mind was preoccupied he had difficulty getting to sleep. On this occasion he had so many worries that he could not focus on one in particular, and he immediately fell into a refreshing slumber.

Wednesday 7 February 1761

Nicolas left the house early in the morning. It seemed strangely silent. Postponing any attempt to solve the mysterious events of the night, he hurried off to the Châtelet, eager to continue his investigations. He had given orders for the remains found in Montfaucon to be deposited in a small closet next to the Basse-Geôle. This was often used to hide the most gruesome or offensive sights from the eyes of the public allowed inside the morgue. No visitor other than Nicolas or Bourdeau was to be let in.

This precautionary measure had proved useful; as soon as he

arrived he was told that a man had reported late at night to the inspector on duty. He claimed he had been delegated by Commissioner Camusot to examine the finds. Despite all his arguments, threats and outbursts of anger he had not been allowed to see the evidence. This confirmed Nicolas's conviction that he was being watched and had been since Monsieur de Sartine had given him this assignment. The individual in question was undoubtedly the mysterious horseman who had been spying on them in the knacker's yard. The first thing that came into his mind was that it was Mauval, Commissioner Camusot's confidant. If his hunch were wrong, he did not rule out the possibility that the spy had been planted by the Lieutenant General of Police, with the task of double-checking his own investigation.

Nicolas continued to believe that Monsieur de Sartine was not playing fair with him. He could understand why but he considered the consequences of this lack of trust, which was a sign of his junior status and insignificance. His superior could not explain certain facts to him, at best for higher motives, at worst because he, Nicolas, was a mere plaything caught up in the workings of higher political interests, a blind pawn moved around a chessboard to mislead the opponent. In fact, Monsieur de Sartine had opened the way for him but without seeking to influence the course of the investigation.

Once more Nicolas's roving imagination led him to constantly question his own ability; he was incapable of simply waiting for events to unfold. Nicolas realised that he still had a lot to learn, but he vowed that he would give as good as he got, with weapons of his own choosing.

He took comfort from this decision and, on Bourdeau's

advice, he gave orders for the human remains to be examined in the torture chamber next to the record office of the court. It was a dark room with a vaulted ceiling, lit only by narrow mullioned windows, whose openings had metal hoods intended to prevent any screams being heard outside whilst stopping anyone from having too good a view of the bloody proceedings down below. Several solid oak tables, chairs and stools provided sparse comfort to the magistrates, police officers and clerks of the court who worked there. What caught Nicolas's attention were the executioner's implements, carefully lined up along the walls. Racks, wooden boards, wedges, hammers, mallets – all of varying sizes – pincers, buckets, funnels, trestle beds, metal rods, swords, execution axes – the whole nightmarish arsenal of instruments of torture and judicial death was here on display. Nicolas could not help shuddering at the sight of this equipment, all the more threatening as it seemed to have been neatly put away by a tidy workman after his day's labour.

Awaiting Nicolas were Bouillaud, the Châtelet staff physician on duty,[2] and his second-in-command, Sauvé, a surgeon, both looking stuffy and impatient. Bourdeau had sent for them early in the morning, one from Rue Saint-Roch and the other from Rue de la Tissanderie. Both of them had obeyed the summons with bad grace, as it upset the regular pattern of their work. They seemed annoyed and looked Nicolas up and down. The young man immediately realised that he had to impose his authority from the outset: above all he must not waste words. Giving the two important figures a dark look, he took the Lieutenant General's commission out of his pocket and, unfolding it, handed it to the two physicians. They glanced at it frostily.

'Gentlemen,' Nicolas began, 'I have asked you here to help throw some light on this matter. In the first place I have to tell you that the opinions you give me must on no account be divulged. They are intended for Monsieur de Sartine who is in sole charge of this case and who relies on your discretion. Do I make myself understood?'

The two doctors silently acquiesced.

'You will be paid your usual fees.'

Two sighs of relief were heard and the atmosphere became more relaxed.

'Gentlemen,' Nicolas resumed, 'here is what was found late yesterday afternoon in Montfaucon, under several layers of snow. The clothes you see were not covering the limbs. We have reason to believe that these remains are those of a man murdered in the night of Friday to Saturday last. We shall first proceed to list the clothes, then you will give your opinion on the bones.'

They all approached the large table. Bouillaud and Sauvé, overcome by the smell, unfolded large white handkerchiefs. Bourdeau took a pinch of snuff. Nicolas would have liked to do the same but it was his job to handle the clothes so he held his breath instead.

'A pair of torn breeches, stained with a blackish matter. Ditto for a shirt, two black stockings, a black leather doublet . . .'

Suddenly inspired, he discreetly searched the pockets of this item. In the right-hand one he felt under his fingers a scrap of paper and a metal disk. He was about to examine them but decided to conceal them in his hand. He resumed his inventory.

'Two leather slippers, apparently belonging to the same pair. The buckles have been torn off. Finally, a carved wooden cane with a silver pommel. Gentlemen, I am listening.'

Bouillaud looked at his colleague hesitantly, then after a sign of encouragement from him put his hands together and stated:

'We have before us human remains. A corpse, if you prefer.'

Nicolas gave him a sardonic look and said:

'I have the greatest pleasure in noting that your hypotheses are in line with my own. We are therefore making great strides. Having stated the basic fact, would you be so kind as to move on to the details. Let's take the head, for instance. I note that the top of the skull is intact, smooth, without any trace of hair . . .'

He leant over the table, pinching his nose and pursing his lips, and pointed to a precise area at the summit of the skull: a darker mark, with a sort of deposit.

'In your opinion what could that be?'

'Congealed blood, without the slightest doubt.'

'The jaw seems to be broken, the teeth have not been found, except for the molars that remained on the bone. The head was severed from the torso. As to the latter, it looks flayed. What's the cause of this appearance?'

'Decomposition.'

'Can you tell me if it's a man or a woman, and above all how long the person has been dead?'

'It's difficult to say. It was covered with snow, did you say? It was doubtless frozen.'

'So what can you conclude?'

'We do not wish to commit ourselves in a case so far removed from the normal run of things.'

'Do you think that any crime is normal?'

'We consider abnormal, Monsieur, the conditions you impose on the exercise of our profession. This secrecy and air of mystery do not suit us. To put it in a nutshell, you have here the fragments of a naked corpse eaten away by frost. There is no more to add. In any case this is not unusual and you seem unaware, Monsieur, that every year the records of the Basse-Gêole provide descriptions of the sorry remains of corpses found on the banks of the Seine that were used by medical students for anatomical demonstrations.'

'But what about the clothes and the blood?'

'The body had been robbed. It was dumped in Montfaucon.'

The surgeon kept mechanically nodding his head in time with the pompous-sounding phrases of his colleague.

'I am grateful for the valuable help that you have agreed to give me,' said Nicolas. 'You may rest assured that Monsieur de Sartine will be informed of your zeal in serving his justice.'

'We do not come under Monsieur de Sartine's authority, Monsieur, and do not forget our fees.'

They left the room rather stiffly. Bourdeau had to step aside to let them by.

'So much for that, Bourdeau,' sighed Nicolas. 'How can we establish the identity of our corpse?'

He had forgotten about the scrap of paper and the round, metal object he had stuffed into his pocket.

'Gentlemen, may I be of assistance to you?'

Nicolas and the inspector turned round, surprised by a soft voice coming from the darkness at the far end of the room. It went on:

'I am so sorry to have taken you by surprise. I was here well before you came and out of discretion did not think it right to interrupt. You know, I am part of the furniture.'

The character stepped forward into the light streaming through one of the windows. He was a young man of average build, about twenty years old, already plump. He had a full, handsome face, with honest-looking eyes, and even a white and well-groomed wig did not make him seem any older. He was wearing a puce-coloured coat, with jet buttons, a black waist-coat, breeches and matching stockings. His shoes were so highly polished that they mirrored the light.

Bourdeau went up to Nicolas and whispered to him:

'It's "Monsieur de Paris", the hangman.'

'I presume you know me,' continued the latter. 'I am Charles Henri Sanson, the public executioner. Don't introduce yourselves. I've known who you are for a long time, Monsieur Le Floch, and you, too, Inspector Bourdeau.'

Nicolas stepped forward and held out his hand. The young man moved back.

'Monsieur, I am honoured, but that is not the custom.'

'Monsieur, I insist.'

They shook hands. Nicolas felt the hangman's hand tremble in his own. His reaction had been instinctive: he had experienced a sort of solidarity with a lad of his own age who, admittedly, practised a dreadful calling but, like Nicolas, served the King and his justice.

'I think I may be of some assistance to you,' said Sanson. 'It so happens that in my family, for obvious reasons, we are well versed in the study and understanding of the human body. On occasion we care for people and reset dislocated limbs. I myself learnt to my cost the usefulness of this science in one appalling instance which also earned me several hours in a prison cell and forced my uncle Gilbert, the executioner at Rheims, to resign his office.'

He added with a sad smile:

'People have a strange idea of the hangman. In fact he's just a man like any other, but one whose position imposes on him greater duties and a greater rigour.'

'What is this appalling instance you refer to, Monsieur?' Nicolas asked, intrigued.

'The execution of the regicide Damiens in 1757.'[3]

In a flash Nicolas could see in his mind's eye the engraving from his childhood, depicting the ordeal of Cartouche.

'In what way was this execution different from the others?'

'Alas, Monsieur, it involved a man who had struck out at the sacred person of the King. He was liable to the special punishment meted out in such cases. I can still see us, my uncle and myself, dressed as is the custom in the executioners' uniform. We had on blue breeches, a red jacket embroidered with a black gallows and ladder, as well as dark-pink cocked hats on our heads and swords at our sides. Our fifteen servants and aides were for their part dressed in fawn-coloured leather aprons.'

He broke off for a moment as if waiting for very distant memories to come back to him.

'I should tell you, Monsieur, that Damiens – may God receive his soul, he has suffered too much – had not only attempted to commit suicide by tearing off his private parts but, prior to his execution, was subjected to torture, in this very room. They wanted him to denounce his accomplices but it was clear that he had none and he merely kept repeating: "I did not intend to kill the King, otherwise I would have done so. I only struck the blow so that God might reach out to him and enjoin upon him to restore all things to their proper place and bring back tranquillity to his estates." He never said anything else, and yet his stomach had been swollen by water, his ankles broken by the boot and his chest and limbs burnt by red-hot irons. He could no longer move nor stand upright.'

Nicolas listened in fascination to this account given in a soft voice by a young man who would probably have gone unnoticed in the street. He gave the impression of both distancing himself from his account and of betraying his emotion by the trembling of his hands and the beads of perspiration trickling down his forehead.

'Once he had reached Place de Grève and been laid out on the scaffold, Damiens had to suffer the punishment of regicides. The hand that had held the knife was burnt over a brazier of flaming sulphur. He raised his head and let out a scream as he beheld his stump. He was then subjected to the pincers. They tore away pieces of flesh, leaving gaping wounds onto which were poured molten lead, blazing pitch and liquid sulphur. Gentlemen, he was screaming and foaming at the mouth and even at the height of his pain shouted, "More! More!" I can still see his eyes – they were bulging out of their sockets.'

Sanson fell silent for a moment. His throat was tight with emotion.

'I don't know why I'm telling you all this,' he continued with difficulty, 'I've never spoken to anyone about it before. But we are of the same age and I know that Monsieur Bourdeau is an honest, upright man.'

'We are touched, Monsieur, by your trust in us,' said Nicolas.

'The worst, however, was to come. The victim was placed upon two beams nailed together in the shape of a Saint Andrew's cross. His upper body was pressed tight between two planks, which were themselves fixed to the cross in order to prevent any of the horses from drawing him in one piece. The purpose, as you will have guessed, was to have him quartered.'

Sanson leant against an armchair and mopped his brow.

'An assistant armed with a whip controlled the horses, four fearsome beasts that I had bought the previous day for four-hundred-and-thirty-two pounds. I was the one directing operations. The horses set off in four different directions, but the joints of the body held firm and the limbs became unnaturally distended as the victim let out a terrible scream of pain. After half an hour I had to command a change of direction for the two horses attached to the legs, in order to inflict on the condemned man what we call in the trade "Scaramouche's swerve". For this the four horses pulled in parallel in the same direction. Eventually the femurs became dislocated, but the limbs continued to stretch without breaking. After an hour the horses were so tired that one of them collapsed; the assistant had the utmost difficulty in getting it back up on its feet. I consulted with my uncle Gilbert. We decided to goad them by whipping them and shouting. They resumed the task. In the crowd spectators were fainting, including the priest of Saint Paul's church who was reciting the prayer for the dying. Others, alas, took pleasure in this sacrifice.'[4]

He stopped and stared down at the ground.

'Was there not a way,' asked Nicolas, 'of cutting short the condemned man's agony, whilst still complying with the formalities of the law?'

'That was what I decided to do. I ordered Monsieur Boyer, the surgeon on duty, to run to the Hôtel de Ville to tell the judges that dismemberment was impossible, that nothing could be done unless the main sinews came away. Through him I requested authorisation to have them cut. Boyer returned having persuaded the magistrates to agree. The next problem was to find the necessary implement. What was required was a sharp knife for cutting into the flesh, as used by butchers. Time was short and I ordered Legris, one of my servants, to take an axe and hack away at the joints of the limbs. He was soaked in blood. I got the quadriga moving again. This time the horses broke off two arms and a leg. But Damiens was still breathing. His hair was standing on end and within a few moments it had changed from black to white. His torso was writhing and his lips tried to say something, but none of us could hear it. He was still breathing, gentlemen, when he was thrown onto the pyre. I have forgotten nothing of that fateful day, and after that I decided to study anatomy and the workings of the human body, in order to perform my duty in the best way possible, without inflicting unnecessary suffering. Every day I pray to Heaven, gentlemen, that no Frenchman may ever strike at the sacred person of our King again. I don't wish to relive all that.'[5]

A long silence followed this account. It was Sanson himself who broke it by going up to the table.

'Before you arrived I took the liberty of examining the remains that your two medical men so promptly dismissed in their usual way. I understand your disappointment and will attempt to open up some avenues of investigation for you. First of all I can tell you, without fear of contradiction, that the decomposition of this body is not due to frost. The most frost can do is dry out and stabilise the state that the body was in at the outset. In fact it has been devoured by beasts of prey, rats, dogs and crows.'

He turned round and invited them to come closer.

'Look at what remains of this leg bone. This piece was crushed by a powerful jaw, a dog's or a wolf's. But the torso, which is almost intact, has been nibbled at by thousands of tiny teeth – rats. If you now observe the head you can still see the marks of sharp beaks. Crows, gentlemen. The place where you discovered the body also tallies with these indisputable facts and our reading of them.'

'And the head, what can you tell us about that, Monsieur?' asked Nicolas.

'Plenty. First of all that it is a man's. Look here, at the base of the cranium, these two bony protuberances that we call apophyses. In children and woman they are not prominent. In addition, a child's head can be recognised by the fontanelles, which are not yet fully closed, and from an incomplete set of teeth. However, here we have the head of a mature individual: see how I can grip it by the apophyses and lift it up? It belongs therefore to a man. Besides, as you yourself observed, Monsieur Le Floch, the jaw has been broken; a bit of it has been taken away by beasts of prey and the remaining part has a clean break caused by a steel or iron implement, a sword or an axe. Take my word for it. Lastly, as vermin do not devour hair, the victim could only have been bald or else scalped, as is customary with the Iroquois, but that seems unlikely. However, I can't find an explanation for the black mark at the top of the skull.'

Nicolas and Bourdeau made no attempt to hide their admiration.

'And what about the torso?'

'The same applies. It has been severed from the body by a sharp instrument, probably the same as that which fractured the skull. There are no internal organs left, only a few dried-up pieces of flesh. The *cavitate pectoris* is also empty of blood, even congealed blood. The body therefore had no blood left in it when it was deposited in Montfaucon. Would you like my conclusions?'

'Monsieur, we would indeed.'

'We have before us the remains of a bald individual, of the male sex, in the prime of life. He was probably killed with a sharp or spiked instrument. Before being deposited in Montfaucon he had been cut at least in two, otherwise you would have noticed a pool of blood on the ground. The body, or what remained of it, has been mauled by vile creatures, which have scattered various missing anatomical parts. This is not surprising; we know that in that foul place a horse carcass can be picked clean overnight. The jaw has been deliberately broken. Finally, gentlemen, permit me to remind you of what you have seen for yourselves: the clothes were not covering the remains. I believe that the dead man could not have been wearing them at the time he was murdered, otherwise they would have been much more bloodstained. In conclusion, I believe that your hypothesis is right: the mutilated body was covered by snow and frost which have preserved it until today in a state I can only describe as fresh – the dark red complexion is proof of this. The process of decomposition began only after you had the body brought to the Basse-Geôle. I may be mistaken, but I believe that the man whose remains we have here really was murdered in the night of Friday to Saturday, then abandoned in Montfaucon just before it snowed at Carnival.'

'Monsieur, I cannot thank you enough for your help. I must tell you . . .'

'You have already done so by listening to me and shaking my hand. Gentlemen, I bid you farewell and remain your humble servant, should you need to call upon my limited knowledge.'

He bowed and left. Nicolas and Bourdeau looked at each other.

'I shall never forget this moment,' said the inspector. 'This young man has amazed me. The young definitely have the ability to surprise me these days.'

'Monsieur Bourdeau, you are a born flatterer.'

'He has solved the business as quick as a flash. It really is Lardin: a bald man, in the prime of his life, the cane, the leather doublet. What do you think?'

'All indications do indeed seem to be pointing us in that direction.'

'You're becoming very cautious!'

Nicolas was aware of an inner voice advising him to think twice. It whispered to him that appearances could be deceptive. He regretted that everything had suddenly become so simple, that everything fitted together like a construction kit. His mind seemed to close up, as if in revolt against certainties when so many other elements in the drama still seemed obscure. He suddenly thought about what he had discovered in the pocket of the leather doublet and feverishly, with Bourdeau looking on in bewilderment, he laid out on the table a folded sheet of paper and a round, metal object.

'Where did you get all this from?' asked the inspector.

'From the dead man's doublet.'

'Lardin's?'

'The dead man's, for now. This is part of a torn-up letter, without a seal or an address.'

Nicolas began to read:

to pay you my respects and to
person who infinitely surpasses the latter
ery pretty, tall and good-looking, for it seems that she
that the sight of her should please you since, in addition, she
has much
to entertain by her conversation. Therefore, I await your visit for
iday and I beg you to find enclosed the disguise necessary for
arnival. I am, Monsieur, your humble servant.

La Paulet

Bourdeau, unable to contain his excitement, began to dance on the spot, shouting:

'The proof, here's the proof! It's the piece of paper that was in Descart's pocket when he came to blows with Lardin in the Dauphin Couronné.'

Nicolas glanced at the metal object. It was slightly rusty and he had to rub it on his sleeve to be able to see the outline of a fish surmounted with a crown.

'That's a funny sort of currency! It's the Dauphin Couronné again.'

'This is a different thing altogether, Monsieur. It's a token for a house of ill repute. You go in, pay the madam in charge and in exchange she gives you a token that you give the girl once . . . once the bottle is empty. Do you follow me?'

Nicolas blushed and did not reply to such a direct question.

'It appears then that this token does indeed come from the Dauphin Couronné. The suppositions are piling up, the evidence is being given to us. Destiny is being far too kind.'

'Pardon?'

'I'm telling you the easy route is not the route to the truth and that fate is offering us some dubious gifts. The fact remains that all this must be carefully checked. Bourdeau, organise old Émilie's release: we'll learn no more from her for the time being. Give her this small sum of money from me. Then hurry to Rue des Blancs-Manteaux and try to find Catherine Gauss, the Lardins' cook. She wants to speak to me and as she has been thrown out of the house I was unable to see her this morning. Meanwhile I'll go immediately to Rue du Faubourg-Saint-Honoré to make the acquaintance of La Paulet.'

'Should we inform Madame Lardin of her husband's death?'

'Provisionally.'

'Provisionally?'

'Yes, but I'll see to it. As for the evidence' – he pointed to what was lying on the table – 'have it put away somewhere cool. I shall keep the letter and the token. Goodbye for now, Bourdeau.'

Nicolas decided to go on foot to Rue du Faubourg-Saint-Honoré. It was a long walk but the weather, although cold, was set fine. Once more, frost had made the ground hard and the young man strode jauntily along the uneven cobbles and the frozen ruts in the streets of the capital. He had always enjoyed walking; it gave him the opportunity to think. In his native Brittany, wandering along the empty shoreline, he liked to see the headlands shrouded in mist on the horizon. He would reach one and then discover another that he would make for in turn. This morning the walk did him good. It cleansed his soul. The image of what were presumed to be Commissioner Lardin's remains haunted his thoughts and became mingled with Sanson's gruesome account.

Something was not right. Why had the body been chopped up, the clothes scattered and everything deposited in Montfaucon when it would have been so easy to throw it into the Seine? Why had the murderer or murderers not gone through the pockets of the leather doublet carefully, in order to remove possible clues that could incriminate them? Clues that on the contrary seemed to have been planted there so that they could be easily discovered. Why had the jaw been deliberately broken and what was this inexplicable mark on the skull? And besides, what was going on in Rue des Blancs-Manteaux? What was Madame Lardin's purpose? Was Catherine's hatred for her to be understood merely as the rejection of a stepmother who had usurped the position of Marie's mother? And this persistent and ever-present horseman, a distant reminder of the threatening figure of Commissioner Camusot? And above all this loomed Monsieur de Sartine, close but unapproachable, who, Nicolas felt, was seeking to put him off the scent.

Nicolas had reached a vast open space that had formerly been marshland. Now a square was being built there, upon which the city fathers wished to erect an equestrian statue of the reigning monarch. The place was usually a hive of activity but the harsh winter had interrupted the work. Along the edge of the river and all around the perimeter, an octagonal enclosure surrounded by a wide ditch was beginning to take shape. Towards the city two enormous symmetrical buildings rose up from the ground.[6] Wooden scaffolding, covered with frost, gave them the appearance of ephemeral crystal palaces. The whole scene was a chaos of monstrous blocks half hidden beneath the snow, an urban glacier riddled with cracks, caves, channels and precipices. It shimmered in the gleaming sunlight and from it trickled icy water that erupted into a display of all the colours of the rainbow.

Nicolas made a long detour along its banks and crossed the gardens that took him to Rue de la Bonne-Morue which intersected Rue du Faubourg-Saint-Honoré at a right angle. A few houses further down he picked out a handsome-looking two-storey building; its sole distinguishing feature was a wrought-iron sign depicting a crowned dolphin.

He lifted the door knocker.

VI

EROS

No shame nor modesty is there,
For Cybele herself is bare
And warbles her lascivious song.
No guest is coy amidst this throng
JUVENAL

A LITTLE black girl, swathed in brightly coloured cottons, opened the door and, in a lisping voice, asked him what he wanted. A small monkey dressed up as a harlequin leapt around her. When it saw Nicolas it quickly ran up to the little girl's shoulders, holding on to the material with its small hands. It clung on to her cap and, bubbling over with anger, began to spit and howl as it eyed the visitor. The young girl brought the animal back under control by tugging its tail. This put an end to its performance and it let out a brief yelp that was answered from inside the house by a muffled, hoarse cry: 'Come in, handsome Messieurs.'

When informed that Nicolas wished to speak to La Paulet, the maidservant gave no sign of surprise and showed him into an anteroom with a polished tile floor and bare walls. A geometrical frieze running along the cornice and an enormous crystal-drop chandelier brightened up a space which was empty except for two seats facing each other, upholstered in grey velvet. She drew aside a curtain of the same material and invited him into a drawing room where, without saying a word, she left him.

The room was spacious, an impression reinforced by the profusion of large mirrors covering the walls. The skirting boards and cornices were encrusted with gilt carvings. Heavy rugs muffled the noise from the street. Ottomans and *bergères* upholstered in daffodil-yellow, white, pink, blue and green silks created a bright, cheerful and spring-like effect. Those walls without mirrors were hung with grey damask and decorated with framed engravings showing scenes that surprised Nicolas by their explicitness. Opposite the windows, a large grey-velvet curtain concealed a sort of dais. Nicolas, whose natural taste had become increasingly sophisticated, was not taken in by this dazzling decor. He had enough time to observe that this ostentatious display of luxury disguised a reality that was more modest. The mediocre quality of the stained materials, the gilt on the carvings that had merely been painted on and the threadbare state of the rugs might have gone unnoticed to a visitor whose eye was drawn to other scenes, but a detailed examination soon dispelled the illusory splendour of this glossy spectacle.

'Do you like her? Do you like her? Naughty boy! Naughty boy!'

He turned. On a perch in the window recess, with a raised foot and its head cocked to one side, a feathered creature which he immediately identified as a parrot was gazing at him. Madame de Guénouel, Isabelle's aunt, possessed one that was always by her side. But it was old, losing its feathers, cantankerous and fond only of its mistress. This one was quite beautiful, the brilliant grey of its body contrasting with the sparkling red of its tail. Its gold-flecked eyes looked inquisitive rather than aggressive. It began to strut solemnly along its bar, warbling and cooing as it went. Nicolas, who in the past had had some unfortunate experiences with other such birds, cautiously offered it the back of his hand in order to give it less scope for a possible attack. Puzzled as to what to do, the bird stopped, ruffled its feathers, then rubbed its beak against the outstretched hand, letting out tiny squeaks of pleasure.

'I can see that Coco trusts you. That's a good sign.'

Nicolas turned round in surprise.

'Coco knows how to choose his friends. I trust him completely. He's like my very own Lieutenant General. But to what does La Paulet owe the honour of the visit of such a handsome young man?'

Nicolas, though ready for anything, could not have imagined the madam as she appeared before him. Almost monstrous in size, a feature emphasised by her short stature, she was far more corpulent than dear old Catherine, who was already well built. This hulk of fat possessed a puffy face into which her eyes seemed to have been embedded. Beneath a knotted headscarf it was plastered with thick layers of lurid make-up. The body disappeared into a shapeless dress of violet muslin with red stripes. The black stone necklace was more like a belt than an item of jewellery. Stubby fingers burst out of their silk mittens. Lastly, the flowing material allowed occasional glimpses of dropsied feet sticking out of old beaver-fur shoes that were worn out and stretched like slippers. This caricature was brought to life by eyes that constantly darted here and there, when the folds of flesh did not cover them up, and which were as cold as those of a reptile on its guard. The parrot, annoyed at the lack of attention being paid to it, began to utter high-pitched little squawks and to beat its wings furiously.

'Coco, stop it or I'll call the watch,' La Paulet teased.

Nicolas, who had no set plan and who, for once, had not been able to imagine in advance his meeting with La Paulet, saw in a flash a possible way forward. It was risky, but he had no choice. With a charming smile he exclaimed:

'Madame, you wanted the police. Here we are to serve you.'

The madam's reaction was beyond anything Nicolas could have hoped for.

'Hell! Camusot is in a great hurry for his little monthly gift. He's early, but he thought he might be forgiven if he sent you here, and I certainly haven't lost out. The strapping fellow that usually comes, that devil of a Mauval, has a look that chills my blood, and it takes a lot to frighten me! He's got such a wicked tongue that I have to do my best not to get into an argument with him. When he comes he takes over the place, plays around with the girls, drinks my wine and disturbs the customers. However sweet-natured I may be, I must really like the police if I put up with that predatory pimp.'

She gave him a leering look that reminded him of old Émilie's in the cab taking them to Montfaucon.

'I know what we owe you, Madame. And the police reciprocate.'

'Yes, yes. I'd like to see the evidence of it. You have to make a living somehow and nothing's ideal. I do favours, I report back, I give warnings and I lend a hand. And I get protection in return. It's a very fair deal for me – I make a profit and so do you. A bit pricey, though!'

'My superiors have a high opinion of you. Do you know any other commissioners, Madame?'

The question was far too pointed and the feint unsubtle. To allay La Paulet's suspicions he was relying on his innocent appearance and his ability to charm. She stared at him for a moment without answering, but the young man's face simply bore a look of naïve ingenuousness and she fell for it.

'Old friends, we are all old friends: Cadot, Thérion, that blasted Camusot and that scoundrel of a Lardin. What a character he is!'

'Is he one of your customers, too?'

'Mine? That's very polite of you, but I've been put out to pasture, even if on occasion . . . No, Lardin's a gambler, you should know, you're part of Camusot's set-up.'

'Indeed, but how did all this come about? I only know the general facts not the details, and you're so kind . . .'

'I'm happy to tell you the whole story – you young people need to learn about things – but before I do so, do me the honour of sitting down. I tire very quickly when I'm standing. It's bad for my complexion.'

Nicolas wondered what her complexion had to do with it; her natural colour could not have shown through the plastered-on layer of white that covered her face very often. Paulet settled back in a wide *bergère* that she filled completely, and invited him to sit down near her on an ottoman. With one hand she pulled towards her a small hardwood drinks cabinet that stood on a pedestal table and opened it up. Several carafes of liqueurs appeared, with their sets of small glasses.

'It's a long story. I'm building up my strength and you're going to keep me company like a proper gentleman. I've got some ratafia that comes straight from Île Saint-Louis. A planter friend of mine gets me some every year. Come on, it won't kill you and it tastes very good.'

She filled two glasses and handed him one of them.

'Madame, I'm overwhelmed by your kindness.'

'My dear boy, with manners like yours, you'll get far – or you'll get nowhere. But let's get back to the point. Lardin is a special case. He was the joker in the pack, you might say. But he wasn't up to it, despite all the Berryers and the Sartines. They wanted him to clean up a business that he was already up to his neck in. When Berryer gave him the task of investigating our little arrangements, Camusot took fright. But I, being La Paulet, kept a cool head. Lardin was a really heavy gambler. He played and lost, that was the rule. But in *faro*, his favourite game, the banker is just an out-and-out rogue and the punter a fool who everyone agrees not to make fun of. You can always change the rules or at least influence someone's luck . . . So the further his investigation advanced, the more unlucky he was at cards. Wham!'

She drank her glass and helped herself to another.

'Wham?'

'Yes, my *faro* croupier had been pandering to him for a long time. He didn't know when to stop, and he was betting more and more heavily. One day he tried to break the bank. Break it like I'd never seen it done before, I swear to you. A fatal move.'

'Fatal?'

'The amount was so big that he couldn't recover. He was ruined and he had to pay up, whatever the costs. I set Camusot on his trail. At least one person was happy! In this business we both go halves, well, two for him and one for me.'

'But will he be able to pay? You say he's ruined?'

'He'll find the money somewhere and pay up, or else . . .'

Nicolas preferred not to dwell on the threat these words contained.

'But, heavens, why did he need to bet so much?'

'Come on, a handsome big body like yours needs another drink.'

She poured him another full glass and filled up her own.

'The story goes back a long way. Lardin and I are old chums. Ten years ago after his first wife died he felt very lonely. He got into the habit of coming to the Dauphin Couronné. My establishment wel-comes the best people. I have courtiers who come here in carriages without their blazons or coats of arms, with unliveried footmen. The house is frequented by the richest clientele. Well stocked as I am, I always kept some new little tart, a dainty morsel, aside for Lardin. You can't imagine the trouble I take to satisfy respectable people! He dined, played a quiet game, then went upstairs with one or other of my girls.'

'Without paying?'

'That was one of our customs. The secret of success is having friends in high places. One evening there was a theatrical performance . . .'

'A theatrical performance?'

'Yes, sweetie, don't put on that bemused look. You see that curtain, it opens onto a stage where we put on special little productions that are, well . . . quite spicy. You don't seem very *au fait*!'

'I'm drinking in your every word, Madame.'

'Drink what's in your glass instead. Some wealthy connoisseurs enjoy seeing live performances of suggestive, saucy little plays. These productions stimulate the most dulled senses. It turns into – are you following me, for heaven's sake, with that dewy-eyed look of yours? – outright debauchery. In short, scenes that would have given even the Duc de Gesvres an erection.[1] One evening there was such an assortment of people that Lardin found himself matched up with a sweet little thing he found irresistible. He had already got through half a dozen bottles of champagne. He fell madly in love with her on the spot. To let him have such a gem on the cheap would have been an insult to God or to the devil, as you prefer. On my advice the girl toyed with his feelings, made him pine and languish. He was withering away. The crafty fellow begged me to act as go-between. Men are like that. I got a tidy sum out of it and we pretended it was payment for petty debts. He married her and his life became hell. She had as many lovers as Paris has parish churches. The bitch is greedy, voracious and coquettish, and she loves fine clothes, her own comfort and good food.'

'But,' said Nicolas, 'she's from a good family, isn't she? She has a relative who's a wealthy man, from what people say.'

La Paulet's eyes widened and she stared at him coldly. She moistened her lips.

'Sweetie, you seem to know more about all this than I do . . .'

Nicolas felt a cold sweat come over him.

'Commissioner Camusot told me that a cousin of hers was a doctor . . .'

The mention of the commissioner seemed to reassure her.

'What Camusot told you was right. The parents of this Lardin woman died of smallpox when she was only fourteen. Her cousin Descart, the doctor, got hold of the family fortune and apprenticed the girl to a milliner. The inevitable happened:

she was ready and willing and gave herself to the first person who came along. That's how she ended up with me, having burnt the candle at both ends, to say the least. Kind soul that I am, I welcomed her with open arms and set her up in society.'

She made a show of wiping away an improbable tear and emptied her glass with the emotion of it all.

'She must really hate this hard-hearted relative, mustn't she?' Nicolas ventured.

'When you get to know women better, sweetie, you'll discover that they don't always behave as you'd expect. Apparently she's on the most intimate terms with him. She knows what she's doing, and I have a feeling that one day she'll get her family fortune back, one way or another. Knowing her as I do, I think she's capable of avenging herself even more cruelly, especially as the devil in question, who's another customer of my establishment, isn't worth the rope needed to hang him. A dirty old man, a puffed-up bigot who needs to be served chocolate with amber and cantharides[2] before he can perform. A skinflint who'll argue down to the last penny, someone for whom you have to provide secret, carefully arranged assignations with play-acting and masks, someone who requires nothing less than the choicest morsels, even if he's not up to doing them credit . . .'

'As bad as that?'

'Worse. Would you believe it, he came last Friday and managed to get into an argument with that blackguard Lardin. They left me with a fine old mess!'

'Was it wise for a man so concerned about his reputation, from what you say, to come here of an evening during Carnival?'

123

'But that's just it, sweetie. Of an evening during Carnival it's quite normal to wear masks and no one should have recognised him. I don't know how all this happened. Anyway, the oddest thing about it is that . . . No, that's enough about that waster. Let's get down to our business instead.'

Later Nicolas would look back on this moment as his real initiation into the police. In the space of a few minutes he had in fact crossed the dividing line between an honest person with firmly fixed and clearly defined ideas of the truth and a hard-bitten policeman who must never lose sight of the ultimate aim of his investigation. This difficult art entails disowning others, being calculating and . . . setting one's scruples aside. He now understood that to make real progress along the difficult path he had chosen, he had to sacrifice everything that until then he had believed to be fine and noble. He was horrified by the realisation of what these choices meant.

He was thinking so quickly that he was not fully aware of how he wrestled with his conscience. Afterwards he never managed to retrieve his train of thought or trace the spark that had set it off. An inner yet unfamiliar voice whispered to him, telling him what he had to do. He surrendered to his impulse, leant towards La Paulet and, grasping both her hands, said to her in a sarcastic voice:

'The oddest thing indeed, Madame, is that you know perfectly well that this meeting was not accidental, and that if Descart was there it was because he had been invited.'

Presumably in response to Nicolas's change of tone, the parrot began to squawk, while La Paulet became agitated and attempted unsuccessfully to free herself from his iron-like grip on her arms. She tossed her head and opened her scarlet mouth as if she were unable to breathe. A fragment of white fell onto her dress and dissolved into a light cloud. In her surprise and anger, her mask had cracked and was breaking into pieces.

'Filthy little beast. Let me go, you're hurting me! Why are you grubbing around like this? You're sneakier than the police informers! It's Descart who told you this, isn't it? I'm going to get him for this.'

'No, it's Lardin,' Nicolas pitched in, waiting for her reaction.

She looked at him in utter amazement.

'It's not possible.'

'And why not?'

'Er . . . I don't know.'

'Well I know something,' Nicolas let rip, 'which is that La Paulet is worried to death, that La Paulet, thinking she was talking to one of Commissioner Camusot's henchmen, got the wrong man and blurted out a lot of significant and detailed information, enough to have the Dauphin Couronné closed down, have good old La Paulet arrested, taken to the Châtelet, where she'd be interrogated by the executioner, found guilty and, broken in body and mind, sentenced to life imprisonment at the Hôpital Général or the Grande Force. All her humming and hawing will be of no use and her protectors will disappear in a flash when they hear of her arrest. In a word, Madame, you were unfortunate enough to mistake me for someone else.'

'But who on earth are you then?'

'I've been sent by Monsieur de Sartine, the Lieutenant General of Police, Madame.'

Seeing La Paulet in a state of collapse, Nicolas realised that he had hooked his fish and that it might be advisable to let it dangle a little on the end of his line. He recalled a rocky inlet at the mouth of the Vilaine, between Camoël and Arzal, where he used to go with lads of his own age to fish for salmon as they went upstream. La Paulet was caught – now he had to make her spit it all out.

'What do you want from me, Monsieur?'

'Come, come, I'm not as bad as all that. You gave me a very warm welcome and your kindness has not fallen on stony ground. But we need to be serious. If you want me to sort things out for you, you must make sure you're on the right side, without any shilly-shallying. That means being on the side of the strongest, the side which gives the best guarantees. In your situation that's not an offer to be sniffed at.'

The fish began to wriggle again and tried a diversionary tactic.

'I can't help you at all. I'm just the poor, innocent victim of evil men. I've obeyed the police. Settle your scores between yourselves.'

'I shall put that matter to one side and come back to it later. What I want to know is why and how Descart came to be here on Friday evening.'

'I've no idea.'

'Was he in the habit of turning up unexpectedly?'

'I suppose so.'

The fish was gaining ground; now it had more room to swim around in, and it was thinking of snapping the line. It was time to make it feel the hook once again. He took out his guardian's watch, which had just struck eleven o'clock.

'I'm giving you exactly three minutes to tell me, in the clearest and most accurate manner, the circumstances of Dr

Descart's visit here on Friday evening. When that time is up I'm carting you off to the Châtelet.'

'Commissioner Lardin had invited him.'

'Only to fight with him afterwards? That doesn't make sense.'

'That's all I know.'

'Or all you want to say?'

La Paulet seemed obdurate. With her closed expression and squat posture she looked like one of those pagan images on the engravings his friend Pigneau had shown him one day, as he dreamt of his future journey to the East Indies. The young man decided to pull the fish out of the water. He waved under La Paulet's nose the fragment of the letter found in the leather doublet of the unidentified body from Montfaucon. He held it in such a way that she could not see that he only had half of it.

'Do you recognise your handwriting and your signature, Madame?'

La Paulet turned away and let out a high-pitched yell. In a fit of frenzy she started to rend her clothes. The cosy drawing room was suddenly thrown into pandemonium. The parrot flew up and bumped into the walls and the chandelier which tinkled, adding to the surrounding cacophony. The little black girl burst in, shouting too, and yelling blue murder. She was followed by the monkey who began to leap and spin around like a whirling dervish. Nicolas remained impassive, got up, grabbed one of the carafes from the drinks cabinet and, aiming at an area of tiled floor between two rugs, shattered it on the floor. His action and the noise it made stunned everybody.

La Paulet stood up. The parrot came to rest on the Cupid above the mantelpiece clock and tried to destroy a candle in a candleholder. The monkey sought refuge under its young mistress's skirt whilst she stood still, her hands on her head and her mouth open to reveal shining white teeth. Nicolas found her face striking, but he could not pin down the fleeting thought that the sight of it suggested to him.

'That's enough,' he said. 'Young girl, bring me pen and paper.'

The monkey was the first to leave the room. It sprang out from under the skirt and crawled quickly along the floor into the hallway. The black girl obeyed and also went out.

'Madame, do you recognise this sheet of paper?'

'I've been merely an instrument for others, my dear young man,' La Paulet answered, recovering her wits. 'Lardin asked a favour of me. The aim was to invite Descart on the pretext of meeting a new girl. Along with the note was a black cape and a velvet mask with silk trimming. I did as I was told. That's all, on La Paulet's word of honour. I beg you to believe me. I'm an honest woman, in my own way. I give to the poor and take Communion at Easter.'

'That's more than enough for me. From now on you're under my protection. Protection free of charge. Look what you gain by this deal.'

The maidservant handed him a tray with a piece of paper, a pen and an inkwell. He wrote a few words and handed the sheet to La Paulet.

'If you need me, or if something happens that you think I should know about, send me this unsigned message.'

She read the piece of paper on which were written these words: '*The salmon is on the riverbank.*'

'What does it mean . . . ?'

'It's of no importance to you, but it means a lot to me. One last thing. Write "I acknowledge myself as being the author of the note sent to Monsieur Descart, inviting him to the Dauphin Couronné on Friday 2 February 1761."'

The effort of forming the letters in her childish handwriting made her poke her tongue out.

'"And I did so at the express request of Commissioner Lardin." Sign . . . Thank you, Madame. This has been a very fruitful conversation.'

Nicolas left the place feeling very pleased with himself, and with a sense of having done his duty. His investigation had made considerable progress, especially as the two cases – one involving gambling and the other Lardin's disappearance – seemed connected. And he now had a very valuable witness. Camusot's machinations appeared in a new light, revealing the collusion between the two police officers. It was clear that Lardin really had fallen into a trap linked to his investigation into the world of gambling, and that he was being blackmailed. His image was considerably tarnished by these discoveries.

As to his wife, Nicolas's impressions were confirmed and he understood better why she seemed so ill at ease each time they met. If her husband really had been murdered, several hypotheses seemed plausible. Either he had been unable to face up to his debts and the threats made by his creditors had been carried out, or else Descart, after his vices had been unmasked, had taken his revenge by killing him. In that case what was Louise Lardin's role? How was she involved?

The positive aspect of all this was that Semacgus seemed in

the clear, having nothing to do with these matters, directly or indirectly, except for his passing fancy for Madame Lardin. Lastly, Nicolas now understood Monsieur de Sartine's reticence and discretion; he had been unsure of Lardin's loyalty and was concerned not to arouse Commissioner Camusot's suspicions.

Nicolas's spirits were so high that he was almost running, leaping over the piles of snow and joyfully sliding on the patches of ice. For once he was impatient to give Monsieur de Sartine a full report, already imagining his superior's surprise and satisfaction.

To get himself as quickly as possible to the Châtelet, where the Lieutenant General held his Wednesday audience, he decided to take a cab. As he was watching the street for an available carriage he heard behind him, muffled by the snow, the sound of a vehicle travelling very fast. He caught a glimpse of a coachman with his face wrapped up against the cold. He motioned to him to stop, but at twenty paces the driver whipped his horse and it broke into a gallop. The carriage was now hurtling towards him. His last conscious movement was to try to leap to one side, but the gap between him and the houses was too narrow. He was struck violently on the shoulder, thrown into the air and fell back down, hitting his head on the icy cobbles. He saw a large flash before his eyes, then he sank into unconsciousness.

VII

SOUND AND FURY

I pall in resolution, and begin
To doubt the equivocation of the fiend
That lies like truth . . .
SHAKESPEARE

'So, Nicolas, how do you feel? You really gave me a scare!'

He tried to open his eyes, put his hand to his head and felt an enormous bump covered with a piece of taffeta behind his left ear. He was stretched out naked in a bed. A young woman in a morning gown sat on a chair next to him, and smiled at him. He pulled the sheet up to his neck and looked at her in puzzlement.

'Don't you recognise me? It's Antoinette, your friend.'

'Why, of course . . . What happened to me? I dreamt I fell off a horse.'

'There certainly was a horse! This morning as I was going out I saw a cab try to run you over. Believe you me, someone wanted to kill you and the cabman went straight for you. You were knocked down and he didn't stop. I ran to you; you were gushing blood and you were so pale I was really frightened. I had you brought up to my room and I called a neighbour who's a barber, and he dressed the wound and bled you. He said you'd

131

only been knocked out. Now you're awake, and I'm very pleased.'

'Who undressed me?'

'What? Modest as ever! I did, and it wasn't the first time . . . You didn't expect me to ruin my bed with all these muddy, bloodstained clothes, did you?'

He blushed. When he first arrived in Paris Antoinette had been an occasional diversion that often made him feel guilty when thinking of Isabelle. The young woman's kindness and simplicity had charmed and touched him. She worked as a chambermaid for the wife of a President of the Parlement. She was always cheerful and discreet, and she had never expected anything from him. He felt a warm friendship for her and had given her little presents – a shawl, a bunch of flowers, a silver thimble – and sometimes in the springtime he had taken her for a meal in a *faubourg* tavern.

'What time is it, then?'

'The angelus has just rung at Saint-Roch.'

'Is it as late as that? I must be off.'

He tried to get up but felt dizzy and fell back onto the bed.

'You need a bit more rest, Nicolas.'

'But what about your work?'

She looked away and did not reply. She shivered; the room was unheated. She got into bed and snuggled up to him. He felt very grateful to her. He discovered again her fragrance and gentleness, and he seemed to be returning to an unfinished dream. He did not see her undress and did not have the courage to refuse her. He went through the usual yet always fresh motions of love-making, but he had never felt so languid. His actions were slow and his sensations exacerbated. Before surrendering to a pleasant torpor he experienced the happiness of this moment of peace without any sense of remorse.

Thursday 8 February 1761

Nicolas was woken by the smell of coffee. He felt refreshed, even if sharp pains still reminded him of the wound to his head. Antoinette was already dressed and she handed him a bowl of coffee and a roll. She had gone out to buy provisions early in the morning. Nicolas drew her towards him and kissed her. She freed herself, laughing.

'Falls do you good. You weren't like this last night. More tender, more . . .'

He drank his coffee without answering, and gazed at her with a mixture of tenderness and embarrassment.

'Antoinette, don't you have lodgings in the President's house any more?'

He remembered a small room and the servants' spiral staircase that he used to climb, carrying his shoes, terrified of being found out.

'It's a long story,' the young woman replied. 'I spent two happy years in that household. The work wasn't hard and Madame was very kind to me. But a year ago a cousin of the Master's moved in with them and began to make advances to me. To start with I laughed it off and took no notice, telling him I hadn't come to this house to get myself into trouble and that I wasn't that sort of girl. In any case he had a young, pretty wife, and he should be looking after her . . .'

Nicolas felt guilty at the thought that it was for him that she had thrown her virtue to the winds.

'From then on,' she continued, 'he never stopped chasing after me, so that one evening in March of last year, when I was leaving Madame's room and going back to my garret, he followed me, grabbed me round the waist and I fainted . . .'

'Then what?'

'He took advantage of me. A short time later my monthlies stopped. I told the President's wife everything, but she's very religious and was very bothered about it. She didn't dare tell her husband because he was so madly fond of his cousin. In the end I was thrown out of the house and onto the street. I gave birth in December and the cousin refused to help me. I gave the child to a wet nurse in Clamart. What could I do, all alone, without support and without references? Madame had refused me everything.'

'Why didn't you tell me? What about the child? Are you sure it isn't mine?'

'You're kind, Nicolas. I've done my calculations and I had stopped seeing you a long time before. That's why I had to make a new life. You'll find out only too soon in your job that I work for La Paulet. Now I'm called "La Satin".'

Nicolas stood up suddenly and grabbed her by the wrists. Always analysing his own reactions, he noted that this way of imposing his will on the women he questioned was becoming a habit. Along with this ironic observation came a feeling of horror at what Antoinette had just told him. What malicious, wicked spirit was directing his life like this? Added to the coincidence of the young woman seeing his accident was the fact that she had now become an important witness in his investigation.

Quick to learn from his mistakes, he was all of a sudden annoyed with himself for not having taken his questioning of La

Paulet further. He could have checked whether the details that Semacgus had given about the evening of 2 February were accurate. His initial satisfaction with what he had done soon disappeared; it had been the work of an apprentice and he was still a beginner at this difficult job. He was too subject to impulse, though he liked to call it intuition. None of this was a substitute for good procedure . . .

So the girl with whom Semacgus had spent the night was Antoinette! He felt awkward and uneasy about this, but also rather ashamed of himself, and sympathetic towards his friend, whom fate had condemned to such a life.

Antoinette, looking pale and scared, had become once more the little girl that she had been not long before. Her ash-blonde hair was pinned up, revealing the delicate nape of her neck which he so loved to kiss. Her face was covered in red blotches.

'Are you annoyed with me, Nicolas? I can tell that you despise me.'

He loosened his grip on her and stroked her cheek.

'Antoinette, what I'm going to ask you is very important. You must promise to answer truthfully. A man's life and reputation depend on it.'

'I promise,' said Antoinette in surprise.

'What did you do last Friday? More precisely in the night of Friday to Saturday.'

'La Paulet asked me to wait for a client.'

'Did you know him?'

'No, she just told me to look innocent and show a touch of class. It was a way of trying to get a few more coins out of him. It was a bit strange . . .'

'What happened that night?'

'The expected visitor didn't arrive and someone else came up.'

'Did you know him?'

'No. Why?'

'Can you describe him?' Nicolas asked, without answering her question.

'He was tall and ruddy-faced, an old man of about fifty, but I didn't have time to look at him properly. He handed me the token and gave me a *louis d'or*, asking me to say that we'd been together until three in the morning, and then he went away.'

'Who saw him leave?'

'Nobody. He went into the garden through the secret door that gamblers use when there's a police raid.'

'What time was it?'

'A quarter past midnight. I said nothing to anyone, not even to La Paulet. At dawn I came back here.'

'Where are my clothes?'

'Are you leaving already, Nicolas?'

'I must. My clothes.'

He was burning with impatience to leave this room, where for some moments he had been stifling, in spite of the cold.

'I brushed them this morning and mended them in places,' Antoinette said shyly.

He got out of bed to dress, then rummaged in his pockets and pulled out the token he'd found in the leather doublet. He showed it to her.

'Do you recognise this?'

She held the object above the candlestick to examine it.

'It's a token from the Dauphin Couronné, but not the usual one. This is the kind La Paulet gives to her friends so they can enjoy themselves for free. Look, there's no number on the back.'

'Did your customer's token have a number?'

'Yes, a seven.'

'Thank you, Antoinette. Here's some money for the wet nurse.'

He stopped, embarrassed, and took her in his arms again.

'That's not for the night. You understand that, don't you? I wouldn't want you to think that . . . It's for the child.'

She smiled sweetly and patted his coat.

Once Nicolas was back out in the street, it was as if something inside him had snapped. The excitement that he had felt as he left La Paulet's was now a distant memory. He was left with the after-effects of recent developments and a sense of remorse that he could not really explain. He also became obsessed by the thought that Semacgus had deceived him: the surgeon would be a suspect again, and one of the most likely if it turned out that the body they'd found really was Lardin's.

Day was slow to break. The thaw was beginning and Nicolas could hardly see three steps ahead. The street was a sort of dark tunnel filled with thick fog. He groped his way forward, wading through filthy muck, bumping into pale, blurred shadows that scurried on or seemed to trudge silently past. Occasionally the layer of fog lifted to reveal the brown walls of the houses. For a considerable time he was forced to feel his way along them.

Crossing the street was a dangerous business, and after the previous day's assault Nicolas was now afraid of hearing a carriage race up behind him in another attempt to run him over. He had never thought so much about his death as he did that morning. He had become aware of the fragility of human beings, even more than he had been in the church at Guérande during his guardian's funeral. Had his head hit the cobbles a little harder he would by now have been among those broken, bloodstained remains laid out every morning on the cold slabs of the Basse-Geôle. He would have liked to take a cab, but where would he find one in all this fleecy whiteness? He would long remember this wander through the city, which seemed to him to last an eternity. Gradually dawn made its laborious appearance. A pale light ousted the darkness from the streets. Nicolas could see faces again, and a semblance of activity started up around him with its usual shouts and calls. After getting lost several times he eventually found himself in Rue Saint-Germain-l'Auxerrois and from there he made his way to the Châtelet via Rue de la Grande Boucherie and Rue Saint-Leuffroy.

As he was walking beneath the dark porch of the building a voice called out his name. He turned round and found himself facing a sort of walking trapezium, the centre of which was formed by a man wearing a tall hat. He seemed to have folded wings on each side of his body. Nicolas recognised Jean, a fellow Breton from Pontivy, and his portable privy. Better known as 'Tirepot', this character had become friendly with him and gave him the benefit of the observations that his job enabled him to make as he travelled the streets of the city. He was not an official police spy but he was a mine of information and anecdotes, a living chronicle of the capital. His information had often proved very useful.

Public conveniences were singularly lacking in Paris and strollers often found themselves caught out on the busy streets when the need was urgent. Short of finding a quiet spot, a difficult thing to do, or relieving themselves in a strange house with all the risks that involved, they resorted to this odd character, who under a loose-fitting, canvas gown concealed two pails suspended on a crossbar he carried on his shoulders. Tirepot had perfected the system by fixing a stool for himself down below his back, enabling him to sit down whilst his customers went about their business, thus making conversation easier.

'Nicolas, have a seat, I've got some important things to tell you.'

'I don't have the time. But stay around and I'll see you later.'

Jean agreed and continued his rounds. His usual shout – 'Everyone knows what they need to do' – rang out under the arches. Nicolas went into the Châtelet. Never had this seat of law and order, sunk in its bluish, sepulchral gloom with its musty smell, seemed so sinister and so deserving of its reputation. A heavy torpor began to numb his senses; he was weary in body and soul, and yet he knew that a hard day's work lay ahead of him. He tried to pull himself together and drive away the dark thoughts that haunted him.

As he began to climb the great staircase he paid no attention to the person who stood motionless on a step, watching him go up. What happened next was swift and sudden. The shadowy figure sprang out in front of him, and at first all he noticed was the sour, stale smell of damp leather. Nicolas was thrown against the wall, his hat fell off and his head, which was still sore, hit the stone surface. His wound started bleeding again and a hand grabbed him by the throat. He could now make out the face of his assailant, who in any case made no effort to disguise himself. It was that of a man still quite young, with a scar running right across his closely shaven head. The initial impression was of someone level-headed and kind but this picture was immediately contradicted by the implacable light in his staring eyes. He pursed his thin-lipped mouth so tightly that the whole of his face, emptied of blood and life, looked like death itself.

The man was holding Nicolas fast. His features changed completely, reverting to their former beauty. Nicolas was terrified to be at the mercy of such a two-faced creature.

'A word of advice, young Breton; you got away with it yesterday, you won't get off so lightly next time. Forget what you know, or else . . .'

The man made a more violent movement and Nicolas felt a weapon strike him near the ribs, but without going very deep into the flesh. He was released and pushed back against the wall, hitting his head again. The man sprang up, bounded down the steps and disappeared.

Nicolas knew he would never forget those pale green eyes. He recognised that lifeless look; it was that of a reptile. He saw himself as a child once more, crouching in the marshes near Guérande, preparing to catch in mid-air a frog he had lured with a poppy petal attached to the end of a string. An enormous grass snake had risen up and, before grabbing its prey, had fixed Nicolas with its cold, unwavering stare.

This new assault, carried out in cold blood in the very building that symbolised the law, proved at any rate the extent to which his investigation threatened some murky interests, and how immune from punishment those behind his assailant felt, to have struck him like this in broad daylight.

Nicolas dragged himself onto the landing. His heart was pounding so fast that he was unable to get his breath back. In the Lieutenant General's anteroom his old friend the usher, sitting at his deal table, did not see him enter. He was completely taken up by one of his favourite activities: he was grinding a plug of tobacco and the result of this operation was then carefully recovered, without losing a single scrap, and placed inside a small pewter tin. Nicolas's hurried breathing made him look up and he let out a cry of surprise when he discovered the young man covered in blood.

'Good God, what a sight, Monsieur Nicolas. I'm going to send for help. Monsieur Bourdeau is looking for you and can't be far away. Mary and Joseph, whatever has happened to you?'

'It's nothing. A wound to the head that has started bleeding again. The head always bleeds a lot. I must see Monsieur de Sartine immediately. Is he here?'

Nicolas had to support himself by holding onto the table to avoid collapsing; his vision was becoming blurred and everything around him was spinning. The usher took a glass flask from one of his pockets and, after a quick look around to check they were alone, offered him a drink.

'Drink it. It's good stuff. Heavens, in this cold I've always got my little stock of rum, like the old salt I am. Come on, it'll buck you up.'

The awful gut-rot made Nicolas cough but the after-effect of the alcohol warmed him and brought some colour back to his cheeks.

'That's more like it. You're already looking better. A bit more life about you now, eh? You want to see Monsieur de

Sartine? Well, you're in luck. He ordered me to show you in, and quickly, if you turned up. He wasn't in a good mood for someone who's always on such an even keel. He was taking it out on his wig, which says it all.'

It seemed that everyone was looking for him this morning!

The usher rapped on the door, waited for an invitation that was not forthcoming, carried on regardless and stepped aside to let Nicolas in.

The familiar room seemed empty. Only the roar of the fire in the grate and the crackle of a log collapsing in a spray of sparks disturbed the silence of the study. The warmth enveloped Nicolas, together with a soothing, languid feeling. Since he had left Antoinette this was the first moment of well-being he had experienced. Motionless and almost in a daze he suddenly noticed the tops of two wigs above the backs of the armchairs in front of the desk. Rooted to the spot, he heard more than listened to the conversation.

'But, my dear fellow, how did we get into this mess?' exclaimed Sartine. 'And this morning I read in a dispatch of a rumour going around London: Lally, under siege in Pondicherry, is said to have capitulated.[1] Our possessions in India are now under threat like those in Canada a year ago . . .'

A shrill voice interrupted the Lieutenant General of Police.

'What do you expect? We were already at war with England and now we've added the alliance with Austria. A land war on top of a war at sea. Trying to do two things at once . . . In addition all this requires gold, a lot of gold, and leaders. Yes, leaders most of all. The army is in chaos. There are too many laws that cannot be enforced; the officers are corrupt, the upper ranks are incompetent and the lower ranks disaffected. There's nothing but disorder, unbridled ambition and court intrigues . . .'

'But wasn't all this carefully weighed up?'

'Carefully weighed up and pondered over, Monsieur. But the lure of the sirens' song was too strong. And when I say sirens . . . Count Kaunitz,[2] the then ambassador of Her Imperial Highness, was the idol of Paris and Versailles. He played to the gallery bringing out his manservants just to powder wigs . . .'

A hand suddenly emerged above the back of the chair, checking the sit of a wig.

'. . . He is courting the good lady, who is being lured with the prospect of imperial recognition.[3] She has suddenly become interested in diplomacy and having a new role to perform. Acting in playlets in the private apartments is no longer enough for her. A show of devoutness and an interest in affairs of State, that's where the future for ageing royal favourites lies! For my part, if I took the liberty of judging the state of France I would conclude that the future of this country is hanging by a thread, and that it's a dilapidated old machine that will, in the end, break into pieces at the first impact. I fear no one can see the danger. That it's deliberate policy, not to want to see.'

'My dear friend, you are very incautious.'

'We are alone and talking to you, Sartine, is like talking to myself. We are old companions. In Paris people are saying that the good lady is collecting anything ever written about Madame de Maintenon . . .'

'That's what they say and it's true.'

'You are in the best position to know . . . But I'm straying from the point. In fact the choice was between war with England and the costs that incurred, or a daring reversal of alliances with the risk of a land war. But these featherbrains imagined that the war would be short. And what were the expected benefits for the Kingdom? All talk and show.'

'What exactly do you mean?'

'Well, of course. Everyone galloped on, heads in the clouds. Oh! The French are birdbrains! Austria held out so many prospects. The Infante Don Felipe, the King's son-in-law, promising to give up his little Italian dukedoms in exchange for settling in the Low Countries. Ostend and Nieuport pledged to France and occupied by our forces, thereby protecting our vulnerable northern border. Think of how promising this agreement was supposed to be, with advantages even for our Swedish, Palatinate and Saxon allies. Lastly, Austria, so full of fine words, agreeing to end its opposition to Prince de Conti's claims to the Polish throne. The good lady already saw herself holding all these fragile threads together. The end of hostilities with the enemy Habsburgs was considered an exemplary model of caution and politics. Think of the claims that were made. That peace would be firmly established and that the alliance would strengthen it. "They" were in a hurry to produce com-memorative plaques and medals . . . The mistake was forgetting about the English and that "Solomon of the North",[4] so highly praised by Voltaire, for whom the spilling of French blood is cause for celebration.'

'The war with England was not of our making,' Sartine remarked.

'True, they didn't leave us any choice. They're pirates, yes, that's what they are.'

The sound of a fist thumping the corner of the desk made Nicolas start. He wondered whether or not to signal his presence.

'They seized three hundred of our ships and captured six thousand sailors, without officially declaring war,' continued the shrill voice. 'And today, as you well know, our navy is in the hands of an incompetent. That predecessor of yours, Berryer, who made a reputation for himself with the good lady by indulging her whims, by telling her all the gossip of the capital and by foiling imaginary plots, is now the minister in charge of that department. And Monsieur de Choiseul wanted a landing in Scotland. A friend of mine, who has served on the King's ships, proved to me, map in hand, the folly of such a plan. What's more . . .'

One of the wigs disappeared and the voice took on a hushed tone:

'What's more, we were betrayed.'

'What do you mean, betrayed?'

'Yes, Sartine. One of my colleagues, an official in the Ministry of Foreign Affairs, was selling our plans to the English.'

'Was he arrested?'

'Of course not. It was important not to tip off London. We are monitoring him now, but it's too late. The damage is done, the disaster has happened and we still have men-of-war blockaded in the estuary of the Vilaine by the English fleet.

Nicolas remembered that in one of his last letters, Canon Le Floch had recounted how, with the Marquis de Ranreuil, he had gone to see the French ships at anchor near Tréhiguier.

'My friend,' asked Sartine in a low voice, 'does this betrayal have any connection with the matter currently exercising us?'

'I don't think so, but the result will be the same. The situation is such that nothing must be allowed to compromise the interests of the King or those of his advisers. Alas, since our defeat at Rossbach[5] nothing must be overlooked. The King of Prussia was taken for an inconsequential fool and look at the result. Everything went to pieces the day that pillager Richelieu – you know his soldiers call him "the Old Pilferer" – negotiated terms with Frederick instead of crushing him.'

'You're unfair on the victor of Port Mahon.'

'A terrible price was paid, Sartine, a terrible price! The marshal's attitude in Germany was worse than a betrayal, it was foolishness. This is what happens when you let a woman run affairs of State from her boudoir. The good lady wanted her friend Soubise to have all the credit for a probable victory over Frederick. What other result could you expect from a tactic drawn up three hundred leagues from the battlefield by her protégé and commissary of the army, Paris-Duverney?[6] Since then successes and reversals have alternated with monotonous regularity. And for what? What interests are at stake now? It makes me weary and sad.'

'Come, come. This isn't like you. We'll win in the end and the King . . .'

'Talking of whom. As someone who sees him, how do you find him?'

'I saw him at my weekly audience on Sunday evening in Versailles. He also seemed to me weary and sad. His face was bloated, his complexion sallow . . .'

'Private dinners, game, wine . . . He's getting too old for all that.'

'The mood was glum,' continued Sartine. 'He paid no attention to the piquant little anecdotes that he has such a liking for and that I constantly feed him. That evening all the talk was about people who had died recently – and preferably suddenly – prayers for the dying and other gloomy subjects. Things often become an obsession with His Majesty.'

'Especially since the assassination attempt.'

'You're quite right. Do you know what the King's response was to his doctor, La Martinière, when he came to examine the knife wound caused by Damiens and reassured him by saying that the wound wasn't deep? "It is deeper than you think, for it goes to the heart." He also quoted his grandfather when he confided in me "that one was no longer happy at his age". And yet he's much younger than Louis the Great was at the time of the military reversals at the end of his reign. Finally he spoke at length of the basilica of Saint-Denis "that kings never see because only their coffins take them there on the day of their funeral". He pressed me, of course, on you know what . . .'

'The good lady bears her share of responsibility in all this. On the pretext of taking the King's mind off his gloomy thoughts, she finds more and more opportunity for entertainments of a particular kind, when she's not organising them herself.'

'Public opinion will turn against her, if our misfortunes continue. The war, the struggle with the parlements and the religious issue – that's quite a list.'

'To return to matters concerning us,' said the stranger, 'is there anything new? It fills me with anxiety to think that . . . Can you give me some hope?'

A long silence followed. Nicolas dared not breathe.

'I've got one of my men on the job. He doesn't know what he's looking for. He's at one and the same time my hare and hound. His greatest advantage is that no one knows him and he knows nothing.'

Nicolas felt his legs give way beneath him; he just managed to catch himself in time but his hand struck the ground. The faint noise sounded as if a thunderbolt had hit the room. Reacting simultaneously but in opposite directions, Monsieur de Sartine turned round to discover a petrified Nicolas, whereas his guest turned his back and hid his face behind a hat. Then the Lieutenant General waved imperiously towards a bookcase behind his desk. The visitor scuttled towards it and pressed its gilt mouldings. The bookshelves swung round, opening up a passageway through which the man hurriedly disappeared. The whole scene had lasted no more than three seconds.

Now, arms crossed, Monsieur de Sartine gazed at Nicolas without saying a word.

'Monsieur, I did not want to . . .'

'Monsieur Le Floch, what you have just done is inexcusable. I put my trust in you . . . On pain of death, you heard nothing. But look at the state you are in. This is what taking up with whores does for you. Well, Monsieur, what do you have to say for yourself?'

Monsieur de Sartine stood up straight, with that triumphant little look in his eye that the satisfaction of showing that he was the best-informed person in France always gave him.

'Monsieur, may I say very humbly that I do not deserve either your anger or your irony. I am truly sorry about what has just happened. I did not do it willingly or deliberately. The usher showed me in, saying that you were looking for me and had ordered that I should be sent in without delay. Dazed by my injury and almost fainting, I thought your study was empty, and when I discovered that you were here with your visitor, I felt it inappropriate to show myself. I didn't know what to do.'

The Lieutenant General remained silent, displaying the laconic disposition that Parisians said could make the dumb talk and the most resolute tremble. Nicolas had never been subjected to it before, his master always having been until then talkative and courteous, even if occasionally brusque and impatient.

'You are misinformed, Monsieur . . .'

Nicolas waited in vain for a reaction to his rejoinder.

'I was not with whores, as you say. Yesterday my investigation into Commissioner Lardin's disappearance led me to a house of pleasure kept by a madam called La Paulet. I presume you know of the Dauphin Couronné. As I was leaving the establishment a cab attempted to run me over. I was knocked down on the cobblestones and lost consciousness. A girl helped me and took me to her room to dress my wound.'

Nicolas did not feel it necessary to expand and to dwell on details of the story that concerned only him.

'This morning I came as quickly as possible to the Châtelet where I hoped to have the honour of speaking to you. As I climbed the grand staircase I was attacked once again by a hired ruffian, who threatened and wounded me, and who I have every reason to believe was Monsieur Mauval. This, Monsieur, is the explanation for the dishevelled and confused state I was in when I came into your room.

He was becoming increasingly excited and speaking more and more loudly. Sartine remained inscrutable.

'This being the case, Monsieur, if I have had the misfortune of displeasing you, or if I no longer enjoy your trust, it only remains for me to return to where I came from. But before doing so, there is something I wish to say to you. Without family or connections, and after being summarily dismissed from a modest position that suited me, I arrived in Paris without anyone to turn to. You gave me a kind welcome and took me into your service. I owe you a debt of gratitude. You placed me in Lardin's household in circumstances that would suggest even to a fool your desire to keep an eye on him. You entrusted me with an assignment that is in many ways extraordinary: investigating Lardin's disappearance. But what I was forced to hear just now has made one thing clear to me: you have not placed any trust in me or shared your ulterior motives with me. I know from what you have taught me that uncertainty is the hallmark of subordination, but you must understand that I was finding my way in the dark, without any information that could have helped me avoid certain pitfalls. Before taking my leave of you, Monsieur, it may be useful for me to give you a final report.'

The Lieutenant General still didn't react.

'The commissioner had disappeared,' continued Nicolas, 'and you gave me full powers to find him. What do we know as of now? On the day he disappeared Lardin was due to attend a rout at the Dauphin Couronné, at the same time as his friend Dr Semacgus. An argument took place between the commissioner and Descart, his wife's cousin. By investigating Descart we have also discovered an animosity between him and Semacgus – professional or some other jealousy. Descart disguises his presence at La Paulet's evening entertainment. Then comes old Émilie, the soup seller, whose horrifying story takes us to Montfaucon. The police visit to the knacker's yard is watched over by a mysterious horseman. The examination of human remains found in the snow proves inconclusive. The corpse is unrecognisable, but Lardin's cane and doublet are found beside it. Our observations give us cause to doubt where the crime took place. In the doublet we found a fragment of a letter and a token from a brothel. These clues may have been snatched during the brawl with Lardin. I continue my investigation, catch La Paulet off her guard and find out that Camusot and Mauval have been blackmailing Lardin over heavy gambling debts. So, Lardin's investigation into Camusot was bound to come to an abrupt end. I discover that Lardin is a regular at the Dauphin Couronné, as is Descart, that he met his wife there when she was one of the "residents", and that she is ruining him financially and is unfaithful to him: most notably she is the mistress of her cousin, Dr Descart. Finally it is confirmed that Lardin asked La Paulet to invite Descart to the evening event, in the course of which he disappeared. In addition I learn that Dr Semacgus did not spend the night with a girl from the brothel and that his black servant, Saint-Louis, has also disappeared. That, Monsieur, together with two assaults against the person of your representative, is the summary of the investigation I submit for your consideration. Today I discover that I was merely a tool for you: I did not know what I was looking for or what lead to follow. I dare to suppose that you have reasons of the greatest importance for treating me in this way. Monsieur, I take my leave of you, begging you to believe that I remain your very humble, obedient and grateful servant.'

Despite his emotion and the throbbing in his temples, Nicolas felt liberated by his speech. The vice gripping his chest was gradually released as these irrevocable words left his lips. What he experienced just then was not far off jubilation. However accurate his summary may have been, he had left out certain details. He was not especially proud of the fact; this pettiness did not improve his opinion of himself, but having burnt his boats it was his way of getting his own back, his response to the humiliation he had suffered. He still felt an underlying anger at having been trifled with by a man he respected, who had entrusted him with a task into which he had put his heart and soul. It was all over, he could now let himself go. His future, his destiny, the next day, everything that had made up his life in Paris, none of it mattered at that moment.

He was preparing to leave the room when Monsieur de Sartine made a sudden, improbable gesture. He pulled off his wig and flung it onto the middle of his desk, then ran his hands nervously through his hair. He went towards the fireplace, poked the dying embers and then walked resolutely towards Nicolas, who was taken aback by the speed at which he moved and could not help stepping back a pace. The magistrate seized him by the shoulders and pulled him towards him. The inquisitive eyes stared at him long and hard. The young man withstood this examination without batting an eyelid. Then Sartine led him gently towards an armchair and forced him to sit down. He handed him a fine linen handkerchief.

'Take this, Nicolas, and press it hard to your wound.'

He stepped aside and went to the door. Nicolas heard him speak to the usher.

'Marie, old fellow, you have your flask, I assume . . . Yes, your flask. Stop pretending not to understand and give it to me.'

There were a few vague mutterings. The Lieutenant General came back in and handed Nicolas a small glass bottle that he was already familiar with.

'Take a sip of this poison. It'll do you good. Old Marie imagines that I'm not aware of his habits.'

Nicolas felt he was going to burst out laughing. The result was that the alcohol went down the wrong way and made him choke. This produced unstoppable hiccups that set off the fit of laughter. Sartine appeared rather worried. He leant against his desk.

'You can be quite insolent at times for a former notary's clerk who wishes to return to that occupation. What eloquence! What fiery passion! What talent! My compliments.'

Nicolas made as if to leave.

'Come on. Don't be childish and listen to me. I didn't think, Monsieur, you could rise to the challenge of the assignment I'd given you. A tricky investigation indeed. You have made rapid and effective progress. I am not easily surprised but you have astonished me. Grey areas remain, however . . . It's true that with me keeping you in the dark you were unlikely to see the light. The secret purpose of all this . . . Oh! It's so delicate to put . . .'

Nicolas realised Sartine's feeling of awkwardness and shared it. To this unease was added his continuing fit of hiccups, only made worse by his attempts to control them. He was convulsed with such an infectious laughter that Sartine joined in. Nicolas had never seen him laugh and he noticed that this outburst made his superior look much younger. He remembered that there were only eight or nine years between them, and this fact reassured him. They became serious again. Sartine coughed, embarrassed at having let himself go in this way.

'It was very wrong of me to underestimate you and to use you as if you were an automaton,' he said, regaining his seriousness. 'You have proved your worth. I shall forget about this misunderstanding . . .'

Nicolas thought that it was a bit rich for Sartine to talk of drawing a line under this 'misunderstanding'. However, admitting he had been wrong made up for it and the 'worth' he mentioned healed his many wounds.

'I see that I must reveal my most secret thoughts to you. You already know many of them. Now listen.'

Nicolas would have listened to anything. Now completely in control of himself, Sartine continued:

'I had given Lardin the task of investigating Camusot, whom my predecessor, Berryer, suspected of corruption in the Gaming Division. The aim was to clean up an Augean stable. It didn't take me long to realise that the commissioner was fobbing me off and that I no longer had control over him. Ranreuil recommended you to me. I placed you with Lardin and what you reported back to me, innocently or not, convinced me of his disloyalty. But there was worse to come.'

The seriousness of his words encouraged the Lieutenant General to put his wig back on.

'At the end of August 1760 Lardin, together with Commissioner Chénon, was called upon in the course of his duties to affix the seals and make a record of the papers of the Comte d'Auléon, the former plenipotentiary in Saint Petersburg, who had just died. This is normal practice for all those who have taken part in State negotiations, and the order came from Monsieur de Choiseul. However, we know for sure that Lardin stole several documents, in particular letters in the King's own hand and in the Marquise de Pompadour's. A few days before he disappeared I sent for him. He threatened – I repeat, threatened – to divulge these items to foreign powers if legal proceedings were taken against him. In the middle of a war, in circumstances that you are aware of . . .'

'But, Monsieur, why did you not have him arrested and imprisoned?'

'I did think about it, but it was a risk I could not take. So I, Gabriel de Sartine, Lieutenant General of Police, had to beg this miserable wretch, who has added treachery to the crime of lese-majesty, to attempt no such thing. I was unaware then of what you have now told me, that in addition to all these heinous crimes he had the vile habit of gambling. I imagined that these stolen papers served him just as a safeguard. We now fear that he may sell them for profit to anyone. Hence the importance of finding out whether Lardin really is dead and, if that is the case, what has become of those stolen letters.'

'Camusot and Mauval must be arrested.'

'Not so fast, Nicolas. That would mean losing any further trace of them for the sake of a foolhardy and pointless sense of satisfaction. You will learn that the protection of the State can sometimes take some very roundabout routes. In addition, Camusot has been with us for such a long time that he knows a great deal about a lot of people. There are risks that a servant of the King must avoid taking. That's not very moral, is it? But remember the words of Cardinal Richelieu: "He who finds his salvation as a private individual is damned as a public figure . . ."'

He stopped talking as if at the mere mention of his name the great cardinal's ghost would suddenly enter the room.

'That is why,' he went on after a moment, 'we need to find out with the utmost urgency whether Lardin is alive or dead.

Can you tell me for certain that the body found in Montfaucon is his? You seem unsure about this . . .'

'The evidence is, indeed, incomplete,' Nicolas replied. 'The only thing I am sure about is that the remains in question were taken from the scene of the crime to the knacker's yard and that . . .'

'That does not satisfy me at all. In such circumstances it . . .'

Monsieur de Sartine was interrupted by a loud knocking on the door. It then opened and Inspector Bourdeau appeared, red with embarrassment. The Lieutenant General stood up straight, his eyes blazing with anger.

'Well! Just bursting in like that! Monsieur Bourdeau, what do you mean by such behaviour?'

'My sincere apologies, Monsieur. Only something very serious could warrant my interruption. I wanted to inform you and Monsieur Le Floch that yesterday evening Dr Descart was killed and everything points to Guillaume Semacgus being the murderer.'

VIII

BETWEEN SCYLLA AND
CHARYBDIS

'Keep your thoughts to yourself and avoid malice lest clouded
understanding
mistake one thing for another.'

THALASSIUS THE AFRICAN

IMPERVIOUS to Monsieur de Sartine's obsessive pacing
around the room and nervous pokes at the fire, Bourdeau
began to recount his day. He seemed proud of the
opportunity to address such an audience.

Charged by Nicolas with the task of finding Catherine after
she had been thrown out of the house in Rue des Blancs-
Manteaux, he had begun his investigation in that neighbourhood. Luck was on his side because a day labourer had come to
pick up a bundle of old clothes that the cook had left with her
landlady. Bourdeau had not been particularly surprised to
discover that Catherine had taken refuge at Dr Semacgus's
home. Armed with this precious piece of information, Bourdeau
drove to Vaugirard but as he explained, somewhat to his
embarrassment, he had stayed too long in a hostelry in the
faubourg where, to warm himself up, he had had a meal of stewed
rabbit accompanied by some table wine that was rather too
young for his taste.

Monsieur de Sartine motioned to him to leave these details aside and get on with his report. Red with embarrassment, Bourdeau described how he had met up with Catherine who was full of praise for the kindness of her host – she said he 'appreciated her cooking and had welcomed her with open arms'. Although the two cooks were both upset, one at having lost her job and her lodging, and the other, Awa, distraught at Saint-Louis's disappearance, they soon became close friends. Awa had been won over by Catherine's jovial ways. They even exchanged recipes and as soon as he'd arrived, Bourdeau had been called upon to judge the success of a poultry pie, a piping hot delicacy that gave off a combined aroma of truffles and nutmeg.

The Lieutenant General brought the inspector back to the point once more with a threatening nod of his wig. In short, Dr Semacgus hadn't been there and Bourdeau, who had wanted to speak to him about Catherine's situation, had waited for him for some of the afternoon. He'd taken advantage of the opportunity to get Catherine to talk and she was quite happy to do so.

According to her, she would have left her position in any case. Madame Lardin, whom she described in the most unflattering terms, had simply brought the crisis to a head. It was one thing for someone like Catherine, who'd been at the battle of Fontenoy with the Marshal of Saxony, to be treated like dirt but quite another for her to witness the depravity of a woman totally without morals. What Catherine loathed most of all was the way she treated her stepdaughter, sweet little Marie. For a long time the mutual affection between Catherine and the commissioner's daughter had prevented the cook from leaving her job, and Lardin, though curt with others, had not been so nasty to her.

In the course of the conversation Bourdeau eventually learnt that not only was Louise Lardin having an adulterous relationship with her cousin Descart and with Semacgus, but also that she had taken up with a sinister-looking womaniser who had been hanging around the house in Rue des Blancs-Manteaux since Lardin's disappearance.

On the stroke of six Semacgus had finally arrived, dishevelled and unable to speak coherently, surprising behaviour for a man who usually possessed such self-control. Eventually it emerged that Descart had just been murdered.

After consoling him, Bourdeau had begged Semacgus to pull himself together and give a detailed account of events.

The inspector told how Semacgus had received a folded note which had been slipped under his door, with a request from Descart for a meeting. He found the initiative unexpected coming from a man with whom relations were anything but good. However, the pressing tone of the note had convinced him that only a serious matter, perhaps one involving medicine, justified an invitation of this type. It was arranged for half past five. He had spent the day in Paris going about his business, then had taken a cab from the Jardin du Roi to return to Vaugirard in order to be on time for his appointment. He had arrived at Descart's early, at about five o'clock. Surprised to find all the doors open, the one to the garden as well as the front door of the house, he had felt his way inside; it was already dark and no lights had been lit. He had hardly reached the balcony over-looking the stairs and the main room when he had stumbled against something that at first he thought was a sack lying on the floor. It was in fact a lifeless body.

Panic-stricken by the turn of events, Semacgus had gone

down into the room and found a candle which, once lit, enabled him to recognise Descart's corpse. It had been stabbed with a lancet used for bleeding. He had stayed there for some time in a daze, then decided to go back to his house to alert the authorities.

Bourdeau had immediately sent for the watch, left Semacgus under guard and hurried to Descart's to confirm the doctor's death and carry out some initial investigations.

It was pitch dark inside the house, since even the candle stub Semacgus had lit had gone out long before. With some difficulty he had found a source of light and carried out a meticulous examination of the corpse that was lying on its side, stabbed near the heart with a lancet. The body was not yet stiff. The crimson face blotched with blackish marks wore an expression of intense surprise, accentuated by a gaping mouth, as if in his final moments the victim had tried to shout something out or say someone's name.

The ground was covered with wet footprints. Bourdeau had given the scene a quick inspection without noticing anything unusual, then had the body removed and taken to the Basse-Geôle, where these gentlemen would be able to see it.

As for Semacgus, Bourdeau had thought it best to have him temporarily imprisoned in a cell in the Châtelet. He was the only witness to the crime and, unfortunately for him, he was also the main suspect, given the stormy relations that everyone knew existed between the two doctors. Finally Bourdeau had left Vaugirard, but not before carefully closing the doors of the house, sealing the exits with sealing wafer and taking the keys with him.

A lengthy silence followed the inspector's account. Monsieur de Sartine had not stopped pacing around the room.

With a wave of the hand he indicated to Bourdeau his desire to be left alone with Nicolas.

'Thank you, Monsieur Bourdeau. Leave us. I have some instruc-tions to give to your superior.'

Hearing this phrase gave Nicolas a pleasure he had difficulty disguising: it was for him the confirmation of his assignment.

'With your permission, Monsieur, I have one small question for Bourdeau.'

Sartine nodded somewhat impatiently.

'Was Semacgus covered in blood?'

'Not a drop.'

'Dr Descart was presumably covered in blood,' Nicolas remarked. 'When Semacgus stumbled across the body his clothes should have become stained with blood, should they not?'

The inspector seemed taken aback.

'Now you come to mention it,' he replied, 'I realise that there was no blood anywhere. Neither on the body nor on the floor.'

'Don't go away, we'll need to speak further. We'll go to see the body and question Semacgus.'

Bourdeau left the room but not before he'd cast an admiring glance at Nicolas. Sartine, who had been slightly annoyed by the episode, resumed speaking.

'All this only complicates things further. Monsieur Le Floch, I firmly intend you to wrap up this case quickly. Don't waste precious time attempting to solve a matter that has no connection with our own. Act with speed, and I will give all the instructions necessary for no one and nothing to put a spoke in your wheel. The main thing, you understand, is the service of His Majesty and the security of the State. Lardin's fate is of no interest to me – it's the risk of seeing the documents in question fall into the wrong hands that worries me. Do I make myself clear?'

'Monsieur,' Nicolas replied softly, 'I now know all the ramifications of the investigation you have been kind enough to entrust me with, but I have to say that all the incidents that have occurred, and the latest one is no exception, seem interrelated to me and all the threads of the plot may be traced back to a single cause. I cannot therefore neglect any lead. All those who to a greater or lesser extent were in contact with Lardin, and especially those who were with him that night in the Dauphin Couronné are liable to be mixed up in one way or another with the serious affair you have agreed to share with me.'

Sartine ignored the young man's remark and went on:

'I must also warn you about something else, even if it goes against the innocent view I suspect you to have of our system of justice. I have been and remain a magistrate. So are you by delegation, thanks to the commission that makes you my plenipotentiary. We must comply with the laws of the State, especially since we proceed only by another delegation of powers, that of the King, the alpha and omega of all authority. We must use it honourably. A judge's power comes from the throne and the ermine on our robes is a symbolic reminder of the coronation cloak.'

He stroked the front of his coat with a self-important air, as if he were wearing his ceremonial gown at a judicial session at the palace.

'In short, I am entitled to retain control over certain matters that involve the security of the State. As you can imagine, the case you are investigating is one of these. This is the price to be paid for the glory and security of the State, especially in a time of war. Every day our soldiers are dying on the battlefield, and anyone with true feeling and affection for their country must shudder at the thought that the enemy might be in a position to jeopardise the reputation of His Majesty and those around him.'

He stared Nicolas straight in the eye and abandoned his solemn tone.

'Everything must remain secret, Nicolas, shrouded in the deepest, most impenetrable secrecy. It is out of the question to stick to the normal rules of procedure that Monsieur de Noblecourt must only recently have taught you. I do not want a magistrate to be appointed for this investigation for the moment; we cannot trust anyone. We must be implacable. If need be, ask me for some *lettres de cachet* for the Bastille: security is tighter there than in our gaols crowded with the rabble, prostitutes and prisoners' families, who come and go without being checked. If you have corpses, then hide them. If you have investigations to make, cloak them in secrecy. You were right to consult with Monsieur Sanson; use him, he is as silent as the grave. If you apply secrecy to everything, this will lead you to the heart of the labyrinth. You are my plenipotentiary, above rules and the law, but do not forget that if you fail and jeopardise my power, my hand will no longer be there to protect you . . . You are your own master. You have my trust and support. Do your best and solve this case swiftly.'

Moved by the aura of grandeur surrounding the Lieutenant General, Nicolas bowed without saying a word. He was going towards the door when Sartine put a hand on his shoulder.

'Nicolas, take care of yourself. Now you know whom you are dealing with. These blackguards are to be feared. Don't do anything foolish. We need you.'

Intrigued by all this commotion, old Marie bombarded Inspector Bourdeau with questions as he waited for Nicolas in the anteroom. The usher was very put out at not being told anything so he concentrated on his pipe, enveloping himself in an acrid cloud of smoke. He puffed away furiously, with rapid, hissing intakes of breath.

Nicolas wanted to take Bourdeau off to the Basse-Geôle to examine Dr Descart's body but the inspector objected that he, Nicolas, was in a sorry state; his wound had still not stopped bleeding, his clothes were torn, and in his present condition he could easily have another collapse. He needed to eat something and restore his strength. Bourdeau assumed that Nicolas had not had any food since their meal the previous evening.

Nicolas did indeed admit that nothing had passed his lips except a glass of ratafia at La Paulet's, a cup of coffee at Antoinette's and two sips of the usher's gut-rot; his stomach felt very empty.

Bourdeau first took Nicolas off to Rue de la Joaillerie to a dispensary run by one of his friends, whose main customers were the men of the watch when police operations turned rough and resulted in a few injuries. The physician cleaned up the head wound after Nicolas had given himself a quick wash. He dipped some lint into a dark, stinking ointment and smeared it on the wound, adding pompously that it was not any old quack remedy. The initial burning sensation immediately gave way to a sort of numbness that surprised the patient, who now had a strip of cloth wrapped round his head, tied so neatly that nothing showed beneath his tricorn. The cut on his side was examined and then given similar treatment. The apothecary covered it with a piece of sticky taffeta.

'That should do the trick,' he assured him, 'and after a few days there will be nothing left to see.'

Nicolas did not appreciate the man's sneering reference to his wound as a 'pinprick worthy of Damiens'. He disliked the fact that a crime of lese-majesty — a shudder ran through him at the thought of it — should be referred to in this derisive way.

As they were leaving the dispensary they came across Tirepot. He had not wandered far from the Châtelet and was patrolling the neighbouring streets as he waited for Nicolas to return. Bourdeau offered to take them to his usual tavern in Rue du Pied-de-Bœuf where they could get warm and restore their strength. The overcast sky gave off a thick, yellowish light that failed to penetrate the narrow, winding streets of the Grande Boucherie. Passers-by appeared, then disappeared like ghosts. All that was visible was the eerie spectacle of their greenish, expressionless faces. The sound of footsteps in the wet snow no longer suggested the sharp, joyful crackle of frost but the scrape of a pickaxe in damp sand, engaged in some foul task.

They were given a hearty welcome by the tavern-keeper who was relighting his stoves. Bourdeau ordered a restorative snack from his fellow townsman, and they were soon sitting down to a meal of bean soup with chunks of bacon swimming in it, followed by a gratin of hard-boiled eggs, generously washed down with several bottles of white wine. Then Bourdeau left them without a word and went off to prepare a home brew of his own. It would act as an excellent tonic, enabling Nicolas to recover from his exertions. First of all he broke up some sugar, then mixed it with pepper, cinnamon, cloves, honey and two bottles of red wine, all of which he warmed up in a large pot. Then he poured the boiling contents into a large bowl, to which he added a further half-bottle of spirits. He set light to the whole thing and carried it back in triumph to his two companions.

Nicolas had already had a considerable amount to eat and drink but he eagerly helped himself to the piping-hot brew, the effect of which, combined with everything he'd drunk already, was to send him off into a pleasant state of drowsiness. He felt kindly disposed towards the world in general, and to those around him in particular. Though normally reserved, he now became voluble. He ventured some jokes that surprised those sitting around the table and eventually had to be helped up by his two comrades, who took him into a back room and made him lie down on a bench. They then went back to their table, asked for some pipes and slowly and contentedly finished off the bowl of flaming wine. It was one o'clock by the time Nicolas reappeared, looking stern and annoyed.

'Monsieur Bourdeau, you are a downright traitor. From now on I shall be wary of your concoctions.'

'Are you feeling better, Monsieur?'

'To tell you the truth, I'm fine.'

Nicolas allowed himself a smile.

'I'd even like a drop more . . .'

Bourdeau's face fell. He pointed pathetically towards the empty saucepan.

'I see. You needed some, too . . .'

Nicolas restrained Bourdeau as he started to rush towards the stove to renew his experiment, and turned towards their companion.

'So, Tirepot, you had something to tell us . . . ?'

'I have that, Nicolas. You know I've got a sharp eye and a good ear. That's how I am. I'm for order and bringing things out into the open. And I won't forget all that I owe you. I wouldn't be here if . . .'

Nicolas motioned to him to stop this story that he knew off by heart. Tirepot had been eternally grateful to him ever since the day the young man had got him out of a spot of bother. After being accused by one of his customers of stealing a purse, he had been saved only by the perceptiveness of the young policeman, who had been able to prove it had been an attempt by a jealous rival to frame him.

'I know, Tirepot. But hurry up and tell us, there are people waiting for Bourdeau and myself and we've already wasted too much time.'

Bourdeau hung his head, pretending to be embarrassed.

'Here we go, then,' Tirepot began. 'Yesterday evening at Ramponneau's[1] I'd put my contraption down and was having a little pick-me-up while waiting for the crowds to come out after supper. That's when I do my best business. Yes, indeed. People are full, and the fuller they are, the more they need to empty themselves. That's life. That's how I make money. Two tough-looking types sat themselves down by me and in no time got through three times as much as we drank just now. One of them seemed to be an old soldier, with a military way of talking, a wooden leg and full of himself as you'd expect from someone used to the sound of gunfire. He downed the wine like nobody's business. These two gallows birds could talk all the slang they wanted, I could still follow what they were saying and I understood well enough that it was about some dirty business, past or future. But what stunned me was that while they were bellowing away, they were handling huge piles of coins, the like of which I'd never seen before. They also talked about selling a carriage and a horse that were apparently hidden in a barn in Rue des Gobelins, in the Faubourg Saint-Marcel. Then they noticed me and left. They could have made trouble for me so I went out the back way just in case.'

'Was the soldier's wooden leg the right or the left one?'

Without being able to explain why, Bourdeau sensed Nicolas's excitement.

'Wait. Let me get my bearings. They were at the table on the right-hand side, one of them level with me and the other one, the veteran, opposite him, his bad leg stretched out towards me. So it was his right leg. 'Yes, definitely. Do you know him?'

Nicolas, his brow furrowed, did not reply. He was thinking and the other two did not dare to interrupt his meditation.

'Tirepot,' he said eventually, 'you're going to search out these two rogues. Get your spies on the job, and this is for you.'

He handed him several silver *écus* and wrote down the expenditure in pencil in a small black notebook.

'You shouldn't, Nicolas. I do it to help you. It's a pleasure and I do it out of gratitude, as true as I'm a Breton.'

'It's not a reward. Thank you for your kind words, but the search you're going to carry out will cost you something and you may lose customers. Do you understand?'

Tirepot nodded without offering any further resistance. But from force of habit he tested the quality of the coins by biting them, much to Nicolas's amusement.

'Do you take me for a forger by any chance? We'll meet up with you again as usual around the Châtelet, as soon as you have some information about those two characters. You'll have to ferret them out.'

When they went outside the world looked just as uninviting and the afternoon had brought no improvement in the weather. If anything it was colder. They hurried off to the Châtelet. Nicolas was feeling better and gave a detailed account of his adventures and discoveries to an amazed Bourdeau. He had the feeling that his drunkenness, followed by a short rest, had sharpened his mental faculties and rid him of melancholy. It was as if the combined effect of a loss of blood and an intake of alcohol had purged him of his anxieties and dark thoughts. The feeling of fragility caused by the two assaults against him had given way to a steely determination.

He took stock of himself, as was his habit. In the final analysis Monsieur de Sartine had shown himself to be almost paternal. With this thought he felt a pang of grief; a picture of Canon Le Floch and the Marquis de Ranreuil came to mind and then faded, giving way to Isabelle's smiling face. He chased away these images and to cheer himself up reflected on the new trust his superior had shown in him. He was able to continue his investigation, which was now no ordinary criminal case but an affair of State. He gave a long sigh of relief and felt determined to see it through, whatever the cost to himself.

They went down into the viewing area of the Basse-Geôle which was crowded with silent groups of worried or grieving families, as well as the simply curious. Bourdeau whispered to him that the body was no longer there and that it had doubtless been taken to the examination room where the doctors on duty habitually performed routine investigations and, in the most puzzling cases, opened up the bodies. This was a small vaulted cellar containing a large stone table with grooves in it for washing down and allowing water to drain off through a hole in the paving of the floor. The room was poorly lit by a few smoking candles, and in it a motionless figure gazed at Dr Descart's body. On hearing the sound of their footsteps he turned, and they recognised Charles Henri Sanson. Nicolas held out his hand which was taken this time without hesitation and even, he thought, with a certain eagerness.

'I didn't expect to have the privilege of seeing you again so soon, Monsieur Le Floch. But judging from the message sent by Monsieur Bourdeau, you wish to have the benefit of my modest knowledge, as I previously offered.'

'Monsieur,' said Nicolas, 'I would have liked to meet you in different circumstances but the King's service makes demands that cannot be deferred. I know I can count on your discretion.'

Sanson raised his hand in agreement.

'We presume that the corpse you are examining has some connection with the remains you were able to tell so much from yesterday.'

Nicolas wiped his brow. It seemed to him that years had gone by since his return to Paris; he was horrified to realise that he had come back from Guérande only four days earlier. He had aged considerably in those four days. Sanson was looking at him with friendly concern.

'We are faced with a new mystery,' he said, swallowing hard. 'The man we have here was found dead, stabbed in the heart with a lancet.'

'It's still there,' Bourdeau interjected. 'I didn't think I should touch the corpse, so I had it brought here as it was.'

'I'm eternally grateful to you for being so careful, Inspector,' said the executioner. 'It will help our examination. Monsieur Le Floch, you are asking for my opinion but I know you to be observant, accurate and able to pick out details. Would you like to be my pupil and offer me your initial comments?'

'Master Sanson, I do indeed have plenty to learn from you.'

Nicolas pulled aside the sheet covering the body. It was now bare except for the shirt pierced by the instrument. The face was frightening. Death's handiwork was apparent in the wrinkled forehead and the deep-set eyes that were still open but darkened by an opaque membrane. The hollowed temples were matched by sunken cheekbones. The man was unrecognisable. Only the lack of chin, made more obvious by the open mouth, acted as a reminder, however exaggerated, of Descart's most striking feature when alive.

'A first impression. We know from the witness who discovered the body and from the inspector, that there was no trace of blood on the victim nor round about. Is it possible to stab someone without spilling blood? In short, I notice that the face seems flushed, the mouth excessively open and that dark stains appear here . . . and again here . . .'

His fingers moved lightly over the face of the corpse.

'. . . of a nasty blackish colour,' Nicolas finished. 'They are strange.'

'Yes, indeed,' Sanson said approvingly, 'you have followed the correct method: dispassionate observation which leads to the right question, without involving the emotions or the imagination. Before you came I studied only the face, and I can already tell you that it taught a modest physician like me a great deal. If that was all I had seen I would have concluded that the victim had been strangled, and perhaps also poisoned. The lancet makes things more complicated.'

Sanson went up to the stone slab. He examined Descart's head, leant over, sniffed, muttered a few inaudible words, then put two fingers into the dead man's open mouth and delicately removed from it something that he carefully placed on his handkerchief. He held out his find to the two policemen.

'What do you think, gentlemen? What is this?'

Bourdeau put on his spectacles. Nicolas, with the eyesight of a young man, was the first to reply:

'A tiny feather.'

'It certainly is a feather. Where does it come from? From a cushion or a pillow? I leave you to work that out. But what can we conclude from this, Monsieur Le Floch?'

'That the victim was suffocated . . .'

'. . . And not strangled, since there's no sign of strangulation around the neck. And, as a man of this age would not let himself be suffocated so easily, it's safe to bet that he was drugged beforehand. There's still a strange smell around his mouth . . .'

'But in that case, Master Sanson, what has the lancet got to do with all this?'

'That's up to you to find out; it's outside my field. But there are some situations in life where truth and simplicity are the best way of fooling people. This *mise en scène* with the lancet seems to me to be intended to lead people astray, and what makes that even more likely is . . .'

He leant over the chest of the corpse again. He slowly drew out the lancet.

'. . . that this lancet did not in fact have the power to kill. It didn't enter the heart and it didn't touch any of the vital organs.'

Nicolas thought for a moment before putting his question.

'But if the blow from the lancet was not fatal, could this careful arrangement mean that the culprit had no knowledge of anatomy?'

Bourdeau smiled. He was following Nicolas's train of thought step by step.

'Probably. It seems to me that the murderer did not want to kill and leave a bloody mess. He then fabricated a cover-up for some mysterious reason that it's your job to elucidate. In doing so he made two mistakes. The first was by wanting to give the impression of a fatal wound to the heart, even though no blood was spilt, and the second was by not striking in the right place. My first instinct was to conclude that he was ignorant of anatomy. However, my second reaction is to say to myself that this whole *mise en scène* was the work of a murderer who had clearly thought through everything he did, and who on the contrary possessed the necessary knowledge.'

'But in that case,' said Nicolas, 'why did he make so many mistakes? Because in both hypotheses the mistakes remain . . .'

'Let me make myself clear,' explained Sanson. 'The murderer uses a drug to make his victim dizzy. He suffocates him, sets the scene and his error with the wound from the lancet gives a particularly vicious twist to the crime. It is deliberate. If he is a physician, he'll take advantage of this to proclaim his innocence by relying on the fact that such a basic mistake could not have been made by a medical man.'

Bourdeau and Nicolas looked at each other, amazed at the young executioner's expertise and the prospects it opened up.

'I haven't forgotten those black marks of yours,' Sanson continued. 'It so happens that when a dead body is lying stretched out, the face turns bluish before very long as the blood stops circulating just below the skin. On the other hand those parts in contact with the ground – the shoulders, buttocks and the backs of the legs – take on a purplish-pink tinge. I conclude from this, too hastily perhaps, that the victim was suffocated face down and maintained in this position for some time. Besides, look how this colouring affects the whole front of the body. This phenomenon occurs about half an hour after death and attains its full effect only after five or six hours. Until then it's possible to delay the process by altering the position of the body but after that the change of colour becomes permanent and quickly darkens, eventually turning a violet-black colour.

'He was lying on his stomach when I found him,' said Bourdeau, 'and we took him away in that position. It was only in the Basse-Geôle that he was turned over, several hours later.'

'That confirms what I've said. We have before us the coming together of two phenomena: a congestion of the lungs due to suffocation and the usual changes to a corpse according to the position of the body. To conclude I would say that this corpse is that of a man who was first drugged and suffocated face down and kept in that position for some considerable time – for more than half an hour in any case – and then clumsily stabbed with a lancet. This last wound was not mortal and, given the cadaverous state of the body by that time, did not result in any loss of blood.'

Nicolas was stunned.

'Monsieur,' he exclaimed, 'I am full of admiration and I thank you for your help. However, I must on behalf of Monsieur de Sartine remind you that this matter requires the utmost secrecy. I believe it will be necessary to open up the body to confirm our presumptions, but what good are our doctors in the Châtelet? Yesterday's unfortunate experience, which was also my first, convinced me that anything out of the ordinary is beyond them. Would you be so kind as to take charge of the operation?'

'I'm not a doctor,' Sanson replied, 'but with the help of my nephew who is finishing his medical studies I could take on the task.'

'Do you guarantee his discretion?'

'As my own, and upon my life.'

After thanking Sanson at length, Nicolas and the inspector left him alone with Descart's body and went off towards the part of the Châtelet that housed the cells. Nicolas, who was deep in thought, stopped suddenly and, taking Bourdeau by the arm, prevented him from going any further.

'I don't wish to question Semacgus now, Bourdeau. As you now realise, he could equally be the agent or the victim of this sinister *mise en scène*. I need more evidence before I can form an opinion about his case. I need to work things out on the ground and go back to Vaugirard, the scene of the crime. I have the impression that you lacked the time yesterday to go through the house in detail and collect evidence.'

'I freely admit that,' said Bourdeau, 'but I wasn't struck by anything unusual. I hope you don't expect me to let you go down there on your own. Now you really will have to be on your guard . . .'

'My dear Bourdeau, don't doubt that I shall be. It's important that you stay with Semacgus. Anything may happen here. As I've no intention of putting him in one of those filthy holes in which his security would be guaranteed only at the cost of his health, I want you to guard him until I question him. However, there is something you can do to help me. Find me a lamp or a dark-lantern. It will soon be night time and I don't want to be wandering around in the dark. Find me a carriage, too.'

While Bourdeau went off to carry out these instructions, Nicolas returned to the duty office. He opened a cupboard full of assorted outfits, wigs and hats. All these items would have been a boon to a second-hand clothes seller; there was enough to dress all the beggars and thieves in Paris. Nicolas chose from this dusty collection, into which all his colleagues delved when some tricky case required them to pass unnoticed in the Paris underworld. Bourdeau reappeared, bring-ing with him a small dark-lantern. With a shy smile he also handed Nicolas a little pistol, a powder flask and a bag of bullets.

'You know how to use it. It only fires one shot, but it's discreet because of its size and it can save your life. It's one of a set of two given to me as a present by a gunsmith in Rue des Lombards. I once did him a favour . . . Please accept it as a gift, and promise that you will use it without hesitation.'

Nicolas shook Bourdeau's hand. He was touched by the fondness shown him by his deputy, who for all his rustic ways was loyal to a fault. He placed the pistol in his coat pocket and, carrying a bundle of clothes, went out of the Châtelet and climbed into the cab that was waiting for him under the archway. He had the feeling of being watched but he could not make out where a look-out might be standing, and he ordered the coachman to drive at full speed to the church of Saint-Eustache.

When the carriage arrived at the church he stopped it outside the main door, jumped out and went inside. He knew the place well as he had often heard Mass there. He loved the immense nave and the roar of the organ resounding under the vaulted roof. He slid the enormous bolt to lock the door. During the week the side entrances were shut and, even if they had been open, the time it would have taken for his potential pursuer to get there still left Nicolas ample opportunity to carry out his plan to the full.

He sought refuge in a dark corner of a side chapel, emptied his pockets, shed what he was wearing and slipped into another set of clothes, over which he put a threadbare greatcoat. He was unrecognisable thanks to an ancient wig, dark glasses and a Regency hat. He checked his disguise in a small pocket mirror. To complete the picture he smeared his face with smoke-black from a taper-stick. Holding on to the pistol hidden in his pocket he drew back the heavy bolt, risking everything. Mauval stood before him. Once more Nicolas was struck by the coldness of the man's expression despite the exertion of the chase. He took the initiative, saying in a quavering voice:

'What a strange idea to bolt the door! Please help me to open it, Monsieur. That rogue who just came in rudely bumped into me.'

Mauval pushed him aside unceremoniously and rushed down the nave. The cab had waited for Nicolas, and it immediately headed off towards the Seine.

IX

WOMEN

'Well, then, let's have a serious talk.

When will all the stuff and nonsense you're saying about me end?'

MARIVAUX

ARKNESS was falling by the time Nicolas arrived in Vaugirard. He would have liked to have kept the carriage to be sure of getting back to Paris but the coachman, despite the offer of a substantial sum, refused point-blank to wait for him. He claimed he was not in the habit of hanging about late at night, especially when there was snow in the offing. Nicolas paid the fare and left it at that. He was alone in the deserted lane.

By now it was pitch dark and there were howling gusts of wind. Deafened by the noise, he felt vulnerable again, and yet he had well and truly thrown off his pursuer. For some time he remained motionless in the shadows, alert to the least sign of danger. He became increasingly uneasy. He had never liked the dark and as a child, when Joséphine sent him out after nightfall to fetch logs from the bottom of the garden, he would sing hymns at the top of his voice. He would carry out his task as fast as the weight of his load allowed.

Another memory came back to him. One day his godfather, the Marquis de Ranreuil, had told him how he had panicked when crossing the trenches under enemy fire at the siege of Philipsbourg. Under the hail of bullets whistling around them, his commander, the Duke of Berwick, had shouted to him: 'Chin up, Monsieur, and just pretend!' Fear, the marquis had explained, was often simply a sign of the terror of being afraid. You had to go beyond it, and in the heat of battle it would disappear as if by magic.

Despite the painful memories it evoked, the image of Isabelle's father had a positive effect on Nicolas. After several attempts with the tinder-box he managed to light the little dark-lantern, although its flame flickered hesitantly in its fragile receptacle.

He opened the gate and went into the garden. So it was back to the beginning, and only two days after Descart's and Semacgus's violent argument in this same place. The return of the frost had made the ground hard and preserved the disorderly traces of footprints. Nicolas imagined the comings and goings of Bourdeau and the men of the watch, the removal of the body, the stretcher and the cart rattling along the badly surfaced road. He stopped halfway to the house, which was even more sinister-looking than he remembered. The pale glimmer of the lantern played faintly upon the dark façade with its casement windows still shut. Nicolas had always been responsive to the hidden mystery of stone, to its ability to instil in him feelings of attraction or repulsion. Did he owe this aspect of his character to his Celtic ancestry, or to the experiences of his youth?

A particularly strong gust of wind brought him back to reality. He started, as if rudely awoken from a dream. The tiring day and the dull throbbing pain of his injuries, which seemed to beat in time with his heart, made him want to get through this task as quickly as possible, but he knew he needed to be extremely thorough. He had not wanted to offend Bourdeau but his job of the previous evening had been botched and carried out in a rather perfunctory way. He hoped that, as they had gone around, the officers and guards had not disturbed the scene where the drama had taken place, destroying valuable clues for ever.

Nicolas checked that the sealing wafers had not been broken and opened the door. He took one step forward and found himself back on the landing from which the staircase led down into the main room. For the moment all he could see were the spot where Descart had been found and the bronze handrail. Beyond was darkness, out of range of the dim beam of his lamp.

The strangeness of the residence struck him even more than it had on his first visit. It did not have a cellar and the room in which Descart saw his patients had its foundations in the basement, which explained the high position of the windows. It had more in common with a crypt than a house.

He examined the landing carefully but noted nothing unusual. Next he went to the right-hand staircase, scrutinising each step. He did the same on the other side, then walked down into the room. First he looked for the candelabra on the chimney-piece and lit them. The large ivory Christ with its arms closed suddenly emerged from the gloom.

Nicolas first noticed footprints that had left dirty black stains on the tiled floor and then, looking up, he saw before him a scene of desolation. The room had been totally destroyed. The large table that Descart used as a desk had been cleared of the papers and the objects covering it, and they were now strewn across the floor. An overturned inkwell had spilt out a pool of black ink, into which someone had trodden. The straw-bottomed chairs were intact, but three upholstered armchairs had been ripped open, disgorging their stuffing and horsehair. Specimen jars and books had been swept off the shelves by some angry hand that had then systematically smashed the glass and ripped off the bindings. Medical instruments lay everywhere. The cupboards had received similar treatment.

Nicolas continued his investigations. To the right of the fireplace a door opened onto a corridor leading to a kitchen, a dining room, a small drawing room and a laundry. Another staircase led up to the first floor. This strange layout meant that the back of the house was once again at ground level. All the rooms were in the same state of systematic destruction and Nicolas couldn't help treading on broken items.

He began with the first floor. Everywhere he came across the same spectacle: mattresses slashed open, clothes and bed linen lying strewn across the floor, broken ornaments and furniture forced open. Nicolas noticed that valuable watches and other expensive items had been left untouched by the wreakers of all this damage. And yet they had been searching for something. On the floor he even found a small velvet purse full of *louis d'or*. Any possible hiding place had been scoured, stripped and smashed. Even the paintings had been turned round. What could they have been hunting for in such a brutal fashion?

Some black marks attracted Nicolas's attention and he set off to follow them. They were evident everywhere and led him to the staircase. It was quite obvious from the identical footmarks going up and down that the stranger who had overturned and broken the inkwell had then gone to the upper floors. He followed the ones that went down, stopping to retrace his steps when the pattern became unclear and confusing and shining his lantern in order to examine them more clearly. He even jotted them down in pencil on a small card. In this way he was able to reconstruct down to the smallest detail the movements of the intruder, who seemed to have acted alone.

Nicolas had now recovered his composure and was able to concentrate all his efforts on the search. The last place he entered was the laundry, a closet piled high with discarded items and he was struck by a blast of freezing cold air. An old stool had been placed up against the wall, beneath an open window. The matting of the stool was marked with inkstains. There were still some marks left on the cob wall, which had been scraped in several places. After turning the house upside down the intruder had escaped through this window.

Nicolas shuddered as he realised the significance of this observation. If the man had fled through here it was because the doors were closed and sealed. This meant that the intruder was still in the house when Semacgus had discovered the body and that he had decided to hide in order to search the house later, without fear of being disturbed. So the person concerned must have been Descart's murderer.

Nicolas remembered that Semacgus had told Inspector Bourdeau that he had arrived half an hour before the time arranged for his meeting; he had perhaps disrupted the murderer's plans. In any case this hypothesis seemed to clear Semacgus. However, there was still plenty left to explain, starting with the ransacking of the house, which could not be attributed to Semacgus unless he had had an accomplice. Bourdeau had noticed nothing and when he had closed the doors the house had been intact.

So anything was still possible and the number of conceivable scenarios grew with each new theory. What could someone have been looking for that was so precious that they took no notice of jewellery and silver?

Nicolas looked at the window thoughtfully. He climbed onto the stool and measured the opening with a piece of string. He carefully noted the position of items in the room, put seals on all the windows and then, certain of having forgotten nothing, snuffed out the candles, closed the door and resealed it.

Once outside he walked around the house to the laundry window, which was about a yard above the ground. Nicolas knelt down on the frozen earth. There were hollow imprints in the ice and these marks were much clearer than those found in the house. He sketched down the impression they had made and examined them with a puzzled look. The footprints went across part of the garden amongst the pear trees and up to the boundary wall. It was not difficult to climb up the wall.

Nicolas fastened the lantern to his coat and propped himself upon a protruding stone from which he was able to examine the top of the wall. He was hoping to find traces of blood, proving that the intruder had injured himself on the pieces of broken glass set into the mortar covering. There were none. Nicolas did however pick up a button with a fragment of material attached to it, and he carefully tucked it into his pocket.

Not wishing to risk injury by attempting to climb the wall, he went through the gate and locked it. In the lane the same imprints appeared and then petered out amongst ruts made by carts. The biting cold took Nicolas by surprise. He was alone, without any means of transport and holding a lantern that threatened to go out. He checked the time by his watch: it was seven o'clock. He decided to go to Semacgus's house to question Catherine. It was also a good excuse to see the cook again, as he was very fond of her. Moreover, in addition to the horse that pulled his stolen carriage, Semacgus also owned a saddle horse and Nicolas intended to borrow it to get back to Paris.

Suddenly a faint whistling caught his attention. At first he thought it was just the effect of the wind in the trees but the sound came again and a barely audible voice spoke:

'Don't be afraid, Monsieur Nicolas. It's me, Rabouine, one of Bourdeau's men. I'm behind the bush, in a small tool shed. Don't turn round. Pretend you're adjusting your boot. The inspector sent me here yesterday evening. What a night! I haven't moved since. Fortunately I had a bottle of spirits and some bread. I'm good at planning this sort of expedition. The main thing is to stay put. You never know.'

Nicolas was annoyed with himself for suspecting Bourdeau of negligence. On the contrary he had made judicious arrangements that might prove useful. He should not have taken at face value the inspector's lack of insistence in coming with him. His deputy was not the sort of man who would leave him to face the threat of danger on his own. He knew that Rabouine would come to Nicolas's help if need be.

'Pleased to see you, but how did you recognise me?'

'To start with I mistook you for someone else, you know, a stranger. Your disguise is very good. But when I saw you come out and replace the seals I thought to myself, "That's our Nicolas." You couldn't help me up, could you? My fingers are numb, I've got frostbite and I've run out of food. It looks as if it could be a hard night.'

'You can go home. I hope your time on watch has at least been useful.'

'I think it was. Last night about an hour after the inspector and the men of the watch had left, a stranger appeared on the top of the boundary wall of the garden, in fact right where you were just now . . .'

'Can you describe him to me?'

'To tell the truth I didn't see much. He seemed both heavy and light.'

'What do you mean?'

'There was something that didn't quite fit. The man seemed heavily built but I could have sworn he was very agile. He wore a mask and was dressed in dark clothes. He was walking carefully.'

'Carefully?'

'As if he was choosing where to step. It surprised me because the ground wasn't yet frozen.'

'Didn't you follow him?'

'Monsieur Bourdeau had ordered me not to move under any circumstances and I didn't think it right to disobey.'

Nicolas managed to hide his disappointment.

'You've done well. You can go now. Nothing's going to happen here this evening. But do me a favour: find me a carriage and send it round to Dr Semacgus's, near the Croix-Nivert. It's the only respectable house in the area, surrounded by hovels. The coachman can't miss it.'

He handed him a few coins.

'This is for you. You've done a good job. I'll tell Bourdeau.'

'The inspector has already paid me, Monsieur Nicolas. But I won't say no to the tip. I don't want to offend you. It's a pleasure working for you.'

Nicolas started to walk along the icy lane. The uneven ground was full of bumps and frozen puddles that made him stumble and slip. Several times he almost twisted an ankle and once he fell. In his current state it would have been the last straw if he had hurt himself. Fortunately he soon reached the surgeon's house. It consisted of a series of low buildings that formed a U-shape around a courtyard enclosed by a high wall.

He pushed open the main door without difficulty. It was never locked, since the master of the house claimed that 'the door of a medical man should always be open to those in distress'. The kitchen, in the corner where the outbuildings joined the house proper, was dimly lit by a flickering light.

Nicolas approached the glazed door, opened it slightly without making a noise and came upon a mysterious scene. Near the tall chimney-piece with its roaring fire crouched Catherine. She was holding Awa, who was half-naked with her head tilted back, and seemed to be singing a lullaby to her new friend. Awa was groaning faintly, her skin glistening with sweat, and sometimes she arched her back and writhed, uttering inaudible words. Her whole body then bent and started to shudder to such an extent that Catherine had great difficulty supporting her.

Looking up, Catherine let out a scream when she saw Nicolas and attempted to stand. She let go of Awa who fell to the floor unconscious, and then looked around for some item with which to defend herself. Nicolas did not understand her reaction at all.

He had completely forgotten about his sinister-looking outfit and his coarse, grimy make-up. But Catherine was not the sort of woman to just stand there helplessly. In her younger days as a canteen-keeper she had been involved in various dirty tricks, ambushes and brawls with soldiers or a civilian rabble and she had always come through them with flying colours. Grabbing a large kitchen knife from the table, she lunged at the stranger. Meanwhile Awa began to have convulsions, whilst being spattered with blood gushing from a beheaded cockerel that lay on the kitchen floor.

Nicolas avoided the blow and let Catherine pass him, carried by her own momentum, so that he was now behind her. He managed to grab her around the waist and was then able to speak into her ear.

'So, my dear Catherine, is this how you welcome Nicolas?'

The effect of his words was immediate. She dropped her knife and tearfully threw herself into the young man's arms. Sensibly he sat her down on a chair.

'Well! How you treat your friends, and dressed up like that!'

'Forgive me, Catherine, I'd forgotten all about the disguise.'

He took off his felt hat to reveal his head swathed in a blood-soaked bandage.

'My God, Nicolas, what has happened to you, my poor little thing?'

'It would take too long to explain. Tell me instead about this witches' sabbath. Is Awa ill?'

Catherine seemed embarrassed. She twined around her finger a long wisp of grey hair that poked out from the mob cap which crowned her old snub-nosed face. Eventually she made up her mind to speak.

'She is not ill. She wanted to talk to her demons.'

'What do you mean, her demons?'

Catherine started to rattle off the story.

'In her country people have strange ways to talk to the spirits. She prepares a sort of herbal tea that she breathes in. Then we behead a cockerel. She starts to dance like a possessed woman. She capers about like a goat. Then the poor thing looks at the pool of blood. She lets out a scream and starts to tear at her face. I have much trouble calming her down. She is still very agitated.'

'But what is the purpose of all this?'

'She wanted to find out what happened to Saint-Louis. Well, the way they do. She is a good girl and I like her very much. Do you know, she has a way with eggs . . .'

Nicolas, who knew that Catherine could go on for ever about culinary matters, stopped her immediately.

'So what did she conclude from all this witchcraft?'

Catherine was so frightened she crossed herself.

'Never say that word. It is how they do things. We must not judge them. We know not their customs. Perhaps ours seem as strange to them. You know, Nicolas, I have travelled much and have seen many things I do not understand.'

Nicolas admired the common sense and kind-heartedness of this simple woman. She went on:

'To see how dejected she is since, I do not think the reply was favourable. What misfortune. And poor Monsieur Semacgus who has been arrested. Nicolas, you will get him out, yes?'

'I will do my best to uncover the truth behind everything that has happened,' the young man replied cautiously.

Awa, though still stretched out on the floor, seemed to be calm again. She was resting, as if drowsy. Nicolas took

Catherine's hands and looked her straight in the eye.

'Tell me about Madame Lardin,' he said. 'And don't hide anything from me because I already know enough to be able to tell what is true and what is not. In any case you left a note that I found in the kitchen on Tuesday evening, under my plate . . .'

'You must know how that woman really was. She was unfaithful always to poor Monsieur Lardin. He could not have done more to make her life pleasant. Clothes, finery, jewels, furniture – all his money went on her. And the evil creature, the more he gave, the more she wanted. And also there were her fancy men; Descart, poor Semacgus and a gallant with a scar across his face. That one, he really frightened me. She opened her legs to all of them, the bitch! And always more and more demands. She really stuffed her belly. Monsieur I liked very much. He was good to me, even if he was surly and hard on other people, and on you too, my poor Nicolas. Even if he also had his faults. He went with whores when she would not have him. He gambled very much at *lansquenet* and *faro*. The more he gambled the more he lost. He came back to me in the early morning, always in a shocking state . . .'

'But in that case how could he keep up such a standard of living?'

Catherine took out her handkerchief and wiped her eyes. She sighed, then spat on the piece of material and tried to wipe the grime off Nicolas's face as if he were a child. He let her do it, and for a moment he thought he was back in Guérande; old Fine's face superimposed itself on Catherine's.

'It was I who helped him. All my savings went to him. Being a cook in the army is not enough to live on. Sometimes there is something extra from booty or looting but only when you have a winning streak. Once my old man was dead I inherited a small property that I sold. It was a tidy sum and I kept it for later. The commissioner went on at me so much that in the end I gave it to him in dribs and drabs. For the last year he has not even paid me my wages. I kept the house going by mending clothes in the neighbourhood. Then there was Marie. She was so sweet that I did not want to give up – it was for her that I did not leave earlier.'

'You did in the end . . .'

Catherine sighed.

'On Tuesday, two days ago, I hear the evil woman tell Marie to pack her bags. She wants her to go the next day to her godmother in Orléans, someone completely unknown to us. Marie is screaming, crying and pleading with her, the poor lamb. I get very worked up and join in and I give the lady a piece of my mind. She is all high and mighty and treats me like dirt. I cannot make any headway with her. The wicked thing has a tongue like quicksilver, and whatever I say she has an answer for. Then she goes for me claws first and nearly strangles me. I have bites and scratches all over.'

She showed him her big arms covered with marks.

'She threw me out there and then, despite little Marie's pleas. What could I do? I was at my wits' end by the time I left. I spent the whole night thinking where to go. I thought of Monsieur Semacgus. He has always been so good and kind to me, so I decide. The next day I come here. I say to myself, "Even if he had fallen into the clutches of that evil creature like the others, perhaps he will understand."'

She stroked Nicolas's forehead.

'You know, Nicolas, I have nothing left. I am a poor woman and getting old. I am still strong and I can be of help to people.

What will become of me? There is no cure for my situation. At my age it is easy to get into hardship and fall on hard times. I would rather die. I will throw myself into the Seine. I will not bring disgrace on anyone as I have no family.[1] It is a pity because with my little nest egg I could have scraped by.'

Catherine's poor, plain-looking face crumpled and her tears began to flow again. She hiccuped as she attempted to pull herself together and her ample bosom heaved with despair. She did not cry, she simply let out a controlled, rasping sigh. Nicolas could not bear to see her so distressed.

'Catherine, stop. I promise to help you. You can rely on me.'

She sniffed and looked at him, her face suddenly beaming.

'But first,' he continued, 'you must answer my questions. Do you feel up to it? It's very important.'

She nodded, now calm and attentive.

'On the night Commissioner Lardin disappeared were you at the house in Rue des Blancs-Manteaux?' Nicolas asked.

'No, definitely not. That Lardin woman gave me the evening off. I stayed with my landlady eating fritters and listening to revellers yelling in the street. I went to bed at about eleven o'clock and the next day I was in my kitchen by seven, relighting my stove.'

'Nothing in particular struck you that morning?'

'Wait a minute . . . Madame woke up very late.'

'Later than usual?'

'Yes, at about midday. She told me she had caught a cold. And that did not surprise me. Her ankle boots were soaking wet. Ruined by the snow. I pointed it out to her and I got told off as usual. She said that she had gone to vespers. Vespers, wearing Carnival clothes and a mask!'

'Did that surprise you?'

'Yes and no. From time to time she did go to church to give herself airs and graces. Not for the good Lord, for sure, but to be seen, of course, and to eye up the men. She even said it had been the church of Petit-Saint-Antoine. But dressed like that . . .'

'She could have gone to Blancs-Manteaux church.'

'Exactly what I thought. With the weather as it was on Friday it would have been much easier just to go across the road.'

'There's something else I want to ask. Were you responsible for the commissioner's clothes?'

'He would not let anyone touch them. He always had papers in his pockets. I washed his shirts and underclothes.'

'Who was his tailor?'

'You know him, Nicolas; it is Master Vachon, who fitted you out when you arrived in Paris so oddly dressed.'

Nicolas had detected an air of embarrassment about Catherine. She was clenching her hands so tightly that the skin was turning blue. He ventured to probe a little deeper.

'How do you know there were papers in his pockets?'

She began to cry silently.

'Catherine, I must have an answer. You must understand that it may help me in my investigation. If you can't confide in me, who can you confide in?'

'I always searched his clothes,' Catherine continued, sobbing. 'When he had big winnings he threw the coins loose into his pockets. Rather than letting everything be lost again, I put aside a small amount for household expenses. I got into the habit when I saw he never counted the money. But, Nicolas, I swear to you, it was never for me. I am no thief.

She held up her head defiantly.

'But I would be quite entitled to reimburse myself for my advances and my unpaid wages.'

'And among these papers did you notice anything in particular?'

'Nothing, except the day before he disappeared. I have not thought about it since but it may be of importance. Perhaps it is, perhaps not. There was a scrap of paper, with your name in the corner.'

'My name? Do you remember what it said?'

'Oh yes. It was very short and it intrigued me. It was like a proverb. Yes, that is it: "Do two make three? Enfolded in these arms, some seek their solace." '

'And you haven't seen this piece of paper since then, have you?'

'Never. No more than I have seen Monsieur.'

Nicolas considered that there was nothing more he could get out of Catherine. After comforting her once more, he helped her to lay Awa on her bed and left Semacgus's house.

Rabouine had been as good as his word and a cab was waiting for him in the lane. The carriage was shrouded in darkness. The snow softened every sound and accentuated the feeling of captivity in the cramped space inside the vehicle. The snow fell slowly in large flakes sent swirling upwards by an occasional gust of wind, sometimes forming fragile halos around the lights of the scattered houses.

Slumped in the corner of the carriage, his head leaning against the velvet upholstery, Nicolas looked out blankly. He was not sorry to have gone to Vaugirard. He had the feeling of having done some useful work. One thing was certain: Descart's house harboured a mystery. Yet he could not be certain whether the intruder had found what he was looking for or had given up. And what exactly had he been searching for?

The ensuing events had not enlightened him at all – except for the discovery that Africa had set up camp with its witchcraft and pagan practices at the gates of the capital. He suddenly remembered an incident from his not-so-distant youth. One day, after he had hurt his elbow during one of the brawls that were such a common feature of the matches of *soule*, Fine had taken him to a woman who ironed coiffes and had a well-established reputation in the area as a bonesetter. While his nurse was crossing herself, the woman had begun a strange chant, then after spinning around several times she had placed a nail in his hand and asked him for a coin. Then she had rested his head on her black skirt, and ten years later he could still remember its strange odour. She had dipped her hand into a pot filled with a sticky substance and had rubbed it vigorously onto the injured part, reciting some words in Breton, which he still remembered: '*Pa'z out ar jug braz, Otro Saint Erwan ar Wirionè Clew ac'hanan.*'[2] His arm, which he had been unable to straighten out a moment before, had miraculously become flexible again. The old woman had warned him that from then on he would know when it was going to rain from a pain in his arm, and that it would not go away when he was old. That time had not yet come.

So poor Awa had merely been following her own custom in order to try to find out her companion's fate. Nicolas had not forgotten about Saint-Louis either, but as time passed there seemed to be less and less hope of finding Semacgus's servant.

The conversation with Catherine had confirmed what

Nicolas already knew about Madame Lardin and her loose morals. According to his servant, the commissioner had been reduced to the undignified roles of deceived husband, penniless gambler and unscrupulous master. However, his character seemed to Nicolas to have quite another and a more disturbing dimension which, in her simplicity, this kind-hearted woman had failed to realise. As to the cryptic phrase found in Lardin's coat pocket the day before he disappeared, he really had no idea what it could mean.

Once again Nicolas contemplated the magnitude of his task. His head was still buzzing with Monsieur de Sartine's words. He suddenly thought about the King, who must also be waiting for news from his Lieutenant General of Police. He had a new awareness of the dramatic background to this whole affair: the war that was still going on, the soldiers on the battlefield in the snow and mud, the heaped-up corpses and the flocks of crows. A shudder ran right through him.

Nicolas decided to return to Rue des Blancs-Manteaux. He needed to change and to tidy himself up: he had a thick growth of beard and it was time to renew his bandage. He also needed to inform Madame Lardin of the evidence that apparently confirmed her husband's death. It would be interesting to assess the nature and intensity of the putative widow's grief.

He thought about Marie. What had become of her? Would she be there to greet him or had she already gone off to her godmother's? Nicolas had come to a decision that was both practical and ethical: he could no longer remain at the Lardins'. Being in charge of the investigation left him no choice. It was impossible for him in all conscience to be both their investigator and their lodger. He was already planning to have the area around the house put under watch if Bourdeau, who was always so precise and careful, had not already arranged it. On the other hand he had to have someone to see to his washing and he did not know whether Louise Lardin had found a replacement for Catherine or whether she was now living alone, anxious to rid herself of everyone around her.

He had been so taken up with these thoughts that he was back in the city before he realised it. The lights were brighter and more numerous. As his carriage neared the Seine it was surrounded by shouting and laughter, and it passed through a group of masked revellers making a hullabaloo. One of them climbed onto the footboard, and with one hand brushed the snow away from the window. In his death's head mask he then pressed his face up against it, and for several long minutes Nicolas had to endure a confrontation with the Grim Reaper, who had been dogging his every step for the past few days.

Soon he was back in Rue des Blancs-Manteaux. It looked just as peaceful and deserted as before, except that there was someone huddled in the church doorway. Uncertain who it might be, he pretended not to have noticed anything. It was either a beggar or one of Bourdeau's spies. The inspector really did think of everything. Beneath that placid appearance he hid a wealth of experience and policing expertise. It could not possibly be someone tailing him, unless his enemy was a mind-reader and had predicted Nicolas's return.

Setting aside this mystery for the moment, he put his key in the lock and noticed that it had been changed and that he could no longer get in. He decided to use the knocker, an operation he had to perform several times.

Eventually the door opened and Louise Lardin appeared,

holding a lighted torch and looking surly. She was wearing a ball dress with a loose back, off-white in colour with silver embroidery. The tight-fitting and low-cut bodice revealed her powdered bosom. The skirts of the dress were rounded and extended at the back by an ample train which was raised over the pannier. This allowed the whole petticoat to be visible, as well as two or three layers of enormous flounces. Her face, excessively powdered and made up, was dotted with beauty spots, with cheeks highlighted in bright red and lips painted vermilion. Two large tresses arranged in a loop fell down the nape of her neck onto her shoulders.

'Is it you, Nicolas?' she said in a shrill voice. 'I thought you'd disappeared too. Judging by your clothes and appearance, you've merely fallen into bad company. Whatever the case, I have decided to ask you to leave this house. Gather up your rags immediately. I'm not in the mood to take in vagrants.'

'This is what I wear for my work, Madame, when the circumstances warrant,' replied Nicolas. 'Your judgement is perhaps too hasty. As to your desire to see me off the premises, I'd already made up my mind to leave anyway. It's quite obvious that I am not welcome here.'

'All you needed to do was to make yourself wanted, Nicolas.'

The suggestiveness of the remark made the young man blush.

'Let's end the conversation there, Madame. I'll leave tomorrow morning; in this weather and at this hour it would be difficult for me to find shelter for the night. But before I go I have some serious matters to discuss with you.'

She did not move, but remained firmly in the middle of the hallway.

'To reply in kind, Madame, allow me to express my surprise at finding a woman whose husband has disappeared dressed up for a ball.'

'You are very insolent all of a sudden. It so happens that I am indeed wearing a ball gown and that I was about to go out to enjoy myself and have a good time as a woman of my age is entitled to do. Does that satisfy you, lackey?'

'That would no doubt satisfy a lackey but it in no way satisfies a representative of the Lieutenant General of Police.'

'You are getting too big-headed, Monsieur.'

'You, Madame, are becoming very irritable and seem barely interested in the sad matter that brings me here.'

Louise Lardin straightened herself and adopted a provocative pose, resting both hands on the panniers of her dress in a way that shocked Nicolas. In a flash the veneer of respectability cracked to reveal the harlot who had been so much in demand at La Paulet's.

'Sad matter? Have you taken it into your head to talk to me about those grisly remains you've dug up from the rubbish at Montfaucon? Does that surprise you? I'm better informed than you thought. It's my husband, isn't it? What difference do you expect it to make to me? You went grubbing about in the filth and you got your money's worth. What were you expecting? Did you want me to act the part of the distraught widow? I never loved Lardin, and now I'm rid of him. I'm free, free and I'm off to the ball, Monsieur.'

Nicolas suddenly found her very attractive in her vivacity, transformed by a kind of pride. She was getting excited, and around her the train of her dress swished through the air with a faint rustle of satin.

'As you please, Madame, but first you will have to answer some questions, which to judge from your reactions so far should not prove too upsetting for you. My task has been made easier and I'll come straight to the point. I should add that I expect someone as high-minded as you to give me straightforward answers. Otherwise I will regrettably have no alternative but to resort to other means.'

'So be it, Monsieur Apprentice Commissioner . . . I yield to the threat of force, for fear of torture . . . But be quick. There are people waiting for me.'

'Last Friday evening you went out. Where did you go and at what time did you come home?'

'Why should I remember any particular day? I don't keep a record of my activities.'

'I should point out to you, Madame, just to jog your memory, that it was the very evening your husband disappeared.'

'I think I went to vespers.'

'At the church of Blancs-Manteaux?'

'Where else can you go to vespers?'

'At that church or another?'

'Oh, I see that old battleaxe of a cook has been talking to you . . . I went to the Petit-Saint-Antoine.'

'In a black cape and a mask?'

'And what if I did? A real lady who ventures out after nightfall during Carnival is putting her virtue at risk unless she wears clothes appropriate for the occasion.'

'And this cape was meant to protect you from the snow, was it?'

She stared at him and moistened her lips.

'It wasn't snowing. It was to shelter me from the wind.'

Nicolas stopped talking. There followed a long silence until Louise Lardin asked in a husky voice:

'Why do you hate me, Nicolas?'

She drew near him. He was struck by her fragrance, a mingled scent of hair powder, make-up, a hint of irises and something stronger that dominated the rest.

'Madame, I am merely doing my duty, but I would have preferred it to have taken me to a house other than this one, where I have been welcome for so long.'

'Everything can be as before with a little effort on your part. My husband is no more. What can I do about it? What must I do to convince you that I know nothing about the cause of his death?'

Nicolas did not want to be diverted. He tried another approach.

'They say that the new Dauvergne motet sung that night at the Petit-Saint-Antoine was very beautiful.'[3]

She avoided the trap.

'I've no taste for music and I don't know anything about it.'

'What did you do yesterday? Did you stay here?'

'I was with one of my lovers, Monsieur. Yes, I have lovers, as you know full well. What else would you expect of a fallen woman, and a kept one at that?'

A tiny particle of powder came away from her face and fell onto her bodice. The sincerity in her voice made her seem pitiful.

'Does that satisfy you?'

'I'm grateful to you for your frankness,' replied Nicolas, blushing slightly. 'Would you mind telling me the name of this man?'

'To prove I'm being genuine I can tell you that it was

Monsieur Mauval, a man who knows what love is and, as you are aware, knows how to punish interferers.'

Nicolas ignored the insult, but noted the threat. The world suddenly seemed very small to him.

'At what time did he meet you?'

'At midday, and he left me very early this morning. I feel ashamed for you, Monsieur, for subjecting me to this inquisition.'

'I was forgetting, Madame, to express my condolences on the death of your relative.'

He had risked this glancing reference, hoping to catch his opponent off guard and find the chink in her armour. It was to no avail. Louise Lardin did not appear to know about her cousin Descart's death.

'A husband forced upon you is not a relative,' she replied. 'Besides, this sudden concern of yours does not impress me. On that note, Monsieur, I must leave you, since I can hear the carriage coming to collect me. I hope that by tomorrow morning you will have left my house.'

'One more word, Madame. Where is Mademoiselle Marie?'

'At her godmother's in Orléans: she has decided to turn her back on the world and become a novice with the Ursuline Sisters.'

'That's rather a sudden vocation.'

'The Lord moves in mysterious ways.'

'Where was Marie the night the commissioner disappeared?'

'In town, at a friend's.'

'Madame, who killed your husband?'

She half-smiled, wrapped herself in a cape with a fur collar and twirled around.

'The streets are dangerous during Carnival. He must have encountered some masked murderer.'

She went out, slamming the door behind her, without so much as a glance in Nicolas's direction.

Nicolas remained rooted to the spot. This duel had drained him and tired him even more. Either Louise Lardin was innocent and her comments merely bore the hallmarks of cynicism and amorality, or she was an actress without equal. He believed also that this desire to provoke and this determination to flaunt her sinfulness were perhaps an attempt to hide something else. How could anyone suspect someone who denounced her own lack of morals in the strongest possible terms? Nicolas was not accustomed to confronting an opponent of this nature. His youth was a drawback and the range of his experience was too limited. He had barely begun his collection of characters. He liked things to be done according to rules and found cynicism disconcerting, the product of a twisted mind. And yet during the past week so much had happened to him, and so quickly. He found Louise Lardin's remarks offensive, an insult to the rules governing social behaviour. Another idea crossed his mind: perhaps Louise's attitude was in essence merely the last attempt of a lost soul to avoid falling into deeper degradation, and her sincerity the homage that vice pays to virtue.

But this was hardly the time to philosophise. Nicolas was alone in the house and he had to take advantage of it. He set aside any scruples he may have had: they were of little consequence compared with the importance of his assignment. In the library someone – the commissioner, Louise or another individual – had cleared out all the papers. Madame Lardin's bedroom had nothing to offer either. He looked thoughtfully at the rumpled

202

sheets. An empty bottle and two glasses seemed to provide evidence of the antics of two lovers. The shadowy figure on the look-out in Rue des Blancs-Manteaux, if he was indeed one of Bourdeau's men, would perhaps have some information about the timetable of Mauval and his mistress.

Nicolas carefully examined the clothes and the shoes and did the same in Marie's bedroom. There, something surprised him. The young woman's wardrobe seemed complete. Had she left without any luggage? He compared his sketch of the footmarks found in Vaugirard with a pair of muddy ankle boots. They matched.

In the end tiredness got the better of him. Nicolas went slowly up to his garret and remembered that the following day he was due to leave the house for ever. He had been neither happy nor unhappy there; his only concern had been to learn and to do well during the months of his apprenticeship. It would take its place amongst his memories and regrets, along with all the other things and people left by the wayside, because life or death or a small inner voice had decided it and there was nothing he could do.

He collected up his clothes and prepared his portmanteau. As he delved into the pocket of the coat he would be wearing the next day he came across a small piece of paper folded into four. He opened it and first of all saw his forename in the corner of the document, then deciphered the words he already knew:

> *Do two make three?*
> *Enfolded in these arms*
> *Some seek their solace.*

So, when Nicolas was still in Guérande, Lardin had wanted to leave him this cryptic message. But why? And what did it mean? It was while he was thinking about this that the young man fell asleep, overcome with tiredness.

X

TWISTS AND TURNS

Quippe series vinculorum ita adstricta ut
Unde nexus inciperet quoque se conderet
Nec ratione nec uisu perspici posset
For the set of ropes was so well bound
that it was impossible to decide either by reasoning or by looking
where the intertwining started and where it was hidden.

QUINTUS CURTIUS

Friday 9 February 1761

Lying on the ground, he felt the sun glow red upon his closed eyelids. After a wild race across the moorland he had tied his horse to the remains of a broken-up boat half buried in the sands. The sound of the surf had made him drowsy. And suddenly the familiar noise had stopped: he had never noticed until then how the ocean's movement could cease. He needed more air, sat up and opened his eyes, but shut them again immediately, dazzled by the light. A whirlwind of sensations came over him and he found himself in bed, chilled to the bone. The previous night, after the ordeals of the day, he had sunk into unconsciousness fully dressed. He had not bothered to close the shutters as he normally did, and a ray of winter sunlight now shone upon his face. He stretched carefully, like an animal, limb by limb. A good night's sleep had rid him of the pain, leaving in its place a numbness and stiffness reminiscent of the fatigue felt by an out-of-practice rider after a day in the saddle. As he did every morning, he took a deep breath to drive away the fears of the night and felt ready to face a new day.

Nicolas ached and felt dirty. He was in need of a good bath, but this was easier said than done. After some thought he decided to use the resources available. Catherine used a large wooden, hooped tub for soaking the washing, and that would have to do. He would light the kitchen stove and heat some water. Cheered by this prospect, he went over to the window. In the foreground the garden was a blanket of white on which could be seen the criss-crossing traces of birds and cats. The day was magnificent and cold. Further away, on the roofs of the neighbouring houses, the snow sparkled with glints of blue.

He finished his packing by gathering up the modest objects he valued so much: a tiny naïve engraving of Saint Anne; his law books; four volumes of the *Grand Dictionnaire de police* by Delamare; an ancient copy of the *Curiosités de Paris* by Saugrain the elder in a 1716 edition; a customary of Paris; an old missal that used to belong to Canon Le Floch; the *Almanach royal* for 1760; two volumes of the reflections of Father Bourdaloue, of the Society of Jesus, concerning various matters of religion and ethics; *Le Diable boiteux* by his fellow Breton Le Sage, born in Sarzeau, which, like *Don Quixote*, he had read over and over again throughout his childhood; a broken fan, a gift from Isabelle; and lastly a hunting dagger, given to him by his godfather the marquis on the day he had killed his first boar. He still had bitter memories of how disapproving and outraged people had been that this honour was being bestowed on a foundling of low birth. He had bought an old studded leather trunk second-hand for a modest sum which, together with his portmanteau, was all he would need to move his possessions.

Where would he go? He had to find lodgings that were not too expensive. In the meantime he had thought of asking Bourdeau to take him in, but apart from the fact that the inspector lived with his wife and three children in cramped accommodation it seemed to Nicolas rather undignified to call on the help of his deputy. It risked putting him in an awkward position that might jeopardise their good relations, which he valued above everything. Père Grégoire would certainly be happy to welcome him back to Rue de Vaugirard, but the prior of the monastery might refuse; Nicolas's way of life and the irregular hours his job obliged him to keep did not seem compatible with the routine of a monastery. Of course he could approach Monsieur de Sartine, but his superior preferred to remain aloof from these practical details and Nicolas did not want to risk having to face that ironic look he knew so well. He had to sort things out for himself.

All of a sudden he remembered an offer made some time ago by his mentor, Monsieur de Noblecourt. The former procurator at the Parlement of Paris, a widower with no children, had been quick to notice how cold Lardin was towards his pupil. On several occasions he had suggested to Nicolas that he share his epicurean solitude by occupying a pleasant bedroom that no one used. At the time Nicolas had turned down the offer because, even if the Lieutenant General of Police had never said it in so many words, he considered himself to be on official business in the house on Rue des Blancs-Manteaux. Regular questioning by Monsieur de Sartine had confirmed this impression. But now the more he thought about it, the more the possibility of calling on

Monsieur de Noblecourt's help seemed a godsend. He was, moreover, truly fond of the kindly and witty old magistrate. Feeling reassured, he decided to have his bath.

The house was silent and there was nothing to indicate that Louise Lardin had returned. Nicolas relit a candle before venturing into the darkness of the staircase. With the instincts of a sleuth that were becoming second nature to him, he carefully examined the steps, and then the tiled floor in the corridor. No traces of snow or mud were visible. It was clear that no one had entered the house since the previous evening.

He went into the pantry to prepare for his bath. First he needed to relight the stove. He knew where Catherine kept the kindling and the charcoal needed for this operation. He was immediately overcome by a sweet, cloying smell that pervaded the room. He thought that there must be a dead rat in a corner or under a piece of furniture, poisoned by some of the arsenic bait that the cook regularly put down. His search proved fruitless and he tried to ignore the smell. He blew on the glowing fire, which crackled cheerfully. All that remained was for him to fill the pot from the indoor fountain and wait until the water warmed up.

The wooden tub was kept in the cellar alongside bottles of wine, jars of grease and a supply of fat and hams – the latter being protected by cloth sacks that Catherine guarded jealously. Nicolas opened the Gothic-arched door onto a stone staircase that led down into the cellar. The room had been part of the original foundations of an earlier building, now no longer standing. Once more the same acrid smell took Nicolas by the throat. He went down the steps and held up his candle: on one of the butcher's hooks hung a shapeless bulk wrapped in some brown jute material. A pool of congealed blood had spread across the floor beneath it.

Holding his breath because of the appalling stench, with his heart racing, and knowing all too well what he was about to discover, Nicolas tugged at the sack. It fell onto the floor to reveal a wild boar, half decomposed and hung by its forelegs. Had the beast been left behind by Catherine, or had it been put there since? He knew game had to be hung until it was tender, and in his early childhood he had been haunted by the vision of the waterfowl that the marquis sent to the canon, who was very fond of this strong-tasting meat; their heads had been riddled with worms and Joséphine would wait until their beaks dropped off before she cooked them. However, he had never known this process taken to the stage of putrefaction. On the floor there were many footprints, some of which came to a stop in front of a large wooden frame with bottles arranged along its shelves. He looked at this long and hard. As soon as he'd found the tub he went back upstairs, anxious to escape the confined atmosphere and the stench, and returned to the pantry where the water was beginning to boil.

Nicolas undressed and glanced towards a large shining copper saucepan, which he had often used as a mirror. He looked a frightening sight with his growth of beard and his body covered with bruises and grazes. He removed his dressings: the wounds to his head and side had healed over well; the apothecary had done a good job. He poured the boiling water into the tub, but the water fountain was now empty. He opened the door leading out into the garden and, shivering with cold, filled a jug with clean snow in order to cool down his bath. He added a little potash,[1] which Catherine used for doing the washing, squatted down in the tub and poured water over himself with the ladle. The warmth of the water relieved his aches and pains. He slowly drifted off into a pleasurable state of torpor that gave him an enjoyable moment's respite.

As someone who railed so bitterly against the new fashions in cleanliness, his guardian the canon would not have missed the opportunity to criticise this pleasure. The subject, along with the philosophers of the Enlightenment and Diderot's *Encyclopédie*, was a source of heated and unending debate between his guardian and his godfather. The canon maintained that nothing intimate could escape God's notice, and that propriety required that on going to bed you should hide your body from yourself. For him personal care should not involve the use of water and should disregard the body except for the face and hands, the only visible parts. All effort should be concentrated on keeping under-garments clean. The marquis, who delighted in these friendly sparring matches, chortled and in Voltairean vein referred to the unholy smell of clerics of every persuasion. He said that as a form of purgatory he would like to see them immersed in a bath of soapy water. His military career had proved to him the usefulness of what was now known as 'hygiene'. The marquis even claimed that he had escaped epidemics thanks to this habit. This was why he had encouraged Nicolas to adopt his ways. At the Jesuit school in Vannes the young man had suffered from not being able to satisfy what had become for him a daily necessity.

He eventually got out of the tub and dried himself carefully. He had the impression of having shed his former self in the bath water. The scabs of his wounds had been softened by the warm water. He decided to sacrifice an old shirt in order to make some lint, a belt to hold in place the dressing for his side and a bandage for his head. He remembered that Catherine kept ointments and medicinal vinegar in a drawer in the sideboard, and sure enough he found there a small phial of 'Roman liqueur', with instructions for its use wrapped round it. He washed his wounds with it, redid his dressings and, after shaving, put on fresh clothes. He decided against having something to eat or drink as the smell was still just as persistent and made him feel queasy. He put everything back in place, went upstairs to get his luggage, and after checking that he had not forgotten anything, he left his apprentice's garret.

He now needed to find a carriage to transport his belongings. He could leave his luggage in the doorway and go to look for a coachman touting for custom, but that would incur the serious risk of finding nothing there when he came back. And he could not reopen the door once he had shut it, as he did not have the new keys.

His thoughts then turned to the shadowy figure of the day before. He opened the door and looked out at the portal of the church of Blancs-Manteaux. The man was still there, stamping his feet and clapping his hands. Nicolas motioned to him. He hesitated and looked first one way then the other before crossing the snow-covered street, and Nicolas immediately recognised him as one of the informers used by the police department. He asked him to go to Rue Vieille-du-Temple, near Saint-Anastase hospital, to find him a carriage. Meanwhile he, Nicolas, would keep watch. The man confirmed that Louise Lardin had not returned home.

A cab soon appeared and the informant got out. Nicolas put

his luggage on board and gave the coachman his mentor's address in Rue Montmartre, at a place called 'Pointe Saint-Eustache' opposite the church of the same name. The magistrate owned the five-storey house and rented out the upper floors, retaining only the main living areas on the first and second floor. The ground floor was shared by a bakery and the servants' quarters occupied by Marion, the housekeeper, and a footman called Poitevin, who was almost as elderly as his master. Nicolas thought that he might be able to recover the clothes he'd hidden in the half-light of the side chapel of Saint-Eustache, if they had escaped the keen vigilance of the beggars who haunted the building.

The carriage moved in silence, but for the bells on the horse that tinkled merrily. The city was emerging from the heavy pall of cloud and mist that had covered it for days. Once they reached the market of Les Halles, the throng became more and more dense and the vehicles were almost at a standstill. Eventually the carriage passed Pointe Saint-Eustache and entered Rue Montmartre.

Nicolas was pleased to see the tall mansion of the former procurator of the Parlement of Paris once again. Pot-bellied and lopsided, it seemed firmly rooted in the Parisian soil. Over the years its side walls had widened and bulged, like those of a beached galleon. The curved line of its balconies with their wrought-iron ornamentation looked like the lips of a giant statue and seemed to be breaking into an enigmatic yet kindly smile. Nicolas felt cheered by the sight; he liked this house. After paying the fare he set down his luggage in the archway of the carriage entrance, where the smell of bread from the neighbouring bakery wafted through the air. He went up to the first floor and knocked on the door. Old Marion's wrinkled face creased with pleasure when she recognised him.

'Oh! Monsieur Nicolas. How lovely to see you. The master was complaining only yesterday that you'd stopped coming to see him. You know how fond he is of you.'

'Good morning, Marion. I would have come to pay him my respects earlier, if circumstances had not prevented me.'

A small water spaniel, a frizzy grey ball, shot up like a firework and began to jump around Nicolas, yelping happily.

'Just look how delighted Cyrus is to see you!' said Marion. 'He knows exactly who his friends are, and the master's. I always say that animals have more common sense than we do . . .'

A voice could be heard enquiring about the visitor.

'I think the master's getting impatient. He's having his hot chocolate in his bedroom, as usual. Follow me. He's going to be so pleased.'

Monsieur de Noblecourt's bedroom was a handsome-looking room, with pale-green panelling set off with gold. It overlooked Rue Montmartre through two glazed doors that opened onto the balcony. The master of the house had often described to his pupil the pleasure he took each morning in daydreaming as he drank his chocolate, dressed in his floral chintz morning gown and wearing a crimson skullcap. From daybreak he would watch the street activities multiply, and cast a philosophical eye over the thousand and one incidents of everyday life. He would drift into a pleasant state of drowsiness, the warmth of the exotic beverage and the particular languid feeling it produced sometimes sending him into a blissful sleep. Cyrus went to and fro between Nicolas and his master, then jumped onto the magistrate's knees.

'The sun and Nicolas have returned, alleluia!' exclaimed the old man. 'My dear child, sit down. Marion, quick, a chair and a cup. Bring us as fast as you can some hot chocolate and some of those soft rolls from my tenant the baker.'

Beneath the skullcap beamed a chubby face, with surprisingly pale eyes. To the right of his large, ruddy nose was a very noticeable wart, which Nicolas, who had not forgotten his classical education, compared to Cicero's. His witty, greedy mouth was set between drooping, blotchy jowls and a chin that had once been prominent but was now enfolded in a triple layer of flesh.

'You see how devout I am in my habits, if not in anything else,' Monsieur de Noblecourt continued. 'I surrender to old age as it creeps up on me, gradually and gently . . . Soon I shall no longer move from this chair. I'll have another one made, an old-fashioned wing chair with a tray, and on casters, why not? I could have it turned into a commode and I'd never get out of it. After all, one year when the winter was extremely harsh Marshal Luxembourg's wife had a sedan chair brought up to her drawing room to protect her from draughts. I'll stay where I am and one morning Marion's ghost – incidentally she is much older than I am – will find me slumped over my cup of chocolate.'

Nicolas knew his old friend well. All this was mere provocation, intended to make him react, and he would have gone on if necessary until Nicolas did so.

'I find you in very high spirits for someone soon to succumb to gout, Monsieur,' he replied. 'Your cup has nothing to fear. Here you go again imitating your friend Monsieur Voltaire – your contemporary unless I'm mistaken – who for the last quarter of a century has been proclaiming that he won't survive another year and that the combined forces of all his ailments will forthwith snatch him from the admiration of Europe and the veneration of his friends. You are the stuff that centenarians are made of. I should add that you have an obligation to your younger friends. Who will they have to talk to if you desert them? Real gentlemen are too few and far between for us to allow them to disappear.'

Monsieur de Noblecourt began to clap with delight and Cyrus showed his approval by barking.

'Very well, Monsieur. I give in. You know your audience and how to flatter people. It is in the nature of things for the pupil to one day surpass the master. But I'm an old chatterbox. Nicolas, you owe me some explanation for your sudden disappearance.'

He stroked the spaniel with a still-plump hand. When it had calmed down, the animal rolled over and spread out its paws to reveal its pink belly.

'Monsieur, the death of my guardian required me to return to Brittany. After paying him my last respects, I returned to Paris to a difficult situation. You presumably know about Commissioner Lardin's disappearance. Monsieur de Sartine has put me in charge of the investigation.'

After he had expressed how much he shared Nicolas's grief, the former procurator's round face and mild-mannered expression suddenly changed. He was wide-eyed and open-mouthed. The discovery that his pupil had advanced so rapidly in his career produced in him a mixture of surprise and disbelief.

'What a piece of news! Monsieur de Sartine's representative! That's far more important that Lardin's disappearance. Lardin was a friend, admittedly, but I preferred to keep him at arm's length. I even saw him last week.'

Marion interrupted him firmly by setting down on the card table another pot of chocolate and a cup and saucer in Rouen china, as well as a plate of the famous soft rolls and a pot of jam.

'I see, Nicolas, that you have friends in the right places. I myself am not allowed such fruity delicacies.'

'I should think not!' exclaimed Marion. 'You can have some if you help me peel quinces, as Monsieur Nicolas did one day last September. In any case, you're too greedy.'

Marion poured out the piping-hot drink and continued her recriminations under her breath. The cups filled with a foaming, light-brown liquid that exuded the warm aroma of chocolate and the subtle hint of cinnamon. Cyrus jumped onto Nicolas's knees, knowing how kind the young man was towards him. Nicolas, whose hunter instinct was ever alert if unobtrusive, and whose mind was still focused on one thing, waited until Marion had left the room before bringing the conversation around to Lardin.

'On which day did you say you met with him?'

'Last Thursday.'

'So it would appear that you were one of the last people to have seen him.'

'It was only a brief meeting. He seemed extremely gloomy, even more so than usual. You know him. Secretive, spiteful, restless. Not a very likeable person. But a good policeman all the same, and that's why we got on with each other. Last Thursday he was the same as ever. Still, I felt sorry for him as he left. He seemed distraught out of all proportion.'

'What about Madame Lardin?'

Monsieur de Noblecourt seemed lost in contemplation of some delightful apparition.

'The lovely Louise? It's some time now since I paid her my

respects. She's a tasty morsel, though near on thirty, but I'm too old for that. However, with her it must be said that age doesn't come into it and whether it's a lusty young lad or a grisly old man it all goes down the same way, so to speak, provided there's the sound of silver . . .'

He emphasised his words by winking so energetically that his skullcap was disturbed and slipped across his forehead. The old man took a sip of chocolate, wiped his mouth, helped himself to a roll then put it back down with a sigh and leant towards Nicolas. He went on in a whisper:

'I smell a rat, my dear child. I'm not so cut off from society as to be unaware of the rumours circulating about Lardin. Or naïve enough not to have understood Monsieur de Sartine's motives in lodging you with this diabolical couple, against all reason.'

He stopped, but Nicolas remained stony-faced.

'Don't tell me that the Lardin woman hasn't made advances to you?'

This time Nicolas turned bright red.

'Well, well,' said the old man, 'as much as that? Dear, dear. But I don't want to know about it. There was a curse on that house. Don't ask me why, but I felt it coming. I had a feeling Lardin would come to a sad end, either from his secret debauchery or from some all-consuming passion. The coveting of flesh or money, the "leech" as Solomon calls it, is a sign of the times we live in. We want unbounded pleasure. If it were possible to move through walls and delve into the most secret places we would discover the depravity going on there. As an elderly sceptic, an epicurean if ever there was one, I survey the time in which I live and stigmatise its morals after I have punished its crimes.'

He shook his head sadly as he looked in turn at the bread and the jam. Cyrus had jumped down and was trembling with excitement as he watched his master's antics. After checking that Marion was not in the vicinity Monsieur de Noblecourt promptly grabbed half a roll, smeared a thick layer of jam over it and gobbled down the whole thing in two greedy gulps.

'My presence really made things very uncomfortable for the Lardins,' said Nicolas. 'Now it's become impossible. Without giving away the secrets of a very tricky investigation, I can say that it must be as obvious to you as it is to me, the person in charge of the enquiry, that I cannot continue to stay in a place where I am supposed to act as judge while still being obliged to them.'

'*Opum contemptor, recti pervicax, constans adversus metus,*'[2] quoted the magistrate with a self-satisfied look. 'You certainly cannot remain at Rue des Blancs-Manteaux.'

'I left this very morning and I've come to ask your advice, as I'm unsure whether . . .'

'My dear Nicolas, I share Monsieur de Sartine's high opinion of your personal qualities and your education. I had already offered you my hospitality here. Treat this as your home. There's no need to thank me as the pleasure is all mine. Marion, Marion!'

He clapped his hands, unleashing an outburst of joy in Cyrus, who started to spin around the bedroom like a top before rushing off to look for the housekeeper.

'Monsieur, I am overwhelmed by your kindness and I don't know how . . .'

'Come, come . . . Here are the rules of the house. This is an annex of Rabelais's abbey of Thélème, where freedom and independence reign. You will stay in the bedroom on the second floor. I know that you're not scared of books, and the walls are lined with them. They are the overflow from my library, which is already full. You will have your own entrance; a door leads on to a small staircase that goes down to the servants' quarters. Marion and Poitevin will be at your service. You will have lunch and dinner with me whenever you wish or whenever you can. I am only too aware of the constraints of your job because I have experienced them myself. Consider this house a haven. Where is your luggage?'

'Downstairs, Monsieur. You can be sure that I will do all I can to avoid being a burden to you for too long. I shall look for . . .'

'Monsieur, that's enough. I shall get angry with you. So the ungrateful fellow is already talking of leaving. I require your obedience. Devote yourself unsparingly to your task and don't answer back.'

Marion appeared, escorted by an impatient Cyrus who had gone to fetch her from the pantry.

'Marion, from now on Monsieur Nicolas will be one of us. Prepare the blue bedroom. Ask Poitevin to take our friend's luggage upstairs. Secondly, on Sunday I shall be hosting a lunch. We'll also have a little music. There will be five of us, with Nicolas and his friends: Père Grégoire from the Carmelites, and that young seminarist, Monsieur Pigneau, you introduced me to one day at a concert of sacred music; lastly we'll have Monsieur Balbastre, the organist at Notre-Dame.[3] I'll give you invitations to send out. As for the meal, I'm relying on you, Marion, to do me proud. Priests and musicians are the biggest gourmets of all, with the possible exception of magistrates.'

Marion listened to her master with visible satisfaction,

clasping her hands with pleasure. She went away as fast as her old legs could carry her to give Poitevin the good news.

Nicolas was delighted to discover the new bedroom that was to be his. An alcove housed a small bed, and was framed by two bookcases set into the thick wall which were full of books from floor to ceiling. Books always seemed to mount a silent guard around him. As a child he had spent many hours in their company, in the loft of the house in Guérande, and later in the marquis's library at Ranreuil. Nothing bad could happen to someone who was protected by row upon row of companionable bindings. It was enough to simply open a volume to release the music of its words, always soothing but never the same. A roll-top desk, an armchair, a washstand and a small chimney-piece completed the furnishings in the bedroom, and it was decorated with blue floral-patterned wallpaper. Nicolas had never lived in such luxury. There was no possible comparison with the garret at Rue des Blancs-Manteaux.

After the successful outcome of his visit to Rue Montmartre, and with the help of the fine weather, Nicolas returned to the Châtelet filled with contentment. He searched the area around the gloomy building closely, but there was no sign of the person he was looking for, wise old Tirepot. No doubt his investigations had yet to produce anything. The truth was that they required considerable caution. Nicolas knew that this bold type of approach often put the lives of the informers at risk. It was not fair to criticise them for taking their time and exercising extreme caution when their investigations led them to the heart of Paris's criminal underworld.

As soon as he arrived he asked the chief gaoler which cell the inspector had put Semacgus into. He was told that Monsieur Bourdeau had spent the whole night locked up with an unknown prisoner registered under the name of Monsieur d'Issy. What was more, the inspector was still there. It was a cell for prisoners with privileges, so it was reasonably comfortable and meals could be brought in from outside the prison. Nicolas admired his deputy's foresight.

After giving his name, the young man went into the room and was struck by the stale odour emanating from the straw and the acrid smell of sleeping bodies. On top of that the whole place reeked of cold smoke. Semacgus and Bourdeau must have indulged in their shared liking for tobacco. The inspector sat in a frock coat with his cravat undone and his grey hair unkempt. Semacgus was lying asleep on his straw pallet with his tricorn over his eyes. On the table were chicken carcasses, two glasses and three empty bottles, proof that the tragic events in Vaugirard had not in the least dulled the appetites of the two companions. Nicolas felt that this was hardly the behaviour of a suspected murderer. He corrected himself immediately. The observation could just as well suggest the cold-heartedness and insensitivity of a hardened criminal. He took it as a lesson. There were two sides to everything: at face value judgements could be made either way. He now grasped the unreliability of eyewitness reports, which were always subject to mood and first impressions.

He looked at the sleeping Semacgus and asked Bourdeau to go and wash, and then to come back to him. He wanted to be alone with the suspect. Bourdeau obeyed, though not without showing his disappointment at being sent away. In fact Nicolas had his own reasons for not wanting a witness to his interview with Semacgus. He justified it, though not very convincingly, by telling himself that he needed to maintain an air of mystery, and therefore his authority, in the eyes of his deputy. The reality was rather more prosaic: since he had not told Bourdeau the whole truth about his adventures the previous day and the night he had spent at La Satin's, he did not want to be caught red-handed disguising certain facts.

Nicolas hesitated for another moment before shaking Semacgus by the shoulder. He was reluctant to disturb the sleep of a man threatened by such serious accusations and towards whom his feelings had never wavered. Semacgus sighed and straightened up, knocking his hat to the floor. The fleeting expression of fear on his face disappeared when he recognised Nicolas.

'Monsieur Bourdeau's wine has a stronger narcotic and soporific effect than the most concentrated opium solution,' he yawned. 'Goodness, I was in a deep sleep. But you're looking very serious, my dear Nicolas . . .'

He got up, took a chair and sat astride it.

'It's presumably thanks to you that I've been put up in this room. I'm grateful for it.'

There was both gratitude and irony in his voice.

'I think you can indeed thank me for it,' Nicolas smiled. 'You might have spent the night in one of those delightful locations known as "Barbary" or "The Chains". Or, better still, we could have received you in "Comfort's End", famous for its reptiles and filth, or even "The Pit", an inverted cone in which, with your back bent and your feet in water, you would have had ample time to meditate on the disadvantages of not trusting your friends.'[4]

'Oh, I see. I take that as a jibe in my direction, but it's one that requires some sort of explanation from you.'

Nicolas sat down on the other chair.

'I didn't want anyone else present at this conversation,' he continued. 'It's not an official interrogation. That will come later perhaps, but for the moment I simply wanted to talk to you about certain events in the most open way possible. Don't see this as malice or slyness on my part. You may well consider it somewhat ingenuous, but that is a part of who I am that I wish to preserve for as long as I can. However, that particular fortress is under attack and you are partly responsible . . .'

Semacgus listened without any particular sign of emotion.

'You have not at any point played straight with me. Ever since our meeting in the Basse-Geôle you have been evasive, vague and secretive. Let us go back over things, if you will. You told me that you left La Paulet's at three o'clock in the morning. Such preciseness surprised me at the time, coming from someone who'd been at a rout. From that moment on you were a suspect . . .'

'In Lardin's murder?'

'A suspect. You're the one who has referred to the commissioner's hypothetical murder, and for the second time. You are also guilty of concealing the truth, since you stated that you had fallen for Louise Lardin once and once only. However, it appears from reliable evidence that your relationship with your friend's wife continued and is perhaps still going on as we speak. Lastly . . .'

Nicolas took out of his coat pocket a blank piece of paper and pretended to read from it:

' "Declared having received one *louis d'or* to state and

223

affirm that the aforesaid stranger had stayed with her until three o'clock in the morning and not to admit that he had left well before. Questioned on this point said and repeated that the aforesaid stranger had left, without anyone whosoever having been able to see him, via the secret door into the garden through which gamblers withdraw in the event of a police raid. Questioned as to when he left, the aforesaid prostitute replied: 'A quarter past midnight.'" The name of this prostitute is La Satin. There's no need to ask whether you know her, is there?'

'Nicolas, you're asking the questions and giving the answers. What's more, does all this have anything to do with Dr Descart's murder?'

'That remains to be proven, I admit. I'm simply trying to make you understand that a magistrate who didn't know you and who was examining your testimony with respect to Lardin's disappearance would, in all sincerity, have reason to doubt your statements. Now imagine this same magistrate coming across you again in a murder case and, what is more, the murder of a man with whom you had, to say the least, stormy relations, and that this was common knowledge. Piece together this whole combination of circumstances and impressions and you can draw your own conclusions about the outcome. You should realise then how lucky you are to be dealing with me, a friend, who as it happens has discretionary powers over the investigation into both cases and who hopes that you have nothing to do with either of these two tragic events. So consider my position and decide whether the moment has come to be open with me about what really happened and how you were involved.'

A long silence followed this speech which Nicolas had delivered in an assertive tone, frequently emphasising his words by hitting the grimy surface of the table with the palms of his hands. Semacgus stood up with a thoughtful look on his face, took a few steps around the cell, sat down again and then, with a sigh, began to speak.

'I'm touched, my dear Nicolas, by your words and by the feelings behind them. I hadn't realised how lucky I was to have a friend as the investigator. Forgive me, but your rise has been so swift that, despite the respect I have for you, I was far from trusting in your abilities, as the circumstances warranted. So I beg you, let's forget all about my past equivocation. I'm ready to answer all your questions. But I warn you, what seems obvious can sometimes be misleading. These are the words of an innocent man.'

'My friend, that is what I wanted to hear. I'm first going to ask you to explain – Bourdeau has already provided me with details of the discovery of Descart's body – the circumstances that led up to you meeting him on the evening of the day before yesterday.'

Semacgus thought for a moment, then began:

'At about nine o'clock someone rang my doorbell. Awa, who waits incessantly for news of Saint-Louis, rushed to the door. On the floor she found a letter folded into four and closed with sealing wax. Not knowing what to do with it she brought it to me immediately. I opened it . . .'

Semacgus rummaged in the cuff of his right sleeve and took out a small note that he handed to Nicolas.

'No address,' he noted. 'No mark on the sealing wax. Let's see . . . "Come to the house this evening, I shall be waiting for you at half past five. Guillaume Descart." The piece of paper has been torn . . .'

'That's how it was when Awa gave it to me. But Descart was thrifty, not to say miserly.'

'Could Awa have cut a piece off?'

'Impossible. She can't read, and look at the whole thing: the folds match up, even with the traces of sealing wax.'

'That's true. What was your first reaction on reading the note? Descart's writing must have been familiar to you.'

'Yes, indeed. During the period when we saw each other more frequently he would send me clients who were unworthy of his skills. So I recognised his writing perfectly well. To tell the truth I was puzzled by how laconic the letter was, but he was an odd character and I took the invitation at face value, as a request for a talk. I did rack my brains about the purpose behind it. Our last meeting – you were there – had come to an abrupt end. I wasn't really expecting an offer of reconciliation.'

'You said to Bourdeau that only something serious, something concerning the exercise of your profession, could explain this request to meet.'

'True, it was possible that he wished to inform me of the current state of his application to get me, a navy surgeon, banned from practising medicine. He delighted in this sort of provocation.'

'Why did you arrive at Vaugirard early?'

'I had to leave a herbarium of tropical plants at the Jardin des Plantes. I'd left myself plenty of time. The weather looked threatening, so I went back to Vaugirard and I didn't think it a crime to turn up at Descart's a little in advance.'

'When you discovered Descart's body, did anything strike you?'

'I was beside myself, because I immediately realised the trap

I'd fallen into: I was a ready-made suspect. I confirmed that he was dead. I saw the lancet. It reminded me of our argument about bleeding and that in this way the weapon used for the crime would also constitute evidence against me. I saw nothing else. Don't forget that all I had to see by was a candle stub.'

Nicolas made no attempt to break the silence that had fallen. Semacgus put his head in his hands.

'My friend,' said the young man, 'certain facts known to me alone lead me to believe that your account is truthful. But now you are going to have to account to me for what I can justifiably call a pack of lies. At what time did you leave La Paulet's establishment last Friday?'

'You're asking me a question and you already know the answer.'

'I wanted to hear confirmation of it from your own lips. That doesn't explain why you concealed it from me the first time. Why all the play-acting with that prostitute?'

'You are forcing me to admit something that I wanted to hide from you so as not to compromise a third party . . .'

'With whom you have not broken off relations and who you continue to see . . .'

Semacgus stared at Nicolas.

'I am no longer surprised that Monsieur de Sartine put you in charge of this enquiry. You stay one step ahead of the game. You'll be a formidable adversary for the criminal fraternity.'

'Don't flatter me, Semacgus. Explain rather why you went to find Madame Lardin that night. Her husband had just walked out of the Dauphin Couronné in a rage and you must have thought it very likely that he would go back home?'

'You're making me go into the sordid details, Nicolas. It had always been agreed between Louise and myself that when she put a lighted candle in the window of her bedroom it meant that the coast was clear. Also, knowing Lardin, it was a safe bet that in his anger he would do the rounds of all the gambling dens until dawn. So there was not much risk for me.'

'Until what hour did you stay in Rue des Blancs-Manteaux?'

'Six o'clock. I very nearly bumped into Catherine who was just starting work.'

'Have you seen Madame Lardin again since that day?'

'No, not at any point.'

'You knew that Descart was her lover, you told me so. Didn't that embarrass you at all?'

'You're cruel, Nicolas. Passion makes us do many things that morally we disapprove of.'

'You told me before that Catherine also knew about Descart. Do you think she shared this knowledge with Marie?'

'Without the slightest doubt. Anything that could harm Louise was a blessing as far as Catherine was concerned. She had no secrets from Marie, who hated her stepmother. Beneath that prim schoolgirl look of hers, and despite her age, she has a very passionate temperament. She adored her father, and he felt the same way about her.'

Nicolas was thinking. Was it possible that sweet little Marie . . . He thought again about the footprints found in Vaugirard which were such a close match to the shoes found in the young woman's bedroom in Rue des Blancs-Manteaux.

'Semacgus, how can you love Louise Lardin?'

'I don't wish you to know the reasons. All I will say is that the worst thing is to love someone you have no respect for. Nicolas, do you have any news of Saint-Louis?'

'None at all and I don't want to raise your hopes on that score.'

Semacgus bowed his head and turned towards the wall, downcast.

'My friend,' Nicolas continued after a silence, 'there's one more thing I have to ask you. For your safety as well as for the proper conduct of the investigation I need to keep you under lock and key. I'm hoping for a successful conclusion as soon as possible. I have no confidence in the cells in the Châtelet because anyone can get in. I'm going to have you taken to the Bastille. I can assure you it's preferable. Your life depends on it. Staying in some cells here is as good as taking a dose of arsenic – it inclines some people to strange acts of suicide, and this is a fact. The investigation then stops and the true culprits are never punished. These two cases involve some pretty unsavoury characters.

'What else can I do other than put myself in your hands?'

'Nothing, I agree. But don't lose confidence. Work on your book. I'll see to it that you have everything you want in the Bastille. Give me a list of what you need. To the outside world you will no longer exist; that will reduce the risks. Trust me.'

Semacgus gave Nicolas a look of resignation. Nicolas said goodbye to him, carefully locked the cell and set off in search of Inspector Bourdeau. He eventually discovered him in the duty room sitting down to a bowl of soup, courtesy of old Marie.

Nicolas felt guilty at having had to exclude the inspector from his interview with Semacgus in such a cavalier fashion, but Bourdeau spared Nicolas's embarrassment by silently handing him two letters. One bore his address written in tall, firm handwriting and was closed with a red wax seal bearing a gold device with a blue stripe inlaid with three silver sardines.[5] He

229

recognised it as Monsieur de Sartine's. The other, in a delicate hand, made his heart jump for joy. He counted the number of days that had passed since his last meeting with Isabelle. It had been more than a week, which was the time needed for mail to get from Guérande to Paris. The letter must have been posted the previous Saturday at midday or on Monday. He put it away in his shirt, next to his skin, intending to read it later at leisure. He opened the Lieutenant General's letter. The message was laconic and said that the weekly audience the King accorded to Monsieur de Sartine every Sunday at Versailles had been postponed because His Majesty was accompanying Madame de Pompadour to her château at Choisy. This circumstance 'provided extra time to clear up swiftly the matter in question'. He ended by encouraging Nicolas 'to spare nothing and no one in order to succeed'. By the time Nicolas had finished reading it Bourdeau had become more amenable, since his sulkiness never lasted very long. Without a word Nicolas gave the inspector Descart's note and, while his deputy was examining it, he had to restrain himself from taking Isabelle's letter out again.

'What do you make of it, Bourdeau?' he asked.

'I think, Monsieur, that this piece of paper might well belong to the main part of a letter and might have been cut out afterwards, for a particular purpose.'

'I see that we're in agreement on this point. What we still have to discover is who pieced it together, and why. I must congratulate you on the trouble you went to in Vaugirard. I saw Rabouine and he was very useful, just like your man in Rue des Blancs-Manteaux.'

Bourdeau turned pink with pleasure and seemed to have fully recovered from his disappointment.

'The man gave me a report after he'd been relieved,' he said. 'He saw Madame Lardin go out at nine o'clock and . . .'

'Impossible,' exclaimed Nicolas, 'he told me himself that he hadn't seen her come back all night. Or else he fell asleep, which he couldn't be blamed for in this cold.'

'I was about to point that out to you. My man assures me he didn't fall asleep and I'm inclined to believe him. I've often put him to the test and never had any cause for complaint.'

'Come on, we must find the answer. Every mystery has an explanation. Increase the surveillance of the Lardins' house. Perhaps we should have the commissioner's wife followed. What do you think?'

'I took the liberty of organising it this morning.'

'You're brilliant, Bourdeau.'

'So brilliant that the important facts are kept from me.'

Nicolas had spoken too soon. He bit his lip. He still didn't have enough experience of people. However, he managed to find a way out of the situation by bursting out laughing.

'Monsieur Bourdeau, you're a fool. Didn't you understand that I wouldn't have got a thing out of a man of Semacgus's age and character if I'd questioned him in front of a respectable man of his own age like you? I thought you'd realise that it was nothing personal. Just to prove it, here's a summary of the situation. Semacgus lied to us. He left the Dauphin Couronné at a quarter past midnight to be with Madame Lardin, and he stayed with her until six o'clock. As for the Vaugirard business, I'm convinced he's not involved. Rabouine must have told you that there was someone in the house when you were at the scene of the crime and that they subsequently went through it from top to bottom. So my dear Bourdeau that should be enough to repair the damage to your self-esteem.'

Bourdeau nodded without answering.

'Talking of Rabouine and the other informers, Monsieur,' he went on, 'I must give you a statement of expenses and fees I have paid myself, since Monday, in connection with the two cases that concern us. I advanced the sums spent from my own pocket. You have here the details of the operations and their cost. The statement needs to be signed by Monsieur de Sartine, then sent to the head of the financial and legal office of the Inspection of Accounts who ultimately sends out a money order for the appropriate amount. It's a slow process.'

'An investigation that's out of the ordinary incurs expenses that are out of the ordinary too. Monsieur de Sartine has given me the wherewithal as far as expenditure is concerned.'

With great concentration Nicolas examined the piece of paper handed to him by Bourdeau. Printed on the left were the reasons for the expenses and on the right were columns giving the breakdown of time spent by the officers and constables of the watch, as well as their totals. He was intrigued to see the extra expenditure incurred by the officer (Bourdeau) and his observers as well as the number of cabs and sedan chairs used as transport during the investigation. The activities of the various informers were also set out, as well as the fees for Sanson and the two doctors at the Châtelet. Plus the travel costs to Montfaucon and Vaugirard, as well as the special-privilege cells for old Émilie and Semacgus. The overall total amounted to eighty-five pounds, which Nicolas wanted to pay out of the contingency fund from Sartine. He realised that his lump sum of twenty *louis d'or*, which already had quite a dent in it, would not be enough. He divided up what was left and gave half of it to Bourdeau.

'Here's an advance. I'll see about the rest. Give me a receipt.'

Bourdeau scribbled a few words on the back of the statement of accounts.

'I'm going to give you a note for Monsieur de Sartine to inform him of the latest developments, to ask him for money and to request his signature on a *lettre de cachet* so that Semacgus can be kept safely at the Bastille. You will take him there under armed guard. I am not concerned that he'll try to escape, rather it's for his own protection. We simply do not know who we are dealing with. Meanwhile I have certain things to verify. I forgot to tell you, Bourdeau, that I've moved. I couldn't remain with the Lardins, given the circumstances. In any case Madame Lardin literally threw me out. So for the time being I'm lodging with Monsieur de Noblecourt in Rue Montmartre. You know him.'

'My house is at your disposal, Monsieur.'

'You're very kind, Bourdeau, but you have a family to think about.'

Nicolas sat down to write the note for Sartine. He took leave of the inspector and left the Châtelet. Eager to discover the contents of Isabelle's letter, he strode off towards the Seine.

XI

FAR NIENTE

As one who in his journey baits at noon,

Though bent on speed, so here the archangel paused

Betwixt the world destroyed and world restored.

MILTON

THE Seine flowed at Nicolas's feet. The banks were covered with an uneven layer of frozen snow and mud, revealing in places the oozing sludge. The grey, rushing waters sped past too quickly to be followed by the naked eye. Tree trunks uprooted further upstream rose and fell in the swirling floodwater. A counter-current roared up the banks then retreated down the sheet of ice like backwash. If he closed his eyes Nicolas could imagine himself beside the ocean. This impression was strengthened by the shrill cries of hovering seabirds, their wings spread out against the wind, on the lookout for carrion drifting in the current. Only the smells that came from the thawing sludge loosened and quickened by the water destroyed the illusion. Gazing at the river had not stilled the doubts that raced through Nicolas's mind. For the third time he re-read Isabelle's letter. The words swam before his eyes. The message seemed so worrying, confused and contradictory that he was unable to make out what it meant:

Nicolas

I am entrusting this letter to Ribotte, my chambermaid, for her to take to the postal service in Guérande. I pray to the Lord that it will reach you. My father has been in an extremely sombre mood since you left and has been watching me very closely. Since yesterday he has been in bed and refuses to speak. I have sent for the apothecary. I do not know what to think about that awful scene. My father used to like and respect you. How did it come to this?

As for me, I am still distressed to be separated from you once more. I do not know if I am right to confess to you the pain your sudden departure caused me. The only small consolation I have for my suffering is the fondness that I know you have for me. However, I believe your soul to be tender and kind enough not to pursue a heart that is not free to follow its own inclination. I no longer know what I am saying. Farewell, my friend. Send me news of yourself. It will help relieve the sadness which overwhelms me. No, forget about me instead.

Château de Ranreuil, 2 February 1761.

Once again the young man attempted to tease out the reasons for his unease. The joy of receiving a letter from his friend had gradually turned into a nagging anxiety as he read on. His foremost concern was for his godfather's health. All else was just a source of uncertainty, made worse by the choice of words and the turns of phrase. During the two years he had spent in Paris he had had the opportunity to go to the opera. Isabelle's letter could have come straight out of a badly written libretto. The feelings expressed seemed forced. Without being able to say why, he suspected her of a kind of play-acting, almost a form of flirtatiousness that was inappropriate to the seriousness of the situation. He remembered having a similar impression when they had been reunited at Château de Ranreuil. The scene they had both enacted then was a familiar one in the repertoire: the lovers' tiff, so common in the comedies of Monsieur de Marivaux. Was it possible that his total commitment was matched only by Mademoiselle de Ranreuil's play or pretence at passion, intended simply to offer her the superficial emotions of a sentimental comedy? Perhaps he had invented a lover for himself without weighing up the risks of indulging in such a dream. In his heart of hearts he sensed that a love that needs protecting like a land under threat, that has to be explained and defended in the way a barrister would address a court of law, is perhaps a love that cannot last. And had he not himself become involved in this attachment too lightly and thoughtlessly, simply because they had been children together and because he was attracted by the aura of a powerful and noble family? How could he have dared to believe that a foundling could have aimed so high, and aspired to go so far beyond his station? A wave of bitterness swept over him, unleashing too the pent-up resentment of past humiliations. Occasionally he began to hope again, and Isabelle's words immediately took on a different meaning. Eventually he decided to postpone this inner debate, and after wandering for a while lost in his thoughts, he found himself once again in front of the Hôtel de Ville.

He had wasted a considerable time on these idle musings. He was annoyed with himself, then decided that in fact he had nothing more pressing to do at that moment. He chose to go the long way. Leaving the Hôtel de Ville on his left he walked along the river, reached the church of Saint-Gervais and, avoiding the bustle of the Marché Saint-Jean, arrived at the beginning of Rue

Vieille-du-Temple. The workshop of Vachon the master tailor did not look out onto the street. One had to go through the carriage entrance of a mansion whose owners had been forced by straitened circumstances to rent out their ground floor and outhouses to craftsmen. The tailor had recently explained to Nicolas that as his professional reputation was already well established, the fact that his shop was tucked away in a cobbled courtyard was a positive advantage to his wealthy customers. Carriages could drop off their occupants at the tailor's door, without them becoming the object of misplaced popular curiosity or dirtying themselves in the muck of the street.

Nicolas's visit had several aims. He wanted to renew his wardrobe which was showing signs of wear and tear and had been depleted by the loss of the clothes he had left behind in Saint-Eustache, and he was also planning to make Master Vachon talk about another of his customers, Commissioner Lardin.

When Nicolas opened the door he was struck by the drawbacks of the location for the shop's interior. The darkness had to be addressed by having more light in the workshop, and this could only be achieved with the use of a very large number of candles. So to the unsuspecting customer this temple of elegance seemed like a brilliantly lit chapel. Dressed in grey, Master Vachon was holding forth and at the same time hitting the ground with one of those canes that had been fashionable in the previous century. His remarks were addressed to three apprentices who sat cross-legged on a pale oak counter, surrounded by a sea of material.

'What wretched times, when the King tolerates this vile breed of financiers,' Vachon was proclaiming. 'All it needed was for a Comptroller General of Finance to burden us with excessive taxes for it to provoke the most idiotic reactions. Everyone is now of the opinion that we are all impoverished. So people become excessively mean, not in order to prove the minister wrong, but as a joke. And since in France everyone just follows the latest fashion, they all try to outdo each other with their economising. So no more folds, gentlemen, no more gussets, no more ornaments: everything has to be taken in, coat tails shortened, fronts low-cut to save on material . . . The thread, you dolt, longer thread . . . I never stop telling you, but it's like talking to the wall.'

He thundered at one of his apprentices who in the face of the storm crouched down until he almost disappeared amidst the satin.

'Then there's the embroidery. Thriftiness not to say miserliness there, too. The master jewellers are in despair: precious stones are being replaced by mere sequins, aventurine glass and paste, that appalling foreign invention.[1] Oh! What a life! . . . Thank you so much Monsieur de Silhouette![2] We'll hang up an effigy of him, like a shop sign. The tradesmen curse him and . . . Well, if it isn't Monsieur Le Floch honouring us with a visit.'

Monsieur Vachon bowed and his sallow, aged face broke into a charming smile. He was a tall, thin man of about sixty, and for such a loud voice to come from a body as puny as his was always a surprise.

'Good day to you, Master Vachon,' said Nicolas. 'I can see that you are in fine fettle, if your fieriness is anything to go by.'

'I beg you not to repeat my words. You know how touchy tradesmen are when their interests are threatened.'

'I would never dream of it. I've come to renew my wardrobe. I'm thinking of a coat for the daytime, something strong and hard-wearing, a greatcoat, breeches and perhaps something a bit more daring, more elegant, that can be worn both around town and at the opera. But you know about these things better than I do and it's your advice I'm after.'

Vachon bowed once more, set down his cane and contemplated the mountains of material stored on the shelves. He kept looking back and forth between the different cloths and the customer.

'A young man . . . Often goes out . . . Something comfortable. This brown cloth looks as if it should suit you. I suggest it for a braided coat, with olive-shaped buttons to stop it flapping about in the wind, and the same for the breeches. Don't mention the word greatcoat again. They're good enough for travelling provincials and for cavalry soldiers, but they're no longer fashionable. A frock coat is what you need, a handsome frock coat in woollen cloth, lined and overlined. It'll be very warm for this freezing cold winter. I'll make you – and, as it's you, for the same price – two cloaks instead of one, never mind Monsieur de Silhouette. For what we'll call the formal coat I have an idea. What do you say to this?'

He carefully removed from its silk-paper wrapping a dark-green velvet coat, discreetly highlighted with silver embroidery.

'I was left with this magnificent garment on my hands after the sudden departure of a Prussian baron. He was about your size. There'll be just a few adjustments to make, and I will need to remove the insignia that was embroidered to order. Would you like to try it on?'

Nicolas followed him into a closet furnished with a cheval

glass. After removing his clothes he put on the green coat without paying much attention. When he raised his head to examine himself in the mirror he thought he was looking at a stranger. The coat fitted him perfectly. It made him look slimmer, bringing out the elegance of his figure. This new person, who gave him a guarded, surprised look, reminded him of those unapproachable lords he had secretly observed as a child in Marquis de Ranreuil's drawing room. He turned and walked back into the shop. Vachon, who was reprimanding one of his apprentices, stopped suddenly, and everyone held their breath at the nobility of the sight, heightened by the shining decoration on the chest. For a moment Nicolas felt as if he were in another world. The tailor broke the spell. He seemed embarrassed.

'It suits you only too well, I mean perfectly. All you need is a sword and you could appear at court in Versailles. What do you think of it?'

'I'll take it. Have the embroidered insignia removed and let out the breeches a little. When can it be ready by?'

'By tomorrow. I'll have it delivered to you at Commissioner Lardin's. How is he?'

Nicolas was delighted. Without being asked, Vachon had given him the opening he was after.

'Is it some time since you last saw him?'

'It was just after Epiphany. He's not one of my customers but he came to order four black satin capes with masks to go with them, and also one of those leather doublets he's been so keen on for years.'

'Were they all the same size, these capes?'

'Identical.'

'Did you deliver them?'

'Certainly not. The commissioner came to collect them at the very end of January. But you're worrying me, Monsieur. Were they not satisfactory?'

'I might as well tell you now, Master Vachon, that Monsieur Lardin has not returned home since 2 February and the police – yours truly – are searching for him.'

Nicolas had thought that the abruptness of this announcement would have provoked some comment from Master Vachon. But none came. After his initial stupefaction, all he talked about was trivial details, taking measurements, giving obsequious assurances that no effort would be spared to satisfy Monsieur de Sartine's protégé, who left him his new address.

As soon as he was back in Rue Vieille-du-Temple Nicolas decided to go on to Rue des Blancs-Manteaux, which was quite near. He immediately spotted the new police spy who had just come on duty, and he went over to him. Madame Lardin was at home. As soon as the rumour of the cook's dismissal had spread around the neighbourhood, several matronly looking women and one young one had come to offer their services. The spy, who was a handsome young lad, had got into conversation with them quite easily; they were only too pleased to give him a bitter account of how roughly they had been treated. Received by a surly and disdainful Louise, they had been told that 'no one is needed in this house' and the door had been promptly slammed in their faces. During the last night he had spent in the house Nicolas had noticed how shabby it had become. For instance, Catherine would never have left game to go off in the cellar. A thousand and one details about the inside of the house were evidence of its total neglect. How could someone as refined and demanding as Madame Lardin tolerate such domestic disorder? Nicolas strongly sensed that she no longer wanted any witnesses in her house. That was why Catherine and he had been thrown out, and Marie sent away.

The spy also told Nicolas that someone who looked like Commissioner Lardin had appeared at the door of the Blancs-Manteaux church. He had rushed inside the building as soon as he'd caught sight of the lookout who had immediately run after him, but in vain. Clearly the monastery had other exits. When asked why he thought it had been the missing person, the lookout replied that he had recognised the leather doublet so typical of the commissioner but he had not been able to glimpse the man's face.

Having had nothing to eat since Monsieur de Noblecourt's hot chocolate and soft rolls, Nicolas was feeling famished. However, there was still something he had to do. Now that Descart was dead, who would inherit his property and money? According to what some people had said, La Paulet in particular, it constituted a considerable fortune. Luckily Nicolas had heard the Lardins mention the name of Descart's notary in connection with the sale of an orchard in Popincourt; the commissioner had decided to part with it because of his heavy debts. His name was Master Duport, and his practice was in Rue de Bussy on the Left Bank. As the weather was still fine, Nicolas decided to go there on foot. The air was clear and ice-cold and burnt the throat like a swig of brandy. The radiant early-afternoon sunlight was reluctant to fade. The city seemed renewed by the brightness and the frost. Not wishing to linger too long in the district of Saint-Avoye, the young man took the shortest route, with the intention of having a bite to eat at one of the stalls in Rue des Boucheries-Saint-Germain.

As he walked, he pondered on the morning's events. It was perfectly clear that Monsieur de Noblecourt had his doubts about Lardin. He suspected some strange goings-on involving the couple and he made no secret of their marital discord.

As for his visit to Master Vachon, it proved at least two things. The first, which he had not thought particularly important at the time, was that Lardin had owned several leather doublets. The remains of the one that had been discovered in Montfaucon constituted an important piece of evidence concerning the commissioner's death and seemed to confirm the identity of the body. This observation was given a strange twist by the account of the informer at Rue des Blancs-Manteaux. The second thing was Lardin's order for four black satin capes. Why *four* Carnival outfits? Nicolas could perfectly well understand who three of them were intended for: one for Lardin, one for Semacgus and one for Descart. That was the right number for the 'party' at the Dauphin Couronné. But who was the fourth one for? Louise Lardin had also gone out that Friday evening – Catherine was quite sure of this – wearing a black satin cape. Was it one of Master Vachon's or a different one? If it were one of the tailor's, why had the commissioner given it to his wife? There was something very mysterious here. Nicolas did not remember seeing the cape when he had done his search of the bedrooms in the Lardins' house. He would have to question Catherine again to find out what she had done with the garment, or else . . .

He crossed the Seine at Pont-Neuf and reached the crossroads at Bussy via Rue Dauphine. He liked this district, and he had often walked its length and breadth when he was staying at the Carmelite monastery. He thought fondly of Père

Grégoire, whom he would be seeing again the following Sunday at Monsieur de Noblecourt's luncheon party.

Nicolas thought it tactless to disturb the notary at lunchtime and so he headed towards the adjacent street of Boucheries-Saint-Germain. He knew what to expect there and had discovered that a Paris butcher's shop was a world of its own. The profession was governed by regulations and by the customs of a corporation that jealously guarded its rights and privileges. He had been surprised to learn that the prices were fixed by the Lieutenant General of Police, according to the going rate for cattle on the hoof. Selling weights and their accuracy were also checked by the authorities. Nicolas had had to deal with various affairs of this sort. The police cracked down severely on street vendors selling meat illegally with no indication of where it came from. The butchers always maintained that the meat was stolen, rotten and unhealthy, to which the street vendors retorted that they had their own customers and that their prices were cheaper than the master butchers' who were members of the guild. He had also had to deal with innumerable disputes involving the department of the Lieutenant General of Police, the butchers and their customers. The eternal problem of 'making up the weight' exercised the people both in the central districts and the *faubourgs*. They were particularly incensed when non-edible parts were sold along with the edible ones.

A stream of half-frozen blood in the street indicated to Nicolas that he had reached his goal. He went through a carriage entrance leading into an open alleyway with meat stalls. In the next courtyard was a slaughterhouse, a scalding room and a melting house, and beyond that stables containing cattle and sheep. The butchers were seeing to the preparation and sale of offal, parts that the ordinary people liked because they were cheap.

Nicolas was on his way to eat at an establishment owned by Monsieur Desporges, part of which had been rented out to a tripe seller who welcomed her hungry customers around a few tables with benches on either side. She served tripe, offal, trotters, liver, lungs and spleen, cooked in many different ways. Nicolas ordered a bowl of tripe, which he was extremely fond of, but the hostess, old Madame Morel, had joined the long list of the young man's admirers and she quietly advised him to try another of her specialities, a fricassee of pigs' trotters. She was careful who she offered it to because she was not allowed to serve this meat, which only pork butchers had the right to sell. The trotters were cooked in stock, which according to her made them more tender. The meat then came away from the bone. Then it would be seasoned with spices and chopped onions and fried in fat and butter that had been melted until it was almost brown. It then had to be fricasseed vigorously and quickly, and stirred about twenty times. After it had been reduced, a ladleful of stock would moisten the whole thing in no time at all. A little mustard would be diluted in some verjuice and vinegar to bind it, before the whole dish was served piping hot.

It was ready in an instant and Nicolas followed her recommendation with such enthusiasm that he had three extra helpings. He felt restored, warmed up and ready to face a notary. This wholesome fare always gave him renewed energy. He enjoyed the habits of ordinary people. He had often shared their company and part of his charm lay in his effortless ability to find the right word or to behave in just the right way and this earned him their loyal support, even though he was not always aware of it.

*

Nicolas had been wise to get his strength back. Master Duport was one of those self-important people who was not easily taken in. He began with a flat refusal to reply to Nicolas's polite questions about Descart's financial status and the existence of a will. The scrivener was almost on the point of calling in one of his clerks to throw the intruder out onto the street. Though he would have preferred to use his own authority to get his way with this man, Nicolas had to resign himself to brandishing Monsieur de Sartine's warrant, after which the notary agreed, albeit with bad grace, to respond to Nicolas's questions. Yes, Monsieur Descart was a man of considerable wealth, made up of land and farms situated in the Hurepoix, at Saint-Sulpice-de-Favières, as well as of bonds in the Hôtel de Ville. He also had a significant sum of money in a bank account. Yes, he had drawn up his last will and testament, only quite recently, at the end of 1760. It appointed Marie Lardin, the commissioner's daughter, as sole legatee.

Nicolas was stunned by what he had just heard. Shortly before his death, then, Descart had felt the need to put his affairs in order. But instead of doing so to benefit his only known relative, Louise Lardin, he had chosen the commissioner's daughter, who was not his blood relation . . . It was difficult to separate this fact from Lardin's attempt to communicate after he had disappeared by means of that cryptic message. From beyond the grave each of them was sending a mysterious signal to the living. Why had Descart made a will in favour of sweet little Marie, who was nothing to him? Had he, that hypocritical and depraved bigot, been captivated by her charm and innocence?

Or was there something more sinister lurking beneath the apparently unassuming character of the young woman? Had Descart wished simply to prevent his money falling into his mistress's clutches, once her unfaithful and rapacious nature had revealed itself to him? None of this implied that he was expecting to die.

Nicolas was still thinking about this as he hurried back across the Seine and along to the Châtelet. Bourdeau was not there: he had gone to escort Semacgus to the Bastille. He had left a message giving a concise summary of the results of Sanson's examination of Descart's body. The victim had been poisoned by a pastry filled with arsenic. Descart had probably fallen unconscious before being finished off by asphyxiation, smothered with a cushion. Nicolas was struck by the sophisticated nature of this murder which combined two ways of killing, plus some careful rearrangement intended to cloud if not conceal the cause of death. Everything seemed destined to be masked, even the Grim Reaper himself, like some Carnival nightmare.

He left the Châtelet and for the first time since he had got back to Paris felt at a loose end. It was already late; darkness was falling and there was a bitter chill, made even keener by a strengthening wind. He allowed himself a stop at Stohrer's, the pastry shop, in Rue Montorgueil, where he gorged on his favourite *babas*. When he got back to Monsieur de Noblecourt's he found Marion near the fire, watching over the double broth that the magistrate took before going to bed. He was having supper in town. Nicolas retired to his new domain. He put away the little luggage he had, got undressed and chose a book at random from all those around him. It was *Vert-Vert* by Gresset. He opened it and came across the following lines:

A famous name is but a tempting charm
A modest lot is better proof 'gainst harm.

He smiled bitterly. Suddenly the sadness caused by Isabelle's letter and the gloomy thoughts it had engendered in him resurfaced. Along with that came the vision of the elegant young man in Master Vachon's mirror, the image that was both his and someone else's, at once seductive and threatening. Nicolas let go of the book and stretched out. The candle in the alcove began to smoke. A long black column rose up to the beams, gradually creating a stain on their lacquered surface. He looked at it thoughtfully. He got up to snuff out the wick after moistening his fingers, then lay down again, haunted by an idea that he could not quite pinpoint, but which was gradually forming. The mark on the beams reminded him of something – and suddenly he saw again the dark mark on the top of the skull of the corpse in Montfaucon. With this discovery he fell asleep.

Sunday 11 February 1761
Nicolas had let Saturday drift by, enjoying his idleness. After getting up late he took advantage of the splendid weather to wander around Paris. His meanderings had taken him to churches and then to the Old Louvre, where he had admired the shop windows full of prints and paintings for sale. In the late afternoon he had eaten in a tavern near Les Halles. On his way back he had been unable to avoid gangs of children shouting and hitting him with a 'rat bat'.[3] He'd had to call on the services of a brusher to remove the chalk marks from all over his clothes. He had slipped back into the house utterly exhausted, and had read until late.

The next morning he had attended High Mass in Saint-Eustache, a church he loved for its vast proportions and the resonance it gave to the mighty roar of the great organ. It was well past midday by the time he returned to Rue Montmartre. He was greeted by a harmonious sound. He tiptoed into Monsieur de Noblecourt's library. It had been temporarily turned into a music room. Dressed in a loose-fitting morning gown with a paisley pattern, the head of the household was accompanying two other musicians on the violin. Much to Nicolas's surprise the first of them, also playing the violin, was Père Grégoire. Nicolas had never been aware that music was one of his passions. The other, small with sharp features and an outrageously blond wig, had to be Monsieur Balbastre, the organist of Notre-Dame, who was playing away on a harpsichord. His friend Pigneau stood near the instrument, lighting up the scroll of the score with a sconce. Slightly embarrassed at being the only person in the audience, Nicolas sat down in a *bergère* and became engrossed in the music. At first it was the expressions and gestures of the performers that held his attention. Frowning and flushed with concentration, Monsieur de Noblecourt seemed to be struggling. Sometimes, however, he would make appreciative sounds at the unexpected improvisations of the harpsichordist. Père Grégoire looked even more absorbed in the performance of this task than he was when measuring out the amounts of herbal extracts or brews for the Carmelite liqueur. He was keeping time by tapping the floor with his right foot. For his part Balbastre was the perfect picture of a virtuoso. He played his instrument almost without looking at the score and his fingers flew over the soundboards of the harpsichord in a frothy shower of muslin cuffs.

The trio's sonata was coming to an end. After the performance there was a long silence. Monsieur de Noblecourt let out a great sigh before removing his wig and wiping his brow with a large handkerchief he'd taken from his sleeve. Suddenly he saw Nicolas. There followed a moment of confusion, of exchanges of greetings and introductions. Nicolas embraced Père Grégoire and Pigneau, who were both delighted to see their friend again. Nicolas greeted Monsieur Balbastre with all the respect owed to a celebrity by a young man no one had ever heard of. He blushed with embarrassment when introduced as Monsieur de Sartine's 'promising new confidant'. Marion and Poitevin interrupted these courtesies by bringing some wine, and each guest sat down and began cheerfully to clink glasses with his neighbour. Pigneau, who was in the habit of discussing with Nicolas the quality of the concerts they went to, questioned him about what he had heard. In this way the young man learnt that the trio had been playing a sonata for bass continuo by Monsieur Leclair. Balbastre cut the seminarist short to stir up a controversy about the lower registers of the accompaniment.

At that moment Marion re-entered the library and approached her master to whisper something in his ear.

'Why, of course!' replied Monsieur de Noblecourt, 'bring him in and lay a place for our unexpected guest.'

A dashing gentleman barely older than Nicolas entered the library. Greeting the gathering with a casual wave of his hat, he handed his sword to Poitevin, who had shown him in. He stationed himself at the harpsichord, having lovingly stroked the lacquer of the bentside, and took stock of the audience. Even his white wig could not disguise his youthful, playful look. His face with its heavy brows, Roman nose and well-defined lips of ironic cast was pleasant to look at. His coat of very pale pastel blue reminded Nicolas of the one Master Vachon had offered him.

'My friends, I am delighted to introduce to you Monsieur de La Borde,[4] First Groom of His Majesty's Bedchamber.'

There followed another round of greetings. Even Monsieur Balbastre seemed charmed by the affability of this visitor, who gave Nicolas a piercing look at the mention of his position with the Lieutenant General of Police.

'To what do I owe the pleasure of this visit, Monsieur?' asked the magistrate. 'Your visits are so infrequent and we would like to see you more often. My friendship for your father now extends to his son. Consider this house your own.'

'You are too kind, Monsieur. It so happens that I have the day off, which has given me the opportunity to call on you. The King has decided to go to Choisy with Madame de Pompadour. I am officially on duty, but he was kind enough to give me leave. When the King is away everyone deserts Versailles. And so here I am inviting myself to lunch.'

While the conversation was getting under way, Pigneau, who was far better informed about court etiquette than Nicolas ever suspected, whispered to him that the term 'groom' should not be misinterpreted: Monsieur de La Borde was an important figure. As one of the four first grooms of the king's bedchamber, he was in complete charge of all domestic arrangements, and above all enjoyed the incomparable privilege of constant access to His Majesty. When on duty, he even slept at the foot of the royal bed. In addition he was considered to be the King's favourite, had the reputation of being wealthy and attended intimate suppers in the private apartments. He gave a final touch to this portrait by adding that he was said to be a close friend of Marshal Richelieu, himself First Gentleman of the Bedchamber.

Nicolas felt in awe of someone so close to the King; he would have expected some special distinguishing feature to have marked out the beneficiary of such a privilege. But Monsieur de Noblecourt had extricated himself from his armchair and was inviting his guests to go through to eat.

Out of politeness each wanted to let the others go first. They entered a rectangular drawing room with windows looking on to the street. An oval table had been laid. The opposite wall was furnished with display cabinets, bookcases and a large dresser with a marble top on which the wine was kept cool.

'Gentlemen, no formalities. We are among friends,' declared the magistrate. 'Nicolas, as the youngest person present, will sit opposite me. Père,' he said to Grégoire, 'on my right. Monsieur de La Borde on my left. Messieurs Balbastre and Pigneau on either side of Monsieur Le Floch.'

Père Grégoire said grace and everyone sat down. Marion entered, carrying an impressively large tureen that she put down in front of her master, who himself served his guests while Poitevin poured the wine, white or red according to preference. There was a momentary silence while each concentrated on savouring the first course, which Monsieur de Noblecourt described, with a glint in his eye, as a pigeon bisque. Then he resumed conversation with Monsieur de La Borde.

'What is the news from Court?'

'His Majesty is very concerned about the siege of Pondicherry. The Marquise is doing her best to divert him from his melancholy. She is also trying to restore his energy. You presumably are not aware – Paris is so biased – to what lengths this lady goes. She is scoffed at and satirised, but no one takes any notice of all the good things she does. Let me tell you that she bought from her private purse thousands of shares in armaments for warships. She has a passionate interest in all sorts of projects. I can even tell you in confidence, we are all gentlemen of honour . . .'

He cast an eye around the assembled guests.

'. . . that only yesterday evening she was saying to me how sorry she was to be a woman at such a time as this, and how concerned she was to see so many people whose main aim should be the public good and the service of the King, doing nothing but criticise . . .'

'Dear friend,' de Noblecourt interrupted, 'how is your friend the marshal?'

'Extremely well, although in his old age he has started to seek out remedies from a whole host of doctors and quacks. He divides his time between Bordeaux, of which he is governor, and Paris, where he follows the sessions of the Academy just as closely as the latest news from the theatre. And when I say the theatre, I mean actresses . . .'

Marion and Poitevin appeared and cleared the table. For the next course they brought a ragout of batallia with truffles, cooked in the embers and served in a folded napkin, and a large plate of warm Hanover ham. After breathing in the delicious aroma gently steaming from the crust of the first dish, Monsieur de La Borde raised his glass.

'Gentlemen, let us drink to the health of the procurator, who is entertaining us royally, as always. What is this delicacy?'

'It's a ragout of specially chosen meats, capon-filled cocks' combs, calf sweetbreads with cloves, rabbit kidneys and slices of calf's leg with morels.'

'And this wine, well the red is as good as the white. Such refinement!'

'It's a burgundy from Irancy, and the white is a still champagne that I have sent from Vertus.'

'I was right to call your table royal,' exclaimed La Borde. 'His Majesty questioned me recently about what his grandfather Louis the Great used to drink. I looked into it with the butler-in-ordinary. We examined old records. For a long time Louis XIV drank champagne, then Fagon, his doctor, convinced him that this wine was affecting his stomach because of its excessive acidity and recommended burgundy, which the stomach digests at a more leisurely rate and is less eager to get rid of. So he began to drink wine from Auxerre, Coulanges and Irancy.'

'I like Irancy,' said Noblecourt, 'because of its clear and rich colour, its fruity aroma and its cheeky sprightliness.'

'We are rather close to Lent to be tickling our palates so much,' Père Grégoire commented.

'But we're not quite there yet,' said Balbastre, 'which enables our host as a defender and champion of our traditional cooking to show it in its true colours. There are so many new-fangled recipes these days.'

'You speak as brilliantly as you play and compose,' said Noblecourt. 'This is one of the great debates of our time, a crucial controversy. It angers me, gentlemen, when I read works that tell us what we should think about this or that. La Borde, do you know Marin?'

'I know him very well. He's a true artist who began his career at the home of Madame de Gesvres, then was head cook for

Marshal Soubise, another inveterate gourmet. His Majesty likes him and Madame de Pompadour simply adores him. He enjoys cultivating the senses . . .'

'Essences? Then I consider him a colleague,' exclaimed the Carmelite apothecary.

Everyone laughed at the good monk's mistake. He was lost in contemplation of the wonders on his plate.

'Yes, that's the cook I mean,' said Noblecourt, 'and I regret to say that I do not share His Majesty's opinion.'

He got to his feet as promptly as his portliness would allow, hurried across to one of the bookcases and took out a volume full of paper bookmarks.

'Look, here is *Les Dons de Comus* by François Marin, Paris, 1739.'

He feverishly searched for the right page and began to read aloud:

' "Cooking is a kind of chemistry, and the science of cooking consists of breaking down, digesting and quintessentialising different types of meat and deriving from them juices that are nutritious yet light, mixing them together and combining them in such a way that nothing is overpowering and everything can be tasted." I won't go on with this twaddle. In my opinion what matters is that meat should be meat and taste like meat.'

He grabbed another book, which was also crammed with bookmarks.

'This, gentlemen, is my bible: *Lettre d'un pâtissier anglois au nouveau cuisinier françois*, by Dessalleurs, Paris, 1740. Listen: "What can be the attraction for those with a real taste for food of a chemical composition made up of reasoned quintessences and from which all traces of terrestriality have been systematically removed. The great achievement of the new school of cooking is to make meat taste like fish and fish taste like meat and to make vegetables taste like nothing at all." That's exactly what I think of these damnable, nay heretical novelties.'

He went and sat down again, still brimming with indignation.

'I enjoy seeing a love of cooking taken to this degree of intolerance,' said La Borde. 'It reminds me of a small volume entitled *Le Cuisinier gascon*, published anonymously in 1747. I have reason to believe that its author was Monseigneur de Bourbon, Prince de Dombes, who often dabbled in cooking at the King's private suppers. Besides, the King, the Queen, the royal princesses and various dukes of the realm – Soubise, Guéménée, Gontaut, d'Ayen, Coigny and La Vallière – all tried their hand at some time. In this book the recipes of the new school of cooking were all saddled with ridiculous names: green monkey sauce, veal à la Neuteau in donkey droppings, chicken à la Caracatacat and other such inventions.'

'Gentlemen, I'm a happy man,' Noblecourt went on. 'The food is excellent and the guests sparkling. So, unlike Monsieur de Montmaur, I can say, "I have provided the meat and the wine and you have provided the Attic salt."'

But as all those present were not participating equally in the conversation, he changed the subject.

'And what does Monsieur de Voltaire have in store for us?'

Balbastre jumped at the opportunity.

'He continues to vent his spleen on the English, not only because they're our enemies but because they have claimed in writing that Shakespeare is infinitely superior to our Corneille. Our great man has put it eloquently: "Their Shakespeare is infinitely inferior to a street performer."'

'Sarcasm clouds judgement,' Nicolas ventured. 'There is some very fine writing by this English author, and passages that stir the soul.'

'Have you read Shakespeare?'

'Yes, and in the original, at my godfather's, the Marquis de Ranreuil.'

'So police underlings read literature these days!' exclaimed Balbastre.

Nicolas immediately regretted mentioning, if accidentally, the name of this respected man with whom he had broken off all contact. Pigneau's pained expression hurt him. What cruder way could he have found to push himself forward? He had deserved Balbastre's barb. Sensing the unease, Monsieur de Noblecourt once again diverted the conversation by giving a running commentary as he confidently and expertly carved the fowl. Monsieur de La Borde, who all the time had been looking at Nicolas with a kindly eye, gave the old magistrate his assistance.

'Monsieur Procurator . . .'

'Why such formality? You want something from me.'

'Certainly I do. Would you be so kind as to show us your cabinet of curiosities?'

'What? You've heard of it?'

'The whole town and Court know of it and you yourself talk about it often enough.'

'Touché! In fact it's not so much my cabinet as my father's, since he was the one who started it. I simply followed in his footsteps. During his travels he developed an obsession for collecting anything he thought was out of the ordinary. I did the same when it was my turn to travel.'

The meal continued with the promise of this visit. The guests began private conversations. Pigneau, knowing his friend's weaknesses and his fits of melancholy, managed to persuade him that Balbastre's comment was more light-hearted than offensive. There were desserts in plenty and the table was covered with fruit pies, marzipan cakes, jams and jellies. Liqueurs were served and after lunch a pleasant feeling of drowsiness came over everyone.

Monsieur de Noblecourt clapped his hands and invited his guests to return to the library. He headed towards a door which opened on to a private room and took a small key fastened to his watch chain to open it. To begin with the visitors could see nothing, as the room had no windows. He lit two candlesticks on a small table. Three of the walls were furnished with display cabinets containing a host of unusual and ill-assorted objects. They formed a collection of shells, dried plants, ancient weapons, exotic china, primitive fabrics, stones and crystals in strange shapes and colours. More disturbing were specimen jars that preserved, in a cloudy solution, spongy whitish blobs of shapeless matter. But what caught the visitors' attention more was a relief tableau with an elaborate wooden gilt frame. It showed a graveyard in the dead of night: half-open coffins revealing decomposing bodies and swarming masses of worms and crawling creatures were sculpted and chiselled in wax, and so realistically that the whole scene seemed to come to life before their eyes.

'Dear God, what is that horrible thing?' asked Père Grégoire.

Monsieur de Noblecourt remained pensive for a moment, then replied:

'My father used to travel a great deal in his youth, especially in Italy. I'm going to tell you a story. In 1656 a certain Zumbo was born in Palermo, Sicily. While a pupil of the Jesuits in Syracuse he was struck at an early age by the macabre decorations that adorned the sanctuaries of the Society, presumably a reminder of their motto *Perinde ac cadaver*.[5] After his ordination he soon became skilled in making scenes with anatomical wax figures. You have one of them here before you. These representations of the corruption of the flesh drew attention to the spectacle of death, in order to show the faithful scenes that in real life would have filled them with horror and disgust.'

'But what was the purpose of all this?' Pigneau asked.

'The aim was to encourage repentance and to convert people. Zumbo travelled around and worked in Florence, Genoa and Bologna. In Florence he produced several such scenes of human decay, in particular one of smallpox commissioned by Grand Duke Cosimo III, whose son-in-law, the Elector of Bavaria, suffered from this disease. In 1695 my father met him and purchased this work, *The Graveyard*. At the time he was working with Monsieur Des Noues on wax heads and on a woman who had died in childbirth, whom he had succeeded in preserving beneath the wax. He managed to render nature to perfection by using this coloured substance. He came to Paris and was received by the Academy of Medicine, to whose members he showed his work. After becoming involved in a legal dispute with Des Noues, who claimed to be the inventor of the procedure, he died in Paris in 1701.'

Everyone fell silent, contemplating the unspeakable and no longer paying any attention to the other curiosities. Nicolas, less affected than the others because he had seen much worse things in real life, suddenly noticed a large crucifix placed against one of the display cabinets. He questioned Monsieur de Noblecourt, who smiled.

'Oh, that's not one of the curiosities, but as I don't want to be suspected of being a Jansenist I've put this gift to one side. It was, would you believe it, a present from Commissioner Lardin. I hadn't realised he was so devout or so eager to convert others. I still wonder about his reason for giving it to me and the purpose of the esoteric little message that accompanied this kind gesture. I still haven't worked out its meaning.'

He unfurled the piece of paper that was rolled around the wood of the cross. Nicolas discovered to his amazement a message matching the one found in his coat in Rue des Blancs-Manteaux.

Carefully you open them
After so much searching

'Look at the riddle,' Noblecourt continued. 'The arms of this Jansenist Christ are closed, presumably to open people's hearts better. That's the interpretation I give it.'

'Will you let me have this piece of paper?' Nicolas asked in a low voice.

'Of course. I understand that all this may be important.'

The merriment of the meal had vanished. The visit to the elderly procurator's cabinet of curiosities had opened up a Pandora's box. It was as if each guest had put on a mask and retreated into sadness and silence. Noblecourt tried in vain to make his friends stay on but gradually each one took his leave. Monsieur de La Borde said goodbye to Nicolas with a strange 'We are relying on you.' After promising Pigneau and Père Grégoire to see them more often, the young man remained alone with Monsieur de Noblecourt, who looked worried.

'I'm too old for these sorts of gatherings,' he sighed. 'I've over-indulged. I'm afraid I'll have an attack of gout and then be told off by Marion, quite rightly as usual. I shouldn't have given in to La Borde's inquisitiveness. I conjured up the devil and broke the spell.'

'Don't be sorry, Monsieur. There are certain things that some people cannot face up to.'

'Wisely spoken. What's more, I noticed that you showed little emotion at that spectacle.'

'I've seen worse things than a wax representation and . . .'

Marion suddenly burst into the room, looking outraged.

'Monsieur, there's an Inspector Bourdeau asking for our Nicolas.'

'Go, Nicolas,' said the magistrate, 'but take care of yourself. I have a premonition of something nasty. It must be the gout. It is the gout!'

XII

THE OLD SOLDIER

'The soldier's lot is such a sorry one that it makes the heart bleed; he spends his days wretched and despised; he lives like a chained-up dog intended for combat.'

THE COUNT OF SAINT-GERMAIN

BOURDEAU was waiting beneath the carriage entrance. He came straight to the point, explaining to Nicolas why he had disturbed him: Tirepot had picked up the trail of the two suspects and had sent a messenger to say he was tailing them. As soon as he had run them to ground, he would make contact. Bourdeau's man had already gone off to meet him, and the inspector had come to collect Nicolas to take him back to the Châtelet where all the information would be pieced together.

Nicolas approved his deputy's arrangements and now, in a hurry himself, wanted to send for a carriage. Foresighted as ever, Bourdeau pointed to a cab waiting in the street. They would go back to the duty office to await developments, and put on disguises to be ready for any eventuality. Nicolas took his cape and tricorn, then got into the carriage. They rapidly reached their destination since on that Sunday afternoon in late winter Paris was almost deserted. All they came across were a few groups of masked revellers intimidating some frightened citizens. This reminded Nicolas that it was exactly a week since he had got back from Guérande.

Sitting at a small table in the duty office, Bourdeau gave a detailed account of Semacgus's move to the Bastille. The surgeon had received a friendly welcome from the governor, who already knew him because he had had occasion to dine with him at Monsieur de Jussieu's. He had been given a large and airy cell with a few items of furniture. Bourdeau had gone back to Vaugirard to pick up clothes and books from a list that Semacgus had given him. Catherine was still consoling Awa, who by now was convinced that she would never see Saint-Louis again. Bourdeau had made use of the visit to check that the seals on Descart's house were still intact, and that no one had attempted to break in. In any case his spies were keeping a constant watch on the doctor's residence. As for the reports from Rue des Blancs-Manteaux, Bourdeau was beginning to doubt the sanity and the zeal of his informers. They spoke solely of Madame Lardin returning home when no one had seen her leave, and of her leaving when no one had seen her come home. That side of the mystery was deepening. Mauval had been spotted entering the house several times. Having finished his summary Bourdeau took out his pipe, looked at it thoughtfully, then concentrated on producing a cloud of smoke that in the slowly gathering dusk plunged the room into even deeper darkness.

Nicolas could not shake off the lethargy induced by the delights of Monsieur de Noblecourt's table. He couldn't stop thinking about his clumsy comment, an act of pretentiousness which he now realised was merely a sign of his own insecurity.

Balbastre had not wanted to hurt his feelings; he had simply ventured a witty remark amidst the sparkling conversation that was the hallmark of a free society. The young man was conscious of how lucky he was to meet men of taste and tact, a reflection of the polished manners of the Court. Revisiting his own weakness, he realised the progress he still had to make before he achieved self-control and could prevent the first gibe directed at him, and the first slight to his self-esteem, from reopening the wound. He was aware that this over-sensitivity was an essential part of his make-up, and something he would have to live with. He had never had the opportunity to talk to anybody openly about it. At one point he had intended to confide in Pigneau but, however kind he was, his friend was still a man of the cloth and tended to treat anything that was said in confidence as if it were spoken in the confessional. He could only see Nicolas's moral suffering in the context of a faith that took little account of private sorrows, or rather urged that they should be transcended by adoration of the divine.

Drowsy from the effects of the meal, Nicolas began to dream. He was at Château de Ranreuil, near the moat. Isabelle had slipped on the grass and had fallen into the water: she was floating motionless amongst the reeds. On the bank Nicolas was holding out his hands towards the young woman but he was unable to move. He was shouting out in despair but not a sound came from his lips. Suddenly the marquis appeared, his face twisted with hatred, clutching a large crucifix with which he was attempting to hit the young man. He felt a sharp pain in his shoulder . . .

'Calm down, Monsieur. It's me, Bourdeau. You fell asleep. Were you dreaming?'

Nicolas shuddered.

'I was having a nightmare.'

Night had fallen and Bourdeau had lit a candle that glimmered and guttered.

'Tirepot has made contact. Our two fellows are currently sitting at a table in a seedy tavern in Faubourg Saint-Marcel, near the horse market. They seem to be regulars. We need to be quick. I've informed the watch and they'll meet us there.'

He handed Nicolas a hat and some old clothes. He himself ran his fingers through the dust on the top of a chest and then rubbed it over his face. He invited the young man to do the same. Their faces now made them look like little Savoyard chimney sweeps. Nicolas picked up the cast-offs that had proved so useful during his investigations in Vaugirard. He wanted to take a sword but Bourdeau dissuaded him, pointing out that this weapon did not go with the rest of his outfit, and that the little pistol he had given him was ample guarantee of safety and discretion. When all was ready they got into the cab driven by one of Bourdeau's aides. The inspector ordered him to take the quickest route, which meant going over Pont au Change, crossing Île de la Cité, reaching the Left Bank via Petit Pont, then speeding towards Porte Saint-Marcel and entering the *faubourg*.

The bumpy ride made Nicolas feel drowsy again; he tried to marshal his thoughts. Something was preying on his mind, as if it were trying to send him a message that he was unable to decipher. He thought back to the lunch in Rue Montmartre and to the astonishing discovery of another message from Lardin that was just as incomprehensible as the first. He found it difficult to explain why the commissioner had chosen to make contact with two acquaintances who were not close friends, and who might have had reason to mistrust him: Monsieur de Noblecourt for reasons of caution and reticence, and Nicolas because of his subordinate status. He would have to re-read and compare the two messages. He tried in vain to determine at what point he had become uneasy and doubtful, and what particular detail had triggered his current uncertainty. He relived the episode of the cabinet of curiosities. He saw again the strange crucifix. It vaguely reminded him of something, and he vowed to give the matter some more thought.

Bourdeau respected his silence and continued to surround himself in wreaths of smoke. In his wisdom, he always seemed to know when his superior needed absolute quiet. It was now pitch dark and the lighting was poor because the wind had blown out many of the candles in the street lanterns. Nicolas had heard Monsieur de Sartine think aloud about the changes he wished to make to lighting in the capital to improve the safety of its inhabitants. He also complained of the ever-increasing number of street signs and awnings that cast too much shadow onto the cobbled streets and created areas of dark that were a breeding ground for thieves, pickpockets and other villains. What was more, the awnings, which were often damaged by the weather, tended to fall down and cause accidents.

Occasionally the noise of the carriage lessened, as if it were going over a carpet. A pervasive, musty smell told them that they had just gone past the mansion of some wealthy invalid. The servants of the house had spread dung and straw in front of the door to muffle the noise of the carriages. Elsewhere, ice-covered potholes caved in and the windows were splashed with muddy water. They encountered more groups of masked revellers who bombarded the carriage with little sacks of flour, but Carnival was almost over and the spirit had gone out of it. Shrove Tuesday would signal the end with a bonfire that finished on Ash Wednesday, the start of Lent.

Once they had gone beyond the city limits, Nicolas had the feeling of entering a frozen desert. The *faubourg* showed itself in its most eerie light. The faint glimmer of the lantern revealed high walls that gradually gave way to indistinct bulky masses. These were religious or charitable institutions, which were numerous in this part of the city. Where nothing had been built, it was left to the imagination to conjure up abandoned areas in which ghostly thickets covered the land with tangled undergrowth, dense with claw-like and frost-encrusted brambles. Small walls reared up, protecting orchards, gardens and yards. The traffic had stopped. Suddenly a nocturnal creature fluttered against the window on Nicolas's side, pecked fiercely at the glass, then disappeared. He thought about Monsieur de Noblecourt's premonition, and at the same time he sensed Bourdeau's anxiety as the inspector trembled beside him.

Tirepot's messenger had got there before them; he intercepted their carriage near the churchyard of Sainte-Catherine. The tavern they were heading for was close by, in Rue du Cendrier. Their guide pointed out a large, badly lit hovel set back from the road. As they approached it a familiar voice greeted Nicolas from behind a collapsed cart by a woodpile:

'Here you are at last!' Tirepot murmured. 'I'm freezing here, waiting for you. Pretend you're passing water. Your two fellows, an old soldier called Bricart and his crony, Rapace, a former butcher, are sitting at the corner table on the right as you go in. Be careful. It's a pretty seedy place.'

Nicolas pretended to do himself up.

'The watch have been informed and are on their way. You stay out of this. I don't want you to be seen. Off you go now.'

Nicolas went back to Bourdeau, who was rehearsing his role. He began to limp as he rammed his big hat on.

'Take my arm and hide your face. Keep out of the light.'

They pushed open the door of the tavern and went inside. The room was in semi-darkness. The beams of the low ceiling were blackened with smoke. The only furniture on the uneven mud floor was a dozen or so painted wooden tables with rough-hewn benches on either side. Here and there poor quality tallow candles provided some dim light. The customers were an odd assortment of rag-pickers, beggars and two washerwomen from the toll-gates, who had hoisted their skirts to warm their backsides by the meagre fire. The tavern-keeper was breaking up lumps of sugar and from time to time stirred a large pot hanging from a hook in the fireplace, in which a thick concoction of assorted scraps and roots was bubbling away. One of the human wrecks went up to him and, after paying, received a bowlful of the soup together with a hunk of black bread mixed with bran. Rapace and Bricart seemed in the middle of a lively conversation. There was a growing collection of wine jugs on their table. Lurching around, Bourdeau pushed Nicolas into a dark corner to the left of the fireplace. The spot was well chosen; it allowed a general view of the room and the entrance, but also of the exits to the back. The inspector banged his fist on the table and in a hoarse voice called the host who came to take their order. They asked for two bowls of soup and a pitcher of brandy and paid up immediately. Bourdeau put down his pipe and spat copiously on the floor.

'Monsieur,' he whispered, 'you need to drink the brandy in one go, throwing your head back. Now, crumble the bread into the soup and grab the spoon with your whole hand. Make sure you're sprawled across the table, and make as much noise as possible while you're eating. To finish it, drink what's left straight from the bowl. Let's be careful. Anyone with an ounce of common sense could see through our disguise. This is going to be a treat.'

He gave him a grotesque wink.

Nicolas became uneasy when he saw the meagre fare arrive. He would long remember this day, in the course of which he had gone from the heights of culinary excellence to the depths of scraps and left-overs. Bourdeau gave him a look of encouragement. He tried to follow his advice and slumped over the grimy wooden table. The bread he had dipped into the broth gradually disintegrated and small flakes of it floated to the top. The first spoonful almost made him pass out, and to settle his stomach he took a quick swig of alcohol. Old Marie's 'pick-me-up' in the Châtelet was sweetness and gentleness itself compared with the river of fire that flooded his chest. He decided to change tactics. He took his courage in both hands, lifted the bowl to his lips and swallowed its disgusting contents. He followed it with another glass of brandy. Bourdeau had difficulty stopping himself laughing out loud. For his part, he had chosen a more devious method: after each spoonful he had a massive coughing fit and spat repeatedly on the floor. In the end Nicolas succumbed to his companion's jollity. Once he had relaxed and had been pleasantly warmed by the brandy he said to himself that up until then, although they had got on easily and well together, he had not paid much attention to the inspector. Their relationship had been confined to professional matters. He had never wondered about Bourdeau's past, his reasons for entering the police force or his family life. Suddenly he felt curious to know more about a man who had always been unfailingly helpful and kind to him. As they waited he seized the opportunity to try to make up for lost time.

'Bourdeau,' he said in a hushed voice, 'you've never told me about how you came to join the police, have you?'

The inspector remained silent for a moment, making no attempt to disguise how taken aback he was by the question.

'No doubt, Monsieur, because you've never asked.'

There was another pause, during which Nicolas thought of the best way of getting back to the subject.

'Are your parents still alive?'

'They're both dead. They died within a short time of each other. Almost twenty years ago.'

'What did your father do?'

He sensed that Bourdeau was more relaxed.

'My father was kennel-keeper of the King's boar hounds. As far as I remember, he was very proud of his position. Until his accident he was extremely happy.'

'His accident?'

'A cornered boar gashed his leg after he had rushed to the help of one of the King's favourite dogs. They had to sever his leg because of the risk of gangrene. His courage was hardly repaid: they resented his failure to save the dog, which had also been gored . . . He had to go back to his village an invalid, without the status of a veteran or a pension. From then on he wasted away, deprived of the hunt, which had been his whole life, and separated from the King, his idol. I watched him die of grief. He never forgave himself for having allowed the dog to die. The King had merely complained and had shown not the slightest concern for the injured man. This is how the great of this world are . . .'

'The King didn't know.'

'That's what they always say. Oh! If the King knew that . . . Nicolas, we are the servants of justice and we obey orders, but as a citizen I'm entitled to my own opinion. The King is a man like any other, with his defects and whims. As a young man my father had been struck by his lust for killing. About forty years ago, when he was an apprentice, he witnessed a scene that affected him so much that he often recounted it, though it reflected badly on the person he revered as a god. The King was then about twelve or thirteen and was very fond of a white doe he had fed when it was only a fawn. It had become used to him, and so tame that it ate out of his hand. One day he had a sudden urge to kill it. He ordered it to be taken to La Muette. There he chased it away, then shot and wounded it. Panic-stricken and whimpering, the poor animal ran towards the King in search of protection. He forced it away a second time and killed it.

Nicolas was surprised at Bourdeau's controlled anger.

'Sensing that his end was near,' the inspector continued, 'my father, who had never asked for anything for himself, reluctantly petitioned his Lordship the Duc de Penthièvre, the Master of the Royal Hunt,[1] and the most honourable of men. Shortly before my father died his Lordship sent me to Paris where, after studying at the college of Louis-le-Grand, I read law. With the proceeds from the sale of my parents' small house, generously supplemented by the duke, I was able to buy my office of inspector and adviser to the King. Thus the damage done by one Bourbon was repaired by another. But what about you, Monsieur? How do you explain your astonishing career?'

Nicolas sensed the hint of irony.

'How did you come to obtain Monsieur de Sartine's support to the extent of representing him and acting on his behalf, with even wider powers than a commissioner? Don't misinterpret my curiosity. But since you were kind enough to enquire about me, allow me to do likewise with equal frankness.'

Nicolas had fallen into his own trap, but he did not regret it. He considered Bourdeau to be sincere and had the feeling that this conversation could only bring them closer together. But it was another Bourdeau he looked at now, someone deeper and more solemn.

'There's no mystery to it and my story's not that different from yours,' he replied. 'I was a foundling, without family or fortune and was recommended to Monsieur de Sartine by my godfather, the Marquis de Ranreuil. Everything followed from that, without me having to take any initiative, except to prove I was competent to perform the necessary tasks.'

Bourdeau smiled.

'You're very much the philosopher. You ask questions without giving answers. I'm not one to question what you're saying, but you must understand that your position is unusual, that tongues in the Châtelet are starting to wag and people are beginning to wonder about you. They think you're a member of a Masonic lodge.'

'What! Why is that?'

'I thought you knew that Monsieur de Sartine was himself affiliated to the lodge of the Arts Sainte-Marguerite.'

'Certainly not. I have no involvement with such things.'

The truth was that the straightforward fellow Nicolas felt he had by then got to know quite well now appeared in a new light. Nicolas was aware of the incongruity of the situation. Since his return from Brittany he had allowed himself to be carried along by events. He had not sensed how much his relations with the inspector had gradually changed. He had himself accepted this shift unquestioningly and happily. Despite his concerns and his conviction that on occasion he was merely being used by the Lieutenant General of Police, he had overcome this ambiguous position by obtaining, as he thought, the total confidence of his superior. Could he rise so quickly from being an instrument to being his confidant? He preferred not to dwell on this, but to throw himself into the fray. However, he fully realised that Bourdeau was not a simple underling, and that it required unusual magnanimity on his part to accept a young man, an apprentice, as his master, so to speak. Despite all his experience the inspector had been prepared to stay in the background and accept orders. Nicolas thought that he had probably failed to ensure that this reversal of roles had taken place as tactfully and as smoothly as it might have. He must not forget the lesson Bourdeau had just taught him. He remembered that instead of using his Christian name as he had before, Bourdeau now addressed him with a deferential 'Monsieur', more appropriate to their new relationship. He nevertheless remained convinced that the inspector was really fond of him, a feeling matched on his part by genuine esteem. He vowed to ensure that he would show it, especially since he was the one who had requested of Monsieur de Sartine that Bourdeau be his deputy.

The silence continued until Bourdeau, swearing under his

breath, drew Nicolas's attention to what was happening in the room. The two suspects had got up and after downing a last glass were on their way out of the tavern. The inspector whispered to Nicolas to count slowly up to thirty. Only then could they themselves leave without raising the alarm, and without running the risk of bumping into the men they were tailing. Bourdeau had given orders to their guide to keep a discreet eye on the two rogues as they left, so as not to lose track of them. He advised Nicolas to pretend to be drunk. They staggered to their feet, leaning on each other, and then left the seedy tavern, knocking into tables as they went.

The cold took them by surprise. It had started snowing again. Bourdeau pointed to the footsteps in the snow and the impression left by the wooden leg. The weather was on their side: all they had to do was follow the tracks. They did not have far to walk; a few hundred feet from the tavern was the entrance to a dead-end, a narrow cart track with faggots of brushwood on either side. A shadowy figure pointed in the direction of the alleyway and disappeared. A wooden gate covered with some kind of awning closed off the access to a piece of land. Through the gaps in the fencing a massive warehouse or barn could be glimpsed in the darkness. No sound could be heard. The inspector whispered in Nicolas's ear that if there were two ways out they ran the risk of letting their quarry get away, and since the constables had not yet arrived they had to act alone and straight away. Nicolas nodded his approval.

Bourdeau pushed the gate gently. It opened with a creak. They groped their way into the enclosure. Immediately Nicolas felt a hood of coarse material being put over his head as the tip of a knife was pressed against his ribs. He heard a dull thud next to him followed by the sound of a body falling to the ground. A voice rang out:

'Hell, this beggar's had it. These loaded sticks are good for smashing heads in. We'll see about the body later. Let's get to work on his mate to find out what they were up to.'

Hands tied, Nicolas was thrust forward. His head was covered with a sack tied tight round his neck, which was half choking him. He realised they were going into a building. Someone struck a light, and he was able to see dimly through the material. They sat him down on a stool and the sack was roughly pulled off him. A torch fastened to a ring on the stone wall lit up a barn cluttered with objects and assorted items of furniture. In the midst of this chaos he immediately recognised Semacgus's elegant cabriolet. Despite his ordeal, he could not help thinking that at last he was nearing his goal or that at the very least a significant new stage had been reached.

His next thought was for Bourdeau. Was he dead? Perhaps these would be his final reflections. He had to find a way of leaving a trace, a message, a clue. But how?

In front of him stood a person of average height with thin, dirty-yellow hair and eyes of differing colours that reminded him of that suave young man who had stolen his watch when he had first come to Paris. His face was pitted with the marks of smallpox. He was pointing a large knife at Nicolas. The other person must have been standing back, and he could not see him.

'Keep your pistol trained on him. Got to be careful. So, my young Monsieur, you've been following us. Grubbing around, eh? Let's have a closer look at what you're hiding.'

He began to search Nicolas methodically. The young man was pleased he had left all his personal belongings behind at the

Châtelet. He hoped that the little pistol tucked away inside the old frock coat would go unnoticed, but the man gave a triumphant grunt when he discovered it.

'Well, what's this, then? Look what I've just fished out.'

He pushed the barrel of the weapon against Nicolas's mouth so violently that his lip split. Nicolas tried to put him off the track.

'Monsieur,' he replied – and immediately regretted this mark of politeness that betrayed him – 'my friend and I were looking for Monsieur Chauvel's house. Could you tell me if it's in these parts?'

'Well, if this fine one here ain't trying to have us on. I reckon he's scared. You hear that, Bricart? Just look at them pretty little hands. All that don't go with the rest. You wouldn't be one of them spies by any chance? And dressed up for Carnival, to top it all!'

Nicolas shuddered. The man did not even bother to disguise their names. It was a bad sign if he were really dealing with hardened criminals.

The other man came nearer. He was older, and had a thick white moustache and a wooden right leg. His clothes were a strange combination of threadbare items of military kit and civilian rags. He was leaning on a cudgel and held a loaded pistol in his hand. He went up to Nicolas to sniff him and stayed by his side.

'Smells of wallflowers. A real swell. Believe me, dear young Monsieur, your number's up and you might as well tell us all you know. Give him a prod, Rapace.'

'Ain't I just going to make him spit it all out. I've got what it takes to make him blab.'

He prodded Nicolas in the chest, right on his wound, which

started to bleed again. The young man could not hold back a cry of pain.

'And sensitive with it. Come on, talk. Talk or I'm going to bleed you . . .'

Rapace was about to continue when there was a sharp, cracking sound. The barn door suddenly burst open and Bourdeau's voice yelled out:

'You're surrounded! Don't move. Throw your weapons down.'

Bricart was flabbergasted and looked all around him, panic-stricken.

'Keep calm! He's having us on. He's on his own,' said Rapace.

He grabbed Bricart's pistol and pointed it at Bourdeau.

'You there, the ghost, hands up.'

While doing what he was told Bourdeau shouted out:

'Over here, watchmen!'

'Shut up or I'll shoot.'

A few seconds passed, agonisingly slowly. They were all frozen in anticipation. Nothing happened.

'For an old soldier, you've lost the knack, Bricart.'

'I just don't understand it. I heard his skull explode.'

'If you don't want me to chop your little friend into bits,' Rapace continued, 'you're going to explain to me what you were looking for.'

The knife was getting nearer to Nicolas's neck, making his heart thump painfully. So everything was going to end here then, in the depths of this godforsaken *faubourg* . . . Suddenly a shot rang out and, with a look of surprise, Rapace fell like a log, a bullet in the middle of his forehead. With a jerk, Nicolas knocked over the stool he was tied to and shoved Bricart, who lost his balance and fell to the floor. Bourdeau leapt forward and threw his full weight onto the old soldier before disarming him. He tied his hands behind his back with a leather strap lying on the floor, then freed Nicolas.

'Bourdeau, I thought you were dead. Thank God, you're safe. I owe you my life.'

'Let's say no more about it. Monsieur de Sartine would never have forgiven me for failing to keep my promise to protect you, and I wouldn't have forgiven myself either.'

'But, Bourdeau, explain this miracle to me.'

'Well, Monsieur, each time I set out on an expedition that might prove dangerous I wear a hat of my own making.'

He showed him a large Regency felt hat. The bottom of it was lined with an iron skullcap, held in place by silk netting.

'But what about the gunshot?'

'The hat again. My little pistol, the twin brother of the one I gave you, is fitted to the side, behind the right-hand brim. They never search hats. Needless to say it takes some getting used to and I've done a lot of target practice to get a result I'm quite proud of. The only drawback is that you can only fire it once because this miracle of design doesn't have a repeat mechanism. I'll get you a hat made to go with your pistol.'

'But why didn't you fire straight away?'

'It would have been very risky. I preferred to wait. What shall we do now? Do we wait for the watch?'

'They should be here very soon. But I've a surprise for you, Bourdeau.'

Nicolas took the torch and went up to the carriage that had been stowed away.

'But you're bleeding, Monsieur.'

'That rogue reopened the wound in my chest, but it's nothing. Take a look at this cabriolet instead. It's Semacgus's. The horse must have been sold already.'

He opened the door of the carriage. The light suddenly fell upon the beige upholstered seat. It was covered with a large stain of dried blood that had dripped onto the floor and formed a blackish pool. The cabriolet had been used to kill someone or transport a body that had been bled dry. The two men looked on in horror.

'I really don't think we're going to find Saint-Louis alive,' said Bourdeau.

Nicolas took charge of operations again.

'As soon as the constables arrive see that they carry out a detailed search of the barn and the land. Not a word must be said about Rapace's death. This cabriolet will need to be taken back to the Châtelet for Semacgus to identify. I'm taking Bricart back for a preliminary interrogation. I'll report to Monsieur de Sartine tomorrow morning. Bourdeau, I'm relying on you to sort everything out here. As soon as you've finished, come and find me. I'm afraid we're not going to get much sleep tonight.'

Tirepot's spy appeared, followed by an officer of the watch and a group of constables. They carried out Nicolas's orders. As he was about to leave he walked up to Bourdeau and held out his hand:

'Thank you, my friend.'

Nicolas felt light-hearted on the journey back to Paris. The numerous signs of deadly danger had now taken on a new meaning. The future, which until then had looked uncertain, now seemed clear. Even the presence at his side of a known criminal could not detract from Nicolas's feeling of relief, to which was added the satisfaction of having done Bourdeau justice. The ordeal had strengthened him, as a mountain stream tempers the red-hot blade of a sword. Death, which he had smelled on Rapace's breath, was now only a distant threat; he felt cleansed and more self-assured. It was as if he had been reborn and now saw things in a different light. The cab, even the pain in his chest and the falling snow all filled him with joy and gratitude. He smiled because his dark imaginings were now giving way to brighter ones and, incorrigible as ever, he had veered from one extreme to the other. He revelled in his euphoria until he reached the Châtelet.

When he had changed Nicolas went to find his prisoner, as he wanted to question him at once. He had often noticed that a suspect had fewer defences if interrogated immediately. It was only later on, when the criminal had had time to think things out, that they were able to put together a battery of assertions and denials. Nicolas had obtained a bottle of brandy from the gaoler. His intuition was telling him to take it gently with Bricart, and only to blow hot or cold and try another tack if the first approach did not work.

When he went into the cell he was struck by the change in Bricart. With the lantern he had brought he could see the old soldier sitting on his plank-bed. The beam of light showed a man huddled up, almost bald, his sallow complexion flecked with brown marks. His face, pitted with old scars, bore the signs of age. His dull eyes were bloodshot and his lower lip flabby and trembling. Nicolas went over to the prisoner and untied his hands. He filled an earthenware cup with brandy and held it out to him. After a moment's hesitation the old soldier downed it in one gulp. He wiped his mouth on the back of his sleeve.

'So now you're all on your own,' said Nicolas. 'You've got no mate to back you up. You alone are charged with a serious crime. If you ask me, there's only one thing you can do: unburden your conscience.'

The man did not react.

'Let's start at the beginning. Bricart can't be your real name. So what is it?'

The other man hesitated. It was obvious that he was weighing up the pros and cons of keeping silent. Or would his desire to relieve his anxiety by talking get the better of him?

'Jean-Baptiste Lenfant, born at Sompuy in Champagne,' he said at last.

'In what year?'

'I never knew. The priest talked about "the year of the great freeze and the wolves".'

'Were you a soldier?'

Bricart raised his head. A visible transformation came over him and, after asking for a drink, he launched into a breathless account of his whole life. Yes, he had been a soldier and for a long time, too, until that damn wound on the battlefield at Fontenoy. When he was twenty his name had been drawn by lot for the royal militia. It was bad luck and he might just as easily have avoided it. He could still picture the scene as he left his village. Many of his friends were in tears, protesting that they were being led to the slaughter. Their mothers were there, wringing their hands. He could still smell the stench of the stinking uniforms that had belonged to those killed in the previous war, or so it was rumoured. He could still feel the weight of the haversack, so heavy that it pulled you back and cut into your shoulders. It was the begin-ning of a long trudge through the winter mud to reach the regiment or the fort. Their clogs fell to pieces, their socks were shredded to bits and by the time they reached the bivouac their feet were bleeding. Some recruits did not survive, others mutilated themselves deliber-ately. For all of them there was the sorrow of having left behind their loved ones, and the homesickness that destroyed all hope. Then each day had followed the next. Things became routine, with moments of happiness amidst all the suffering. There were the mates, the drinking sessions, pilfering that turned into looting, the bellyfuls of stolen poultry and fruit and the girls from the farms and the taverns.

But one day everything came to an end on the battlefield. Why then, why him? It began with a reveille blasting out in the cold dawn. The enemy had begun their attack at five o'clock. The officers of the general staff galloped past in their brightly decorated uniforms. On a hillock in the distance you could see a grey and gold spot and beside it a red one. The sergeant muttered it was the King and his son, the dauphin. For the first and last time in his life Bricart had seen the Marshal of Saxony, so ill from the effects of the pox that he had to be carried around in a wicker chair, his body swollen with dropsy. He was shouting angrily at the officers, whipping up their energy and castigating their indiscipline. Everything got going to the sound of the bugles, and one by one the columns moved up to the front line.

Then, just as suddenly, everything was over. The surprise of the impact, the first impression that nothing has happened, that you've saved your skin and that you'll get up simply covered in earth and in the blood from a mate mown down beside you. Next comes the feeling of soaking in a warm liquid and then, growing stronger and stronger until it makes you scream, the terrible pain from the leg shattered by a cannonball. He was left lying there until nightfall and had put a tourniquet on his thigh himself. He had been half-dead when he was picked up. But before that he had heard the frightening clash of battle, the shrieks, the whinnying of the horses, the screaming that had gradually given way to the wailing of the wounded and the groaning of the dying. Near him a hussar crushed beneath his horse was crying softly, calling out for his mother. He had had to fight off looters, women and even children who snatched from those poor corpses their pathetic riches, including the braid sewn onto their uniforms. Then he had been taken in a cart to a dressing station. The ground was covered with blood and human remains. Surgeons were maiming the poor devils for life. His right leg went. He stayed there for days. Each of the wounded lay in his own excrement, worse than if he had been sleeping on dung. They were all swarming with vermin, and the dead served as mattresses for the living. Yes, he'd been a soldier and they'd made good use of him as cannon fodder.

Now that he was an invalid, with no means of support and no rank, he was left to his own devices with only his threadbare uniform and his wooden leg to comfort him. He went back to his village. His mother and father had died long since, and his few cousins had given him up for dead and his meagre inheritance had been dispersed. Reduced to poverty, he had wandered far and wide, then had the idea that in the big city he would be able to provide for himself more easily. But what could an invalid unfit for manual labour hope for? He could not read or write and was barely able to sign his name. He was afraid of ending up in the Hôpital Général, locked up like an animal amongst the lunatics who were given their food on the end of a bayonet. He knew what he was talking about because he had been caught once and put away in Bicêtre. Miraculously he had escaped and he dreaded the idea of going back there.

Bricart had livened up as he told his story. The colour had returned to his cheeks. But under the influence of the alcohol he became prostrate again, his head slumped on his chest. Nicolas could not help pitying this fellow to whom life had been so cruel. But the time had come to apply pressure and to get either a formal confession out of him, or information likely to help the progress of the investigation. It was essential that Nicolas corroborate the various facts already in his possession. He decided on a direct line of attack. Bricart's reactions would indicate how he should follow up the interrogation.

'You're in danger of something much worse than Bicêtre!' said Nicolas. 'Be a good fellow and tell me what you were up to with Rapace. And to start with, where does the bloodstained cabriolet in your barn come from?'

Bricart huddled up even more. He gave Nicolas a shifty, suspicious look.

'We're dealers, that's all. We buy things and sell them.'

'You can't tell me that you're afraid of being put in the hospital and at the same time claim that you're a tradesman. You're not going to make anyone swallow that.'

'Rapace was the one with the cash. I've got nothing. I just helped him.'

'Doing what?'

'Finding bargains.'

'And the cabriolet, was it a bargain?'

'Rapace was the one who dealt with it.'

Nicolas realised that Bricart had chosen solid ground from which to defend himself: blaming everything on Rapace, who was no longer around to contradict him. The long account of his life as a soldier had merely been a diversionary tactic. By talking about unimportant things he would say nothing about what really mattered. Nicolas needed to attack him from a new angle.

'Does your leg hurt a lot?'

Relieved, Bricart jumped at the opportunity to talk about something else.

'Oh, my dear Monsieur, the bloody thing never gives me a moment's peace. Would you believe it, I still think it's there. I can feel it itching. I even go numb in the toes. Ain't it a shame and an ordeal to have to scratch away at nothing. And the stump still hasn't healed up. It hurts terribly.'

'Your wooden leg looks solid enough.'

'I should say so. It was made from the oak of a sling-cart destroyed at Fontenoy.[2] A carpenter carved it for me. This leg's an old friend who's never let me down.'

He lifted up the tip towards Nicolas, who took hold of the end firmly. Bricart was flung back against the wall and banged his head.

'God, what does this shuffler want from me?' he growled.

'I think you're a lying rogue,' Nicolas replied, 'but I intend to get the truth out of you.'

While keeping hold of Bricart's wooden leg with one hand, he took a crumpled piece of paper out of his pocket with the other. He carefully put the metal tip of the prosthesis onto the centre of the document.

'This is clear proof,' he declared. 'Jean-Baptiste Lenfant, also known as Bricart, I hereby charge you with having been to Montfaucon on the night of 2 February, along with Rapace your accomplice, in order to deposit there the remains of a murdered body. You went there in a horse and cart.'

The prisoner's terror-stricken expression showed he was desperately searching for a way out. Nicolas had already seen this look on a fox caught in a trap, surrounded by angry dogs. He felt no pride at having reduced a man to such a state of panic but he had to make him talk. He let go of the wooden leg, which banged against the plank-bed on its way down.

'You're lying and making it all up,' protested Bricart. 'I don't know anything. Let me go. I haven't done anything. I'm just a poor old invalid soldier. An invalid!'

He was shouting and the light now showed the sweat pouring down his face.

'Would you like me to give you some more precise details?' Nicolas asked. 'Why can I state categorically that you were in Montfaucon that evening? Because I noted down imprints in the frozen snow.' He waved the little piece of paper. 'Imprints of what? Those of a small six-sided object with an irregular outline, which happens to be identical to the tip of your wooden leg. I should add that you were not on your own in Montfaucon . . .'

'Hell. There was only Rapace. Go to the devil!'

'Thank you for confirming that you were with Rapace at the knacker's yard. Even if you'd sworn the opposite I would have told you that a witness had seen you there. For the last time, my only advice to you is to speak the truth. Otherwise people more skilled than me in such matters will drag it out of you by working on your other leg.'

He was horrified by his own brutality. Its sole justification was that he believed his suggestion was Bricart's only chance of saving his life, or at any rate of suffering less. The man before him probably was a criminal, but could you judge his misdeeds without seeing them against the background of a life of misfortune? He imagined Bricart as a child, a young man, a wounded soldier and all that suffering went through his mind . . .

'Fair enough,' the other conceded, 'I was in Montfaucon with Rapace. So what? We were carrying a dead old nag we'd cut up.'

He was struggling to speak, sighing after every word, as if he were short of breath.

'Cutting up a horse in the dead of night? Stop fooling around, Bricart. You know very well it wasn't a carcass but a corpse.'

Bricart was picking at a brownish scab on his bald skull, making it bleed. He was shaking his head as if trying to escape from a cruel and haunting thought.

'I'll tell you everything,' he sighed. 'You don't look a bad sort. Rapace and I were caught stealing wood in the warehouses of the port of La Rapée. To keep us warm, of course. Winter is hard on the poor.'

'Go on.'

'The man who arrested us seemed to know Rapace. He offered us a deal. He asked us to do a favour for one of his friends. He knew everything about us: our names, the barn . . . He was the devil with a face like an angel. As he talked he had a grin on his face that scared the wits out of us. There was no way out of it. On Friday evening at around ten o'clock we were to be waiting next to the building site of the new square at the bottom of the Tuileries, with a cart and two barrels. We were promised a good reward for a few hours' work. He even gave us an advance, in *louis d'or*!'

'So on the Friday . . . ?'

'We turned up as arranged with the cart. What could we do? At ten o'clock precisely we were at the corner of the building site, on the town side. There we saw three people arrive in masks.'

'And the man who'd arrested you, was he there?'

'I don't know. There were three in masks with big black capes. It was Carnival.'

'Did you notice anything in particular?'

'There was a devil of a cold wind. One of the masks nearly fell off. The hood of the cape swelled out. I thought I saw a woman.'

'Then what?'

'They took us to Rue du Faubourg-Saint-Honoré and left us there. An empty cabriolet arrived at about half past eleven. It was driven by a negro. He was the one who had to do all the work while his master was having a good time in a nearby brothel, he told us. He lay in ambush. A man also wearing a mask came out of a house. The negro jumped on him, knocked him unconscious, dragged him into the carriage and stabbed him. Then we went to the edge of the river. He cut up the body on the riverbank. Rapace helped him – he used to be a butcher. We put the pieces in the two barrels. Then he ordered us to dump everything in the knacker's yard and paid us our dues.'

'Did you see the dead man's face?'

'Yes, a bourgeois, of about fifty.'

'Then what?'

'Off we went to Montfaucon. There was a hell of a wind; it looked as if it was going to damn well snow. An awful place. Once we got to the knacker's yard we emptied the barrel and, to be frank with you, we even messed up the head a bit, like the negro wanted us to.'

'Was he there?'

'No, no. He'd left us by the river. He had to disappear to pretend he was the one who'd been killed.'

'Did he say anything else?'

'Rapace did try to find out who the dead man was. All he said was it was a married man who'd got in his master's way.'

'Very well. What time was the meeting on the building site of Place Louis XV?'

'Around ten o'clock, I told you. Then the man was killed at around midnight. After he'd been moved from the riverside we set off for La Courtille. Half past two was sounding on a bell tower. One hour later everything was finished.'

'What did you do with the cart and the barrels?'

'Your men must have found them, if they know how to look.'

'Bricart, your version of events will be checked and you'll be faced with witnesses. I hope for your sake you've been telling the truth. Otherwise I can assure you you won't escape torture.'

The man did not reply. He was lost in thought. Now all Nicolas had before him was an old man on whom he could have taken pity, except that the horror of what he had reluctantly admitted to suggested he was capable of even worse. Nicolas picked up the lantern again and banged on the door for the gaoler to let him out. The cell was left in darkness once more.

*

This interrogation left Nicolas feeling frustrated. Many aspects of Bricart's account seemed odd. If the old soldier were to be believed, then Semacgus was once again the main suspect. In that case Saint-Louis, who was still alive and was acting as his master's accomplice, had run away or was hiding somewhere. Who was this angel with the look of the devil, a description that inevitably suggested Mauval? And what about those three mysterious masked figures who had ordered the murder and its macabre enactment? Was it really a woman that Bricart had seen? The timescale tallied very well with all the witness accounts. He remained puzzled, however, and wanted to be quite honest with himself. Was it possible that his friendship with Semacgus had affected his judgement and was preventing him from admitting that the navy surgeon might be guilty? What worried him about Bricart's account was that it was too polished, too perfect in its detail. Furthermore, it seemed unlikely that the motive for Lardin's murder should have been so clearly expressed, with the risk that the two accomplices might use it against those behind the deed to blackmail them, or to defend themselves if accused . . . As for Mauval, whose baleful influence was again evident, he was so well protected that nothing could be expected from him as a potential witness.

In the end Nicolas kept coming back to Semacgus. Was it possible that passion had led him to crime? Was Louise Lardin his accomplice? Or Descart? Anything was possible, and the worst thing was that everything was inextricably linked. All this uncertainty made his heart pound.

To calm himself he began to write a detailed account for Monsieur de Sartine, just in case he was not able to have access to him the following day. In fact this exercise enabled him to marshal his ideas. Some things had still not become clear in his mind. He tried to pick up the thread of his dialogue with Bricart, remembering what had struck him in passing, what was missing from the account, and the fleeting impressions that had gone through his mind. He was just dozing off with his pen in his hand when Bourdeau appeared with that characteristic expression of his when he was the bearer of news.

'Bourdeau, you've got something to tell me . . .'

'Yes, Monsieur. We have, in the course of our search . . .'

'Found a cart and two bloodstained barrels.'

Bourdeau smiled.

'Congratulations, Monsieur. Bricart talked.'

'Oh, don't celebrate too soon. What he told me doesn't simplify anything, it only makes our task more arduous. Any other discoveries?'

'The place is full of items, stolen no doubt. I've searched Rapace. Apart from odds and ends I only found a broken brass watch.'

Bourdeau handed him a large handkerchief which, once untied, revealed a few sols, a small dark-wood snuffbox, a ball of string and the watch in question. Nicolas immediately launched into the account of Bricart's interrogation. Three o'clock soon struck and they decided to take some rest. Nicolas returned by cab to Rue Montmartre.

Monday 12 February 1761

He had a short night's sleep. He was up by six o'clock. After a quick wash he went down to the pantry where a horrified Marion helped him to change his dressings. He had time for a cup of chocolate and a freshly baked roll. The old housekeeper told him that the day before Monsieur de Noblecourt had suffered a severe attack of gout, as he had predicted. He had been forced to stay in his armchair with his foot wrapped in wadding. It was only towards morning that he had been able to lie down and have some rest. According to Marion it wasn't so much his appetite for food as the white wine which was at fault, and the thirsty prattler had drunk it in copious quantities. She knew from experience its harmful effect on her master's health.

Nicolas went on foot to Rue Neuve-Saint-Augustin. He derived a childlike pleasure from leaving his footprints in the overnight snow that was still virgin and clean. On arriving at the Hôtel de Gramont he asked a manservant if the Lieutenant General of Police were available, and was shown in almost immediately. Monsieur de Sartine, who wore a morning gown, was staring at a large open wardrobe containing dozens of wigs. Nicolas knew that every morning he enjoyed admiring and handling his collection.

'As you have disturbed me so early, Nicolas, you are, I take it, bringing me what I've been waiting for. Don't worry, I am joking. If that were the case I'd know already.'

'No, Monsieur, but I've made progress. I'm following several leads.'

'Several? That means you must think none of them are definite.'

'It would be more accurate to say that we are dealing with several plots, all of them interconnected.'

He gave a brief summary of the latest developments in the investigation. The Lieutenant General listened with his back to

Nicolas, busily grooming one of his treasures with a small silver brush.

'You're trying to pull the wool over my eyes, Monsieur. Everything is crystal clear. Semacgus is in your hands, and what's more he's the suspect in both cases. The circumstantial evidence, not to say the proof, is mounting.'

He swung round and continued his train of thought.

'If everything is connected and if Lardin is dead it should be easy to find you-know-what.'

'I think, Monsieur, that nothing in this investigation is simple and I doubt whether Bricart told me the whole truth.'

'Threaten him with torture and use it if necessary.'

'He's an old soldier . . .'

'First and foremost he's a gallows bird. So none of this sensitivity for him or for Semacgus, who I know is a friend of yours. Don't forget that this involves the King and the State. Leave the sentimentality to our philosopher friends. The very things they criticise in their own country are commonplace in the states of the foreign princes they praise to the skies and expect pensions from. By the way, Bourdeau spoke to me about your accounts. I've ordered my officials to allocate you more funds. Don't economise. The stakes are high. You don't have much time left but you seem to be making progress. Thank Bourdeau on my behalf for having kept you with us.'

Nicolas went back to the Châtelet, his head full of Monsieur de Sartine's words. Should he subject Bricart to torture? The decision was his and it tormented him constantly. He had already been present at some sessions – like other things it had formed part of his apprenticeship at the Châtelet – and he knew that very few of its victims could endure it and all too often it led to false confessions. He remembered having had a long discussion with Semacgus on this subject. The surgeon considered that excessive pain destroyed the ability to reason in those who suffered it, and that torture, which was inhumane in itself, should be abolished like all abuses inflicted by man on his fellow creatures. Nicolas had not been able to find convincing arguments to counter these observations that further undermined his already shaky belief in the practice. The worst thing was to imagine Bricart tortured, his body swollen by water he had been forced to swallow, or his only good leg imprisoned between wooden planks. They would not even be able to drive the wedges in. Nicolas was quite prepared to accept that the old soldier was a criminal, but he still imagined him as a raw recruit, torn from the bosom of his family. Today he was merely an old man who might be experiencing remorse, but Nicolas could see the desperate adolescent that the royal militia had cast into the horrors of war.

With this thought he arrived at the Châtelet where he found Bourdeau putting the finishing touches to his report on the events of the previous night. When he looked up at Nicolas, the young man was struck by the unusual gravity of his expression.

'Monsieur, I have some bad news for you. Bricart hanged himself during the night in his cell. The gaoler discovered the body this morning when he was doing his rounds.'

Nicolas remained speechless for a moment.

'What did he hang himself with?' he stammered at last. 'He'd been searched when he was admitted . . .'

'A leather strap.'

Bourdeau turned away to avoid the look of horror on Nicolas's face. The young man pictured himself again untying the prisoner's hands. At the end of the interrogation he had forgotten the long leather strap that had fallen to the floor. The narrow beam of light from his lantern had prevented him from seeing it.

Bourdeau handed him his report along with the tied handkerchief containing the items found on Rapace. He slipped it all into his coat pocket mechanically.

XIII

IN AT THE KILL

> Where is the wingèd flight
> Or the escape to the depths of the cave
> That would save me from a death by stoning?
>
> EURIPIDES

In the cell nothing had been touched. They gazed at Bricart's body, hanging at the end of its rope like a dangling puppet. The strap, which had been slung around a bar, had been tied with a slipknot. The prisoner had hoisted himself on to the plank-bed, then flung himself backwards with the help of his wooden leg, which remained jammed at right angles to the wall. This accidental arrangement added a grotesque touch, as if the old soldier had been in the process of climbing up the wall. Bourdeau shook his head and put his hand on Nicolas's shoulder.

'This is one of those misadventures that are common in the job. Don't fret about it and don't blame yourself for this mistake.'

'A mistake is just what it is, though.'

'That's not the word I meant to use. Let's call it fate. Destiny offered him a way out. There was no dignified solution for him because he was bound to be tortured and sent to the gallows. As for the rest, let me tell you as a friend that a proper interrogation should never be conducted by one person alone. Haste is a bad counsellor. Another person can see what's been forgotten. You simply thought you were doing the right thing at the time. And, another thing, remember that a man who wants to die will always find a way. In this case it was that wretched strap that served the purpose.'

'Bourdeau, are we certain at least that it was suicide? Someone might have wanted to stop him talking.'

'I did wonder about it. However, I've seen a lot of people who have hanged themselves because I've been involved in dozens of cases of suicide. Without being an expert like our friend Sanson, I do know something about the subject. And it is, I must admit, a tricky one. There's been a great deal of scholarly discussion about how to decide whether someone found hanged committed suicide or was murdered.'

'So what are your conclusions?'

Bourdeau went up to the body and turned it round. The wooden leg fell back down. The body seemed both fatter and shorter.

'Look carefully, Monsieur. The face is bloated and purplish, the lips twisted, the eyes protruding and the tongue seems swollen and clenched between the teeth. The position of the strap has left a mark on the neck, with bruises under the throat. Lastly, the fingers are bluish and tensed, as if the hand was continuing to clutch something. These details are conclusive. There is no doubt that this was suicide.'

'You're right, Bourdeau,' Nicolas sighed.

The situation had to be accepted. Thanks to the understanding way in which the inspector had couched his criticism in the form of advice, Nicolas felt less remorseful.

'Anyway,' said Bourdeau, 'if he hadn't killed himself this way, he would have found another. He had the means.'

He pointed to the bottle of brandy and the cup that had rolled onto the floor.

'I've learnt my lesson,' said Nicolas, 'and I'm more determined than ever to see this through.'

He felt the anger rising within him at this waste of a life that had been shattered twice, but was now destroyed for ever. He vowed to find those responsible for pushing Bricart to the brink. A cold determination now overcame his sense of bewilderment.

'This death, as well as Rapace's, must remain a secret,' Nicolas decreed. 'In the latter case I'm afraid it might already be too late; the real culprits are spying on us. It's essential for them still to believe that Bricart is alive: they'll feel threatened by his evidence or his confessions. We must go on the offensive and take them by surprise.'

'How do you intend to proceed?' asked Bourdeau.

'Let's take stock. We have two definite murders. The first may be Lardin's; the second is Descart's. We have one person who is missing, dead or has run away: Saint-Louis. We have two women. The first is Louise Lardin, married to one of the missing men, and brazenly just pretending to mourn him. She is also the mistress of one of the dead men, Descart, and of two of the suspects, Semacgus and Mauval. The second, Marie, has been sent away or is missing, and it's difficult to know whether she should be classified as a suspect or a victim. Notice that Louise Lardin seems at once to be involved with everything and sure of being beyond the reach of the law. As for Semacgus, his name crops up with disturbing regularity.'

Nicolas was beginning to have his doubts about the surgeon.

He thought back to the initial lies, which discredited everything that had followed, and the repeated protestations of sincerity. Semacgus did not have a solid alibi for either the first or the second murder. He could also be a suspect in Saint-Louis's disappearance since, if he were dead, his master had been the last person to see him. In addition Descart had clearly accused him of his coachman's murder. Nicolas felt he had to free himself from Semacgus's hold over him. The man was all the more elusive because he lived alone and no one knew anything about him.

The last but by no means least of Nicolas's concerns was to get his hands on the King's papers. This was what he would be judged and assessed on. It would be just about acceptable to abandon to their fate some obscure individuals whose presumed guilt could not be proven. The failure to find letters that compromised those in power would never be forgiven. Sartine had made this quite clear to him.

'If I follow you correctly,' said Bourdeau, 'Rue des Blancs-Manteaux requires our close attention.'

'You understand me perfectly. That is where we must concentrate our efforts. On Madame Lardin and then Semacgus. Don't forget those strange reports from our informers positioned around the commissioner's residence, all those unexplained comings and goings. But for us to be effective we need to act quickly. The element of surprise will have the greatest impact and will combine the advantage of the well-laid trap with the thoroughness of a proper search.'

Nicolas had Bricart's body taken to the back of the vault in the Basse-Geôle. It was the third body to be deposited there in a week. What exactly was the connection between the remains found in Montfaucon, Descart's body and that of an old soldier who'd lost his way in life? Once he had worked that out, the mystery would almost be solved. Bourdeau had gathered his men together. Several officers and guards would accompany them. Three cabs set off noisily from beneath the porch of the Châtelet. They had to make their way through congested streets and crowds of people had to move out of the way as the convoy approached.

They closed off Rue des Blancs-Manteaux and men were sent round to the back to prevent anyone escaping through the garden. Accompanied by two officers, Nicolas and Bourdeau went up to the door and knocked loudly. There was a long wait before Louise Lardin appeared wearing a morning gown, with her hair undone. She looked as if she had only just got out of bed. There was a sharp exchange of words between her and Nicolas, but when he informed her of the official nature of the search she seemed to calm down. Bourdeau whispered to Nicolas that she was using delaying tactics. She was presumably attempting to give someone else time to escape. And yet the latest report by one of the spies had said that she was alone in the house.

After requesting her to stay in the dining room under guard, he asked Bourdeau to go up with him to the first-floor bedrooms. Louise's room was a complete mess. The bedclothes were rumpled and the pillows still showed where two heads had rested on them. Bourdeau put his hand under the cover; the bed was still warm on both sides. Madame Lardin had not been alone when they entered the house.

An officer was sent to search the house from top to bottom, beginning with the attic. He came back empty-handed. Nicolas systematically emptied the chests of drawers and the wardrobes. He seized a cape and a black silk mask, as well as some shoes, and put them all into a sheet, which he tied up and sealed. Amongst the commissioner's belongings he could find no sign of the leather doublet or the other cape. Marie Lardin's bedroom did not look any different. However, there was one surprise in store for him: on opening the wardrobe whose contents had puzzled him on his last search, he discovered it was almost empty. Dresses, skirts, mantles and shoes had disappeared. Had Marie returned? Or else . . . He vowed to question Louise about this. In one final inspection he discovered the young woman's missal at the bottom of a drawer in a small marquetry table. He had often noticed this little book with its blue velvet binding, which she took with her to Mass. Why had she left it behind? She was very attached to it because it came from her mother. Intrigued and moved, Nicolas began to leaf through the little book. A note fell from it, identical to the commissioner's mysterious messages. This one said:

> *Restoring to their owner*
> *The secrets of the King*

So Lardin had put a third message in a place where he was sure his daughter would find it one day. Had that been the case? Marie only used her Book of Hours when she went to Mass, at least that was what Nicolas assumed. Bourdeau had not noticed the discovery; he put it away in his pocket. He would need to compare this message with the other two in his possession. He was fervently hoping that the reference to the King might relate to the letters that he had been given the task of finding.

Next Nicolas took Bourdeau up to what used to be his private domain on the second floor. He felt a little nostalgic on seeing it again, but he found nothing suspicious there. They went back to the ground floor for a careful examination of the library. Inside a copy of the poems of Horace they found an invoice from a craftsman, a cabinetmaker, for some work that had been paid for on 15 January 1761. The recent date intrigued Nicolas and he took the document. Had it been deliberately hidden in this book, or was it simply used as a bookmark? It would be no trouble to check what this invoice related to. He kept quiet about this clue, too.

They joined Louise Lardin in the dining room. She was sitting bolt upright on the edge of a chair.

'Madame, I won't bother to ask if you were alone. We know you weren't. The area is under surveillance. Your visitor won't get far.'

'You are very offensive and presumptuous, Nicolas,' she replied.

'That is irrelevant, Madame. I would be grateful if you would tell me what has happened to the clothes belonging to your stepdaughter, Mademoiselle Marie. I would advise you to reply without protest, otherwise you will be made to do so forcibly in the Conciergerie.'[1]

'So I'm a suspect, am I?'

'Answer my question.'

'I gave away my stepdaughter's old clothes to the poor. She has decided to enter a nunnery.'

'I hope for your sake that this point can be confirmed. Now, Inspector, we're going to search the kitchen.'

Louise was about to react but quickly restrained herself.

'You won't find anything there.'

'Bourdeau, give the lady your arm. She will act as our guide.'

The kitchen was freezing cold. Nicolas would have bet that the stove had not been lit for several days. Bourdeau began to sniff with a disgusted look on his face.

'What a stench!' he exclaimed.

'What!' said Nicolas ironically, 'Don't you find this aroma pleasant? Ask Madame Lardin, then, the reason for this filthy smell. She'll tell you, I think, that she's very keen on game that's been well hung.'

'What do you mean?'

'There's some big game down below, in the cellar, just rotting away. How do you explain that, Madame?'

For the first time since they had arrived, Louise betrayed some signs of anxiety. She leant against the sideboard.

'I got rid of my cook,' she replied, 'and I still haven't found anyone to replace her. You, Monsieur, are in a good position to know how skilled she was at her job. I do not stoop to menial tasks around the house. I leave that to the skivvies. As soon as I find someone, everything will be cleaned up.'

'And does the smell not bother you?' Bourdeau asked.

Louise ignored the question and made as if to go out.

'Don't leave us, Madame,' ordered Nicolas. 'Officer, keep an eye on this woman. We're going down to the cellar.'

Nicolas poured some vinegar from a china container. He moistened his handkerchief and suggested Bourdeau do the same. The inspector refused and waved his pipe, which he quickly stuffed and lit.

'I think we're ready. Let's take this candlestick.'

As soon as they were downstairs and despite their

precautions, the smell became unbearable. The boar was in a state of putrefaction. Strips of flesh had fallen onto the ground and were smothered in a slowly moving layer, a wriggling mass of crawling creatures. Nicolas stopped Bourdeau as he was about to move on. He took off his boots, crouched down and with the light from the candle examined the floor. His search led him to a wooden frame with bottles arranged along its shelves. He grasped something and showed it to Bourdeau. It was the squashed stub of a church candle. He stood up again, put his boots back on, called Bourdeau to help and began to clear the bottles off the shelves. Leaning against the wooden structure, Bourdeau suddenly saw it slide along beside the wall to reveal an old door.

'What would I do without you?' Nicolas said. 'You're like Alexander the Great. While the rest of us are struggling in vain, you cut the Gordian knot.'

'I didn't do it deliberately,' the inspector replied, 'but I have a feeling this door has a lot to tell us. You are the one who deserves the credit, Monsieur. All I did was to follow you. You give a very good imitation of a bloodhound on the scent. You really know how to sniff things out.'

'At this very moment I wish I couldn't sniff at all,' Nicolas said, putting his handkerchief to his face again.

They burst out laughing, relieving the mounting tension somewhat. Nicolas pushed the door, which had no lock. They noticed that the frame could be moved aside from the other side. A rope fastened to one side ran through a hole made in the door. One only had to pull it for the loose frame to move along and free up the opening. This was the explanation of the mysterious comings and goings of the visitors and occupants of the Lardin household. The police spies were obviously of no use faced with a system like this, and the stranger who had been with Louise had without doubt bolted this way. It remained to be seen where the exit led.

They went down some more steps. The vile smell of rotting flesh was becoming stronger in the stale underground air. After a few paces they had to turn twice to the left before descending further. Nicolas heard Bourdeau cocking his pistol. They were going through one of those underground passages that have criss-crossed Paris since time immemorial. Hordes of rats seemed to appear at their feet from nowhere, as if queuing up in impatient rows, with the biggest ones jumping over the rest. There had to be some reason for their shrill shrieks and frenzied excitement. The passage led into a vaulted room. Nicolas stopped, stricken with horror at the scene before him. Just as the strips of flesh from the boar had a life of their own, here lay another seething mass only a few paces away from them. Bourdeau, who was behind him, could not stifle a cry. To get nearer they had to kick away rodents that became more and more aggressive, baring their teeth as they squealed. They could see the gleam of hundreds of red dots looking towards the candlelight. Bourdeau pushed Nicolas aside. He had taken a flask of alcohol out of his pocket. He emptied the contents onto his handkerchief, set fire to it and threw it onto the rats nearest them. A few of the beasts began to sizzle, unleashing terror amidst the vile horde. Within a few moments the panic was general and the area temporarily cleared.

Nicolas would wonder for a long time to come whether the vision of that vast expanse of rats was not preferable to the sight that then confronted them. There was a body, that of a human being, though barely recognisable as such. Monsieur de Noblecourt's scenes of bodily decay were pale imaginings compared with the vision of this decomposed and half-eaten corpse. The rib cage had burst open and bones were poking through. The face was unrecognisable but the head was bald. Bourdeau and Nicolas recognised Commissioner Lardin at the same time. There was no doubt about the identity of the corpse. Bourdeau gave Nicolas a nudge.

'Look, those two broken teeth to the front. And the bald skull. It definitely is Lardin.'

'There's something odd,' said Nicolas. 'Look at his stomach, and those rats that have been dead for several days, all around the scattered entrails. Sick?'

'Or poisoned.'

'Poisoned in that case by the viscera of a man who died of poisoning.'

'And who handles poison? Cooks to combat vermin and rodents. Gardeners to get rid of moles, and doctors or apothecaries in their remedies.'

'Catherine wouldn't hurt a fly,' Nicolas remarked. 'Although it didn't go for Louise Lardin, as far as the commissioner was concerned Catherine was one of the few people who had something good to say about him.'

'First of all we need to establish how long he's been dead, and this may provide a useful alibi for some people.'

'Given the state of the body, that's hardly going to be easy. There's still the possibility of suicide.'

Bourdeau was thinking.

'Have you noticed that all the dead man's clothes have disappeared?' he said. 'It's not very common for people in a state of desperation to do away with themselves in such a state of undress.'

'There's no point in wasting words. We first need to find out where this underground passage leads.'

At the end of the vault more steps led up into a gently sloping corridor, narrow and low-roofed. At its far end was a faint glimmer of light. They came across a pile of planks which they cleared away without difficulty. They were now inside a stone building, a sort of disused chapel penetrated by daylight through narrow loopholes. They still had to clamber over heaps of brushwood before finally uncovering a stock of church candles. On one side were tied-up bundles of them and on the other a stack of half-used tapers. They pushed open a door which led into a garden they immediately recognised as that of the Blancs-Manteaux monastery. That explained everything. Their spies could keep their eyes wide open or increase their vigilance as much as they liked, but this passageway enabled a veil of secrecy to be cast over anyone entering or leaving the Lardins' house. That was why one informer thought he had seen the commissioner running towards the church. He had specifically mentioned his leather doublet. But had it been the commissioner, or someone impersonating him so that people would think him still alive? While the commissioner's clothes were still missing the doubt would remain. They turned round and put everything back in place to hide the fact they had been there.

'I've got an idea,' said Bourdeau. 'It may not work but it's worth a try. Imagine that the escapee has been caught. You witness the scene. You go back up on your own to the kitchen. You inform Madame Lardin that her visitor has been nabbed, that he's talked and that I'm holding him under guard. Then we'll see how she reacts.'

Nicolas quickly assessed all the possible consequences of this bold suggestion.

'There's more to be said for than against it,' he concluded. 'I'll spice it up a bit by improvising according to the good lady's mood.'

Silently they went back the way they had come. The rats reappeared but wisely moved aside as soon as the two came near. Bourdeau remained in the cellar and Nicolas climbed the stairs to the kitchen. Closely watched by the officer, Louise Lardin was still leaning against the sideboard. She did not see him straight away. Nicolas thought she looked pale and much older.

'Madame,' he began, 'I don't think there's any need for me to describe what we found in the secret passage of your house. But what you don't know is that we have arrested the person who escaped from your bedroom when we arrived, just as he was attempting to leave the Blancs-Manteaux monastery. He has confessed to the crime.'

Shock, terror and then calculation could be read in succession on Louise's face. She lunged at him, ready to scratch his eyes out. Nicolas had to grasp her by the wrists to protect his face while the officer gripped her around the waist. Eventually they managed to force her into a chair.

'What have you done to him?' she yelled. 'You're wrong, you lunatics. It wasn't him. He's got nothing to do with it.'

She was wild with fury and her whole body arched.

'Who was it, then?'

'The other one, the coward, the pig, the man who wanted me, then didn't. The one with scruples, qualms as he called them.

Who didn't want to deceive his friend. Oh! The man of honour who slept with the wife of someone he owed so much to. The one who came to our rendezvous. He was in the brothel with Lardin and Descart, at La Paulet's, an old friend, as you know. He turned up late and shamefaced, to get under my skirts. He needed it. He couldn't do without me. He thought Lardin was out on the town, so he stayed. But Lardin came back earlier than expected. They had a fight and Semacgus strangled him. Afterwards, what could you expect me to do? The wife, the husband, the lover . . . I was an accomplice. The sentence would be death, for sure. We undressed the body and dragged it into the underground passage. All we had to do was wait for the rats to clean it all up. Then we would dispose of what remained, a little bag of bones to throw into the Seine at night. We had to get that shrew of a cook out of the way because she poked her nose in everywhere. I threw her out of the house as soon as possible before things in the cellar . . . We put the wild boar there, for one smell to cover up the other. I'm innocent. I haven't done anything. I did not kill anybody.'

'So according to you Dr Semacgus was caught in the act by your husband and killed him in a brawl.'

'Yes.'

Nicolas decided to play what he thought was his trump card.

'If Mauval is innocent, why did he confess?'

'I don't know. To save me. He loves me. I want to see him. Let me go!'

She fainted. They laid her out on the table and Nicolas rubbed her temples with vinegar. When she remained unconscious he ordered her to be taken immediately to the Conciergerie, where she could be given medical attention.

Bourdeau, who had been listening to everything from the staircase to the cellar, reappeared. Nicolas sensed that he was impatient to comment on Louise Lardin's revelations.

'It worked,' he said, 'but it's raised as many questions as it's answered.'

'You'll have noted, Bourdeau, that she claims Lardin was strangled. Only when the body has been taken for post-mortem and carefully examined will we know the truth. Besides, our reasons for suspecting the use of poison are perhaps not incompatible with what she's told us. Remember Sanson's conclusions about Descart's death, poisoned then suffocated. There's a similarity here that the facts may or may not confirm. If that were to be the case, Semacgus would be in a very difficult position. He could have killed here as well as in Vaugirard. We cannot rule him out of either case as he had motives to murder both Descart and Lardin. Even though for Descart the medical rivalry and controversy about the use of bleeding seem rather flimsy grounds . . .'

'Are you forgetting that Descart accused him of having killed Saint-Louis?'

'No, but in the version of events I was considering, Saint-Louis wasn't dead but had acted as his master's accomplice.'

'And where does Mauval fit into all this?'

'His presence can be felt everywhere. He's meddling in a business that I'm not at liberty to reveal, but which has some bearing on this case.'

'Oh,' said Bourdeau wryly, 'I know that you have friends in high places and that your investigation doesn't stop at solving Lardin's murder. Our police force has its black sheep and Monsieur de Sartine doesn't want rumours to spread. That's why you suddenly broke with the normal rules.'

Nicolas did not answer. He preferred the inspector to be content with a hypothesis that was not too far from the truth but did not give much away about an affair of State that he was under strict instructions not to divulge. Bourdeau for his part, even if he felt slightly bitter about his chief's discretion, had sufficient experience and self-discipline not to hold it against him. Nicolas was sorry not to be able to call on the inspector for this vital part of the investigation where his talents would have been extremely useful, but he fully understood the Lieutenant General's concern to avoid unnecessary discussion of matters to do with the King. The young man did not enjoy the constant self-control this necessary discretion imposed on him and which, as he understood, would be part of his life from now on. This never-ending effort was a trial; it made him feel somewhat melancholy, but it also gave him new strength. He had long since realised that this was the force that would shape his destiny; what is more, he knew that secrecy was deep down one of the essential features of his make-up. He felt the need for other people, but was also concerned not to let them intrude on his life. Like certain shy animals, his first instinct was to retreat when others tried to come close too suddenly. He had not chosen his job but, if his qualities were developing, that was presumably because it suited his inherent skills.

The body was placed in a coffin and transported to the Basse-Geôle to be examined. A messenger was dispatched to Sanson.

Nicolas, who wanted to prove to Bourdeau that he had learnt his lesson after Bricart's suicide, decided that they would both go to question Semacgus at the Bastille. After he had ordered an officer to keep Louise Lardin in solitary confinement they got back into their carriage to go to the royal fortress. On the way Nicolas thought about the best tactics for questioning Semacgus. There were two pitfalls to avoid: being taken in by a man who had an advantage over him in terms of age and experience, and his feelings of friendship for a suspect in two murder cases.

Nicolas was only dimly aware of the bustle in the streets where house-fronts were being decorated in preparation for the procession of the Fatted Ox. However, although a newcomer to the city, he knew perfectly well that this procession of the animal bedecked with flowers, ribbons and all sorts of adornments often caused problems for the police because of the excesses and debauchery it encouraged in the crowd. The procession set off from the Apport-Paris near the Grande Boucherie opposite the Châtelet, then paid its respects to the Parlement on Île de la Cité. After that it returned to its starting-point, where the animal was then slaughtered and cut up. But sometimes the butchers' boys, the organisers of the festivity who were anxious to make it last longer, did not wait until the last Thursday before Lent to parade but began their celebrations on the Tuesday or Wednesday, taking a different route from the official one, around other parts of the city.

Soon they came within sight of the Bastille. To their left, the square of Porte Saint-Antoine led into the *faubourg*. They turned off to the right and went alongside the ditches. Nicolas shuddered when he saw the four enormous towers overlooking the city. They had to go through several gates at the end of the bridge leading to the main entrance of the state prison. Bourdeau, who knew the place well, reported to the guards on duty and to the head gaoler. The man held out a cold, clammy hand to Nicolas, who only just managed to stop himself recoiling from this cross-eyed and freakish-looking individual who walked with a waddle. He picked up a lantern and led them towards one of the towers.

They went inside the stone monster. The enormous bulk of the fortress became more and more oppressive as its thick walls closed in around them. They might have belonged to some sick being whose symptoms were the discoloration and flaking of the skin. There was no interplay of light and shade; the two elements never mixed. Only a few shafts of daylight managed to pierce the darkness of the vaults, but they spread no further. The narrowness of the openings to the outside was such that these fleeting apparitions faded as swiftly as they had come. However, where for centuries they had struck the stone in the same place, its surface had taken on a whitish-blue tinge contrasting with the dull grey of other blocks nearby. But one's eye could not rest for long on these paler tints. Everywhere, in the corners, nooks and crannies and the dead-ends of this immense maze, strange damp mosses covered the main body of the prison like leprous sores. Coils of fungi hanging in the air like heavy spiders' webs used up the little oxygen there was in this confined atmosphere. Strange mineral concretions, grey verging on green, their sharp points glinting in the light of the lantern, betrayed the presence of saltpetre and salts that oozed from the limestone walls as a result of the constant humidity. It was slippery underfoot in the gloomy passageways, where the rotting, spongy ground, reminiscent of an underwater cave carpeted with seaweed, turned into mud. Everywhere was a dank, pervasive smell that was almost palpable, so oppressive that it was difficult to breathe. It reminded Nicolas of the collegiate church in Guérande when on very rainy days it became a steaming crypt with water trickling down its granite stone walls, and it reeked of cold incense, damp and the clinging smell of decomposition that rose up from the ancient vaults.

To that was added the smell of dirt and grease from the head gaoler's grey twill coat. His gasping breaths and the sound of their footsteps were the only signs of humanity in this deserted place. After slowly turning the key several times, he eventually opened a heavy oak door reinforced with iron bands. Nicolas was surprised by the enormous size of the cell. The room was hexagonal with three steps that led down into it, adding to the impression of height. Three more steps at the opposite end led up to a narrow opening with thick bars. To the right was a bed on which Nicolas saw, to his surprise, white sheets and a drugget[2] blanket. They did not immediately notice Semacgus, who was hidden by the open door. As they entered they found him sitting at a small table practically inside the fireplace. He was writing, and the noise of the lock had apparently not disturbed his work. He called out in a bad-tempered voice:

'Not before time! It's devilish cold in here and I was running out of wood.'

As there was no reply he turned round stiffly to discover a pensive Nicolas, a calm and collected Bourdeau and a deeply anxious gaoler.

He got up and went over to meet them.

'Seeing you, my friends, makes me think I'm going to be taken out to be hanged!' he exclaimed.

'It's a bit early to hang you,' said Nicolas, 'but the purpose of our visit is to question you about some serious developments.'

'For heaven's sake! It looks as if we're going to go over old ground again. Nicolas, you veer from one extreme to the other. Please make up your mind about me and spare me His Majesty's hospitality. I've been doing my sums and it's already cost me a fortune even though I haven't been locked up here for long. Four pounds and four sols for food, one pound for wine, forty sols for the wood that still hasn't come and, pardon me for the sordid details, one pound and two sols for the sheets and a chamber pot. The filthy piece of rag I had for a blanket when I arrived in this palace gave me a delightful rash that makes me scratch until I bleed. However, I mustn't complain. I'm lucky not to be sleeping on straw, but you must admit that it's hard on an innocent man to be deprived of his freedom and as I understand that I've been imprisoned by a *lettre de cachet* I fear that my case may never come to court and that I will rot here until the end of time.'

'Our conversation will probably determine whether you are freed or not,' Nicolas replied curtly.

'I prefer that word to interrogation. You always try a bit too hard, Nicolas. It's just lack of experience, because you're basically a good sort.'

'That's probably because the clarity of your answers is not always what it should be.'

'I'm not very fond of people speaking in riddles. There's always someone who gets eaten up in the end. Your tone is not very friendly, my dear Nicolas.'

'Please remember, Monsieur, that at this moment you are dealing with a policeman.'

'Very well,' sighed the surgeon.

Semacgus walked over to his straw-bottomed chair and sat

astride it as was his habit, with his arms on the back and his chin in his hands.

'I would like to return with you to the events of that evening in the Dauphin Couronné,' Nicolas began.

'But I've told you everything.'

'It took two attempts. And what interests me now is the second part of the evening. One of the girls has said that you left her almost as soon as you went into her room. What time was it, as a matter of fact? Last time you wriggled your way out of the question.'

'How should I know? Between midnight and one o'clock. I don't keep an eye on my watch all the time.'

'At what time did you arrive at Rue des Blancs-Manteaux to meet Louise Lardin?'

'When I didn't find my carriage or Saint-Louis, who was supposed to be waiting for me in Rue du Faubourg-Saint-Honoré, I went to look for a cab, which took me a good quarter of an hour. I must have reached Rue des Blancs-Manteaux at around two o'clock.'

'Could you describe your arrival in detail?'

'As I already told you, when Louise put a lighted candle in the window in her bedroom overlooking the street it meant that the coast was clear. However, that morning there was no candle and this time she was standing at the door wearing a mask and waiting to let me in herself. She had only just come back from a Carnival ball.'

'So the whole family was having a good time!'

Bourdeau coughed and motioned to Nicolas that he would like to speak.

'You said "this time". What do you mean by that?'

'That usually I went straight to her bedroom.'

'So you have a key to the front door?'

'That's not what I said.'

Bourdeau took a step forward and leant over towards the surgeon.

'So what did you say? It's high time you stopped misleading justice, Monsieur. It can be good-natured, but it is fearsome when angry and it is pointing its finger at you.'

Semacgus looked at Nicolas, but the young man clearly nodded his approval of his deputy's words.

'To tell you the truth, I came in through the monastery of the Blancs-Manteaux, through a garden gate. I hadn't mentioned it before because the detail didn't seem important. Louise had asked me to be discreet about this matter.'

'The Blancs-Manteaux monastery?' roared Bourdeau. 'What's that got to do with the Lardins?'

'The cellars of the monastery link up with those of the house. During the day you can go in through the church, which is open. At night through the garden gate, which I have a key to. Then you go through a disused chapel, down into the cellar, under the street and back up into the vault of the pantry.'

'And that particular morning?'

'Louise explained to me that, because of the recent snowfall, it was wiser not to go the usual way. That was why she was waiting for me.'

'Did that not surprise you? It was a rash thing to do.'

'I should remind you that I had on a cape and mask and that I could have been mistaken for Lardin. Besides, it was a serious point because the commissioner could also come back via the monastery and notice the footprints in the snow.'

'So Lardin knew about this passageway. Who else?'

'In the household? No one. Neither Catherine, nor Marie nor Nicolas, even though he lived there, knew this secret. None of them had noticed it, I'm convinced of that.'

Nicolas did not reply. He let Bourdeau continue the interrogation. He owed him that, and he was not unhappy to be able to sit back and think without having to intervene.

'Why did you repeatedly conceal this fact from us?'

'It was the Lardins' secret and I'd given my word.'

'Do you know, Monsieur, whether Commissioner Lardin realised that you were aware of this secret passage?'

'He certainly did not.'

'At what time did you leave, and by which route?'

'At around six o'clock, as I already told Nicolas, and through the front door.'

'By staying so long in the house, were you not taking the risk of being caught by her husband? Did you tell Madame Lardin about the commissioner's argument with Descart in the Dauphin Couronné?'

'She had assured me that he would not come home that night, and that as a precaution she had bolted both the cellar and front doors from the inside. So even if Lardin turned up unexpectedly he would have had to use the knocker to be let in. She had even planned to justify this unusual precaution by saying she was frightened that wild groups of masked revellers might suddenly turn up. Occasionally some of them burst into people's houses and carry on with their silly pranks.'

'But why block the passageway in the cellar? It was improbable if not almost inconceivable that revellers would come in that way if it was supposed to be secret. Her husband would have commented on that.'

'The fact that you have asked that question shows you know very little about women. Her aim was not to think about how odd it would be for revellers to come up through the cellar. Having the doors locked – as they most certainly were – made her feel quite secure. I don't see the use of picking up on contradictions she wasn't aware of herself. Besides, at the risk of being discourteous to the lady, at that particular moment her mind was on other things . . . You must excuse me for interrupting this civilised conversation but Phoebus is here to visit me.'

Semacgus rushed to the window and pressed his face to it. A ray of sunlight struck the wall at this spot and he took a sensual delight in its radiance.

'It's the only moment of sunshine,' he explained. 'I take advantage of it to treat my rash. I need a point of reference. What's the time? They took my watch away when I was admitted and the sun doesn't stay long enough for me to tell the time by it.'

Later Nicolas would remember having behaved like an automaton, driven by an irrepressible urge. He rummaged feverishly in his coat pocket and pulled out the packet of items found on Rapace. He took out the little brass watch and, as Bourdeau looked on intrigued, passed it to Semacgus without saying a word. The moment he took it he let out a scream and threw himself upon Nicolas, grabbing him by the shoulders.

'Where did you find this watch? Tell me, I beg of you.'

'Why do you ask?'

'It so happens, my dear policeman, that I know this watch

very well. I bought it myself as a gift for Saint-Louis. He played with it like a child and never stopped marvelling at it every time it struck. And now you're showing it to me again. I repeat my question: where did you find it and where is Saint-Louis?'

'Give me back that watch,' Nicolas said.

He went over to the window and examined the object closely. He was thinking so fast and so hard that he could hear his heart pounding. Everything was becoming clear. Why had he not realised before? And to think that this vital piece of evidence had been lying in his coat pocket and that he might not have thought of it, might have left it there and never have known. The little brass watch was broken and the hands were stuck at four minutes past midnight. So the range of possibilities was very narrow. Either the watch had already stopped, or it had been broken during some incident, or at a later time. If, contrary to what Bricart had said, Saint-Louis and not Lardin had been killed near his carriage, the watch might have been broken at the time of his murder. Now, if it had stopped at four minutes past midnight it was completely impossible – and there were plenty of witnesses – that Semacgus was responsible for the murder since he was at that very time at the Dauphin Couronné. Nicolas frantically ran through the consequences of this discovery.

Unaware that they already knew of it, Semacgus had just revealed to them the existence of the Blancs-Manteaux passageway, even if to an extent it had been forced out of him. It was true that confiding this information could also be an attempt to put them off the scent. Nicolas had learnt not to underestimate the navy surgeon's intelligence. Besides, the complexity of the murders of Lardin and Descart could lead to the most contradictory conclusions. He looked at Semacgus, who had sat down again. The surgeon seemed strained and suddenly older. Nicolas felt an instinctive pity for him, but prevented himself from expressing it. He had one final card up his sleeve: he felt the bitter need to use it.

'Semacgus, there's another very serious matter of which I must inform you. Commissioner Lardin's body was found this morning in the underground passage of Rue des Blancs-Manteaux, half eaten by rats. Louise Lardin expressly accuses you of having killed him. She claims he caught you playing your amorous games and the two of you had a fight.'

Semacgus raised his head. He looked pale and dejected.

'The woman will spare me nothing,' he sighed. 'I never saw Lardin that morning. I have nothing to do with his death. I'm telling you the truth. I feel as if I'm talking to the wall. You haven't answered my question. Where did you find this watch?'

'In the pocket of a poor devil who, in addition, was in possession of your bloodstained carriage. We have to leave you, Semacgus. Have no fear: if you are innocent, justice will be yours. Bourdeau and I guarantee it.'

He went up to Semacgus and held out his hand.

'I'm very sorry about Saint-Louis but I think there's little hope of finding him alive.'

They went out, impatient to get away from the Bastille where the surgeon and his gaoler seemed to be the only living souls. They were eager to get back into the open air and to escape the oppressive atmosphere of the place. The cold and the sun, which had reappeared, did them good.

Nicolas was pleased to discover that the inspector shared his opinion. He, too, had noted the constant ambiguity of what Semacgus said. The ironic detachment he had shown since the very beginning with regard to this business could only work against him. The only thing that could not be doubted was his unswerving affection for his black servant. And yet there was nothing in his statements to make them question the truth of what he had said. However, Bourdeau added, it was always the same story with the confounded fellow. You wanted to believe him even though all the unanswered questions left plenty of room for suspicion. The result was that, according to the moment or the mood, he seemed to be either a very clever impostor or a bungling innocent.

Nicolas enlightened Bourdeau on the incident with the watch. He thought it wiser to keep Semacgus in solitary confinement until the circumstances of Lardin's death became clear. Bourdeau remarked that Mauval should at the very least be questioned but he did not pursue the idea, much to Nicolas's relief. That would have meant going into details that he was not able to give.

As they talked, he was thinking that, even if the Lardin case was becoming clearer with the discovery of the commissioner's body, the same could not be said for the case involving the King's papers. And what about the messages Lardin had left? Would more be found, and for whom would they be intended? Had they been written before or after he disappeared? What was his motive in giving them to those close to him? Was it to further complicate the dangerous game he was playing? Nicolas was still convinced in his own mind that these messages were a kind of last will and testament. The mention of the King's name showed how important they were. The more he thought about it, the more certain he was that they were the key to the mystery. But there was considerable danger in drawing attention to this search. In the shadows lurked Mauval and the person directing him and others as well. Overtures had probably been made to agents of the warring powers. Paris was full of English, Prussian and even Austrian spies; France's allies were always on the lookout for possible ways of exerting pressure to strengthen the alliance and influence operations.

There was still the matter of finding Marie Lardin, whose exact involvement was unclear to the young man. He had not been convinced by her sudden and convenient religious calling and he felt sorry for the young woman, who was still a child. He remembered their last meeting that night on the staircase at the Lardins'. Then Marie's face faded in his mind before Isabelle's. Had he read the letter from Guérande in the right way? As he already knew, emotions were not always easy to put into words. Why did people have such difficulty expressing their feelings? He remembered a sentence of Pascal's that he had learnt at school: 'Words arranged differently have different meaning and meanings arranged differently have different effects.'[3] What until only recently had seemed to him full of artfulness now suddenly became touching in its awkwardness. He preferred to try and banish this thought. Nothing should distract him from his task.

Seeing Nicolas so blank-eyed and deep in reflection, Bourdeau had refrained from disturbing him. But the clatter of their carriage was already resounding beneath the archway of the Châtelet. Nicolas took Bourdeau off to the duty office. Commissioner Desnoyers from the district of Saint-Eustache was looking up some records. They had to wait for him to finish.

'We are at a crossroads,' Nicolas said. 'We need to decide which way to go.'

'You think Saint-Louis has been killed, don't you?'

'I don't think anything. I know that the watch given to him by his master was in the possession of Rapace and Bricart. What's more, if the remains found in Montfaucon are not Lardin's, who do they belong to? Why not to Saint-Louis? We must go by what we know and the facts in our possession. If the remains are those of his coachman, this doesn't necessarily clear Semacgus of the crime, quite the reverse. Remember Descart's allegations. In the case of Lardin, his wife's accusation is categorical. I think the law will follow its usual course so that for her and for Semacgus the use of preliminary torture will be inevitable. There are three deaths involved.'

'And what about Descart's murder?'

'The same thing applies. If we can pinpoint the time of Lardin's death then at least Descart can be ruled out, even if in his present state it doesn't make much difference to him. Have you sent for Sanson?'

Bourdeau nodded.

'Then we'll be able to clear Lardin, who also had every reason to want to eliminate his wife's cousin. As for Semacgus and Louise, we cannot exclude the possibility that they are guilty. We have yet to determine the reason why the mysterious murderer ransacked the doctor's house in Vaugirard.'

'And what about Mauval? You're still forgetting Mauval . . .'

'I'm not forgetting him at all; he's involved in everything, as I said before.'

'He seems to enjoy an extraordinary degree of impunity.'

'And because of that we must be certain before we strike.

You must never miss with a snake. You won't get a second chance. For the time being I need to think things over and give Monsieur de Sartine an account of the latest developments. Bourdeau, I want you to hurry Sanson up and report back to me as soon as possible. Check that Louise Lardin is kept in solitary confinement and that her cell is properly guarded. I don't want her to be eliminated.'

Just as they were about to go their separate ways, old Marie appeared. A young woman who 'looked a bit like a whore' was asking for Nicolas concerning an 'important and urgent matter'. Nicolas asked for her to be shown in and requested Bourdeau to stay. Nicolas recognised La Satin immediately. The brown cape she was wearing barely concealed her flimsy, very low-cut dress and her delicate ballroom shoes. Her make-up had come off and her cheeks were red with cold or emotion. Nicolas took her by the arm and offered her a seat. He made the introductions. Bourdeau lit his pipe.

'What are you doing here, Antoinette?'

'Well, Nicolas,' she said in a plaintive, childlike voice, 'you know that I work at La Paulet's. She's not an evil woman; she has her good points. The other evening . . .'

'Which evening?'

'Two days ago. I was in the corridor up in the loft where I was going to hang the washing to dry when suddenly I heard someone crying in a vacant room. I tried to find out who was there but the door was locked. What was I to do? I preferred not to get involved. The less you pry into other people's business, the better. But the following day I got caught up in it in spite of myself. La Paulet sent for me and gave me some of her very own ratafia. As you know she's very keen on her pick-me-up. She used to be very beautiful in her time; she's slept with marquises, but now she can't stand the sight of herself in the mirror.'

'So what did she want from you, then?'

'She simpered, said all sorts of nice things to me and in the end asked me to do her a favour. She'd been given a novice.'

'A novice?'

'Yes, that's what we call the new recruits, the virgins, the ones who are new to the game and untrained in its ways. They're choice morsels, very sought after by the madams. Not like an old hand who pretends she's still untouched. She's a healthy young thing who won't pass on the pox to the man who has her. There are plenty of takers, including some very grand ones. So La Paulet wanted me to soften the novice up, to prepare her and convince her to make the sacrifice. Apparently she was refusing to do so and threats and blows hadn't done the trick. They'd thought I might persuade her gently to agree. What could I do? La Paulet promised me a nice tip if I succeeded. Before answering I thought through the pros and cons of the whole thing. What decided me was that perhaps I could help the poor girl. Added to that I'm always short of money for the little one and the wet nurse. So, anyway, La Paulet took me up to the second floor, to the room where I'd heard the crying and left me alone with the poor little thing who seemed to come from a good family. She heard me out but wouldn't have anything to do with it. I could quite understand. She told me the whole story. She'd been kidnapped at night, bundled into a carriage and taken to La Paulet's. She had no idea what was going on or what was being done to her. Since then she'd been threatened until her head was spinning in order to make her give in. Won over by my openness and trusting in me, she begged me to do something for her. At first I said no, because it was too dangerous. With Mauval roaming about the house every day and being in fact the real master of the Dauphin Couronné I was taking a big risk. But she promised me she would protect me if she managed to escape. When she mentioned your name I gave in. I felt sure you wouldn't let Mauval do me any harm. I had to come to find you in the Châtelet to warn you that she's in great peril. Nicolas, there's not a moment to lose. Mauval has arranged a special game of *faro* this evening for a very select gathering, and she's to be the prize!'

Nicolas took his sword and attached it to his belt. He motioned to Bourdeau who was already checking his pistol.

'Old Marie,' he said to the usher, who had remained at the door, 'I'm leaving Antoinette in your care. You will answer for her with your life.'

'I could have chosen worse,' the old man said with a smile.

Nicolas and Bourdeau ran down the steps of the grand staircase. Their cab was still there. It set off at full gallop.

XIV

DARKNESS

'We started a deer and killed a wolf more or less as generals win
battles, that is to say we ran towards the noise, saw the enemy dead
or wounded on the ground, took fright and retreated in an orderly
fashion.'

ABBÉ BARTHÉLEMY

NICOLAS had just explained to Bourdeau the nature of
his relationship with La Satin. The inspector had
made no comment. The carriage had had to slow
down because despite the shouted warnings and a few cracks of
the whip it was impossible to force the pace without running the
risk of knocking down passers-by. Nicolas found the journey
interminable. He mulled over the latest developments.

So Mauval was holding Marie Lardin prisoner – the 'novice'
could only be her – and was intending to hand her over to the
highest bidder. Then she would be forced to engage in the vilest
of trades, or even worse be forcibly taken off to the Sultan's
harems or sent to the American colonies. It was obvious that
there was a scheme afoot to get rid of her, and thus Lardin's
heiress, and more unexpectedly, Descart's. Yes, this
complicated plot had certainly been well prepared. Nicolas
imagined the scene when the notary enquired about Marie so
that she could claim her inheritance. No one would have been

able to find her. Not having heard from her stepdaughter since her sudden departure for Orléans, Madame Lardin would have become worried. Monsieur de Sartine's police enjoyed a good reputation, but it was not unknown for an ordinary traveller to disappear without trace. At the other end of her intended journey a message or forged letter would be conveniently discovered, apparently lending credence to the young woman's recent calling to become a nun. But ultimately her fate would remain a matter of pure speculation. Gradually people would lose interest and then all would be forgotten.

Nicolas suddenly felt his stomach turn. He had to swallow the bitter bile filling his mouth. His heart began to race and he broke out in a cold sweat. Bourdeau turned towards him and examined him. Nothing could be read from the inspector's placid expression.

Trying to overcome his sudden indisposition, Nicolas wondered once more about the true character of his deputy. There were really two Bourdeaus. One was a jolly fellow who enjoyed life, a good husband and father, someone giving every outward sign of being happy with the routine of his job and the little pleasures of a simple and uneventful existence. The other, a character of greater depth, concealed a capacity for secrecy and even dissimulation honed by extensive contact with criminals. The young man wondered about the enigma of the human character. People were judged on appearances but it was difficult to find the flaw that revealed the truth about someone. Since leaving Guérande this question had haunted him constantly. Innocent looks might well disguise the truth. The Marquis de Ranreuil, Isabelle, Semacgus, Madame Lardin, Mauval and even Monsieur de Sartine had given him ample proof of this. At best, faces were mirrors that reflected your own questions. Thus every secret confided, every attempt at friendship and every giving of oneself came up against the invisible wall of other people's defences. Every individual was alone in the world and this solitude was the common lot.

Nicolas watched with unseeing eyes the busy passers-by in the street. What was he doing here himself, an accidental newcomer to this city, and what was the real point of this frenzied pursuit of an unseen enemy that he had been engaged in over the past eight days? Why had destiny chosen him and for what ultimate purpose, when he could have stayed in Rennes carrying out the routine, reassuring tasks of a notary's clerk?

They had reached Rue du Faubourg-Saint-Honoré. Nicolas knocked on the body of the carriage to stop it. They had left the Châtelet in such a hurry that they had not yet prepared a plan of attack. Bourdeau had not wanted to disturb Nicolas's reverie. They now needed to decide what to do.

'I know this place well,' Nicolas said, exaggerating slightly. 'If Mauval is around, we need to be careful because he's dangerous. The best thing is for me to go into the Dauphin Couronné on my own and try not to arouse any suspicions.'

'I wouldn't think of letting you go on your own,' Bourdeau answered. 'We'd do better to wait here for reinforcements. Remember what happened in Faubourg Saint-Marcel. We mustn't make the same mistake twice. Let's wait for the officers.'

'No. Time is short and our best weapon is surprise. You're the key to my plan. I know from La Satin that the house has a secret exit leading into the garden. I want you to station yourself there. If Mauval is inside he'll avoid a direct confrontation. He slipped through our fingers this morning and he must be convinced that we've come in large numbers. So he'll try to escape through the back. That's where you'll nab him. You're the one I'm worried about. Be on your guard. He's a treacherous devil. We'll send the coachman off to fetch help.'

After being suitably instructed the man turned the carriage around and Nicolas and Bourdeau went their separate ways. The young man headed off towards the Dauphin Couronné. He knocked on the door several times. A spy-hole with a grille opened and he was subjected to close scrutiny by a person he could not see, who eventually opened the door. Nicolas was expecting to see La Paulet or the little black girl and was surprised to find instead a tall, elderly woman swathed in black veils, her face plastered with a thick layer of ceruse, with garish rouge on her cheeks. Her trembling hands, covered with floss-silk gloves, rested on the pommel of a cane. The overall effect was of a widow or even a nun who had swapped her convent clothes for more secular dress. She raised her head and gave him a sidelong glance.

'Good day, Madame. I'd like to speak to Madame Paulet.'

'Monsieur,' she replied in a husky, simpering voice, 'Madame Paulet is in town at the moment, attending to business. Perhaps you would like to wait for her. She shouldn't be long.'

She bowed and stepped back a little to let him in. He recognised the hallway and as he expected was shown into the yellow drawing room. Its appearance had not changed. The shutters were closed and hidden by heavy curtains. The room was poorly lit by a single candlestick placed on a pedestal table. What had seemed on his first visit to be the height of luxury now struck him as vulgar and dirty. In the shadows he noticed the parrot cage and went up to it, intrigued by how calm and quiet the bird was. It was then that he noticed it had been replaced: instead of the feathered creature there was a china imitation.

'Monsieur will have known Coco, I assume,' said the old woman, seeing his surprise. 'Alas, he has left us! He died of shock. He was a funny little creature who talked so well. Too much, sometimes.'

She cackled and went towards the door.

'I must go. I have things to do. Madame Paulet won't leave you waiting for long.'

Nicolas sat down in a daffodil-yellow *bergère*. He could have decided to force his way in and search the house from top to bottom, with the risks that might entail for the young woman being held prisoner. But as the old woman did not know him it was better to wait patiently for La Paulet and make her admit to what she had done. That would also give the reinforcements time to arrive.

After about ten minutes he stood up, went towards the fireplace and looked at himself in the mirror. He had aged and was looking tired and drawn. As he continued to stare at himself he suddenly felt a sort of tingling between his shoulders. A shudder ran through him. He could sense that someone was looking at him. He moved imperceptibly to the side and eventually in the right-hand corner of the mirror he saw the old woman's face as she moved silently towards him. She had thrown back her veils to reveal a doll-like face but her eyes were now wide open, and in their green glint Nicolas recognised Mauval and could see his murderous determination. He knew even before seeing the weapon that his enemy was about to thrust a sword into him. He stood stock still, not moving a muscle. He had to avoid doing anything that showed he was on his guard.

In an instant he knew what could save him. As a hardened player of *soule* he had learnt how to dive to the ground and take a fall. He had to reverse the situation and put his aggressor in a position of uncertainty. Admittedly Mauval's advantage was that he had Nicolas in front of him but, if he lost sight of him, then they would be back on an equal footing.

Nicolas suddenly threw himself onto the pedestal table. The piece of furniture collapsed, knocking over the candlestick. Nicolas deftly put out the candle. The room was now in total darkness. As he touched the ground, Nicolas had pushed the pedestal table towards his aggressor in the hope of confusing him and slowing his progress. He rolled to the side. Silence hung over the room like a pall.

For a moment he considered shouting out to alert Bourdeau, but he immediately thought better of it. Would his deputy hear him and could he get into the house? Mauval would have taken every precaution. He was annoyed with himself for falling into this trap and decided that the first thing he had to do was protect himself from behind, and so avoid being pinned to the wall like a butterfly on a board.

Crouching near the fireplace, he groped around and felt some cold metal rods: fire tongs. He managed to get hold of them and, taking care not to knock anything over, hurled them across the room. They brushed the chandelier, which tinkled discreetly, then there was a snapping sound and a chiming of crystal. One of the wall mirrors must have smashed and fallen down. There was a rustle of fabric, a thud and the sound of a piece of furniture being knocked over. Nicolas prayed to heaven that his adversary did not possess a tinder-box. He reassured himself, however: the first person to strike a light would reveal himself.

With his back to the wall, Nicolas settled down to wait. There was a serious risk of him becoming drowsy and losing his bearings in this fearsome place. He was under no illusions. This was a fight to the death: Mauval could not afford to let him live. He still clung to the faint hope that Bourdeau would intervene in time, or that the watch would arrive in great numbers.

The curious thought occurred to Nicolas that he was like Phineas tormented by the Harpies. Would Zetes and Calais arrive in time to get him out of this predicament? This idea gave him food for thought. According to tradition the blind old king had only a staff with which to fight off the monsters that might attack him. He had a sword. All of a sudden he had the idea of combining defence with attack, making use of a stratagem suggested by this mythological reference.

He slowly unsheathed his weapon, placed it on the floor and then just as cautiously removed his frock coat. Moving to the right, he felt his way along the wall until he reached the window near to the parrot cage. Occasionally he stopped, his heart pounding, to peer into the threatening shadows in an attempt to find out whether Mauval, too, were planning something. It was likely that he had chosen the same way of protecting himself by staying with his back to a wall, probably near the door.

At last Nicolas felt the marquetry table on which the cage stood. He went closer, opened the mesh door and took out the china bird. He put it down on the table, then froze at the sound of distant creaking floorboards. This noise was followed by the scraping sound of furniture being pushed or dragged. He needed to act as quickly as possible and use speed to surprise his aggressor. He draped his frock coat over the cage as if making a scarecrow, and tested its weight to be sure he could brandish it.

What was to follow would require the perfect coordination of extremely difficult movements but Nicolas felt relieved: he had weighed up the pros and cons and now the die was cast.

After putting down his sword, he took hold of the cage by the middle and lifted it up. He took the china parrot in his right hand and immediately hurled it violently across the room; Coco's death had not been in vain. At the same time as he heard it shatter against a wall, he distinctly felt his enemy make a sudden move, knocking over another piece of furniture. Then holding the cage covered by his coat in one hand and his sword in the other, he moved forward, finding his way along the wall on his right. On that side at least he was protected against any attack. Moving sideways he attempted to reach the door. A blade swished through the air and slashed his coat. There was Mauval.

For a moment the shock of it took his breath away. Nicolas had the feeling that he was not going to be able to reach the door to defend himself in broad daylight in an honourable combat. If there were no way out, then chance alone or the hand of God would direct the battle and decide the outcome, which would reward neither courage nor skill. For some unknown reason, fate would determine the result of this absurd uniting of their two destinies.

Nicolas took a large stride to the left. He assumed that Mauval had understood he intended to get to the door. He was anticipating the next attack that logically should come from his right. Not content to merely teach him the rudiments of fencing, the Marquis de Ranreuil had also introduced him to chess. He remembered that you always needed to think five or six moves ahead before deciding where to put your pieces. The problem here was that he was only vaguely aware of his opponent's positions.

He heard a blade being driven into the tapestry on the wall. He had to resist the temptation to respond. He had a different plan and decided to remain where he was. The cage was not very heavy, but the added weight of his frock coat made it unbearable and he felt his arm getting numb and beginning to tremble. Soon he would get cramp. He began to swing it backwards and forwards to produce a slight noise and specifically to deceive Mauval with the resulting displacement of air. Suddenly there was another thrust where he was not expecting it, to his left. It grazed his shoulder, making him let out a cry that he had the presence of mind to transform into the moan of someone who has been wounded. He ducked immediately and the next lunge went just over his head. He stood up again and rattled the cage loudly. Mauval had presumably come nearer to finish off his victim. He must have been able to sense the frock coat in front of him, and as he had not suffered a counter-attack might believe that Nicolas were seriously wounded. His sword sank into the coat between two bars of the cage, without touching the young man. Nicolas swung round sharply, trapping Mauval's weapon. Since he now knew precisely where his adversary was, he struck out with the point of his sword and felt the weapon slide over a hard obstacle then enter a body. He heard a long sigh and the sound of something collapsing in a heap. For a moment he suspected a ruse similar to his own. He began to move towards the door again, fearing another attack. But nothing came and eventually he reached the handle and turned it feverishly. The door opened and, after drawing aside the velvet curtain in front of it, he was bathed in the red glow of sunset entering the hallway through the bull's eye above the door.

As he turned back towards the drawing room, Nicolas

noticed amidst the overturned furniture a motionless, shapeless mass on the floor. Taking a candlestick and lighting it, he went further into the room. The mirrors that faced one another showed countless reflections of his image. He cautiously approached the body huddled up under its veils, felt it with the tip of his sword and then nudged it with his foot. The corpse rolled over to reveal Mauval's face. His green eyes were now staring vacantly, and beneath its grotesque coating of make-up his devilish face looked angelic once more.

Though emptied of feeling, the eyes seemed to gaze accusingly at Nicolas who could not bear their stare; he closed them. He observed the precision of his sword-stroke, which was straight to the heart. And yet only chance had guided his hand. It was at this moment that he realised he had killed a man. All the tension of the struggle dissolved and an immense weariness came over him. Admittedly all he had done was defend his own life but nothing, no possible argument, could dispel the feeling – the remorse even – of having taken the life of a fellow human being, and he knew already that this feeling would haunt him for ever. At the same time he knew that from then on he would have to learn to live with the pain and the memory of it.

The young man tried to pull himself together and set off in search of Bourdeau. At the end of the hallway a door opened onto a pantry extended by a closet that led into the garden. He came across Bourdeau who was waiting there, looking anxious.

'Good God, Monsieur, you seem very pale. So I was right to worry. What happened to you?'

'Oh! Bourdeau, I'm so pleased to see you . . .'

'I can see that. You look like a ghost, not that I've actually ever seen one. You've been a very long time.'

'I killed Mauval.'

Bourdeau made him sit down on the stone sill at the base of the house.

'But you're wounded! Your coat's torn and you're bleeding.'

Nicolas felt the pain just as the inspector pointed out his wound.

'It's nothing. Just a scratch.'

He then launched into a graphic account of his fight with Mauval. Bourdeau nodded his head as usual and patted him on the shoulder.

'You've no reason to blame yourself. It was him or you. That's one blackguard less. You'll get used to this sort of encounter. On two occasions I've had to defend myself in similar circumstances.'

They went back into the house. Nicolas led the inspector into the main drawing room. Bourdeau commented admiringly on the precision and cleanness of the sword-stroke, to Nicolas's considerable embarrassment. After the inspector had searched him, they took down one half of the stage curtain from the little theatre and threw it over Mauval's body. In addition to a few *louis d'or* and a snuffbox decorated with a miniature of Louise Lardin, they found an opened note. The sealing wax had been broken. In Nicolas's own handwriting it bore the sentence: 'The salmon is on the riverbank', which Nicolas immediately recognised. It was the password he had given La Paulet if ever she needed to contact him discreetly. On a scrap of paper they also found Monsieur de Noblecourt's address. As Bourdeau remarked, here was proof that the man clearly had evil intent towards Nicolas.

Remembering the main purpose of their raid on the Dauphin

Couronné, they rushed up to the second floor. Of all the doors leading off the corridor, only one resisted their efforts to open it. In response to their banging Nicolas could hear muffled wails. Bourdeau moved his companion aside, took a tiny, carefully crafted metal rod out of his pocket and inserted it into the lock. After a few unsuccessful attempts he managed to loosen the bolt. Lying bound and gagged on two straw mattresses on the floor were La Paulet and Marie Lardin.

When they had freed them from their bonds, Marie began to sob uncontrollably, like a child. La Paulet, her broad snub-nosed face now bright red, seemed to be choking, and her ample bosom was heaving as she cried out plaintively. Eventually she managed a few faltering steps, looking down at her swollen feet.

'Oh! Monsieur, we are so grateful to you.'

Her face took on a frightened look and she glanced anxiously around her.

'Don't worry, Madame,' said Nicolas, who had noticed her expression. 'But you have some explaining to do. You are party to a crime. This young woman has been abducted, forcibly taken to your establishment, kept locked up in appalling conditions and threatened with being sold into a life of infamy. For the least of these crimes, Madame, you could be branded with a fleur-de-lis on the steps of law courts and imprisoned for life. So you see how important it is for you to be honest. Tell the truth and it will be taken into account, I give you my word.'

'Monsieur,' replied La Paulet, taking his hand and squeezing it repeatedly, 'I know you're a gentleman. Have pity on a poor woman forced against her will to take in this poor little lamb.'

She looked towards the corridor for a second time.

'That monster did the whole thing.'

'What monster?'

'That devil Mauval. I'm just the poor supplier. I'm good to my girls. I'm well established and have a quality clientele. I've always paid my dues to the police. And if there is illegal gaming it's with Commissioner Camusot's blessing. I lost my temper the last time you came. But, my dear young man, you pushed me to the limit. Just ask Mademoiselle how I defended her tooth and nail when I discovered she was Commissioner Lardin's daughter. I wouldn't hear of it. And then that Mauval beat up the errand boy to steal my message from him. He feared you might come and wanted to set a trap for you. I was adamant that I'd have nothing to do with it, and then he hit me . . .'

She showed him her bruised cheek.

'Then he threw me in here, just as you found me. If that's not proof enough of my innocence, what is?'

'It's only proof that you were afraid of things going too far,' Nicolas remarked curtly.

Between sobs Marie confirmed part of what La Paulet had said. They were interrupted by a great commotion. A sudden fear overcame the madam. After whispering something in Nicolas's ear, Bourdeau went downstairs. The reinforcements they had expected had arrived at last. The inspector had asked his superior to detain the two women while Mauval's body was being taken away. It was better for the moment to keep his death secret. When La Paulet enquired about his would-be assassin, Nicolas remained evasive. He was convinced that she had told him almost all she knew as honestly as she could. La Satin was right, she wasn't an evil woman, even if her trade put her on dangerously familiar terms with the world of crime.

The three of them, he and the two women, stayed in the room

without saying a word. Nicolas did not want to question Marie in front of someone else. After a considerable time Bourdeau came back and signalled to Nicolas that all was clear. They left the Dauphin Couronné, Bourdeau in one carriage with La Paulet, and Nicolas in another with Marie. The young woman had calmed down, although she let out the occasional long sigh. She looked at Nicolas admiringly.

'Please forgive me, Mademoiselle, but I must ask you a few questions.'

'Please allow me first to thank you, Nicolas. I realise that the girl passed on my message . . .'

She gave him a sidelong glance.

'Do you know her well? Have you known her long?'

Now he was the one under interrogation . . . He hesitated for a moment, but did not think it right to hide the truth.

'She's a very good friend and I've known her a long time.'

Marie looked at him with contempt.

'So you're just like the rest of them . . . And with a woman of easy virtue!'

Nicolas exploded.

'Mademoiselle, that's enough! Here you are, free once more. I don't know whether you realise what you've escaped, but there's one thing I'm sure of: in some circumstances it's better to rely on certain women of easy virtue than on respectable ladies. And the least you can do when you owe them your safety is to be grateful that they felt pity and that they kept their word. Would you now kindly answer my questions and tell me how you came to be at La Paulet's?'

'I don't know, Monsieur,' replied the young woman, who had stopped calling him Nicolas. 'I found myself locked up in that room, where you found me. I was completely dazed, ill, my head was hurting. La Paulet wanted to persuade me to involve myself in the vilest of trades. Then this girl came to convince me. As I was crying she felt sorry for me and I tried to bribe her. I had nothing to lose. Either she would do what I asked or she would refuse, in which case I'd hardly be any worse off.'

'Do you have any idea on which day you were abducted?'

'My memories are muddled. I believe it was Wednesday of last week. I think my stepmother had overheard our conversation that evening when I tried to put you on your guard, if you remember, Monsieur.'

'I remember very well. Another thing: did your father at any time send you a message?'

She responded indignantly.

'You've been searching my room. What right had you to do that?'

'Not only your room, the whole house. But I assume from your reaction that you did indeed receive something. This is an important detail. Answer me.'

'A note whose meaning I didn't understand that won't make any sense to you. He slipped it into my hand the last time I saw him, the day before he disappeared. Do you have any news of my father?'

'Do you remember the words of that message?'

'It was something to do with what was owing to the King. I don't know what it was referring to. My father simply urged me to keep this piece of paper safe. I put it in a drawer and forgot about it. But why this barrage of questions, Monsieur? What about my father?'

Nicolas had the impression she was about to throw a tantrum, like a child. He felt sorry for her. There was no reason to hide the truth from her. It was hardly as if she were a suspect and two witnesses, La Satin and La Paulet, could confirm her account.

'Mademoiselle, you must be brave.'

'Brave?' she said, sitting up. 'You don't mean . . .'

'I deeply regret having to inform you that your father is dead.'

She bit her fist so as not to scream.

'It's Descart! It's him! I told you. She made him do it. My God, what will become of me?'

'How do you know it was murder?'

'She talked about it, she did, with him.'

The young woman started crying again. Nicolas handed her his handkerchief and let her calm down.

'You're wrong. Descart is dead too, murdered, like your father.'

'So it's Dr Semacgus.'

'Why do you think it's him?'

'It has to be one of my stepmother's lovers. The doctor always gave in to her.'

'Or your stepmother herself.'

'She's far too crafty to compromise herself.'

She continued to sob and he did not know how to calm her. He gently wrapped his frock coat around her. She slumped onto his shoulder. He did not dare move and this was how they remained until they reached the Châtelet.

Nicolas gave Bourdeau the task of taking down La Paulet's and Marie's statements. The brothel-keeper of the Dauphin

Couronné was to be kept in solitary confinement until the case could come before a magistrate, according to the normal procedure. La Satin could return home providing she kept quiet about the affair. As for Marie Lardin, she would be taken to a convent and would stay there until the end of the investigation. It was not appropriate for her to go back to the house in Rue des Blancs-Manteaux on her own until the circumstances of her father's murder were known and her stepmother was no longer under suspicion.

Bourdeau offered to take her to the Convent of the English Ladies[1] in Faubourg Saint-Antoine where he knew the Mother Superior. He questioned his chief about what he was planning to do. Nicolas smiled and replied with a hint of irony that he was going back home full of good intentions and would meditate on the insignificance of life while staring up at the ceiling. In any case it was getting late and night was falling. He needed to tend to his wounds, he had to find out how Monsieur de Noblecourt was, and he felt very hungry.

Nicolas's casualness was only a pretence, but he quite enjoyed keeping Bourdeau guessing. On his way to Rue Montmartre he went over the main stages of his investigation. The connection between certain facts still eluded him. Despite his exhaustion and the shock he continued to feel at the death of Mauval, he knew that thinking things over quietly and having a good night's sleep would clear his mind. He was famished, but he did not want to satisfy his appetite in one of those mercenary Parisian establishments that cater for the lonely eater. He felt the need for home comforts.

Night had fallen. The cold was intense by the time he crossed the porch into the magistrate's house. He was delighted to find the familiar smell of warm bread wafting through the air. He took Marion and Poitevin by surprise as they sat talking at the pantry table. A large steaming pot was simmering on the stove. This familiar scene reassured him just as much as the smell in his nostrils. He enjoyed being welcomed like the prodigal son in the Bible. Monsieur de Noblecourt was still unwell, but he had constantly been asking after his lodger. He would be pleased to see Nicolas.

The young man went up to his room via the hidden staircase, taking with him a jug of hot water. He wanted to have a quick wash and tend his wounds before going to see the procurator. He was delighted to find the clothes he had ordered from Master Vachon. By the light of his candle the handsome green coat was resplendent with all its embroidery. When at last he entered the library, joyfully greeted by Cyrus who barked and jumped around, he discovered his host slumped in his armchair with his right foot wrapped in wadding and resting on a tapestry cushion. Monsieur de Noblecourt was reading and had to make an effort to turn towards Nicolas.

'God be praised!' he exclaimed. 'Here he is at last! My premonition was wrong. I've been on tenterhooks since yesterday. I've had the darkest thoughts. I can even say that each attack of this wretched gout brought on a fit of anxiety to match. Fortunately my fears were misplaced.'

'Less than you think, Monsieur, and I can thank you for urging caution, which is undoubtedly what saved my life.'

Nicolas then began a detailed account of all that had just happened. This was no easy matter because the old man constantly interrupted him with exclamations and questions. He managed to keep going with his story, however, until Marion interrupted them by bringing her master a cup of clear broth. The magistrate suggested that Nicolas should eat the boiled beef he was not allowed, and all the vegetables. There should also be a good bottle of burgundy brought up from the cellar just for the young man. This suggestion was taken up enthusiastically.

'Marion has sentenced me to death by hunger!' sighed the magistrate. 'Fortunately,' he added, pointing towards a book he was reading, 'I make up for it by devouring *Le Cuisinier* by Pierre de Lune. I nourish myself by salivating. Did you know that this grand master of the art of cooking was superintendent of the kitchens to the Duc de Rohan, the grandson of the great Sully? He's the inventor of the *bouquet garni*, stewed beef and the *roux*. What's more,' he added, eyeing longingly the ancient bottle that Marion was putting on the table, 'I'm not allowed wine. When I've had my fill of reading about food, I take up my good old copy of Montaigne. Listen: "Pain will surrender on far better terms to someone who stands up to it. We must resist and stiffen our resolve against it." I'm doing my best. Good grief, I notice this account of my sufferings has not affected your appetite. That's the sign of a clear conscience.'

Nicolas looked up, embarrassed at having been caught gorging himself. The warm, tasty food was giving him renewed energy.

'My humble apologies, Monsieur. Today's events . . .'

'. . . have made you ravenously hungry.'

'Monsieur, may I ask your advice on all this?'

The aged procurator looked down, screwing up his eyes. He seemed deep in thought. His flabby jowls drooped around his chin, like a ruff of flesh.

'The truth is,' he said, nodding his head, 'that nothing has been resolved. However, you now possess pieces of information that you still have to fit together. Think long and hard about the circumstances of your investigation. Weigh up impartially the evidence and the assumptions. Then let yourself sink into a deep sleep. Experience has often taught me that solutions occur to us when we least expect them. And my final piece of advice is this: for the truth to be revealed you need to shine a light. If you don't have a light, just pretend.'

He looked at Nicolas with a glint in his eye. This small satisfaction caused him further pain that made him wince and groan feebly. Nicolas realised it was time to allow his elderly friend to rest. After wishing him goodnight he went back to his room. He lay down on the bed to think. Sometimes the way the case was unfolding seemed clear, at other times its different aspects crowded his mind and became jumbled up. He kept going over the same suppositions, but they led nowhere.

To calm himself he decided to examine the three messages left by Lardin. He spread them out on the writing surface of the roll-top desk and re-read them several times. The sentences danced before his eyes and their contents continued to suggest to him something that he could not manage to pin down. Exhausted, he mixed up the scraps of paper as if he were shuffling cards and he left them there. Then sleep overcame him.

Tuesday 13 February 1761

A hand was hovering over pieces of a puzzle lying on the floor. His brow furrowed with concentration, he was trying to put together the word CAT. He took the first letter, then the second . . . He looked up, pleased with himself. He had, however, forgotten the T and, like the verger in a church, the canon was impatiently tapping his cane on the echoing kitchen flagstones. Eventually he pointed out to him the missing letter. The familiar voice said to him: 'Now everything is in the right order.' But already his guardian was mixing up the pieces of the puzzle again and giving him another word to assemble. As he knelt down, Nicolas could see the canon's clogs and the threadbare and mud-spattered braid at the bottom of his cassock. Fine was singing an old Breton ballad while plucking some poultry. He was surprised by the grating music that accompanied the gentle lilt of the refrain.

It was at this point that he woke up. He went to the window and drew the curtains. From Rue Montmartre rose the plaintive sound of a hurdy-gurdy played by a peasant from the Auvergne dressed in a sheepskin and accompanied by his black dog. His guardian's words were still echoing in Nicolas's head when he noticed Lardin's three pieces of paper spread out untidily on the desk. Without looking, he mixed them up again and then examined them. How could he not have noticed it before? Everything became clear, or at least he had a new lead that was bound to prove successful. There was now an explanation for Lardin's determination to leave these cryptic messages behind. But nothing was definite for the moment. At the very most, as in the fairy tale, there was the trail of pebbles left to show the way.

He was ready in an instant. He burnt his throat as he gulped down the cup of chocolate that Marion had hurriedly prepared for him. The old servant bemoaned the fact that he had left her so little time to whisk the drink. This process was necessary, she claimed, for it to develop its smoothness and to bring out its full aroma. Marion had long since taken to the young man, and peeling quinces together the autumn before had marked for her the beginnings of an affectionate bond between them. She trusted him wholeheartedly and was touched also by the respect he showed towards her master. Poitevin, who shared Marion's liking for Nicolas, gently but firmly made him take off his boots. As quick as a flash he cleaned and then polished them. Finally he shined up the leather by brushing hard and applying plenty of spit. Tearing himself away from the creature comforts of the Noblecourt household, Nicolas rushed cheerfully into the cold air of the fine, icy day which greeted him.

He went first to the Châtelet, where he wrote a message to Monsieur de Sartine. Its purpose was to request his presence that very evening at six o'clock to preside over a general confrontation with all the suspects and witnesses. Then he had a lengthy discussion with Bourdeau. They needed to bring Semacgus from the Bastille and Louise Lardin from the Conciergerie, to summon Catherine the cook, and of course the commissioner's daughter. For the time being and without any further explanation, Nicolas delegated to his deputy responsibility for taking any decisions or initiatives in his absence.

Once this was arranged he went down to the Basse-Geôle and spent some time considering the remains found in Montfaucon, which were now part of a macabre collection that included the bodies of Descart, Rapace, Bricart, Lardin and Mauval. These corpses gathered together in one place offered a terrifying image of the destructive effects of vice, self-interest, passion and destitution that had finally produced this spectacle of human decay. It was painful for him to see Mauval again. His face, now that it had been cleaned, seemed serene and younger-looking. What tragic combination of circumstances had brought together in this same resting place people so different and distant from one another in life? He again leant over the unidentified body found in the knacker's yard as if attempting to discover its secret and to obtain some confirmation from it. This was how Sanson found him. Their conversation was lively. They examined Lardin's body, then Descart's. Their words were interspersed with long silences. Eventually Nicolas left the chief executioner, having invited him to attend the session at the Châtelet that same evening, to be presided over by the Lieutenant General of Police.

Nicolas had a busy day going from one place to another. He had taken a carriage and travelled the length and breadth of Paris. First of all he had been driven to Rue des Blancs-Manteaux. He carefully examined the Lardins' house once again, then crossed the Seine to visit the practice of Master Duport, Descart's notary, but also Lardin's. He was given a frosty reception, responded in kind and eventually obtained what he had come for. He went back through the city into the heart of Faubourg Saint-Antoine. He got lost in the maze of streets and dead-ends in the district where joiners worked. After many wrong turnings he had to ask passers-by for directions, but their information was contradictory. He finally managed to locate the cabinet-maker whose name was on the invoice discovered in Commissioner Lardin's library. The craftsman's papers and accounts were completely disorganised. After a lengthy search the man eventually managed to give Nicolas information about the order in question. Having had his intuition confirmed, he allowed himself a break in a *faubourg* tavern, treating himself to one of those wholesome dishes he was so fond of. All that was missing to make his enjoyment complete was the friendly presence of his companion Bourdeau, always game for this type of revelry.

Having satisfied his appetite, Nicolas sent the carriage away and walked back via the Rue Saint-Antoine. Amidst the crowd of craftsmen and day-labourers he allowed his mind to roam. Sometimes he was beset by doubts about the validity of his initiative. Was he well enough equipped to justify summoning everyone to appear before Monsieur de Sartine? Then Monsieur de Noblecourt's words came back to him and restored his determination to succeed. He knew that he was not only trying to secure the successful outcome of the investigation, but also his future in the police force. A mistake would consign him for ever to a lowly position, especially as it was still so soon after his phenomenal ascent. Monsieur de Sartine would not forgive his failure, as it would reflect badly on him for having put a young and inexperienced man in charge of such an important case. What mattered to the Lieutenant General of Police was not so much to arrest ordinary criminals as to resolve an affair of State that closely involved the King and the safety of the realm in wartime. He was perfectly aware of the particular reasons why his superior had taken it upon himself, perhaps too lightly, to trust him. Nicolas owed it to himself not to disappoint him. But convinced as he was, deep down, that he had given of his best, even risking his life in the process, his doubts were more a way of warding off ill fortune than a justified fear.

He returned to the Châtelet on the stroke of five. He felt alert and determined. His inner deliberations had culminated in his decision to act and to bring things to a head without too many qualms.

Bourdeau had become concerned about his absence and showed his relief when he saw him, but was careful not to enquire how he had spent his day. He had preferred to present Nicolas's request orally and in person because he knew how the Lieutenant General reacted when he suspected he was not being paid all the respect owed to his position. Once more Nicolas acknowledged his deputy's wisdom.

Monsieur de Sartine had indeed balked at the proposal foisted upon him, but in the end he had been swayed by the inspector's arguments: he would not regret a session in which everything was to be clarified.

Bourdeau looked at Nicolas, whose expression showed neither approval nor concern at this way of putting things to Sartine. But he went on to congratulate him. Now the room needed to be made ready. With the help of old Marie a row of stools was set up in the Lieutenant General's office. It was not quite the dock but it was not far off it and, he said, it would make the suspects more uncomfortable. There was a lengthy discussion with Bourdeau, which resulted in old Marie being invited to take part in the proceedings. The three of them went in and out of the office several times as if to inspect it. As the appointed hour drew near, Nicolas became more and more excited.

The suspects and the witnesses began to arrive one after the other, and were then put into separate rooms so they could not communicate with each other. Six o'clock sounded on the nearby bell tower. The sound of brisk footsteps on the stairs heralded Monsieur de Sartine's arrival, punctual as ever. He beckoned Nicolas to follow him into his office. No sooner had he got inside the room than he rushed over to the great fireplace and started to poke the fire furiously. The young man waited calmly until this ritual was over.

'Monsieur,' he began, 'I do not appreciate being told what to do or being summoned to my own office. I sincerely hope you have good reason for behaving in this way.'

'I merely suggested organising a session that I considered so vital to our investigation that it could not take place without you,' Nicolas replied deferentially. 'Besides, your presence here means you must have judged this to be the case.'

Monsieur de Sartine's tone mellowed.

'I take that to be a good sign. But, Nicolas, will it at least lead us to settle the matter we both have on our minds?'

'I think so, Monsieur.'

'In any case make sure you remain discreet about this.'

He went behind his desk and sat in the great red damask chair. He took out his watch and looked at the time.

'Get through it quickly, Nicolas. I'm expected for dinner and my wife would not forgive me for missing it.'

'I shall have everyone brought in immediately. But I fear, Monsieur, that your dinner will go begging . . .'

XV

HUNTER AND QUARRY

Come, you shadows, out of eternal gloom;
Look now upon the day of victory.
May deep despair and cruel rage at last
Assemble you as one upon this stage.
Step forward then and tremble at your fate.

QUINAULT

EMACGUS was the first to appear, and was even ruddier than usual, though impassive. He was followed by La Paulet and La Satin. The madam looked downcast but her small eyes, sunk in folds of flesh, were darting around like those of an animal at bay. Antoinette betrayed her surprise at finding herself next to the navy surgeon. Louise Lardin, in a grey skirt and loose-fitting black jacket, without wig or make-up, seemed to have aged several years. Her tousled hair already showed the first signs of grey. Marie Lardin, in mourning clothes, was nervously fidgeting with a small handkerchief. Catherine Gauss supported her whilst glowering at her former mistress. Sanson slipped in like a shadow and stood almost unseen against the wall in the recess next to the fireplace. Bourdeau remained at the door.

The witnesses took their places on the stools provided. The Lieutenant General of Police went around the desk and sat on its edge, swinging one leg and toying with a silver stiletto. In the centre of the room and directly opposite him stood Nicolas, holding on to the back of an armchair. Old Marie brought two extra candlesticks. In their light the young man's silhouette cast a long dark shadow right down to the far end of the room.

'Monsieur Le Floch, you may begin.'

Nicolas took a deep breath and launched in:

'Monsieur, the investigation you put me in charge of is coming to an end. I think I can confirm that the necessary evidence has now been assembled to come close to the truth and to identify the culprits.'

Sartine interrupted him.

'The aim is not to come close to the truth but to attain it. We await your explanations, Monsieur, though as my friend Helvétius put it,[1] truth is sometimes a light that shines in the fog but fails to dispel it.'

'There has been plenty of fog in this case, from the very start,' Nicolas said. 'Let us go back to the beginning. Commissioner Lardin had disappeared. You put me and Inspector Bourdeau in charge of investigating his disappearance. We proceeded as usual, but at first could find nothing. Then, thanks to the testimony of an elderly soup seller, old Émilie, we discovered some human remains in the knacker's yard at Montfaucon. I should point out in passing, Monsieur, the efficiency of an administration that enabled information gathered by Temple police station to be passed on to us.'

Monsieur de Sartine gave an ironic nod of acknowledgement.

'I am pleased, Monsieur, by your observation concerning the efficiency of my police force, which is indeed the envy of Europe. But continue.'

'We examined these human remains closely and they taught us several things. They were of an individual who was bald, male and in the prime of life. He was killed by a bladed instrument, then cut up and deposited in Montfaucon where his jaw was smashed. Our examination showed that the body was taken to the knacker's yard before it started to snow and freeze. From this we were able to tell that the body had been left there the very night that Commissioner Lardin disappeared. In addition we found clothes belonging to the missing man near the body. Everything therefore pointed to the remains discovered being those of the person we were searching for. However, there was still some doubt in my mind. I had the impression that everything had been planned and arranged as if some outside agency wanted to make it easier for us to identify these remains. Every piece of evidence was intended to prove that they were indeed Lardin's. I noticed, however, one detail: a black mark on the top of the skull, which I shall come back to. The way in which the jaw had been so savagely smashed also cast some doubt on the first supposition.'

Nicolas paused to get his breath back and then went on:

'The investigation also involved the family and friends of the missing man. We quickly learnt from Dr Semacgus that Lardin had organised a supper party in a bawdy house, the Dauphin Couronné. In the course of that crucial evening Dr Descart and Lardin quarrelled and both left the brothel at about midnight. As for Semacgus, he is said to have stayed with one of the girls until three o'clock in the morning and then been unable to find his black servant Saint-Louis, who had also disappeared. When he was questioned, Descart made no reference to his evening at the Dauphin Couronné and accused Semacgus of having killed his coachman. It was common knowledge that there was a rivalry between the two men, who had previously been friends.'

'So far, Monsieur,' Sartine said impatiently, 'you've told me nothing that I didn't already know.'

'Our investigation at the Dauphin Couronné provided new leads. It appeared that, from the beginning, the Lardin couple had suffered the after-effects of Louise's turbulent youth and that Descart, Louise's cousin, had embezzled her parents' fortune and was thereby the cause of this debauched youth. Because of his unhappy domestic situation, Lardin sought pleasure by paying for the services of La Paulet's wanton women. Being an inveterate gambler and plagued by a wife with expensive tastes, he had lost a fortune and had fallen victim to blackmail by criminals.'

Concerned about the dangerous direction Nicolas's account was taking, the Lieutenant General of Police was nervously tapping the edge of his desk with the stiletto.

'I shall say nothing about these criminals,' Nicolas continued, much to Sartine's relief, 'nor about their motives. One of them, though, did interest us. His name was Mauval and his haunting presence had been noticed as he spied on us in Montfaucon. It so happened that this Mauval was Louise Lardin's lover. It was also the case that Descart had been lured into a trap at the Dauphin Couronné. Enticed by the propositions made by La Paulet, who encouraged his desires, he was bound to come across Lardin.

A muffled voice could be heard protesting:

'I was responding to demand,' said La Paulet. 'The customer gives the orders.'

Nicolas ignored this interruption.

'The meeting and the quarrel seemed therefore part of a cleverly arranged plan. We discovered from another witness that, far from leaving the establishment in the Faubourg Saint-Honoré after three o'clock in the morning as he had first stated, Dr Semacgus had left at around midnight to share the bed of Louise Lardin. So no one had an alibi for that night. Descart and Lardin disappeared at about midnight. Semacgus slipped away at the same time. Saint-Louis, Semacgus's coachman, was nowhere to be found. Louise Lardin, who had allegedly gone to attend vespers that evening, was unable to demonstrate beyond doubt where she had been until very late that night, as proved by her cook's testimony regarding the state of her shoes, which were ruined by snow or rain. The mystery was still unsolved but one of these characters, Dr Descart, was soon to meet a violent end at his house in Vaugirard. The initial results of the investigation into his death were ambiguous. He seemed to have been stabbed by a lancet for bleeding. Everything pointed to Dr Semacgus, who had been invited by Dr Descart to meet him at the very time he died and who had ample opportunity to kill him. Or was it a diabolical plot by this same Dr Semacgus? Had he intended this clue to point the finger of suspicion at him in such an obvious way that he would appear completely innocent? And what about the mysterious figure whose hopping footsteps had been noticed by one of our informers, and had left small imprints on the frozen ground that I noted down? The only conclusion from all of this was that Descart could no longer reasonably be considered one of the suspects. So what then?'

'Exactly. What then?' said Sartine.

'Well, Monsieur. We are dealing with a Machiavellian plot in which the culprits are sometimes the victims.'

'Your words are becoming more and more confused, Nicolas.'

'Everything has been done to make the situation so complicated that it is almost impossible to unravel. The first false trail is the body in Montfaucon. It was not Lardin's. We found his body yesterday in the cellars under Rue des Blancs-Manteaux.'

Catherine let out a scream.

'Poor master, poor Marie.'

'Whose, then, were the macabre remains in the knacker's yard and what was the reason for trying to put us off the scent like this? It is in fact a long story. Imagine, Monsieur, Commissioner Lardin, after a long and distinguished career, a man with an uncontrollable passion for gambling who has to provide for his young wife, a flirtatious and pleasure-loving woman. He squanders considerable sums of money and falls into the hands of blackmailers. His situation becomes so desperate that his own servant is forced to help pay the household expenses. He is cornered.'

Nicolas gave his superior an insistent look and Monsieur de Sartine nodded approval.

'Lardin decides to disappear. He hopes that his disappearance will enable him to remake his fortune and to flee abroad where he intends to settle. He prepares a criminal plan. His wife, Louise Lardin, has a very rich cousin, Dr Descart, whom she loathes. The doctor needs therefore to be accused of the commissioner's murder, after which he will be tried and executed and his property confiscated and transferred to his victim's wife, who is at the time his natural heiress. Madame Lardin agrees and gives herself to Descart to justify the suspicions against him.'

'It's not true. You're lying. Don't listen to him.'

Louise Lardin had interrupted Nicolas, and Bourdeau had to restrain her from clawing at his face.

'It is the truth, Madame. Descart was drawn into a trap at the Dauphin Couronné. La Paulet had dangled the prospect of an attractive new recruit. He was made to put on a mask and a cape for his Carnival disguise. Lardin arranged to be there too, with Semacgus, because there needed to be a witness to the quarrel. Descart arrived and was duly provoked. There followed a struggle, and Lardin took advantage of it by tearing off a piece of Descart's pocket, which would be useful incriminating evidence for the future. The doctor ran off, and Lardin followed close behind . . .'

'What about Descart?' asked Monsieur de Sartine.

'He disappeared into the night and returned to his house where he lived alone. If accused of the crime, he would have had no witness and no alibi.'

'You really make it sound as if you were there, Monsieur.'

'Once again, Monsieur, your police force is well organised. I shall continue. During this argument, two criminals in Lardin's pay – Rapace, a former butcher, and Bricart, a disabled former soldier – knocked Saint-Louis unconscious and slit his throat in Semacgus's carriage. Then on the banks of the Seine they chopped the body into pieces that they put into two barrels. They transported the whole lot to Montfaucon, where an eyewitness saw them abandoning it along with the commissioner's clothes and his cane. The snow that fell later in La Villette than in Paris, covered up the remains.'

'How can you be so sure? That's not what I read in the reports.'

'In the reports you read what the witnesses were prepared to tell you. In fact I am in a position to state that the body found in Montfaucon really was that of Saint-Louis.'

Nicolas took a piece of card from his pocket. He went up to one of the candlesticks and held the item over the flame. The smoke immediately left a black mark on the paper.

'This was how it all dawned on me one night,' he said, 'as I watched my candle flame blacken the beam above my head.'

'What you are saying, Monsieur, is so abstruse that I'm beginning to doubt your ability to think straight. Explain yourself.'

'It's very simple. You remember that black mark found on the skull in Montfaucon. I found it even more intriguing because our witness on the spot, old Émilie, had seen Rapace and Bricart strike a light from a tinder-box and burn something.'

He turned towards Semacgus.

'Monsieur, how old was your servant?'

'About forty-five, as far as you can tell with an African.'

'In the prime of life, then?'

'Certainly.'

'He was bald, wasn't he?'

'In spite of his name, taken from his place of birth, Saint-Louis had remained a Mahometan. That was why he kept his head shaved except for one lock of hair in the middle, which according to him would allow his God to pull him up on the day of his death.'

'We all know that Commissioner Lardin was bald underneath his wig,' Nicolas continued. 'If someone had wanted to pass off Saint-Louis's body for Lardin's, this distinctive characteristic would have to be removed. So it was burnt. But a black trace of it remained, which caught my attention.'

'But,' Sartine objected, 'the man was black . . .'

'That is precisely why his body had to be taken to the knacker's yard, where it would be gnawed and devoured by hordes of rats, birds of prey and stray dogs until it was unrecognisable and the bones were picked clean. And why do you think the jaw was smashed and the teeth scattered? Because Lardin's teeth were in very bad condition, unlike those of Saint-Louis, whose beaming smile is still remembered by those who knew the faithful servant. But it was important that the body should be identifiable, hence the presence of clothes and items that had belonged to Commissioner Lardin.'

Monsieur de Sartine nodded silently, before asking:

'What about Descart's murder?'

'I'm coming to that, Monsieur. Dr Descart was found dead in the doorway of his house, stabbed in the heart with a lancet for bleeding. That at least was how the murderer wanted it to look. I repeat that the victim was not in fact killed in the doorway of his dwelling, that he had not been stabbed in the heart but close to it and that the wound observed was not the cause of death. A medical expert . . .'

He turned towards the fireplace where only Sanson's shadow could be seen.

'. . . has given a learned demonstration of how, far from being stabbed, the doctor was in fact poisoned and then suffocated with a cushion. Of that we are certain. But who could have wanted Descart dead?'

He went up to Semacgus, who was looking down at the floor.

'You, Doctor. You were Descart's exact opposite. Your way of life and your outspokenness were in contrast to his hypocritical piety. You may argue that those are not grounds for killing him. But in addition to this there was your professional rivalry. You belonged to opposing schools of thought and we know how much hatred such quarrels can generate. Besides this, Descart threatened your interests. You were at risk of being banned from the medical profession as you were only a navy surgeon. Your whole life would have been turned upside down. What is more, you were rivals for what convention forces me to call Louise Lardin's affection. He had caught you with her. I know very well that you claim to have discovered the body but there is nothing to prove that you didn't arrive a few moments earlier and commit the crime. You returned home leaving time for your small-footed accomplice to . . . let's say . . . set up the scene.'

Monsieur de Sartine let out a little sigh of relief.

'Your constant lies do not help your cause, Semacgus,' Nicolas continued. 'You are a suspect but too many assumptions crowd out the truth. Everything points to your guilt. However, in this *mise en scène* there are many reminders of the still life laid out in Montfaucon. The truth resides perhaps in a hidden lie.'

Semacgus was unable to control the twitching of one of his eyelids.

'Luckily for you there is this invitation from Dr Descart, which on reflection has no justification. It's a torn-off scrap of paper, undated and unsigned and with no address, which arrived at your house in very odd circumstances. I am not saying it's a forgery; there is no doubt it is in the doctor's handwriting. But I maintain that it is a part of a letter sent by Descart to his mistress Louise Lardin, the contents of which have been misused to invite Dr Semacgus to the house in Vaugirard. That means, Monsieur, that I accuse Madame Lardin of the murder of her cousin Descart.'

'I have no doubt, Monsieur Le Floch,' said Sartine, 'that you will immediately back up this bold statement with conclusive proof, as you are moving very quickly from one culprit to another . . .'

'Nothing could be simpler, indeed. Why is Louise Lardin a suspect in her cousin's murder? Let us think it through with her. I am convinced that the plot at the Dauphin Couronné was prepared and hatched by Lardin with his wife's full agreement. But the commissioner was unaware of something that Louise Lardin had discovered by chance. I deserve no credit for finding it out because all I needed to do was put some pressure on Master Duport who was, I should emphasise, both Lardin's and Descart's notary. He told me that he had informed Madame Lardin – though he immediately regretted doing so, given her reaction – that her cousin Descart had just drawn up a will that left his estate to Mademoiselle Marie Lardin. I do not believe that this piece of information was passed on to the commissioner. On the other hand it gradually took over Louise Lardin's mind and gave rise to a diabolical idea: getting rid at a stroke of a husband she despised and a cousin she loathed. She would help the commissioner make his disappearance plausible in order to murder him more easily. At the same time she would implicate Semacgus in a killing of which he was innocent. Descart had to be disposed of because ultimately there was nothing to guarantee that he would be accused of the commissioner's murder. There were too many unknown factors. Lastly, in an ever more vicious attempt to confuse matters, Louise Lardin had worn her stepdaughter's shoes when she went to Vaugirard. As she has bigger feet she walked awkwardly, a fact noted by a police spy who saw her leave Descart's house after she had ransacked it to find . . .'

Monsieur de Sartine began to cough. Nicolas stopped himself in time.

'To find . . . the will. What was the point, you may ask, of going to so much trouble? She needed to have some escape routes. Should the situation become dangerous for her, the accusation could be turned on Marie Lardin, the new heiress. Once Descart had been eliminated Commissioner Lardin's daughter had to be got rid of at all costs. That was why she was drugged and then abducted and taken to the Dauphin Couronné, destined for a vile trade that would dishonour her and ensure that she was never heard of again. At that point Louise Lardin, the grieving widow and distraught stepmother, would reap the rewards of her crime, entering into Descart's inheritance and disappearing with her favourite lover, the blackguard Mauval.'

Louise Lardin rose to her feet. Concerned about her intentions, Bourdeau approached her.

'I protest!' she exclaimed. 'I protest against the abominable accusations of this Le Floch fellow. I am innocent of the crime. I had the misfortune to have lovers. That much I admit. But I killed neither my husband nor my cousin. I have already told Monsieur Le Floch that the commissioner was killed by Dr Semacgus during a struggle after my husband had found us together on the morning of Saturday 3 February. My only mistake was to give in to his pleas to conceal the body Monsieur Le Floch found in the cellars of my house.'

'It is quite natural for the accused to protest their innocence,' Nicolas continued unperturbed. 'But I hadn't finished my demonstration and we need to go back over the details of the commissioner's death. It so happens that Louise Lardin displayed, one after the other, two contradictory attitudes to her husband's disappearance. First she played the role of the loving and worried wife, then, in the second stage she showed the cynicism of a courtesan now free to boast of her debauchery and to admit her estrangement from a husband she despised. The second attitude was a response to suspicions that had arisen as a result of the investigation. She had to face up to them. In doing so she deflected these same suspicions, which then became difficult to sustain against a woman capable of such frankness. We find once again this evil intelligence at work, this making use of the facts to render them meaningless. So what did Commissioner Lardin really die of? Monsieur de Sartine, with your permission I would like to question the man best placed to enlighten us.'

He pointed towards Sanson. Monsieur de Sartine signalled his agreement and the executioner appeared in the flickering torchlight. Of those present, only Semacgus and Bourdeau knew what lay beneath the exterior of this very ordinary-looking man, whom Nicolas avoided calling by name.

'Monsieur,' he asked, 'what did Commissioner Lardin die of?'

'Carrying out a post-mortem on his body provided clear proof that he died of arsenic poisoning,' stated Sanson. 'Dead rats found near the body had perished in the same way after feeding on him. The details of the post-mortem . . .'

'Spare us the details,' said Sartine.

'Might the substance employed,' Nicolas continued, 'be the same as that used for Descart's murder?'

'Exactly the same.'

'In your opinion, for how long had Commissioner Lardin been dead?'

'Given the state of the body and the place where it lay, it's difficult to give an answer. However, I think the body had been there for more than a week.'

'Thank you, Monsieur.'

Sanson bowed and went back into the shadows. Nicolas turned towards the Lardins' cook.

'Catherine, were there rats in Rue des Blancs-Manteaux?'

'You know very well there were, Monsieur Nicolas. A real plague. I never stopped trying to get rid of them.'

'With what means?'

'I had a jar of arsenic.'

'Where was it?'

'In the pantry.'

'It is not there any more. It would be a very odd sort of struggle between a deceived husband and his wife's lover that ends in poison being swallowed. What Madame Lardin has told us is not credible. Her husband was poisoned as a result of a carefully hatched plot, for plot it was from the very beginning, as I shall now prove.'

Monsieur de Sartine had gone back to his armchair and, cupping his chin, was staring admiringly at the young man fired up by his demonstration.

'There was a plot, as I say,' Nicolas continued, raising his voice. 'I assert that Mauval, Louise Lardin's lover, was given the task of recruiting the two blackguards who were to slit Saint-Louis's throat. He arranged a meeting between them and those behind this plot on the building site of Place Louis XV. There they were to meet three people wearing masks and black satin capes. Carnival provides useful opportunities . . . Master Vachon, your tailor, Lieutenant General, but also Lardin's, made four black capes for him to order. But let us do our sums. At the Dauphin Couronné Semacgus was, on an evening such as this during Carnival, already wearing a mask. Lardin, also in a mask and cape, makes one. Descart wore a mask and cape – the one La Paulet sent him, along with the invitation – and that makes two. What about the other two? One for Mauval makes three. And the other for Louise Lardin, four.'

Louise Lardin got up, foaming at the mouth, and started yelling.

'You're lying, you bastard. Prove it.'

'A strange request from someone who's supposed to be innocent, but there's no point in shouting. I shall prove it. Let us examine the sequence of events that evening. At around ten o'clock Rapace and Bricart were waiting at Place Louis XV with a cart and two barrels. Soon after that three masked strangers joined them. Instructions were given and an advance on the reward was paid. They were driven to Rue du Faubourg-Saint-Honoré, near the Dauphin Couronné. A carriage arrived shortly before midnight. Semacgus went into the brothel. This is when his coachman, Saint-Louis, was lured into a trap and stabbed. The two accomplices cut up the body beside the river and put the pieces into the two barrels. When questioned the two criminals tried to claim that it was Lardin who had just been killed. However, at midnight Semacgus, Lardin and Descart were together. We now know when Lardin was killed and, in addition, the exact time at which Saint-Louis died. His watch, which was broken in the struggle, was found in Rapace's pocket.

It had stopped at four minutes past midnight. Between a quarter past midnight and one o'clock in the morning Descart, Lardin and finally Semacgus left the Dauphin Couronné. Lardin was the first to arrive back at Rue des Blancs-Manteaux. He was the second victim of the plot after Saint-Louis. He was poisoned by his wife and Mauval, who had hurriedly returned from Place Louis XV. His body was put in a secret underground passage where it would be eaten by rats and quickly become unrecognisable. A few days later some game was hung in the cellar to cover up the suspicious smell. Everything was then done to make life impossible for the cook, Catherine Gauss, who might have suspected something. Marie Lardin would be abducted and I myself, the lodger, would naturally be thrown out of the house. Yes, there was a plot and I maintain and uphold my accusations against Louise Lardin.'

Louise looked him up and down contemptuously. Then she turned towards Sartine.

'I appeal to you, Monsieur. None of this is true. Let me be shown the proof as promised.'

'So be it, Madame. You want the proof, but I've got something much better than that – a witness. You remember the meeting arranged at the building site of Place Louis XV and those two men with whom you negotiated the gruesome murder of an innocent man. Remember the storm that was brewing that evening, with westerly gusts heralding that snow would come in the night. You cannot have forgotten that one of those gusts undid your hair and almost tore off the mask covering your face, revealing enough at least for one of the men in question to remember your features. In some situations details imprint themselves on the memories of even the least observant people.

Louise Lardin was wringing her hands and shrieking:

'It's not true.'

'You know very well Madame, that, unfortunately for you, I am not lying.'

Nicolas turned towards Bourdeau.

'Inspector, please bring in the accused.'

Bourdeau opened the door, raised his hand and gave a signal. Then the heavy silence hanging over the assembled company was broken by the ringing echo of faltering, unbalanced footsteps resounding on the flagging of the ancient building. The noise became louder and merged with the pounding of the hearts of those present. Suddenly Louise Lardin got up, pushed Nicolas aside and, grabbing the silver stiletto Monsieur de Sartine had been toying with some time earlier, stabbed herself in the heart with a loud cry and collapsed. In the doorway stood old Marie, aghast and with a cane in his hand.

Nicolas broke the appalled silence that followed this scene.

'She knew that Bricart had seen her face that evening. She also knew about the old soldier's disability and the sound of his wooden leg. She was sure that he was going to recognise her.'

'It is appropriate that a case as grim as this, based entirely on falsehood and deception, should end so dramatically,' exclaimed Monsieur de Sartine.

With the help of old Marie, Bourdeau quickly ushered out those present and, after Sanson and Semacgus had confirmed she was dead, sent for assistance and a stretcher to remove Louise Lardin's body. It would join the other corpses that lay in the Basse-Geôle, including those of two of her victims and of Mauval, her lover.

*

Nicolas and the Lieutenant General of Police stayed behind alone. There was a long silence between the two men until in the end Nicolas said:

'I think La Paulet should be released, Monsieur. She could be useful and she's played fair by us. She is, as we know, rather a good backup for the police. As for the rest . . .'

Monsieur de Sartine was by now on his feet. He went up to Nicolas and put a hand on his shoulder. Nicolas stifled a cry: it was the shoulder that had been wounded by Mauval's sword.

'My compliments, Nicolas. You have unravelled this plot with a shrewdness that justifies the opinion I have had of you from the beginning. I leave it to you to judge who should be prosecuted or pardoned. With regard to La Paulet, you're right. The policing of a great city can only be carried out by making use of the weakest or the most influential members of society. We must not think ourselves above this. But I have one question for you: who gave you the idea of the *deus ex machina* in the last act? Even I turned towards the door to look.'

'The idea was inspired by a comment of Monsieur de Noblecourt's,' Nicolas replied. 'His advice to me was "just pretend". A woman like Louise Lardin would never have confessed, perhaps not even under torture. I needed to find a way of catching her out when her defences were down.'

'That reassures me about my capacity to judge people,' Sartine continued with a smile. 'In the end it's thanks to me, who entrusted you to Monsieur de Noblecourt, that all this has been resolved. What is more, with our old friend the only dead you'll find in his cellar are the bottles he likes to get through in the company of his friends.'

Pleased with his quip, he allowed himself a quick comb of

his wig, opened his snuffbox and offered Nicolas a pinch. The young man accepted and helped himself. This interlude was followed by a sneezing session that left them feeling relaxed and very pleased with themselves.

'So now,' Sartine continued eventually, 'not only do you decide who I give audiences to but you also try to deprive me of my supper. I hope the reasons you're going to put forward will justify this impertinence and will not leave me, so to speak, hungry for more explanation. Mind you, to have one particular matter cleared up I would gladly fast for a whole week. Nicolas, do you have the King's papers?'

'You will have them, Monsieur, if you agree to follow me. It will take us two hours. You will still have time to join your dinner party. There's bound to be something left to eat and drink.'

'That's adding insult to injury!' Sartine exclaimed. 'But what can I do? I must submit to his every whim. Come on, let's go.'

Nicolas paused for a moment.

'Lieutenant General, I have one request to make of you, to right a wrong.'

'As things stand now, my dear Nicolas, if the request is reasonable you may assume I will agree to it, and if it is impossible I will agree to it anyway.'

The young man hesitated once more before saying:

'I would like Bourdeau, who conducted this investigation alongside me and whose help has been incalculable, to be involved in its ultimate conclusion. I would understand your reluctance, but I'm sure that we can trust him.'

Monsieur de Sartine began to pace up and down his office, then instinctively started to poke the fire even though it had gone out long before.

'I'm a man of my word,' he said eventually, 'but you are putting me in a very difficult position. You are a formidable opponent, Nicolas. It must be the contact with criminals that has made you so tough. However, I understand and share your feeling about Bourdeau. No one is more devoted to you than he is and, if I am to believe the reports, he saved your life. He has shared the suffering, so it is only right that he should share the glory. Who said that?'

'Joan of Arc at the coronation of Charles VII in Rheims, Monsieur, about her standard.'

'Nicolas, you never cease to amaze me. You really are a worthy pupil of our Jesuit brethren. You deserve to move in higher circles . . .'

They left the room. In the main hall they found Semacgus and Bourdeau. After bowing low to the Lieutenant General, the doctor held out his hand to Nicolas.

'I wanted to express my gratitude to you, Nicolas. You didn't spare me, but you've saved my life because without Louise's confession I was done for. I shall never forget the lesson. Treat my house at the Croix-Nivert as your own. Catherine considers you a son. I am keeping her; she's big-hearted, and Marie Lardin has decided to go to Orléans to live with her godmother.'

Monsieur de Sartine was becoming impatient. Nicolas beckoned to Bourdeau.

'Will the inspector do us the honour of accompanying us for the epilogue to this case?' Nicolas asked.

'Upon my word,' said Bourdeau, his face suddenly beaming, 'I would have bet a hundred bottles of Chinon that there was something more to all this!'

*

The Lieutenant General led them towards his carriage. Nicolas ordered the coachman to go to Vaugirard. During the journey he hardly had time to assess the scale of his triumph. Under Sartine's wary eye, he outlined to Bourdeau the affair of State linked to the criminal case that had just been resolved. Then each of them withdrew into silence. Nicolas was prey once more to doubt, his eternal enemy. Although he was sure of himself and of his deductions, and convinced he was nearing his goal, he dared not imagine the consequences of failure in these circumstances.

The Lieutenant General toyed with the lid of his snuffbox, snapping the clasp shut at regular intervals. The coach-and-four hurtled through dark and deserted streets. Soon they were in Vaugirard. Nicolas gave the coachman directions to Dr Descart's house. The place still looked just as grim. They had scarcely stepped out of the carriage when Bourdeau began to whistle a strange tune. In the shadows, on the other side of the road, exactly the same tune could be heard in reply. A spy was there, keeping watch on the house. The inspector went off to speak to him and came back saying that everything was in order and that no one had attempted to get in.

After breaking the seals Nicolas opened the door. He struck a light from a tinder-box and picked up a piece of candle that lay on the floor. He lit it and handed it to Bourdeau, asking him to do the same with the candelabra to illuminate the main room. Sartine looked in horror at the appalling mess in the house. Nicolas cleared the top of Descart's desk with a sweep of his arm and laid out three pieces of paper. He then fetched an armchair and a chair and invited his companions to sit down. An inscrutable-looking Monsieur de Sartine complied without comment.

'Monsieur,' Nicolas began, 'when you did me the honour of letting me into a State secret that I had begun to suspect as the criminal investigation proceeded, I set myself the task of doing all I could to solve this matter too. I had little to go on at first. You told me that Commissioner Lardin had been required in the course of his duties to go through the papers of a plenipotentiary who had just died, and had stolen several very important documents to do with the interests of the Crown, thus threatening the security of the State. Once in possession of these papers Lardin was in a position both to ensure his own impunity and to set up an odious blackmail scheme. However, due to the extent of his gambling debts, he was himself at the mercy of Mauval, the agent and henchman of Camusot, head of the Gaming Division, who is corrupt but beyond the reach of the law.'

Sartine looked at Bourdeau and sighed.

'I won't dwell on the danger of these documents being divulged to foreign powers, nor on the fact that it was impossible, Monsieur, for you to take action against the perpetrators of this crime of lese-majesty. But I was convinced that the case of Commissioner Lardin's disappearance had to be closely linked to the existence of these State papers that had been . . . let's say . . . mislaid.'

'Why was that?' asked Sartine.

'The constant presence of Mauval during the investigation, his spying, his threats and assaults on me could only have been for a very good reason. Lardin was dead, but his murderers had not managed to lay their hands on the documents which the commissioner had endeavoured to hide from them.'

'Explain to me how they could have learnt of their existence.'

'The plot, Monsieur, the plot. When Lardin planned to

eliminate Descart in agreement with his wife, he informed her that he was in possession of papers that would be extremely valuable for someone to sell. He made it clear to her that these papers were the ultimate guarantee of their impunity. However, the man still retained an element of caution. He added that he had concealed these papers in her cousin Descart's house. Where better to hide them than in the house that would be passed on to Louise Lardin, Descart's natural heiress and the wife of his alleged victim? However, he was careful not to tell his wife exactly where he had put the papers.'

'Nicolas, this is wonderful! It sounds as if you were there! Were you by any chance behind the door and under the beds listening to everything? On what have you based such a confident account of the details of this tale? Is this why you've brought me to this godforsaken suburb?'

'On my intuition and my knowledge of the people I've been proud to unmask. There was in fact one imponderable and unexpected element in this well-oiled mechanism. A tiny grain of sand, a stumbling block . . .'

'Oh, really? What is it? This is like listening to the worst kind of empirical philosopher!'

'Conscience, Monsieur, conscience. Commissioner Lardin had long been an outstanding member of your police force. He had spent many years in harness, giving of his best in the fight against crime. Something of this had stayed with him. He was not absolutely sure of the loyalty of a woman whose wanton ways he knew and accepted. He tolerated her relationship with Mauval, but could he really trust this demonic couple who had embarked on this evil enterprise alongside him? In any case his motives don't much matter. However, I do believe that in a sudden act of lucidity and duty, or with a premonition of his impending death, he wished to leave a trail that would lead to the stolen letters. This trail, Monsieur, is on the table in front of you.'

Sartine leapt out of his armchair and eagerly began to read the three pieces of paper laid out on the table.

'Explain yourself, Nicolas. This makes no sense – I can't make head or tail of it.'

'First I need to tell you how these notes in Lardin's handwriting came into my possession. I found the first in one of my coats, the second was sent to Monsieur de Noblecourt along with a gift, and the third was entrusted to Marie Lardin who was told how valuable it was. At first sight the whole thing doesn't tell us very much.'

'What about at second sight?'

'They are very informative and I'm going to prove it. Naturally you will already have noted that it mentions returning the secrets of the King.'

'Is that all you need?'

'It's not all I need but it points me in the right direction. I spent a long time searching before I arrived at my conclusions. I moved the papers around as my guardian the canon used to do with the pieces of a puzzle.'

'What on earth has your guardian to do with this?' Monsieur de Sartine asked impatiently. 'Do you want me to die of apoplexy before your very eyes?'

Bourdeau retreated into the shadows, looking worried.

'I mixed them up time and again,' Nicolas continued, arranging Lardin's notes in a different order.

Do two make three?
Enfolded in these arms
Some seek their solace.
Carefully you open them
After so much searching,
Returning to their owner
The secrets of the King

'And what am I supposed to make of this gibberish?' said Sartine. 'Have we come here for rhymes, rebuses or anagrams?'

'Examine the capital letters at the beginning of each sentence, Monsieur. What do they spell?'

'D . . . E . . . S . . . C . . . A . . . R . . . T. Well yes, they spell Descart. But where does that get us?'

'It gets us here, to Vaugirard. It was not for nothing that Lardin devised so many stratagems for these notes to reach their intended recipients. He clearly intended that the secret should be discovered, and that the search should be directed towards this house.'

'How did you possibly deduce that just the word Descart could lead us to what we're searching for?'

'Thanks to Monsieur de Noblecourt's cabinet of curiosities, Monsieur.'

'Oh dear,' said Sartine, turning to Bourdeau, 'I think he's lost his senses again. You told me he was wounded yesterday. It must be the loss of blood.'

This time it was Nicolas's turn to show his impatience.

'In this cabinet of curiosities, one of the most famous in Paris . . .'

'And with which I am very familiar,' Sartine went on,

'because I've been subjected to our friend's innocent quirk of always wanting to reveal its horrors to his guests at the end of a fine meal.'

'Monsieur, a few days ago I noticed in that strange setting a large ebony crucifix with its arms closed. It's one of those Jansenist items that would prevent you from obtaining a certificate of confession. I was struck by its appearance. It reminded me of an image I had come across earlier. I questioned Monsieur de Noblecourt. The crucifix in question had been given to him recently, much to his surprise, by Commissioner Lardin. Our friend had found a note wrapped round its base, the very same note that you have before you, beginning with the words "Carefully you open them". Then, when I carried out a search of the Lardins' house with Bourdeau, I discovered among the commissioner's papers an invoice from a cabinet-maker in Faubourg Saint-Antoine for two unspecified items. As I couldn't get the image of the crucifix out of my mind I sought out the craftsman in question. After I had got lost several times, I reached my destination and the man found the order: two ebony crucifixes, each with an ivory Christ . . .'

'We are caught between Scylla and Charybdis,' said Sartine. 'I don't know what's stopping me getting back into my carriage.'

'Curiosity and hope, Monsieur,' replied Nicolas with a smile. 'The craftsman himself expressed surprise at the nature of the work required for one of the items in question. According to him he had been asked to completely hollow out the main part of the cross and to fit it with a lid equipped with a secret catch, a sort of pen box for concealing jewels, *louis d'or*, precious stones . . .'

'Or letters,' Monsieur de Sartine continued, suddenly calm.

'Or letters. So I had a name and an object, even if the

craftsman had refused to reveal the mechanism to me. That might have been enough, but I wanted to solve the mystery of Lardin's notes. Let us look at them again, if you don't mind. "Do two make three?" I translate somewhat freely as "for the pair of crucifixes there are three messages". "Enfolded in these arms" is a reference to Christ with his arms closed. The rest is obvious. "Carefully you open them, after so much searching, restoring to their owner the secrets of the King." This Christ will return the King's papers.'

A long silence followed Nicolas's demonstration, disturbed only by the guttering of candles and the roar of the wind in the fireplace. Monsieur de Sartine and Bourdeau looked on in fascination as Nicolas got up like a sleepwalker, took hold of a candelabrum and went towards the fireplace. He stopped, raised his arm and the light illuminated a great ebony crucifix. On it was an ivory Christ with arms closed, Commissioner Lardin's last gift to his wife's cousin. Bourdeau hurried over, grabbing a chair, and with one foot on the mantelpiece took down the object, creating a cloud of dust as he did so, and placed it respectfully on the table. The young man invited Monsieur de Sartine to examine the object. The Lieutenant General's fingers were trembling and all he could feel was the smooth surface of the wood. He looked at Nicolas in desperation.

'Are you certain of what you have suggested?'

'It cannot be otherwise, Monsieur.'

Now it was Nicolas's turn to examine the crucifix. The mysterious words rang in his head: 'Carefully you open them.' He leant over the ivory Christ and noticed that the Saviour's hands were not nailed to the wood of the cross. He took hold of them and tried to press them down. The arms yielded with a clicking sound and the whole object rose slightly. He turned the crucifix over. A small wooden panel had opened up, revealing a small space filled with tightly packed papers. He stepped aside.

'If you please, Monsieur.'

Sartine took the bundle of letters from their hiding place. He beckoned to Bourdeau to bring some light and began to leaf through them, reading them out.

'Draft orders to be sent by His Majesty to the Comte de Broglie and to the Baron de Breteuil, twenty-third of February 1760. Letter from the Duc de Choiseul to the Marquis d'Ossun, the King's ambassador in Madrid, tenth of March 1760. Minute of a letter from Madame de Pompadour to Her Royal and Imperial Majesty in Vienna. Copy of an intercepted letter from Frederick II, King of Prussia, to his sister the Margravine of Bayreuth dated seventh of July 1757 . . . "Since, my dear sister, you have just taken upon yourself the noble task of working for peace, I beg you to agree to send Monsieur de Mirabeau to France. I shall willingly defray his expenses. He may offer up to five hundred thousand crowns to the King's favourite . . ." '[2]

He looked up thoughtfully.

'Still the same old story of Prussia attempting to bribe the lady. No proof . . . But if it were divulged at the present time . . .'

He collected himself, thrust the bundle of papers into his coat and looked the two policemen up and down sternly.

'You've seen and heard nothing. On pain of death.'

Nicolas and Bourdeau bowed and made no reply.

'Monsieur Le Floch,' Sartine continued, 'for the second time this evening I express my thanks to you, but this time I do so in the name of the King. I must leave you. I have to go to Choisy without delay. In this time of misery and war you have given me the great privilege of being a bearer of good news. The King will not forget this.'

He went up the stairs four at a time and disappeared into the night. Then they heard the sound of the carriage leaving at a fast trot. They looked at each other and burst out laughing.

'We deserved that,' Bourdeau said, 'and it's only fair. You were extremely impertinent towards the Lieutenant General; you really had to be sure of yourself there. Monsieur, thank you for allowing me to be present at all this. I shall never forget it.'

'My dear Bourdeau, we're about to go back to ordinary duties. Events thrust us into prominence. After the success of our investigation we are returning to obscurity. The King has been saved. Long live us! Since everyone has given up on us I have a wicked suggestion to make. We are a stone's throw away from Semacgus's house. He can't refuse us anything. We're going to invite ourselves to supper. I can already smell the aroma of Catherine's cooking from here. And, if nothing's ready, she'll kill the fatted calf for us.'

Then the two friends disappeared into the cold February night.

EPILOGUE

Two months went by. Normality reasserted itself. Nicolas continued to be employed as a supernumerary in various police tasks. Usually he teamed up with Inspector Bourdeau, but they never referred to the events they had taken part in; these were now cloaked in silence. As all guilty parties were dead, no legal measures had been taken.

Nicolas carried out his day-to-day tasks conscientiously. The Lieutenant General of Police had withdrawn the special commission that for a time had given him unlimited powers. There were fewer audiences with the Lieutenant General, and even then they were only for administrative purposes. The young man felt no resentment about this. The thrill of the investigation over the previous weeks had given way to a period of contented calm. The life he was leading suited him. He enjoyed living at Monsieur de Noblecourt's where he was surrounded by affection and had numerous opportunities to meet the friends of the former procurator of the Parlement, and so extend his circle of useful connections.

He had resumed contact with Pigneau and listened

indulgently to his missionary plans. He regularly visited Père Grégoire, who was always pleased to see his former boarder. Lastly, Semacgus's house was another haven where he often went on Sundays. Catherine strove to lavish her culinary care and attention upon him. The surgeon, whose conversation and knowledge had always fascinated him, engaged Nicolas in interminable discussions from which he learnt a great deal. As for Guérande, he tried not to think about it. After a lengthy inner debate he had decided not to reply to Isabelle's letter. His life in Paris, his recent but gradually increasing experience of social relations and his realisation of the gulf between the daughter of a marquis and an orphan without name or fortune, was at once a source of pride and a reason to give up all thought of her.

Nicolas still visited Antoinette, though he would have liked her to change her way of life. But she was becoming increasingly self-assured and for her the attraction of easy money was too hard to resist. This friendship therefore took the form of the normal dealings between a policeman and a prostitute, even though they were still fond of one another. Nicolas had twice come across Commissioner Camusot, who still held his post but was no longer head of the Gaming Division. Rumour had it that this demotion was the result of the case in which Nicolas had played an important role. He felt that people had become envious of him, or deferential towards him. Bourdeau, always on the alert for rumours in an establishment he knew so well, told him the gossip and added ironic comments of his own. Nicolas listened, laughed and took no further notice. He had none of the ambitions people ascribed to him.

At the beginning of April Monsieur de Sartine informed him rather bluntly of the death of the Marquis de Ranreuil. The news caused him bitter grief. So he had not been able to make peace with his godfather to whom he owed so much, and without whom he would still be mouldering away in a dusty office in Rennes, doing a job without a future. The Lieutenant General hardly gave him time to come to terms with his feelings. He studied him briefly, then announced that the following day the two of them would be going to Versailles as the King had expressed the wish that Monsieur Le Floch be presented to him. There followed a long series of recommendations about court manners, appropriate dress, the wearing of a sword and the punctuality required. Nicolas had never seen his superior look so nervous. Monsieur de Sartine eventually ended their conversation with an abrupt 'Your good looks will make up for everything. Breeding always shows.'

That evening Nicolas asked Marion to brush the green coat which he had never had the opportunity to wear. Monsieur de Noblecourt lent him his court sword and the cravat of Bruges lace he had worn at his wedding. Nicolas declined supper and went up to his room. His grief, which he had held back because of the announcement of his audience with the King, now came pouring out. So many images from the past flooded back to him: returning from the hunt, playing chess, the lessons the marquis had taught him and all those insignificant moments of ordinary happiness. All these memories had helped to make him the person he was. He could still hear the authoritarian voice of his godfather. The elderly aristocrat had always shown him unrestrained affection. Nicolas felt sorry that unfortunate circumstances had come between them, leading to an irreconcilable rift. A dim image of Isabelle came to him and then disappeared, leaving in its place blank despair.

The next day brought a host of things to do. The house in Rue Montmartre was turned upside down in the frenzy of preparation. Nicolas attempted to dull the pain of his grief by concentrating on the details of his attire. A barber was sent for to shave him, and then for the first time the young man had to conceal his own hair beneath a powdered wig. When he had put on his coat and tied the precious cravat, he looked at himself in the mirror and failed to recognise the sombre-looking man he saw there. A cab took him to the Hôtel de Gramont, where he was due to meet Monsieur de Sartine. He waited for some considerable time in the main drawing room. The Lieutenant General at first took him to be a stranger. Then, hands on hips, he walked round the young man nodding approval. He was delighted and complimented him on his outfit.

In the carriage taking them to Versailles Monsieur de Sartine respected Nicolas's silence. He took it to be a sign of the understandable emotion the young man felt at the prospect of such an important event. In fact, though Nicolas was familiar neither with Versailles nor the Court, that feeling was far from his mind. He gazed upon the busy streets with total detachment. One day all these anonymous passers-by would disappear, all these people moving about without so much as a glance at their carriage whose movements he himself observed without making out their faces. They, Sartine and himself, were like living ghosts. The future was nothing more than the gradual approach of a mysterious end that would come in due course. What was the purpose, then, of an existence that regretted the past and feared endless sorrows and grief?

They were nearing Versailles. Nicolas summoned up all the resources of his childhood faith and sighed as if to relieve the weight of things unsaid that was crushing him.

Monsieur de Sartine misinterpreted Nicolas's reaction. He had been waiting for a signal to break the silence that he obviously found so oppressive. Good-naturedly he sought to reassure Nicolas. He held forth about the Court as only an insider could. During the present reign Versailles, he said, had lost the splendour it had enjoyed under Louis XIV. The King was frequently absent and then it was truly deserted, with nobody there except those who were obliged to remain. On the other hand, when the King was in residence, the courtiers flocked there and hunted with him, but as soon as they could they hurried back to Paris and its pleasures. Most of the ministers now resided in the capital.

Nicolas admired the immense avenue that crossed a town with buildings scattered amidst parks and gardens. The crush of carriages grew. He leant out of the door and in the dazzling brightness of that spring day glimpsed a massive, impressive building thinly veiled in mist. The blue of the slate, the flashes of gold, the light-yellow stone and the red mass of brick heralded the royal palace. Soon the carriage reached Place d'Armes, filled with a host of other carriages, sedan chairs and pedestrians. It went through the first monumental gates decorated with the coat of arms of France and entered the first courtyard. It stopped in front of the second gate that restricted entry to the royal courtyard. Sartine informed Nicolas that this protected part was called the 'Louvre' and that only carriages or sedan chairs with red caparisons, showing that the occupants enjoyed the 'honours' of the palace, could enter it. They got out of the carriage, which the coachman stationed to the side. Two guards in blue jackets with long gold and silver braided stripes and red lapels saluted them before they headed off towards the buildings to their right.

Nicolas, feeling lost, followed Monsieur de Sartine who was hurriedly making his way through a crowd of onlookers and courtiers. He had the feeling he was entering a gigantic maze of galleries, corridors and staircases of all sizes. The Lieutenant General was a frequent visitor and found his way around with ease. The young man's state of confusion was comparable only to that he had experienced two years earlier on his arrival in Paris. His discomfort was further increased by the thought of all those stares directed at him, a stranger accompanying such a daunting figure. He felt constricted in the coat he was wearing for the first time. The foolish idea suddenly occurred to him that someone might suspect it had been ordered for someone else. He was not at all aware of the route they took, and he found himself in an enormous room amidst a dozen or so people who were gathered round a tall man being helped by a manservant to remove a blue coat with gold braid.[1] The man then removed his shirt and was dried. A little old man, powdered and bejewelled, was handing him a change of clothes. The man recited some names in a monotonous voice to an usher. Sartine nudged Nicolas sharply, telling him to doff his hat. It was then that he realised he was in the presence of the King. He was surprised that the few people present continued to talk amongst themselves in low voices. A man whom he did not immediately recognise approached him and whispered in his ear:

'I am delighted to see you again, Monsieur. You are present at the removal of the King's boots. My compliments. His Majesty is in the process of choosing who will have the honour of dining with him.'

He also greeted Sartine, who made no attempt to conceal his surprise at seeing Nicolas on friendly terms with Monsieur de La Borde, First Groom of the King's Bedchamber. The expression on his superior's face reassured the young man. He was not the only person to be experiencing surprise. The King's voice rang out.

'Richelieu,' he said, speaking to the little old man, 'I hope you have made your peace with d'Ayen about which of you is in charge of placing the guests at the riding school ball. Consult Durfort.'[2]

'I shall comply with Your Majesty's instructions. However, Sire, may I observe –'

'That the hunt was not successful,' the King interrupted. 'Two stags missed at Fausse Repose. A third took refuge in the doe pond. It took us three attempts to shoot it. We are not pleased at present.'

The old marshal nodded and forced a smile. As the King had finished changing he headed towards a small staircase and those present watched him disappear from view, bowing as he left. Before Nicolas had had time to think, La Borde was already leading them away.

'We are going to the private apartments,' he explained to him. 'The King wants to hear in the privacy of his own rooms your personal account of a certain investigation. His mood is not good today. The hunt did not succeed in making him forget his worries. But have no fear, all will be well. Speak confidently and don't be shy, because if you hesitate the King will withdraw into himself. Be agreeable without being long-winded, but say enough to keep up his interest. Deep down the King is kindly, especially towards the young.'

They found themselves in an anteroom with a fairly low ceiling, then went through a gallery decorated with large paintings. La Borde explained that the King had wanted exotic hunting scenes. There were representations of animals and people from far-off lands that Nicolas had never had the opportunity to see.[3] A manservant showed them into a drawing room with white wood panelling set off with gold. The room gave an impression of balance and harmony. Seated in a red damask armchair, the King was drinking a glass of wine that a lady had just poured him. They all bowed, holding their hats in their hands. The King gave them a faint wave. The lady held out her hand to Sartine, sat down in turn and gave a noble bow in response to the greetings of other guests entering the room.

'So, Sartine,' asked the King, 'how fares your city of Paris?'

The Lieutenant General of Police duly responded to the monarch's question and the conversation began. Nicolas felt strangely composed. He was unable to believe that he was in the presence of his sovereign. He saw before him a distinguished-looking man, with well-defined features and a gentle expression accentuated by large eyes. Instead of surveying those around him the King was staring into space. The face, with its high forehead, gave an impression of great dignity. Signs of age and tiredness were, however, evident in the bloated, sagging cheeks. His pallid complexion was marked in places by sallow patches. He spoke in a low voice, looking listless, almost dejected. Occasionally Nicolas was aware of the King glancing at him quizzically then immediately looking away.

Sitting next to the King the lady, whom Nicolas assumed to be the Marquise de Pompadour, seemed quite unlike the image he had in his mind of the King's favourite. He was surprised by what she was wearing: a sort of tight-fitting jacket, buttoned up to the neck. The sleeves hung down to her wrists and hid her hands. He remembered all the nasty comments he had heard about how appropriate this attire was for a lady not renowned for the beauty of her hands or the attractiveness of her bosom. Her ash-blonde hair was half covered by a hood attached to the cape of her dress. Its greyish, iridescent colour matched that of the King's coat, contrasting with the blue of the Order of the Holy Spirit. Her face, with its perfect oval shape and large, wide-open blue eyes, had nevertheless been too rouged for Nicolas's liking. Yet the overall effect was almost austere. He recalled the rumours that the marquise wanted to model herself on Madame de Maintenon. She was smiling but her expression remained fixed. He concluded that her appearance concealed worry and suffering. Occasionally the marquise cast a look that was both adoring and anxious towards the King, who for his part showed his fondness for her with numerous small gestures of affection. Nicolas was breathing more easily; he felt as if he were at a family gathering.

'So here is your protégé, Sartine, to whom we are much indebted. La Borde has spoken to me of him.'

The Lieutenant General did not hide his astonishment.

'I had not realised that Monsieur Le Floch was so popular, Sire.'

The King beckoned to Nicolas.

'Monsieur, I wish to hear your personal account of a matter close to my heart. I am listening.'

Without a second thought Nicolas plunged straight in. His future was probably at stake and in his situation others would have seized this opportunity by drawing on all their personal resources and making every effort to charm. He chose to speak simply, clearly and colourfully, though not overly so, suggesting rather than describing, not asserting himself too much and giving Monsieur de Sartine far more credit than he deserved. The King interrupted him several times, asking for more details about the post-mortems on the bodies, before giving up the subject at Madame de Pompadour's request, since these morbid details horrified her. Nicolas managed to be sparkling yet modest, and dramatic when the situation required. What he said was interesting without being overlong. The King, engrossed in the account, seemed suddenly younger: there was a brightness in his expression once more. Nicolas concluded his account and stepped back a pace. With a charming smile the marquise held out her hand for him to kiss, a hand that to the young man seemed feverish.

'Thank you, Monsieur,' she said, 'we owe you a great deal. His Majesty, I am sure, will not forget the services you have rendered us.'

The King got up and took a few steps.

'The King is the first gentleman of the Kingdom, as my forbear Henry the Fourth used to say, and will reward in a manner befitting the son of one of his most faithful servants, one of those noble Bretons, who three years ago spared no effort in the fight against the English.'[4]

Nicolas understood nothing of this: it was as if the words had been addressed to someone else. Sartine remained impassive. La Borde was open-mouthed. The marquise looked at the King in surprise.

'I did indeed say the son of one of my servants,' the King went on. 'Monsieur,' he said, looking at Nicolas, 'your godfather, the Marquis de Ranreuil, who has just died and whose service I do not forget, presented me with a letter in which he officially recognises you as his natural son. It is my great pleasure to inform you of this and to restore to you the name and titles that are yours.'

A long silence followed these words. Nicolas threw himself at the King's feet.

'Sire, I beg Your Majesty to forgive me, but I cannot accept.'

The King jerked his head back.

'On what grounds, Monsieur?'

'To accept, Your Majesty, would be to betray the memory of my . . . my father, and would deprive Mademoiselle de Ranreuil of an inheritance that is rightfully hers. I renounce it, as I do my title. I have already had the good fortune to serve Your Majesty. I beg to be able to continue to do so under my own name.'

'So be it, Monsieur.'

He turned towards the marquise.

'Here is a very rare example and one that restores our faith in human nature.'

Then, turning again towards Nicolas, he said:

'The marquis wrote to me that you were an excellent huntsman, as he was.'

'Sire, I did my apprenticeship under him.'

'You will always be welcome at my hunt. La Borde, Monsieur Le Floch is to have the privilege of hunting the stag. He is to be exempted from wearing the beginners' uniform.[5] For the rest, Monsieur de Sartine will make my wishes known to Monsieur Le Floch.'

The audience was at an end. They withdrew. In the gallery, the First Groom of the Bedchamber congratulated Nicolas.

'The King has admitted you to his hunt. He knows you are a Ranreuil and honours you as such. You have the honours of the Court and the right to ride in the King's carriages.'

Nicolas followed Sartine as if in a dream, and he was not sure he wanted it to end. They returned to their carriage. Sartine was silent until they had left the palace.

'I had warned the King that you would say no. He didn't believe me.'

'You knew all along, didn't you?'

'All along, since your arrival in Paris. Monsieur de Ranreuil loved you. He was very unhappy about the situation he had created. Imagine his anguish at the fondness between you and Mademoiselle de Ranreuil, your sister, and in honour of his memory try to forgive decisions that at the time you could not understand.'

'I sensed there was a mystery.'

'Another example of your intuition!'

'And what about my mother?'

'She died giving birth to you. You need know no more than that. The marquis was married. She was of noble birth and would have been disgraced.'

'May I ask, Monsieur, why you thought I would say no?'

'I have been observing you since your father entrusted you to my care. You are very like him. But what he obtained by birth you have had to earn by your talent. You have already proved that you were able to overcome your weaknesses, despite the misfortune of your birth. If I have sometimes seemed to mistrust you in a way you found hurtful, it was more a reflection of my concern than a judgement on your worth. I do understand you, Nicolas. I was orphaned at fifteen, without wealth or connections. I was Spanish on my father's side. He was the intendant of Catalonia and I was sent off to the college of Harcourt, where from an early age contempt and disdain were heaped upon me. Humiliation is the most powerful of social mechanisms. The nobility opens its doors, but it is often an illusion. And, if we are to believe our philosopher friends, it might be better to be one of the common people in these changing times. Whatever the case,' he added with a smile, 'it was not very diplomatic to turn down a title that was your due in the presence of a favourite born a Poisson. Fortunately for you she did not seem to take offence.'

He took a bundle of papers out of his coat and handed them to Nicolas.

'Read this.'

The young man was not sure he understood the meaning of the words before him and Sartine had to explain.

'His Majesty in his great goodness has seen fit to give you as a token of his satisfaction the position of Commissioner of Police at the Châtelet. The cost of the commission has been paid and you will find a receipt for the fees. The only condition the King attaches to this favour is that you should report directly to me. He intends to use you without any intermediary for matters exclusively related to his service. I dare to presume, Commissioner Le Floch, that this condition will not be too burdensome to you.'

'Monsieur, without you . . .'

'Let's forget about that, Nicolas. It is I who am indebted to you.'

For the rest of the journey Nicolas was unable to control the flood of emotions surging through him. When the coach had entered Paris he asked Monsieur de Sartine's permission to get out at the College of the Four Nations[6]; he wanted to return to Rue Montmartre on foot. The magistrate agreed with a smile. The Seine and, on the other bank, the Garden of the Infanta and the Old Louvre were bathed in the glow of dusk. The air was light, scented with the perfume of grass and flowers. The wind blew away the foul smells of the riverbanks. Small clouds, pink, grey and golden, drifted over the city. Shrill cries heralded the arrival of the swallows.

It was a moment of peace. The thorn that had for so long been embedded in Nicolas's heart and flesh plagued him no more. In the chaos of this world he had found his place. He had set aside the temptation of assuming a rank whose value was dependent on the prejudices of others. From now on he would be his own judge. Having come to terms with the past, a new life was opening up for him, one that he would form with his own hands. He remembered with affection Canon Le Floch and the marquis. Their shades could feel satisfied. He had proved himself worthy of their love and their teachings. The bittersweet image of Isabelle resurfaced as the happy memory of a shared childhood. For a long time he looked towards the setting sun. Over there, far away, ocean waves were breaking upon his native land. He walked back along the *quais* as far as Pont-Neuf, whistling an aria from an opera.

NOTES

CHAPTER III

1. The name given to the morgue situated in the basement of the Châtelet.

2. A card game in which the banker plays alone against any number of players.

3. A meal in which the meat course and the dessert are served at the same time.

CHAPTER IV

1. The Jansenists represented Christ with arms unopened on the Cross.

2. The medical service for the French navy was founded in 1689 and was largely made up of surgeons. Doctors, holders of degrees in medicine, were trained in the universities whereas navy surgeons were trained in schools of surgery in Rochefort, Toulon and Brest. Throughout the eighteenth century doctors attempted to prevent surgeons from practising medicine or even tending the sick.

3. L. Batalli. Italian doctor and author of *De Curatione per sanguinis missionem* (1537).

4. G. Patin (1605–1672). Professor of medicine at the Collège de France.

CHAPTER V

1. First mentioned in Europe in 1533, this tuber was introduced into Spain in 1570, and later into Italy, Germany and Ireland. Present in France from 1616 onwards, the potato became a source of controversy: it was claimed to cause leprosy. It was Parmentier (1737–1813) who popularised the vegetable during the reign of Louis XVI. The King was said to eat some at every meal.

2. The doctors and surgeons of the criminal courts of the Châtelet were on duty one week in four.

3. Robert François Damiens (1715–1757). A soldier, then a domestic servant, he struck Louis XV an inoffensive blow with a pen-knife to remind him of the duties of his office. His punishment was commensurate with the fear felt by

the Sovereign, who in the moments following the attack thought he had been mortally wounded. The author has taken numerous details from the well-researched study by Martin Monestier, *Peines de mort. Histoire et techniques des exécutions capitales des origines à nos jours*, Paris, 1994.

4. Casanova, who witnessed the execution from a window overlooking Place de Grève, has left a graphic account of it.

5. Charles Henri Sanson's words are all the more remarkable since it was he who executed Louis XVI on 21 January 1793. He resigned his office immediately after this execution and set up a foundation for the annual celebration of a Mass of Atonement in the church of Saint-Laurent.

6. The buildings referred to are the symmetrical mansions of the Ambassadeurs Extraordinaires, later to become Hôtel de Crillon and Hôtel de la Marine.

CHAPTER VI

1. A famous eighteenth-century case. The Duchesse de Gesvres attempted to have her marriage annulled because of her husband's impotence. The case had still not been settled at the time of her death in 1717.

2. Aphrodisiacs used in the eighteenth century. An excessive amount of powder of cantharides (a tropical fly) could prove fatal.

CHAPTER VII

1. (1702–1766). A French general of Irish descent. After the failure of the siege of Madras, he capitulated at Pondicherry after heroically defending it. He was accused of treason, sentenced to death and executed. His son obtained his rehabilitation with the help of Voltaire.

2. (1711–1794). The Chancellor of Austria.

3. The 'good lady' here refers to Jeanne Poisson, Madame de Pompadour.

4. Frederick II, King of Prussia.

5. A French defeat in which Frederick II crushed Marshal Soubise and the forces of the Holy Roman Empire.

6. (1684–1770). A financier and friend of Madame de Pompadour.

CHAPTER VIII

1. A fashionable Paris innkeeper.

CHAPTER IX

1. During the *ancien régime*, people who committed suicide were sometimes tried and even sentenced to be hanged on the gibbet and their family disgraced. Even if this practice had gradually disappeared, traces of it remained in the popular consciousness.

2. 'Since you are a great judge, Monseigneur Saint-Yves de la Vérité, listen to me.'

3. Violinist and composer (1713–1797). he was Superintendent of the Royal Music in 1764 and a member of the French Royal Academy of Music, of which he was three times director.

CHAPTER X

1. A product used instead of soap for doing the washing.

2. 'Contemptuous of wealth, firm in virtue and steadfast in the face of fear.' (Tacitus, *Annals*, Book IV, 5).

3. (1727–1799). A French composer and organist.

4. The most famous dungeons in the Châtelet. As early as 1670 Louis XIV had decreed that 'the prisons of the Châtelet should be healthy' but it was Louis XVI who decided to abolish them in 1780.

5. The coat of arms of Antoine Gabriel de Sartine. Recently ennobled (Comte d'Alby) he wanted them to include a representation of the fish formerly sold by one of his ancestors, a grocer, which sounded like his patronym.

CHAPTER XI

1. Glass paste imitating precious stones.

2. (1709–1767). The Comptroller General of Finance in 1759. He launched the fashion for portraits obtained by tracing the outline of a profile and filling in the whole with black.

3. During Carnival children were accustomed to marking passers-by with a piece of cloth cut into the shape of a rat and rubbed in chalk.

4. (1734–1794). Louis XVI's First Groom, then a farmer-general. He died at the guillotine during the Terror.

5. Just like a corpse.

CHAPTER XII

1. (1725–1793). Son of the Comte de Toulouse, himself the legitimate son of Louis XIV. He succeeded his father in this office in 1734.

2. A cart for transporting a cannon.

CHAPTER XIII

1. Where preliminary torture was carried out during the preparation of a criminal trial, and where those accused of criminal offences were imprisoned.

2. A cheap material made of light wool.

3. *Pensées*, I, 23.

CHAPTER XIV

1. A convent situated in Rue de Charenton in Faubourg Saint-Antoine, where young foreign girls of noble birth were brought up.

CHAPTER XV

1. (1715–1771). A French philosopher. He was a farmer-general and contributed to the *Encyclopédie*.

2. At the time there were many rumours of attempts either by Austria or Prussia to bribe Madame de Pompadour, Louis XV's favourite. Frederick II had asked his sister, the Margravine of Bayreuth, to approach the lady at Versailles via an emissary, her Grand Chamberlain the Chevalier de Mirabeau.

EPILOGUE

1. A hunting coat worn at Versailles. Each hunting ground and each type of hunt would have a particular coat.

2. The Master of Ceremonies.

3. There were two paintings by Van Loo (an ostrich hunt and a bear hunt), two by Parrocel (an elephant hunt and a buffalo hunt), two by Boucher (a tiger hunt and a crocodile hunt), one by De Troy (a lion hunt), one by Lancret (a leopard hunt) and one by Pater (a Chinese hunting scene). Most of these paintings are now on display in the Museum of Amiens.

4. In 1757 the Breton nobility mobilised against raids by the British.

5. The grey hunting coat worn by beginners.

6. Palais Mazarin.

Acknowledgements

First I wish to express my gratitude to Jacqueline Herrouin for all the skill, attention to detail and patience she showed in typing up the text. I also wish to thank Monique Constant, *conservateur général du Patrimoine*, for her help, trust and encouragement. I am grateful to Maurice Roisse for his intelligent and careful checking of the manuscript. As a tireless walker through the streets of Paris, he was my investigator on the ground. My thanks also to Xavier Ozanne for that indispensable technical touch. Finally, I wish to pay tribute to the historians whose works have constantly accompanied and assisted me in the day-to-day task of writing this book.

Sofia, May 1997